BODY OF TRUTH

During her 15-year career as Ireland's State Pathologist, Marie Cassidy became known to the Irish public as a trusted figure whose expertise helped to solve murders and clarify unexplained deaths. In over 30 years of practice, she performed thousands of postmortems and dealt with hundreds of murders. She has witnessed the burgeoning role of forensic science and the impact that has had on death investigation and the expectations of the general public, while embracing new technology and welcoming the input of experts in the other sciences. She retired at the end of 2018 to spend more time on the other passions in her life, her family and writing.

Marie's number one bestselling memoir *Beyond the Tape* was published in 2020. *Body of Truth* is her first novel.

MARIE CASSIDY

BODY OF TRUTH

HACHETTE
BOOKS
IRELAND

First published in Ireland in 2023 by
HACHETTE BOOKS IRELAND
1

Cataloguing in Publication Data is available from the British Library.

Trade paperback ISBN 978 1 399703598
Ebook ISBN 978 1 399703604

Typeset in Sabon LT STD by Bookends Publishing Servies, Dublin.
Printed and bound in Great Britain by Clays Ltd, Elcograf, S.p.A.

Hachette Books Ireland policy is to use papers that are natural, renewable and
recyclable products and made from wood grown in sustainable forests. The
logging and manufacturing processes are expected to conform to the
environmental regulations of the country of origin.

Hachette Books Ireland
8 Castlecourt Centre
Castleknock
Dublin 15, Ireland

A division of Hachette UK Ltd
Carmelite House, 50 Victoria Embankment, EC4Y 0DZ
www.hachettebooksireland.ie

To all the women I've ever known and have yet to meet.

I

People associated death with silence. With hushed tones and murmured condolences.

In Dr Terry O'Brien's experience, death was always accompanied by noise: sirens blaring, doors slamming, orders given, questions asked, the rustle of paper suits and, finally, the clang of metal as the knife drops onto the table.

Death and noise. Two constants of the pathologist's working life.

In the mortuary, of course, such intrusive sounds could be drowned out by the radio, which was, at that precise moment, playing the Commodores' 'Three Times a Lady' at full volume. The stereo was a rather grubby piece of equipment that spent its days wedged between boxes of gloves and rows of glass specimen jars on top of a cupboard that lined the wall of the mortuary. Getting into that cupboard and giving it a good clear-out and restock was next on the list of jobs Terry had been systematically working through since she'd taken up the position of temporary state pathologist in the Dublin State Mortuary a few weeks ago.

But it would have to wait for now.

There were other more pressing matters to be dealt with.

The mortuary was where, as Terry was wont to say, 'all the real work happened' in law enforcement. It was a long high-ceilinged room, its floor and walls tiled in a patchwork of mismatched greys.

Various lights and magnifying glasses hung on extendable, manoeuvrable arms from the ceiling, and as well as the aforementioned cupboard, the walls were lined with sinks, workstations and backlit display boards.

To Terry's left, behind a glass panel, was a viewing gallery, where investigating officers and other interested parties could watch proceedings.

This morning, there was standing-room only remaining in the gallery. *They've come for a show*, Terry thought. *So let's give them a show.*

On the table before her lay the body of a man, Robbo Boyle, a bouncer from Cabra who, according to the senior investigating officer, had come out the worst in an altercation with a group of lads to whom he had refused entry to the nightclub where he worked. During the course of this disagreement, he had found himself falling to the ground – to be accurate, he had been flung upon it with some degree of force – causing his head to bounce off the kerb, knocking him unconscious.

The other bouncer on duty said Robbo wasn't down for long before he regained consciousness. When his colleague hauled Robbo to his feet, he saw Robbo was bleeding from the ear, but he also stated there were no cuts to be seen on his head. Robbo insisted he was fine, carried on for the rest of the shift and went home. It was his mother who found him dead in bed the next day when she went to wake him.

Terry knew this script by heart. It was a typical Friday night back home in Glasgow.

Mindful that the man's kin were waiting to identify the body, Terry picked up a ten-inch scalpel and tried to angle her cut as far back as would still allow good access to the skull. She deftly sliced across the top of the head from ear to ear.

And there it was.

'Vinnie, can I get a photo?' she asked the police photographer, pointing to the large bruise under the skin, just above the right ear.

Detective Garda Vincent Green broke off from a deep conversation about last night's soccer match, which he had been conducting with the two scene-of-crime officers present, and positioned himself, camera at the ready, on Terry's right. He'd got used to her style and pace of working by now – detailed, steady, less hurried than that of her superior, Professor Boyd, the chief state pathologist.

With a nod, she placed a ruler beside the large red patch of haemorrhage on the under-surface of the scalp, something that had only become visible once she cut into the skin. Vinnie moved in and took the photograph.

Terry steadied the head with her left hand and drew the blade across the muscle fanning out over the surface of the skull from above the ear. The brownish fibres gaped apart to reveal bleeding on the surface of the skull. Vinnie moved back in and out again, he and Terry swapping places with now practised ease, the intermittent camera flashes the only indication of their endeavours.

Tomas, the mortuary assistant, appeared at Terry's left side and handed her a pair of forceps. With a flick of her wrist, the muscle peeled away from the skull.

'And there it is!' she said.

Vinnie leaned in. 'Got to hand it to you, Doc, you said as much at the house. A fractured skull! Shit, you even got the actual site right!'

Terry shrugged. When the coroner had called her that morning to tell her she was needed for a suspicious death, he'd mentioned the man's profession and that there'd been an altercation. She'd told him what the cause of death was going to be immediately. She'd seen more cases like this than she could count.

'Tomas, you can get on with the skull,' she instructed him. 'Just avoid the fracture. Vinnie, stay with me. We're not out of the woods yet.'

'Yes, Doc. I'm with you.'

The background music was drowned out as Tomas's electric saw cut through the skull. In her peripheral vision Terry saw the two scene-of-crime officers who were in the room cringe and one look away, a slightly greenish tinge washing across his complexion. The crime scene manager Mary Healy, who stood beside the two scene-of-crime officers, was made of sterner stuff. Terry and she exchanged an amused glance.

Like well-drilled dancers her team took up their positions,

Terry with her hands cupped over a bowl right under Robbo's head.

'Ready?' Tomas looked left and right. Two affirmative nods were swiftly followed by the crack of the skull opening. Vinnie's camera clicked and Terry leaned in to have a look.

'An extradural haemorrhage,' she observed. 'He didn't stand a chance.'

The glistening disc of a blood clot, about the size of a chocolate chip cookie – M&S rather than Maryland – slid slowly towards Terry's waiting hands.

'It's a big one, Doc,' Tomas said. 'Reckon a good 150.'

'Big enough to kill him, that's for sure,' Terry affirmed, guiding the clot into the bowl.

Terry glanced at the figures in the viewing gallery. The gardaí crammed into the space had broken into two groups. The one at the back included Detective Chief Superintendent Sinnott, a bear of a man with broad shoulders, a rapidly receding hairline and a prominent paunch, his grey suit doing nothing to hide the strain the buttons of his shirt were experiencing. He'd introduced himself on arrival into the viewing gallery as head of murder squad and made much of Boyd's 'latest protege', which had made Terry cringe. DS Healy had quietly told her, 'A rare visit from the king.'

The officers in Sinnott's group seemed preoccupied, all talking intently. She leaned over the dissecting bench and rapped on the glass to get their attention. Their heads whipped around, startled by the sudden interruption.

She pressed the button on the intercom.

'Sorry to interrupt, gentlemen.'

She caught herself as soon as she said it and scanned the

viewing gallery but, not unusually, there wasn't a woman in sight on the other side of the glass.

Blessed am I among blokes, she thought.

'Just to let you boys know,' she gestured to the body on the table, 'Mr Boyle died from a head injury. He's got a fractured skull and a large extradural haemorrhage, resulting in a blood clot that squashed his brain and killed him. From what I've been told about the circumstances of his demise, it looks like you have a homicide on your hands.'

DCS Sinnott buzzed back: 'Our friend there may not be the only one on the menu today. A body has been found in the Phoenix Park. You'll need to get over there, pronto. The SIO on the case will be there to meet you.'

And with that, he turned his back on her and resumed the conversation with his cronies.

'Well, you're very welcome,' Terry said, realising that, even though she was still holding the button for the intercom, no one was listening.

2

The team broke off to prepare for their trip to the Phoenix Park.

Terry was in her office grabbing her coat and gulping from a half-finished can of Coke when the door was flung open without ceremony and her boss, Professor Charlie Boyd, strode in, closing the door behind him and turning his large brown eyes on her with a laser-like stare.

Boyd was in his late fifties, a tall, lean man with a rugged complexion earned from spending a lot of time outdoors. That morning he was dressed in a dark blue pinstriped three-piece suit set off by a red tie and pocket square, his greying hair, which still had traces of chestnut brown through it, swept back from his forehead.

'Dr O'Brien, I would appreciate a few moments of your time.'

Terry flashed him a smile, though she had a feeling it

wasn't going to do her much good – her boss had the look of a peregrine falcon about to snare a fieldmouse. 'Please have a seat, Prof.'

Boyd cast an eye about Terry's office. 'Where, precisely?'

Terry was exact, meticulous even, in her work in the mortuary, but her personal affairs tended to be a little more chaotic. Her office was an explosion of files, photographs, empty cofee cups and Coke cans, magazines, handwritten notes, sandwich wrappers and half-finished tubes of Polo Mints.

'Let's move that bundle off that chair in front of you.' Terry got up and picked up the pile of case files from the aforementioned chair and placed them against the wall.

Boyd pointedly brushed the seat with the flat of his hand before settling his long frame into it.

'Now,' Terry said, sitting in her own chair and taking a swig from her can. 'What can I do for you?'

'I have heard something that … disturbs me.'

Terry waited. Boyd had a flair for the dramatic, and she knew he was working up to something. When the wait stretched for five long seconds she said, 'Prof, in the job we do we hear disturbing stuff every day. What is it that's so terrible?'

Boyd narrowed his eyes and sat forward. 'What I heard is directly pertinent to *you* and the circumstances of your employment.'

Terry tried not to flinch, but she felt her stomach drop. 'Oh.'

'Yes. Oh.'

'And?'

Boyd shifted in the seat and cleared his throat. 'I was speaking to a colleague of mine in Glasgow yesterday evening. He informed me that you were placed on what he termed "gardening leave" three months ago, due to an irrevocable clash with certain members of your team. Serious and entrenched disagreements over basic practice, apparently.'

Terry put the can back on her desk and gave a hollow laugh.

'Please be serious, Dr O'Brien. This is not a laughing matter. I was under the impression when I signed off on your position that you had left your previous employment because you wished to, in your words, "expand your horizons". Which seems now to be somewhat at variance with the truth.'

'It is *absolutely* the truth,' Terry snapped back, trying to control her annoyance. 'Strictly speaking, I wasn't put on *gardening leave* – I chose to take some time out. But did your friend, who randomly decided to dish the dirt on me, tell you that this disagreement developed over a misunderstanding of the role of the expert witness by those who should know better?'

'You are not being very clear, Dr O'Brien.'

'I was being pressured to alter my report to support the police's theory. In other words, to lie. The procurator fiscal agreed and the guy was done for thieving and not culpable homicide – manslaughter here. Certain high-ranking police officers made it known that I had obstructed their investigation and a killer had walked. I was furious at their attitude and told them so. In no uncertain terms. They logged a complaint, I logged a counter complaint. It all got a bit messy.'

Boyd eyed her but said nothing.

'I was completely honest at my interview,' Terry continued, ploughing on despite her boss's glowering silence. 'I *did* want a change of scenery and to learn about police work in a new jurisdiction, and I also have friends here. All true.'

Boyd sighed and, reaching over, pushed a coffee cup that was sitting close to the edge of the desk out of danger. 'Dr O'Brien, in the interest of fairness, might I say you are, without question, a gifted pathologist.'

'Thank you.'

'You're quite welcome. You are also, however, impulsive and far too fond of the media attention your arrival here has attracted. I do not like the way you manage your team – your overfriendly attitude is unprofessional. I suggest you keep a certain distance from your work colleagues. Ireland is a small country. You hold a very important position, one that garners respect from the public and close scrutiny from the press. The Office of the State Pathologist is not your personal playground. I do not know how things were done in Glasgow,' he elongated the word, treating it as if he found it distasteful, 'but we do things differently here. Am I clear, Dr O'Brien?'

Terry gazed back at him, feeling anger prickling but knowing now was not the time to have this battle. 'You are crystal clear, Professor Boyd.'

'Good. Now I believe you are wanted in the park. I trust you will apply yourself to this case with close attention and no small amount of professional reserve and objectivity.'

'Professional reserve and objectivity are my middle names, Professor.'

Boyd blinked, not sure if she was making fun of him. 'Well. Good. Good day, Dr O'Brien.'

Boyd stalked out and, groaning in frustration, Terry put her head on the desk and practised the breathing exercises her therapist, whom she had left behind in Glasgow, had advised her to use in moments of stress. They didn't work, but they did make her slightly lightheaded.

I think I'll stick with the Coke, she thought, swallowing the rest of the can. She pulled on her coat and made for the car park.

3

The garda car entered the Phoenix Park from the North Circular Road.

Terry was still getting her bearings around Dublin. It would be easier if she had her own car, but that was parked at her dad's place back in Glasgow, and there was no way she was ever getting on a ferry again after the horrendous crossing she had endured a month ago. Her dad had driven them both over to get her settled in. In truth, he just wanted an excuse to visit his old stomping ground.

Perhaps she should get something small to get her around town. She'd have to think about it.

The last time Terry was in the Phoenix Park was when she was about ten years old, and her family had come over from Scotland for a holiday. The ferry from Glasgow had been a nightmare then too, not helped by her dad's mantra: 'Two more vomits and we'll be there.'

One of her father's old school friends from Swords had given them a loan of their mobile home somewhere north of Dundalk. Her aunt Bridie, Dad's sister, and her cousins had rented a caravan on the same site. Terry had loved spending time with her Irish relatives – she smiled when she recalled their antics, running amok, or 'acting the maggot' as Bridie called it, about the caravan park. It was a wonder they didn't get thrown out.

On one of those days, in an effort to keep their boisterous children out of trouble, the O'Brien family had driven down to Dublin to visit the zoo. Truth be told, only her big sister, Jenny, had any interest. Terry had sulked and complained about being away from the beach and her cousins the entire time they'd been there.

Terry forced a familiar feeling of regret back into the depths of her consciousness. Thinking of Jenny always aroused strong feelings in her. It didn't look like that was ever going to change.

At the first roundabout the garda driver took a right turn, away from the main park area. Terry relaxed a little. Her work, either in the mortuary or in the field, was a safe space for her, somewhere she knew the rules and had a tangible, achievable problem to solve. Pathology wasn't like the other areas of policing, where they had to worry about motive and crimes of passion – Terry's job involved getting to grips with the science of what had happened to the deceased.

And science was, in many ways, simple. It told you directly, in a trail of evidence that was easily detectable if you knew where to look, the story of what had happened to the dead.

Even better, science was as honest as the day is long. Science *never* lied, even if people misunderstood it from time to time. Terry, though, was an expert in interpreting the subtler messages left for the living to read.

She tapped the shoulder of the garda in the passenger seat in front of her, who'd introduced himself as Pádraig and the driver as Tony. 'Where are we heading?'

'Farmleigh. You know the big house where all the VIPs stay?' He turned to the driver. 'Were you about when Obama came over? Jaysus, that was a big deal, all the bosses were stressed out of their game. And for all that, there was I was on ground patrol, spent a week wandering, getting paid to do nothing. Never saw them once.' He turned round to Terry. 'Do you remember, Doc?'

'No. I wasn't here then.'

Terry knew all about the visit, though. Her aunt Bridie had come up from Cork to Moneygall, the backwater town Obama's ancestors were supposed to be from. There was no way Bridie was ever going to miss an American president or a pope on Irish soil. Many of her generation seemed to live for such moments, when the eyes of the world were focused on their little island.

As if reading her mind, the garda continued. 'The brother was in the Armed Response Unit and was sent down to Offaly. I mean, everyone wants to be Irish these days. But Moneygall! Who the feck wants to claim that place? Still, good for tourism, I reckon. Only reason I can think of why anyone in their right mind would want to go to *Offaly*.'

The car was stopped at the gatehouse by a couple of security guards, who seemed to take their role a tad too seriously. Only when it was explained that one of the state pathologists was on board did they relent and move the bollards.

'Farmleigh,' the guard in the passenger seat repeated. 'There'll be TV cameras all over the place before we know it, like flies on shite.' He turned back to Terry again. 'They'll be all over you as per, Doc.'

She knew they would. The anonymity that came with a forensic pathology job in Scotland was not replicated in Ireland; here, it seemed, you were part of the story. A fact that, as had so recently been communicated to her, bothered Professor Boyd considerably.

The Irish media had made a huge fuss over her, the broadsheets referring to the new arrival as 'Ireland's glamorous new pathologist' and one of the tabloids going so far as to state that she was 'making murder sexy again', which she thought was rather offensive to the families of the deceased. But she knew responding would just add fuel to the fire.

As they followed the road through the grounds, the handsome Edwardian house – all columns and balustrades – suddenly came into view against a backdrop of pristine blue sky. Once the home of the Guinness family, the mansion sat on seventy-eight acres of what was mostly farmland in the north-west corner of the Phoenix Park.

The house's commanding vista was, that afternoon, marred by a haphazard arrangement of garda cars and vans. The 'death investigation circus' – as that same tabloid had referred to Irish law enforcement's arrival to a murder scene

– had come to town, creating a dark contrast to the unusually warm late summer's day. Terry, the journalist in question had suggested, was the 'alluring female ring mistress'.

You'd swear I asked for any of that nonsense, Terry brooded, recalling once again Professor Boyd's irritation. It was the press who want the personal, rather than the professional, angle. It wasn't her fault if the occasional hack asked what brand of make-up she wore or where she got her shoes. Boyd was never asked stuff like that – it was not a problem men had to deal with.

The driver gave their details to a young guard with a clipboard, who dispassionately lifted the tape stretched across the end of the drive and directed them to the front of the house.

'We'll hang around and take you back, Doc,' the driver said. 'No rush. We'll park over there behind the van.'

Terry thanked them and, climbing out into the sunshine, walked towards the group of detectives standing in the shade of the portico.

She stopped dead. Among the group was Detective Chief Inspector John Fraser, a well-dressed senior detective whom Terry had met at a forensic medicine conference on deaths in custody some months before.

'Fuck,' she muttered to herself. She didn't know he was Dublin-based. It hadn't exactly come up the first and last time they'd met.

Fraser was in his early forties, with a strong, solid build, his hair artfully mussed and a bit long, which was unusual for a detective. There was an assured air about him. There had been drinks and conversation when they met – she found herself relaxed in his company – and eventually, as if by unspoken mutual agreement, they'd ended up back in his room.

It had been … fun. Really good fun. Just what she'd needed, given the drama that was brewing with work back home. The following morning they'd had breakfast together, not a trace of awkwardness or embarrassment, before they disappeared back to their ordinary lives.

She had no idea then they would end up working in the same city in the not-too-distant future. On the night in question, she didn't believe she would ever see him again. It was a one-night stand, pure and simple.

Fraser stepped forward into the sunshine and Terry wondered if he felt as mortified as she did. 'Dr O'Brien.'

'DCI Fraser.'

'It was only a matter of time until our paths collided, Terry. I'm the senior on the case.' At least he had remembered her name.

They looked at one another for a few long moments, then Fraser said, 'Your timing couldn't be better. I was just going to have a look at the site.'

He cast a glance at her feet. Terry was relieved she'd jettisoned her stilettos in favour of her old trainers before she'd left the morgue.

'The body's over beyond the lake there, in the woods near Beech Lane along the north side of the estate. Do you need to bring anything with you?'

Terry looked in the direction the detective was pointing,

hoping for a distant outbuilding where the body might be, but there was nothing but green: grass, bushes, trees, patches of ragwort and rosebay willowherb.

'Nope,' she said.

Terry had encountered forensic pathologists who attended scenes with enough equipment to carry out major neurosurgery. In her experience it was better to keep your powder dry, your mouth shut and your hands in your pockets until you knew what you were dealing with. She could drag half the lab out with her and use none of it. Far more sensible to look at the remains and then send for equipment that would actually be useful.

'We don't know much at this stage,' the DCI continued. 'Some kids on a day out with their mothers found the body. They were walking around the lake, the young lads messing about, throwing sticks in the water, when their dog went missing. They found more than they bargained for when they went looking for it. According to the technical bureau, the body's been there a while. It was probably the smell that attracted the dog. We've got a specialist team talking to the boys and their mothers.'

Those poor kids, Terry thought. But they were not her problem now. She needed to keep her mind on the task before her. Whoever was lying in the woods ahead, all alone, was the person she needed to care about.

'Male or female?' she asked.

'Looks like a woman. But no one's got too close.' The ghost of a smile crossed his lips. Terry knew that some of the burliest police officers were the biggest wimps when it came to death. And this one would be particularly unpleasant. 'There's no sign of a bag or a phone. But you might find something when you have a close look.'

At the far side of the lake was a large white van with 'Technical Bureau' emblazoned on it. As she and Fraser approached, Terry spotted two men in white coverall suits wrestling with a body bag.

'Alan!' Fraser shouted across.

A tall figure appeared at the open doors at the back of the van and looked over, simultaneously pulling back his hood to reveal a mop of thick black hair.

'This is Dr O'Brien, the pathologist.'

The tall man waved and began to walk towards them. Fraser said to Terry, 'This is DI Alan Ahern, head of the ballistics section,' then called over to the approaching detective, 'You crime scene manager today, Alan?'

Ahern grinned. 'Fancied getting out of the office. Mary is busy with the bouncer crime scene, and I thought you might appreciate the A-team turning up.'

He nodded at Terry, pulling down the zip of his white suit to reveal a tight black T-shirt barely concealing an impressive torso, then rolling up the sleeves to display equally impressive biceps. Terry tried not to stare, but she could see why her best friend, Michael, who had told her quite a lot about DI Ahern already, was so smitten. He liked a man with a bit of muscle on him. He also had a blind spot for poseurs.

She and Michael had been best friends since they'd started university in 2008, and he was part of the reason for her recent move to Dublin, where Michael was a scientist in Forensic Science Ireland. It was a job he loved, at least until his break-up with his long-term partner, Paul, who had until recently been the state pathologist. Alas for Michael, Paul had returned to the US, and they needed a replacement. A heartbroken Michael had begged Terry to apply. And she had to admit the timing couldn't have been better, the opportunity coming just as she had decided she needed to get out of Glasgow for a while. Breathing space was what she needed before she made any radical decisions about her future career.

She'd remained close to one of her university lecturers, Professor Rooney, who was a regular speaker at forensic pathology conferences, and was therefore very well-known in forensic circles. He was more than happy to support her application.

'Every cloud has a silver lining,' Terry had told her distraught friend when she'd heard she'd got the job. 'Think of all the horror movies and bottles of wine we'll have once we're neighbours.'

Of course, it hadn't quite worked out like that, as Michael was fond of reminding her. But she'd been as ridiculously busy between settling into a demanding new post and the endless interview requests she had to deal with from the Irish media. But at least Terry and Michael were at long last forensic sidekicks. He liked being a big fish in the little pond that was Dublin, and she could see why. Everyone knew each other and, in the main, there was a feeling of collegiality and mutual support in law enforcement circles.

Not that she hadn't encountered bitchiness and jealousy. But she'd found that everywhere she'd been. In this instance, though, the good outweighed the bad. So far, anyway.

Ahern flashed her a smile. 'Dr O'Brien, I'm pleased to meet you. Mike has told me all about you. He can't sing your praises enough, in fact.'

Mike, is it?

'Nice to meet you,' she said. 'I think Michael may have mentioned you, too. Once or ten times.' She looked over at Fraser. 'You know Michael Flynn, John?'

'I do,' Fraser said. 'A fine forensic scientist.'

Ahern feigned bashfulness and turned back to Fraser. 'This one's well past its sell-by date according to Vinnie. I haven't seen her yet.' He handed Fraser and Terry white protective suits and gestured towards the boxes of surgical gloves sitting on the tailgate of the van. 'Help yourselves.'

Suited and booted, Terry and Fraser set off after Ahern. In a natural clearing ahead, they could see a man hunkered down with his back to them. As they got nearer, it was clear he was focused on something in the ditch in front of him; he turned as he heard them approach.

'Vinnie!' Terry was relieved to see the photographer's familiar aquiline face, his heavily lidded eyes giving the man a permanently thoughtful, hangdog look.

'Just finishing up here, Doc, then you can give it all a once-over.' Vinnie let his camera rest against his chest. 'She's lying in an awkward position so I can't see too much.'

'Definitely female?'

Vinnie nodded. Terry made her way over, carefully placing every step so as not to disturb evidence. The photographer got up and stood back so she could squeeze past.

The smell of decay hit her. The others quickly pulled up their masks, but the flimsy coverings weren't designed for this situation – Terry thought they intensified the stench rather than filtering it out – and they were damned uncomfortable to wear for any length of time. But rules were rules.

She looked back at Vinnie and, sotto voce, asked, 'Dumped?'

He gave a subtle nod. Terry was always careful not to divulge too much to anyone outside her immediate team before she was sure of her facts.

The body was small and appeared slight, long blonde hair the only indication that this was likely to be a female. It lay on its right side in a semi-foetal position, the limbs at odd angles, as if it had rolled into that position. The other side of the ditch was boundaried by a dense hedge and a fence. She looked at Vinnie and nodded across at it. Vinnie nodded in return, silently agreeing with her hypothesis that the body must have been hoisted over the hedge and fence to have landed where it was, in such a twisted, unnatural position.

Gingerly, she slid into the ditch, Vinnie above her, firmly grasping her left arm. She leaned over the corpse and as she did the hair moved, as if of its own accord, revealing a mass of maggots engulfing the woman's face. Their squirming had forced the strands to part.

Shit, Terry thought, *ID is going to be a problem.*

The body looked fully dressed, but Terry couldn't see any staining. She could see tears in the clothing and the woman's fingertips had been gnawed – not surprising, given that she was at the mercy of any passing rodent or other four-legged resident of these grounds.

'Any idea about the cause of death?' Fraser called down to her.

She knew her answer would determine what he did next, so

she just shrugged. 'Not a clue at the moment, sorry. I might, and I mean *might*, have a better idea once I get a good look at her in the mortuary.'

She saw disappointment cross his face, but she was damned if she was going to jump the gun. In contrast to Fraser, the officer beside him looked visibly shocked as he stared at the throbbing mound of larvae.

Not such a tough guy then, DI Ahern, she thought. Crime scenes like this did tend to separate the men from the boys.

'Time of death?' asked Fraser.

'Don't know that either. But I know a man who will be able to help us: your friend and mine Alan, Michael Flynn.'

The two detectives waited for her to explain herself.

'Amongst his many accomplishments as a forensic scientist, Michael – *Mike* to Alan – also specialises in entomology and anthropology – bugs and bones to you and me.' Terry pointed to the maggots that crawled over the woman's face.

'Aha,' Fraser said.

'At any rate, these guys will give Michael a good enough picture, and if you suspect drugs might be a factor in this lady's demise, they might help us there too. Clever little buggers, maggots.'

On the drive over, her garda escorts had regaled her with tales of bodies found in the park and how, in their considered opinion, this was probably just another 'junkie'. Terry hated that term.

'Wait until you have the facts,' she'd told them. 'And the term is *drug user*.'

A collective roll of their eyes had confirmed that she was preaching to the entrenched and disinterested.

A drug overdose was a long shot here, though. Why would someone move or try and conceal the body of a woman who had simply died of an overdose? That didn't make sense. Still, she had to keep an open mind. Terry stuck her arm up. Vinnie grabbed it and hoisted her out of the ditch.

With luck there could be a very simple explanation for this woman's death.

But she doubted it.

4

Terry removed her latex gloves, took out her phone and dialled Michael's number. He answered after the first ring.

'Hi,' she said. 'Busy?'

'When am I not?' he replied, his tone harried.

'I've got something right up your street,' she went on. 'A body's been found in the Phoenix Park. The grounds of Farmleigh.'

Terry knew Michael could never refuse a chance to get out of the laboratory and into the field. He always loved to be in the thick of it. And, of course, he would be delighted to work a case with her – Ahern being involved would be an added bonus.

'It's crucial we get a rough idea of the time of death,' she said, knowing which buttons to press.

Michael responded by heaving a weary sigh and shooting back: 'I don't do rough, as you well know. Entomology is a science. And I don't do *time of death*. But I will tell you when the first fly landed on the body.'

Terry could imagine him pulling himself up to his rather modest height as he spoke. 'I'll take that as a *yes, I'm on my way*, shall I?'

'They'll need to get onto the met office and get temperatures and weather for the last few weeks,' he said. 'I'll know better when I see the body how far back they'll need to go.' He paused a few beats for dramatic effect before saying, 'I'll get my kit together and head over.'

'Thanks, Michael.' She put her phone back in her pocket and turned to Fraser. 'One entomologist on his way.'

Ahern came over to join them at the edge of the ditch. 'That Mike fella is a bit of a dark horse. He was the DNA expert on a case I was on, but I didn't know he was an entomologist too.'

'Not to forget anthropologist,' Terry said. 'Not that he'd let you.'

'Impressive.'

Terry looked closely at Ahern. He seemed genuinely interested. *Maybe Michael's in with a chance*, she thought.

Fraser shrugged. 'Anything that helps me narrow the window of opportunity is appreciated. This is a needle-in-a-haystack situation at the moment.'

'Well, time-of-death calculation is not an exact science. But Michael is your best bet. Particularly if her body was dumped here shortly after she died.'

Terry knew many pathologists who gave the impression they could give a specific time of death and, unfortunately, they believed that they were being helpful, but many an investigation had fallen foul of good intentions. She was well used to griping from detectives when she talked in terms of days since death rather than hours and minutes. But only the people there at the time knew when someone had died. And she wasn't in the business of delivering false hope.

'I wish the time she died was our only issue,' Fraser said. 'Who the hell *is* she?'

They arranged the postmortem for 10 a.m. the next morning, after which Fraser and Ahern left for a conference at the incident room in Kevin Street Garda Station.

She was relieved things didn't feel too weird with Fraser. While she waited for Michael to arrive, she and Vinnie walked to the house, hoping someone would offer them a coffee. One of the guards had told them a couple of rooms had been put aside as a hub for the various teams needed on site. Even at this distance from the mansion they could hear sounds of frenetic activity, a sure sign the media were gathering. It was nigh impossible to keep them at bay once they got a sniff of a story, and this would certainly pique their interest: the body of a young woman found in the grounds of the official state guest house.

As she got closer to the house, Terry thought she had better lose her white suit, which was dirt-smeared and smelled badly, before going in. She pulled down the zip and wrestled her way out of it as Vinnie did the same, and they made their way towards the stately home.

Terry was finishing her coffee and scene notes in one of the small rooms they'd been given when Michael arrived. She watched her friend as he fiddled with a large old-fashioned doctor-style bag – a present, she knew, from his parents at graduation. Mammy Flynn had been so excited at her son studying medicine at Glasgow University that she'd gone out and bought the bag the day he was accepted. She hadn't been so thrilled when Michael switched to forensics. But he did get to keep the bag.

With it in hand, Michael looked around until he spotted Terry. Grinning, he strode over and went to hug her, but she stepped back, giving him a stern look. There was a time and a place for everything, and she was still relatively new here and wanted to maintain a professional veneer.

'Thank you for coming out, Dr Flynn,' she said, attempting a formal air.

Michael's laugh cut through the affectation. 'Your wish is my command, *Dr O'Brien*.'

Despite herself, Terry smiled. Vinnie looked from one to the other.

'We go way back, me and Tez,' Michael said. 'You're Vinnie, right? We met when you were shooting that scene in Dundrum about four months ago. The hammer attack?'

They shook hands.

'Never did find the hammer.' Vinnie sighed. 'Found enough other odds and ends to fill a toolbox, but that hammer proved very elusive.'

Michael turned back to Terry. 'Lead on, Macduff. I guess you're going to be my lovely assistant today?'

In a situation like this, the forensic scientist was the one in charge, the pathologist following his instructions. His slight smirk told her he would enjoy bossing *her* around for a change.

Vinnie led the way, Terry and Michael in quick step behind

him. They reached the wooded area where the body lay, and Terry felt her friend's eyes come to rest on her.

'Are you okay?' he asked quietly.

'I'm fine,' she replied, forcing a brightness into her voice that she didn't feel.

Michael knew about another wooded area, many miles away, which had left an indelible mark on Terry's life. The last time she'd been there had been a sunny day, not unlike this one, but in her mind's eye a permanent darkness hung over those trees, the pall of death always upon them.

Cairnhill Woods in Scotland were never far from Terry's thoughts. How could they be? They were where her sister Jenny had been found, murdered, all those years ago. The hard shell of professionalism was a useful protection at moments like this.

'I saw your fancy boy, by the way,' she said, changing the subject. 'Total poseur, no surprises there!'

'No way, Alan was here?'

'Yes, *Mike*.'

When they reached the ditch where the body lay, Michael set up his gear along the side of it. Vinnie looked on, fascinated, as he lined up glass bottles, some containing clear fluid, and a tape measure, then jumped in.

'Right, Tez. You ready to hand me the bottles?'

Terry noticed the photographer flinch as Michael plunged a thermometer into the mass of maggots just where the eye socket should be. From experience, she knew that the best way to get over squeamishness was just to get into the thick of it. She crouched at the edge of the ditch and turned to

Vinnie. 'You take pics of the maggots as I lay them on the tape to get their length.'

Vinnie, his long face even paler than usual, took a deep breath, swallowed and then raised his camera.

The three worked together in companionable silence until Michael was satisfied he had a representative sample.

'Trowels, Tez!' he said merrily.

Terry rummaged in Michael's bag, then, armed with two trowels, slid into the ditch beside him. Together they followed the trail the larvae had taken as they migrated from the body to pupate, their little bellies full. It took Terry a few minutes to get her eye in – it was no mean feat finding the tiny pellet-shaped pupa cases in the ground around the body that were essential for Michael to calculate the minimum time the deceased had been dead. Not quite the same as when the person died.

A good hour's work later, as the evening was drawing in, her friend stood and stretched. 'Right, time for a shower. Then does anyone fancy a scoop?' He looked from Terry to Vinnie.

'I'll give the drink a miss, if you don't mind,' Vinnie said. 'I want to get a few more photos once the boys move the body.' He reached down from his perch at the edge of the ditch and grabbed hold of Terry's arm and pulled her out. 'Another time, Doc?'

'No worries, Vinnie. Thanks for your help. See you at the mortuary tomorrow morning.'

Terry started back towards the house, her suit, once white, a mottled collection of dark stains from dirt, ditch water and worse.

'Jesus, we don't half stink,' Michael said, following her.

'What's new,' she said, turning back to him just in time to see two white suits hoist the packed body bag up from the ditch. 'So where are these drinks happening – usual place?'

'Where else?'

'Right, let's get cleaned up back at base, then head in.'

5

The Forensic Pathology Department where Terry worked, in the grandly titled Office of the State Pathologist, was part of a complex off Dublin's Griffith Avenue that included Forensic Science Ireland – Michael's domain – and State Toxicology.

A state-of-the-art purpose-built mortuary had been a long time coming and was Chief State Pathologist Professor Boyd's pride and joy, even if he was an outspoken critic of the building's modern edifice – a subject he had held forth on in the bar on more than one occasion when Terry was present.

She understood his ambivalence. This was a fitting repository for the dead, but Charles Boyd favoured Art Deco and Georgian elegance, and she had to agree the building was a bit flash. From the outside it looked more like an art gallery than a hotel for the dead – most checking in for just a couple of nights, the more complex cases often outstaying their welcome.

The front half of the building allowed for everything to be on view, from the outside and the inside. A sweeping staircase led up to the concourse presided over by Mrs Carey, Cerberus, the guardian of Professor Boyd, who divided his time between academic commitments at the university and his position here.

Terry would have bet her bottom dollar that no one who worked in the building had any hand in the design. Beyond this transparency of glass, the true purpose of the place was hidden away: to uncover the secrets of the dead.

Even at this time of evening it was ablaze with lights, but Terry knew the only live occupant was Jimmy, who was on the late shift. He had been the mortuary manager when Boyd's predecessor, Professor Carly, was appointed state pathologist in the early 1980s, and rough and ready as he was, Jimmy would walk over hot coals for Boyd. He didn't seem to feel quite the same way about Terry yet.

If there was no greyhound meeting, he always volunteered for the late shift. She knew he would be in the mortuary office, lying on the couch, a can of Aldi's version of stout in hand, watching the telly. She checked her watch – 7.42 p.m., which meant *Coronation Street*. Who was she to deny him such simple pleasures? Not that he would be likely to take much notice of her wishes anyway.

She went around to the back of the building to the hearse entrance. As she walked down the hall she shouted out, 'Only me, Jimmy. Just getting a shower and I'll be out of your hair. Body will be here in the next hour. PM's booked for ten tomorrow.'

In reply, the sound of the television quietened for a moment and then racked back up to just below nuisance level. Terry knew he'd heard her.

Tomorrow she would set about trying to piece together what had happened to the Farmleigh woman. Whoever she was, she deserved a better resting place than a ditch at the edge of the woods. She deserved a grave with a headstone – they all did – and it was up to Terry to help fill in the blanks, providing the details that should be etched into it.

Michael was late arriving at Mulholland's, his old work local from when FSI was located in town. Then, it had been far enough away from the big chiefs in Harcourt Street to allow them to relax and let their hair down, a necessity given the pressures of the job.

The pub was situated on Dame Lane, a narrow walkway between Dame Street and Grafton Street, within walking distance of both Pearse Street and Harcourt Street Garda Stations.

Terry sat on a high stool nursing a Bacardi and Coke as she waited for him. She'd missed a couple of calls while she was at the scene, both from her dad. She thought about calling him back as she waited for Michael, but the last thing she wanted was a lecture about being in the pub, so she texted a quick 'Sorry I missed you – call you tomorrow x' instead.

Michael tapped her shoulder as she signed off and she almost knocked over her glass with the fright. 'For *fuck's* sake!'

He gave her a quick hug and sat down. 'You can take the girl out of Glasgow but you can't take Glasgow out of the girl,' he said. 'Did you not get me a pint, doll?'

His exaggerated Glasgow accent made her laugh. He was normally so polite – well, as polite as anyone from Larkhall could be. He flashed her the same cheeky grin she remembered from their first encounter so many years ago.

It was during freshers' week at Glasgow University, at an introduction to the drama society. She was with Becs, her friend from as far back as primary school, who was determined they throw themselves into the whole shebang, hook, line and sinker. Becs was small, blonde and super confident; Terry was the complete opposite: tall, lanky, awkward in herself and shy – hardly drama material. Michael had marched up to her as she stood on her own in a corner, shredding a paper cup into confetti, terrified that anyone might notice her.

'Did you hear that?' he said, his voice incredulous.

Terry looked around, hoping that this curly-headed laddie was talking to someone else.

He gestured towards the guy at the top of the room, who was waxing lyrical about the joys of the drama soc. 'Snobby twat. *We only do Shakespeare and serious plays, nothing as frivolous as musicals.* Huh! Bugger that, is what I say.'

'It might be a laugh?' Terry said, although she wasn't so sure she wanted to be prancing about on a stage, performing the Bard.

'Are you joking me?' Michael's response had become their tagline over the years.

They never did join the drama society.

Terry slipped her phone into her bag and gestured for the barman to put on a pint for her friend.

'Like the new look,' she said, leaning across and ruffling

his hair. 'Yuck!' She wiped her hands against each other. His normally unruly mass of curls was straining against a thick layer of gel.

Michael settled on his stool and lifted the glass that landed on the beer mat in front of him. 'Cheers, me dear!'

They clinked glasses and sipped their drinks.

'So, how do you feel about today?' Michael asked as he wiped at an errant drip on his thigh.

'Fine, why?' she said.

He had a serious look on his face. 'That can't have been easy, the body of a young woman in the woods.'

Terry had no intention of going there. 'Give it a rest, Michael.'

He could be exasperating at times, acting like a surrogate big brother, trying to protect her from the workings of her own mind, as if anyone could. She stared down at her drink. When she looked up, the expression of concern on his face made her feel bad for snapping at him. She knew he meant well, that he could see through her 'fake it till you make it' facade. But it didn't help that he kept trying to bring up the past.

'Honestly, I'm okay,' she said, switching on a smile. 'Don't fret so much, you big girl's blouse.' She picked up her glass and held it aloft. 'Pals?'

Michael sighed. 'Pals.'

Terry looked around for a menu. She'd had nothing but coffee and Coke since breakfast and the Bacardi was going to her head. Michael nudged her arm.

'What?'

'Look who just walked in.'

Terry turned to see Alan Ahern, the crime scene manager from earlier on. Michael was staring at him, bug-eyed, his tongue virtually hanging out. As Ahern made his way through the bar, women openly appraised him; a couple that he knew were acknowledged with a hand on the shoulder and the full force of his smile.

'I think your gaydar might be a tad faulty,' Terry said.

'Uh-uh.' Michael shook his head as he waved in Ahern's direction. 'Hands off, he plays for my team.'

'Hello, Mike, and hello, Dr O'Brien,' Ahern greeted them as he approached.

Michael pulled over another stool but Ahern squeezed between their two stools and leaned against the bar.

Poor Michael, Terry thought. He'd been like a love-sick puppy since Paul had packed up and gone back to Boston. Paul had said they should call it a day because he wasn't sure if or when he'd be back in Ireland. His mother had dementia and he needed to care for her. Michael had lost weight since, not from grief, but mainly because Paul had been a great chef, and the one thing Michael loved as much as a muscle-bound man was a good home-cooked meal.

'Let me get you another one,' Ahern said, turning his back on Michael. 'What are you drinking, Terry?'

'Thanks. Bacardi and Coke please.'

'Carlsberg here,' Michael added.

Although Ahern barely acknowledged him, he put the full order in. 'Now, if you'll excuse me,' he said as the barman set about his work, 'I have to use the little boys' room.'

'Are you joking me?' Terry said when Ahern was well and truly out of earshot, watching him flirt his way across the floor. 'You don't stand a chance with that lad, Mikey boy!'

Michael's eyebrows shot up. 'Just because you fancy him doesn't mean he's hetero, hen.'

'I do *not* fancy him. I'm just telling you, from an expert point of view, he's as straight as an arrow.'

'The lady doth protest too much.'

Ahern returned just as the order arrived and tapped his card to pay. Thanking him, Terry hesitated before raising her glass. She still needed to eat! But she closed her eyes and enjoyed the sensation of the cold rum and cola going down.

'So how does working in Dublin compare to Glasgow?' Ahern asked as he pulled his stool over so he was sitting between Terry and Michael.

Terry shrugged and focused on not slurring her words. 'Same job, different people.'

'Well, it's the people you work with that make the difference.' He smiled.

Terry caught sight of herself and Michael in the mirror behind the bar.

Oh God! she thought. *We look like lovestruck teenagers vying to impress the cool guy at school.*

She decided there and then that, good-looking or not, she would not be getting into any kind of relationship with Ahern beyond the professional. She'd already come close to making her job unnecessarily difficult with those kinds of hijinks, and she still had to see how that would pan out with Fraser.

Michael interrupted her musings. 'Did you hear the latest? DCS Sinnott came in to see MacKenzie earlier on about one of his cold cases, wondering if the forensics might match anything to do with the body in the park today.'

Monica MacKenzie was Michael's boss, the director of Forensic Science Ireland. Terry found her a bit irritating, too much of a head-girl-at-school vibe about her.

'Seemingly Sinnott's got some guy called Cleaver in mind,' Michael continued, 'recently released from Mountjoy for aggravated assault, known to be a predator and he has form attacking women in the park. I looked him up – the rag press called him the "Park Prowler". He was in the frame for this murder years ago, but Sinnott never got the chance to properly pin him for it.'

Ahern took a swig of his pint. 'Probably wishful thinking. Bet it was the McCarthy murder – that's always been the one that got away for him. Sinnott wasn't the Super then, just a rookie detective. But he's a sore loser. Always thought Frank Cleaver got the better of him. Sinnott likes to stick his name in the mix for anything from jaywalking to triple murder, bless him.'

'The McCarthy murder?' Terry asked.

'Eileen,' Ahern replied. 'Eileen McCarthy.'

'Anyway,' Michael broke in, 'MacKenzie wasn't best pleased – sent him off with a flea in his ear. We're out the door with cases as it is.'

Terry leaned in. 'So what happened to Eileen McCarthy?'

'Terry, has anyone told you that you've an unhealthy interest in murder?' Michael said, an eyebrow raised.

Terry chose to ignore him.

'She was found dead in her home,' Ahern said matter-of-factly, 'strangled and stabbed. It was 2007 or '08, I think. No one was convicted for it – but there was strong circumstantial evidence that pointed at Frank Cleaver. He and the vic knew each other. They'd met in a pub on the evening she was murdered and she'd rebuffed him, after which he became very agitated and threatened her – the entire pub heard it. And, of course, he had a history of violent sex offences. There was never a smoking gun, though – the entire case against him was circumstantial.'

'So he walked away from it,' Terry said.

'He did, and that was the start of Sinnott's obsession. The Supe's theory was that it was a rape gone wrong – he was convinced the attacker, who he believed was Cleaver, hadn't intended to kill the vic, but that he lost control and the violence escalated to the point she died. Cleaver fit the profile to a point, but there was never enough to prosecute. Her poor family never got any resolution.'

Ahern downed the rest of his pint and rubbed his mouth with the back of his hand. 'Well,' he said, 'I'd better be going. An early start tomorrow.'

Michael's eyes followed him as he glided out the door.

'For Chrissake, Michael, put your tongue back in your mouth,' said Terry as she signalled for the menu.

She made a note to herself to look up Eileen McCarthy's postmortem file. It was probably nothing but her interest was piqued – an unsolved murder was right up her street. And it seemed curious the gardaí might think there was a link with today's case. It wouldn't hurt to have a look, but not until she'd completed the postmortem on the Farmleigh woman.

Better to go into each case with a clear view.

6

It was dark when they left the pub.

Terry had moved on to water, knowing she would need to be operating at her best the next morning, but she was still a little tipsy with only a toasted sandwich from the bar in her stomach. She said goodbye to Michael, who was going in the opposite direction to her, and walked south, past Trinity College and down Nassau Street towards her short-term rental on Northumberland Road.

She crossed onto Merrion Square, now empty and quiet, its park closed for the night, free from the bustle of the day. It wasn't cold, but she pulled her coat around her and kept her head down as she quickened her pace towards home. The Schoolhouse Hotel on her street corner was lit up. She checked her watch – it was 11.30 p.m. The hotel's bar would be just closing.

The only sounds on the empty street were the voices of

two men smoking in the beer garden and a car coming along behind her. It slowed as Terry approached her flat and she fought an irrational sense that she was being followed.

Her job made her hyper-aware of the murder statistics in each city she made home, and the circumstances of these deaths. Which meant she was acutely aware five women had been murdered on their way home from nights out within the past twelve months. She didn't like to think her job made her paranoid. Just careful.

She turned in to the gate quickly and took the steps to the front door of her building two at a time. As she turned the key into her own flat, her phone rang in her pocket. It was her dad's ringtone, 'The One and Only' – Chesney Hawkes's one-hit wonder had been at the top spot in the charts the week she was born, as her father liked to remind her. That was February 1991, and he'd been singing it to her since.

She pushed open the door and fished out her phone at the same time, pressing the green button. 'Hi Dad, just give me a minute!' She switched on the lights and sat down in the bare living room. 'Sorry I missed you earlier – did you not see my text? I had a horrendous day and Michael took me out for a few drinks.'

The words were out before she had time to think. Her dad didn't miss a beat. 'Was that wise, love?'

'Please, Dad. Don't start.'

'I thought you were laying off the booze for a bit, that's all.'

'I was, and now I have a drink from time to time and I can handle it just fine.

'That's what I said and look how that turned out.'

'You're fine now. I'm fine too. There's no need to be worrying.'

'I could have died, you know,' he said softly.

'Well, you didn't, Dad. And then you met Aileen and lived happily ever after.'

'Once an alcoholic, always an alcoholic. I wouldn't call that happily ever after.'

'Functioning alcoholic, Dad. And that's not what I am.'

Don O'Brien was a proper Irishman, the first with a song and the last to leave after one more for the road. The drinking had got out of hand after Terry left home. He was still working as the desk sergeant in Rutherglen Police Station when he had a stroke. She hadn't a clue there was a drink problem involved. It was his friend at work, Big Jim, who'd sat her down and asked her to persuade him to go to AA.

And now, with it all under control, he was evangelical when it came to the booze, apparently worried that a *problem with the drink* was genetic, an Irish trait.

'How's wee Michael anyway?'

Terry smiled to herself. Michael hated anyone pointing out his height. She told him that they'd worked on a case together that day.

'Anything interesting?'

Terry paused. 'It's a young woman, found dead in the woods. Looks like a murder.'

Her father was silent. Then, after a few seconds, he cleared his throat. 'Well, that can't be easy. Are you okay?'

'I'm fine, Dad. This is the job – I can't pick and choose what I work on. Anyway, hopefully we can find out who she is and who did this to her ...'

He sighed. 'It's not your job to find out who did it, Terry – that's up to the police.'

'Yeah, and they always do such a great job, eh, Dad?'

They both knew what she was referring to.

Jenny's death had torn the O'Brien family apart. Not finding her killer had turned out to be the straw that broke the back of her parents' marriage. Their family shrank from four to two within a few years. Terry stayed with her dad when her mother couldn't cope and moved away. From that day till now, he'd had her back.

'They do the best they can with what they have,' her dad said. 'You need to do your own job and take care of yourself, Terry. That should be your priority.'

There was a firmness in his tone that she knew spelled the end of the subject. Her dad was right. She'd hit the bottle when things started to go badly in her job in the Glasgow pathologist's office, which had not helped her situation one bit, further alienating her from an already fragmented team. If it hadn't been for her innate ability, she probably wouldn't have lasted as long as she had.

Becs, Terry's friend from childhood, had been indispensable, always ready with Irn-Bru and a couple of paracetamol. Eventually, one day Becs marched her into House of Fraser, stood her in front of a mirror and said, 'Where has my friend gone?'

For the first time in a long time, Terry saw herself through her best mate's eyes. Where had the once-happy young woman she had been when they first met at school disappeared to?

A new wardrobe hadn't been a panacea, but it had been the start to recovering her old self.

She was, as she was forced to admit when Becs finally persuaded her to enter therapy, someone who self-medicated with alcohol. But she didn't need it every day, not any more, at least. She was managing to keep her drinking under control.

Moving to Dublin was a final bid to put the past behind her, but even now she sometimes felt she'd never be truly free of the fact that her sister had been murdered and whoever had done it was still walking around. She'd barely unpacked since she got here, and the bland rental-property furniture and featureless walls held nothing of her personality, if she even knew what that was any more.

'Hello, dearie,' her stepmum Aileen's voice called out from the other end of the line, bringing her back to the moment.

'Hello back.' Terry raised her voice as she pictured her dad waving the phone in the air so Aileen could hear her. 'Loved the photos of your niece's wedding. Like your hair lighter.'

'Thanks, hen,' Aileen said.

Terry was relieved to feel the conversation winding down. 'Dad …' she said, but this time her father spoke over her.

'I'm sorry, love,' he said. 'For being cross with you.'

His voice sounded forlorn and the feeling of anxiety that had been clinging to Terry since earlier gave way to sadness. 'It's all right,' she said.

'Jenny wouldn't have wanted you so miserable, you know. She'd have wanted you to be happy, to get on with your own life.'

'I am happy, Dad. I am getting on with my life.' She tried to keep the tears out of her voice.

'Ah, sure, I know. And I'm proud of you, pet. You know that.'

'I know, Dad.'

They said goodbye and Terry went to the kitchen and poured herself a vodka.

She returned to the sofa. Outside the window, beyond her own reflection, she could just about make out the silhouettes of trees at the end of the overgrown garden.

She could still hear her sister's terrified voice, echoing through a different grove of trees, screaming out to her, 'Run, Anne Therese! Run!'

7

That night, Terry couldn't sleep. At 6.23 a.m., she got up and wandered into the bathroom. There were dark rings around her eyes, half mascara smudges and half exhaustion. She padded through to the sparse kitchen and made a cup of coffee.

In the sitting room, she switched on the small TV. The body in the Phoenix Park was headlining the news coverage: 'Partly skeletonised remains found in the grounds of Farmleigh House' ran the ticker at the bottom of the screen. Terry reckoned they must have been filming while she was in the ditch, chasing maggots with Michael.

The crime reporter was trying to pad it out, waffling on about general crime in the park. The report package then cut to footage of Terry herself, striding towards the house with Vinnie, the reporter informing viewers that the new pathologist in the department had been called in. Dammit, she wished now she'd kept the white suit on, this was just the kind of shot designed to rile Boyd. After that, the camera zeroed back in on John Fraser in Farmleigh, identified as 'the senior investigating officer'.

Fraser gave a quick statement, saying it was the body of a woman, but not really divulging any other facts. To be fair, that was the truth of it so far. Terry hoped there'd been some developments overnight.

Behind the DCI and the reporter were the usual rubber-neckers, straining the good nature of the police tape cordoning off the area, as well as the patience of the gardaí who were trying to secure the scene.

Off to the side, standing alone by a makeshift memorial made of flowers laid by random mourners, was an older woman, her eyes closed, her hands in swift motion. It reminded Terry of her aunt Bridie, the doyenne of her parish church down in Cork, rosary beads rotating through her fingers with the speed of a fisherman reeling in his nets. But the look on her face was more like that of her mother.

Or what was left of her mother after Jenny's death – broken and haunted, waiting for answers that never came.

The mortuary car park was almost empty when Terry's taxi pulled up at 9.30 a.m. There was just a small white van that she assumed belonged to the Scenes of Crime Unit and, beside it, Jimmy the mortuary manager's grungy old Land Rover. Tomas, the assistant, generally took the bus, and she hoped he was in already.

It was Jimmy who opened the back door, unshaven, definitely unwashed and wearing the brown shop-coat he insisted on keeping as his uniform. 'Oh, it's you,' he muttered, as if he was both surprised and disappointed by her appearance.

Terry gave an internal eye-roll. 'Good morning to you too, Jimmy. Has Dr Flynn arrived yet?'

'The Scottish midget?'

Terry kept walking. *That's the second time Jimmy Finnegan has irritated me this morning*, she thought.

'The forensic scientist,' she said.

'Yeah. He's got Tomas boiling water. Says it kills the maggots. I just usually scoop them up and use 'em for the fishing.'

'Third.'

'Third what, Doc?'

'Nothing.'

Michael was already in the PM room, suited and booted, when Terry walked in.

'Morning,' he said. 'How are you feeling?'

'Fine,' Terry replied. 'How're you?'

'As bright as a daisy in May.'

'Yeah, looks like it,' Terry said.

'Can't believe I had to miss you two out drinking on a school night!' Vinnie joined in.

'We had one drink after work, that's all.'

'If you say so,' Vinnie said.

Terry felt a defensive prickle.

The body was in a worse state than she first thought. Identification was going to be difficult and so might identifying the cause of death. The left side had been exposed, so had borne the brunt of the weather, insects and scavengers. And while the right side had been protected by the base and sides of the ditch, it hadn't been protected from flies, which could get into any nook or cranny. Only the skin around the right ear had survived the onslaught of the larvae that had made short work of the soft tissues on the left side of the face.

Terry and Michael walked around the postmortem table trying to decide the best approach. If this was a murder, she wanted to be sure they collected every piece of relevant evidence, and Michael was there to make sure nothing was overlooked. Two heads were definitely better than one in these situations.

The body looked pitiful lying on the autopsy table – small and dirt-encrusted, like a defenceless child. Michael gave Terry a nod and she swiftly moved into professional mode, swabbing, taping, documenting each step, all the while running through potential scenarios.

She'd thought it might be a sex-related killing when she had first looked down into the ditch. Not necessarily the work of a predatory rapist and killer, but maybe a clandestine sexual encounter turned sour. The job taught her with alarming regularity how easily passion could tip over into violence.

As usual she started with the clothing: plain white T-shirt, no-nonsense white bra, light blue denim skirt and white lace thong. The skirt had ridden up, exposing her left hip. There were small holes, animal teeth marks she suspected, and a few ragged tears around the left shoulder of the t-shirt, as well as a few holes over the left side. She smoothed the material and she could see that the holes were over the left breast. Vinnie took a couple of photos and then Tomas helped her pull the garment over her head. The bra showed the same three holes in the left cup. There was no bloodstaining but a small globule of fat was stuck to the edge of one hole. Once it was photographed, Tomas grabbed the woman's right arm and pulled the body onto its right side to allow Terry to undo the clasp at the back. Tomas lowered the body back onto the table and when Terry wrangled the bra off she saw three stab wounds on the left breast.

'Oh, oh!'

'What have you found doc?' Vinnie handed the bra to Mary Healy, the Crime Scene Manager and keeper of the exhibits and walked back to the table.

'She's been stabbed.'

'But you said there was no blood. Are you sure its not just teeth marks. Rats or something.'

Tomas stuck his head in front of Terry to get a better look, 'Big fucking rats. Sorry doc.'

Terry couldn't help smile. 'Fine Tomas, but I agree.'

She stood back and looked the body up and down, then lifted the scale and laid it on the skin beside the uppermost wound and motioned for Vinnie to take a photo. 'Guess we'll just have to wait until I get inside and see what is going on. But meantime can you take a photo of her pants before I remove them? There's a tear at the left side of the waistband and they're just holding together. The elastic will break when I pull at them.'

'Sure. Can you just smooth the material out so I get the holes on the front of them? What did that?'

'Now that's definitely animal.'

Soon, the body lay naked and exposed. Terry looked over

to Michael. This was a collaborative effort: she was the pathologist and he was the scientist. Neither was going to step on the toes of the other. Only once she had harvested all trace evidence to Michael's satisfaction would Terry begin her own part of the process.

Michael took one last look at the body's hands and gave her a thumbs-up. 'She's all yours, Terry.'

She stood at the end of the table. It was as if a line had been drawn down the body: the ravaged left half bearing the effects of decomposition, the right half moderately preserved.

Terry reckoned the woman had been young and pretty. Her hair was long and very blonde. She did the usual check for identifying features. It was always difficult in these circumstances. She scraped the dark blistering layers of putrefying skin from the back of the right arm, working down from the shoulder. There was something on the back of the wrist.

'Vinnie, can you get a close-up of this area?'

'What am I looking at?'

'I think it's part of a tattoo.'

Vinnie took several photographs. 'It's just at the edge, where a rat or something has been nibbling. Have a look.' He held the camera towards her.

Terry peered at the screen. 'Might be a "c" and an "e" but it could just be the edge of a flower or whatever folk get.'

'Not a fan?'

Terry cocked an eyebrow at him. She turned back to the body. The three wounds on the left breast glared at her. They were oval shaped and the wound margins had an orange waxy appearance. *Odd*, she thought.

Tomas bustled over as soon as she walked to the side of the table. With his gloved hand, he deftly swept the remaining mass of maggots from the head into a bucket, letting Terry have a closer look at the scalp. The maggots' appetite had been voracious, and the skull was exposed. There wasn't a mark on it. The eyes were gone. Terry stepped closer and picked up the scalpel Tomas had laid on the table. She drew the knife across from shoulder to shoulder, then placed the tip in the dip of the neck above the top of the breastbone and continued the cut down to the pelvis, forming a T-shape. Carefully, she peeled back the skin on the left side of the chest. There was no haemorrhage into the fatty tissue. She poked the handle of the scalpel into each hole in turn. The top hole continued through the gap between two of the ribs into the chest cavity, the other two ended on the ribs. She dissected off the fatty breast tissue to expose the front of the ribcage.

There was a hole in the intercostal muscle between the left third and fourth ribs. Tomas handed her a bread knife and she sawed through the costal cartilages, joining the ribs to the breastbone and lifted off the front of the ribcage, exposing the contents of the chest, the lungs and heart. She had expected the lung to be punctured, and it was, but surprisingly it hadn't collapsed like a burst balloon, and there was no blood in the chest cavity. *Curiouser and curiouser*, she thought. Within minutes the contents of the chest and abdomen were being hefted over to the dissection table.

By the time this task was complete, Tomas had stripped back the scalp and opened the skull. Vinnie hovered, camera at the ready, as Terry turned her attention to the preserved neck area. Meticulously, she peeled back the layer of skin and the muscles beneath, checking for bruises, exposing the skeleton of the throat. There was patchy haemorrhage into the soft tissues across the front.

She stopped and beckoned Vinnie over. 'The thyroid cartilage is cracked down the middle.' She pointed to the Adam's apple.

Vinnie leaned in to get a couple of close-ups. When he stood back, Terry nodded at him. 'Got what you need?'

'Yes, boss.'

She began to focus on the dissection, carefully checking the slender rings of cartilage above and below the voice box. 'The cricoid's broken as well, but you'll get a better shot once I've removed the lot.'

Now was the time to check for evidence of sexual assault. In Glasgow, as soon as she mentioned vulva or vagina, or any reference to the female genital area, the mortuary technicians did a disappearing act. Not so here.

'Can you two back up the bed a bit and give me some room?' she told Vinnie and Tommy who had taken up position one at each shoulder. The two gave her a puzzled look but shuffled back a couple of steps. 'Thanks.'

For the next ten minutes she was bent over the body, doing one of the trickiest dissections a forensic pathologist had to do. Sweat dripped down between her shoulder blades as she carefully removed the perineum and internal sex organs. She took the specimen over to the dissection board and examined outside and in for injuries that might indicate she had been raped.

Eventually, she looked up. 'Tomas, any sign of the DCI?'

'No. Want me to check if he's on his way?'

Before she had a chance to answer, John Fraser appeared in the viewing gallery.

Terry signalled for him to move closer to the glass and pressed the intercom button. 'Her throat has been crushed. Probably an armlock. Grabbed from behind or pinned down by a forearm. As to whether or not she was sexually assaulted, her pants were torn, but that could be animals worrying the body. There *was* a bruise on the anterior vaginal wall. But before you run away with yourself, that might mean something or nothing. She may have had recent sexual intercourse, but I can't say if it was consensual or not. Doctors do not diagnose rape. Well, unless the injuries are so horrendous that there is no other explanation. But you get the gist. Maybe the swabs will show something. At any rate, it looks like you've got yourself a murder. But there is something else. She's been stabbed.' She gestured behind her to the body on the table. 'Three to the left breast. But the strange thing is, she was already dead when the injuries were inflicted. They're postmortem, very postmortem, injuries.'

Fraser didn't push the button to activate the microphone in the viewing room, so Terry didn't hear his response, but it didn't take an expert lip reader to interpret, 'Shit!'

8

Once the postmortem was concluded, Terry filled in Fraser further on what she had learned. He listened intently, nodding at various points.

'Thanks, Terry,' he said. 'I mean, *Dr O'Brien.*'

'You're most welcome, *DCI Fraser.*'

He smiled and she could feel herself blush but if Fraser shared her discomfort, he gave no sign of it. They said their goodbyes and he left.

Terry's next job was to update Professor Boyd on the PM results, which meant facing him after yesterday's dressing down. It was the last thing she wanted to do, but she couldn't avoid him forever.

She knew Charlie Boyd had a massive ego. On her first day on the job, approaching four weeks ago now, he'd displayed it in no uncertain terms in front of everyone in the mortuary, and Terry was at the butt of the display. He'd swanned in, three students in his wake, and began pontificating about the PM on the table based on assumptions from the case description. Boyd had not taken it well when Terry updated him with the emerging evidence – far from Boyd's 'folly of youth' theory which had the young hillwalker fall from a high peak, he had more likely died as a result of a minor fall that would otherwise have been survivable, but for the fact of a physiological quirk, an eggshell skull.

He put paid to that theory in no uncertain terms, dressing her down in front of the team. The students could barely keep their mouths closed. He was most firmly putting Terry in her place, showing himself to be top dog. It didn't matter that her 'theory' was spot on.

She knew now that he'd been suspicious of her from the start and the fact that she couldn't go to a scene without winding up on the news was bad news for his ego. He was threatened by her, and that's why he'd gone digging, she was sure of it. But she had to work with him. And perhaps she could use the opportunity to update him on things to glean some information from him about the Eileen McCarthy case Ahern had mentioned the night before. If Sinnott was right, it might help shed light on the Farmleigh murder. He might have a reputation for being gruff and a man's man, but he was, by all accounts, a good cop.

Terry climbed the back stairs to the first floor, intending to drop off her notes in her office before seeking Boyd out down the hall. As she reached her office, she heard his voice booming from the reception area at the end of their corridor. Someone was getting it in the neck.

'It's damned inconvenient. I can't be expected to drop

everything and run over here every time you have a problem – I have other commitments, and they are *all* pressing.'

Terry made her way down the hallway and, seeing the look of misery on Mrs Carey's face, decided to do the office manager a favour. She cleared her throat loudly and both heads turned at the interruption.

'Dr O'Brien,' Boyd said, pulling himself together. 'A word.'

He strode past her, making for his office, 'Who stole his scone?' said Terry to Mrs Carey.

'Pardon?'

'Oh, it was something my gran used to say. What's got him in a tizzy now?'

'He's looking for a file and can't find it. I've told him exactly where it is, but he's not a patient man. I'll go and get it for him in a moment.'

'Dr O'Brien, if you please!' Boyd bellowed from within his sanctum.

Terry followed the sound and stood awkwardly in front of his desk.

'He tapped his desk with a pen and sat silently for a couple of seconds. 'As per our conversation of yesterday, I think you would be better served concentrating on your work than courting the media, don't you agree?'

Was he referring to the news item with footage of her? 'I—'

Boyd cut her off. 'Did I not make myself clear?'

'I made no contribution to the TV report whatsoever, if that's what you're referring to. I arrived at the scene as per your instructions and did my job. I'm not used to cameras lurking around every corner.'

He cut across her. 'Are we any closer to an ID on the Farmleigh remains?'

'We're waiting on DNA and a dental examination.'

'Well, put it at the top of your priority list. There'll be a media circus around this and you need to get a handle on who that woman was ASAP. We need data, Dr O'Brien, not fashion tips.'

'Do you think I don't know that, Professor? Do you seriously believe I court any of this attention? I can assure you, I'm doing everything in my power to establish this poor woman's identity.'

Boyd sniffed and looked uncomfortable. Terry realised he was not used to being spoken to like that. He picked up a sheaf of papers and began staring at them intently.

'May I ask you about something?' Terry said, deciding she might as well capitalise on his discomfort.

Boyd raised his eyebrows. 'What is it, Dr O'Brien?'

'Do you remember anything about the PM on a murdered woman called Eileen McCarthy? It was in 2007 or 2008.'

'I may do,' he said.

'Apparently DCS Sinnott thought a man called Frank Cleaver was the killer, but he never got it off the ground. Cleaver's recently been released from prison for a different conviction. Sinnott has suggested there may be a connection between the McCarthy death and the one at Farmleigh. I was wondering if I might have a look at the PM results.'

Professor Boyd took off his glasses, closed his eyes and rubbed the top of his nose, as if he was exhausted. 'Dr O'Brien, did you not hear what I just said? You have a body with no ID found on state property. I suggest you concentrate on that.'

'That's what I am doing! I just—'

'Enough! Get on with the work you came here to do. Now,' he sat down and opened his laptop, 'I have my own work to attend to. Good day.'

Terry could feel her anger rising. *What the hell was this man's problem?* Not trusting herself to speak, she glared back at her boss and walked out.

9

Terry had just got back to her office when her desk phone rang. 'Terry O'Brien here.'

'Terry, it's Vinnie. Laura, that young doctor we talked about, is here.'

'Young doctor?'

'My friend's sister? She qualified last year and is trying to get onto the pathology training scheme? She's completely obsessed with forensics, wants to be a mini-you? You said to give her your email and you'd give her a chance.'

A vague memory stirred in Terry's head. She sat up. 'Oh, yeah, Laura – we did email, but it's next week she's supposed to come, I'm sure.' Terry started searching frantically through her deleted emails, until she found the last one from Laura – confirming a start date of that very day. *Shit*. 'Vinnie, today is really not the day. This is really not the week. Can she come back on Monday?'

'She's come all the way from Belfast, Terry. She took two weeks' leave from the Royal Victoria to come here. I'm not going to send her away. Come on, you promised.'

Terry rubbed her eyes and counted to ten in her head. 'Okay. Send her up.'

Exactly three minutes later a young woman appeared at her office door.

'Hi, Laura.' Terry pointed to the chair in front of her desk and beckoned her in.

She was small and slim, probably no more than five feet in heels and seven stone soaking wet. She had an oval-shaped, symmetrical face and long, shining dark hair in a plait that hung almost to the small of her back. Under her coat she was wearing a Fun Lovin' Criminals T-shirt. She buzzed with nervous energy.

'Thank you so much for seeing me, Dr O'Brien. I can't tell you what it means to me to have this opportunity.'

'And you think postmortems are for you?' The girl's face turned crimson. Terry smiled at her. 'This isn't everyone's cup of tea. If you'd been at the case earlier this morning you might be reconsidering.'

'Oh! I'm so sorry I missed it, but I just got down and I met Vinnie over at Garda HQ. I didn't want to rock up on my own. Otherwise, I would love to have seen you at work.'

'Well, you're more than welcome at the next one. You know what we do here and if it doesn't faze you then I'm more than happy for you to tag along behind me. If it gets too much, just say. I won't take it personally.' Terry stretched across her desk and shook hands with the young woman. 'Welcome aboard. Now, I can't predict the future, and I certainly can't predict when someone will die. In-between times, I have plenty to be getting on with, and you can help out with that – though I reckon you'll find most of it pretty boring.'

Terry waved her hand towards the mounds of folders, files and papers on her desk, on the floor and piled on top of every surface in the room. 'You can start by helping me tidy this lot up.'

Laura looked about her in utter dismay. 'Oh. Okay. I can do that ... I think.'

'Come on. Let's start with what's on the desk and take it from there.'

'Sure,' Laura said, standing and taking her coat off. 'It'll be a good learning experience anyway. I mean, these are all case files, aren't they? Well, not the empty coffee cups or the sweet wrappers or ... whatever that is ...' She indicated a clump of something that Terry thought had once been a banana. 'But the rest will be good to familiarise myself with, won't they?'

'That's the spirit,' Terry said.

And they began.

IO

He watched the girl get off the bus and walk towards her house. She was wearing the long coat again. Her hair was pulled into a tight bun at the back of her head. He liked it better loose.

She worked in HR for one of the big IT firms. She would be good at dealing with people and their problems, he thought. She would be kind and understanding.

It was easy to lose your cool when you had to deal with stupid people who didn't understand the importance of the job you were doing. The girl would get that, he felt.

She turned in the gate and mounted the steps to her home.

He wondered suddenly if she missed the place where she and her foster sister had grown up, if it was a good home, a happy one. Or had it been like his.

Maybe she was happy without her foster sister.

By the time he'd been released from care, his mother had died. But his sisters were still living in that little house near the river. He'd made a point of visiting them, when the time was right. It excited him to think about it.

He watched the girl fiddling with the lock on the front door and thought about what it would be like to visit her.

11

Terry kicked off her heels as soon as she got home, then took a long shower. It had taken herself and Laura the day to get her office in order, and while she loved the airy spaciousness it now had, she felt as if she was covered from head to toe in dust and grime. The water pressure wasn't as good as her shower back in Glasgow, but it was electric so she could stay as long as she liked. Eventually, towelled and pyjamaed, she padded to the kitchen to cobble together some dinner.

The fridge was sparse, the cupboards more so. She took the last two eggs from a carton, a bit of butter and made herself a small omelette, with a slice of toast and a mug of tea. Then she went into the sitting room and ate it on her lap, with an eye on a talk show on TV.

She wasn't really sure who half the guests were, but the hum of conversation and laughter and occasional clapping and cheering was a welcome distraction. A chef talked about how successful her podcast on traditional Irish foods had become in the US. Terry reached for her phone to check it out and, under the list of 'Popular and trending' podcasts, something caught her eye. *Abandoned: The Search for Justice for Ireland's Murdered Women.*

She tapped on the icon and read the 'About' text underneath:

My journey started with Women's Aid publishing the names of over 200 women killed in Ireland from 1996 until today.

Who killed these women?

The majority were killed by someone they knew. But one in eight of these murders remains unsolved and half of them were young women in their teens and twenties, and no one was brought to account. Young women whose lives were tragically cut short.

And who cares? Well, their families, those who loved and worried about them. And me.

It wasn't just a list of names. Beside each was a photograph. A moment in time captured forever. A reminder of who they were. Abandoned investigates some of the country's most prominent cold cases of unsolved murders.

Terry shuddered. She knew that feeling of loving someone who seemed to be just a statistic to those in power, who never seemed to do enough or care enough.

To the left of the podcast description was an arty-looking image of the host, Rachel Reece. Her face was partly obscured by a baseball cap, half turned, her one visible eye staring directly into the camera, defiant-looking.

There was a quick update at the bottom of the description.

I'm currently working on a new episode on the unsolved murder of Eileen McCarthy. I'm putting out my usual call for anyone who has any information on the case to contact me at rachel@abandonedpod.org

Terry's attention was piqued. There was that name again. She scrolled a little more. There was one more update from six weeks previously:

I'm once again asking for any information my listeners might have on Eileen McCarthy. My requests for interviews with the gardaí have been flatly refused, my emails unanswered. Professor Charles Boyd, the forensic pathologist who carried out the postmortem on Eileen, agreed to an interview but threw me out of his office when I raised some points he didn't want to hear. This is going to have to be a grassroots investigation. I'd appreciate any help I can get.

She was surprised to see Boyd's name. Was that why he'd been so sharp with her earlier when she's asked about the Eileen McCarthy PM?

Next morning, Terry sat in her office finalising her report on the bouncer case, but her mind kept drifting to the notes she'd made on the Farmleigh body. DCS Sinnott seemed to be attributing this murder to a sex offender before she had even performed the postmortem. He obviously thought there were similarities between the Farmleigh case and that of McCarthy. If she could get a look at the McCarthy report, despite Boyd's warning, maybe she could find something that pointed either towards or away from this guy Cleaver that could stop the police wasting their time or give them something concrete.

She was sitting pondering this when Laura breezed in.

'Morning, Dr O'Brien,' she said, taking a seat on the opposite side of the desk.

'I told you to call me Terry.'

'I'll try to remember.'

'Do. Laura, you're into all that true-crime stuff, aren't you?' Laura had mentioned her passion for it during their spring cleaning the previous day.

'It'd be truer to say I'm obsessed by it.'

'Have you heard of *Abandoned*?'

'It's the most-listened-to Irish true-crime podcast, so *yes*.'

'It's good then?'

'Rachel Reece is a "gifted investigative journalist", quote, unquote. She's actually uncovered some clues and leads that were missed during police investigations – well, according to what she says anyway. But, yeah, it's a really good podcast.'

Terry nodded thoughtfully. 'You know she's currently researching one on Eileen McCarthy?'

'Yes. I heard her update.'

'As it so happens, I need to have a look at the postmortem results on that case. It's been suggested it may be linked to the Farmleigh murder. Do you fancy helping me?'

'Sure! What do you need?'

'Someone to do a bit of ferreting. There's a mountain of files out there, and administrative prowess is not to the fore of my skillset.'

'Then I'm your girl. Can you access the records digitally?'

Terry laughed. 'Good question.'

They did a quick search on her desktop, but regrettably the files from 2007 weren't digitised – technological advances seemed to be adopted far more slowly in pathology than other areas – but the catalogue was available, and she was able to find the file number and confirm that Boyd had indeed performed the autopsy, as the podcaster said.

Usually she'd have asked Mrs Carey to retrieve the file, but with Boyd involved – not to mention his having warned her off the McCarthy case – it seemed safer to keep it to herself for now.

The folders in the hall of records were arranged on a series of shelves, abutting one another, which had to be cranked apart to access the files. Facing them was a metal wall. Terry felt claustrophobic, imagining being crushed between the shelves. They walked along the wall which was labelled from the 1970s to 2020s till they located the storage shelf for 2007. They manoeuvred things to open up the space between it and its neighbour, then walked into the gap formed and found themselves in a narrow corridor lined by floor-to-ceiling shelves forming a vertical suspension system, the folders dangling from a metal rod stretching end to end on each shelf. They flicked through the files to the relevant month. And flicked through them again. Laura rechecked the file number, then tried 2006 and 2008, in case it had been misfiled, but it wasn't there either. There could be no doubt about it: the McCarthy file was missing.

Terry leaned back against the unit.

'It's not unusual that someone would request an old file,' she said to Laura, 'particularly if it might have relevance to an ongoing case.'

'Who might have it?' Laura asked.

'I don't know,' Terry admitted. 'Boyd seems the likeliest candidate. I mean, he's close to Archie Sinnott, and Sinnott is the one who's sniffing around the case. And I mentioned the case to Boyd yesterday, too.'

'Is there any way to find out?' Laura asked.

'There is,' Terry said. 'But given my strained relations with the prof it could backfire on me if we're not subtle.'

'Subtlety I can do,' Laura said so earnestly Terry almost believed her.

Five minutes later they were standing at Mrs Carey's desk, while the office manager talked into the phone. After what seemed like forever, Mrs Carey ended her call and replaced the receiver. Only then did she make eye contact with Terry.

'Yes, Dr O'Brien?'

'Mrs Carey, I'm having trouble locating an old file, and I thought, if anyone in this department would know where it was, it would be you!'

Mrs Carey, seemingly unimpressed by the flattery, replied, 'Well, I certainly do not know the location of every old file. But I could probably make a fair guess about most. Would you like me to search the records room?'

From Professor Boyd's office, which was directly opposite Mrs Carey's desk, they could intermittently hear the chief pathologist's voice as he spoke loudly and authoritatively to someone.

'Oh, no – I've had a good look there myself. I thought perhaps someone else might have it, and I was wondering had anyone requested any old files lately – from 2007?'

'Well, I don't remember the exact year, but I did retrieve a number of files for Professor Boyd some weeks back and he hasn't asked me to return them yet, so it's possible he still has them. Would you like me to—?' Mrs Carey picked up her phone as if to call him.

'No! No, it's fine – I can ask him myself later. I wouldn't like to disturb him. Not to worry – I'll catch up with him again.'

'Well, he's not here this afternoon – he has lectures at the university.'

'Okay, thanks. Come on, Laura.'

They headed back to Terry's office before Professor Boyd could appear.

Later that morning, Laura went over to Garda HQ to shadow Vinnie while he catalogued his photographs from the previous day's PM, while Terry finalised the bouncer report, leaving her door open so she could keep an eye and ear on the comings and goings while she worked.

Sure enough, just before one, she heard Boyd's booming voice in the corridor. She waited for five minutes, giving Mrs Carey time to gather her things and leave for lunch, then headed towards Boyd's office. An added advantage to the office manager keeping everything running like clockwork was that you could generally predict where she would be and when.

Sure enough, her chair was empty, an extra cardigan on the back in case of sudden temperature changes, her notepad and pen aligned with the phone, and her navy handbag gone from the coat stand beside the photocopier behind the desk.

Realising her opportunity, Terry quickly slipped into Boyd's room.

The chief state pathologist was a keen birdwatcher and hiker, the walls of his office covered in artfully captured photographs of red kites, avocets and choughs taken during his excursions to the mountains and lakes of Ireland. The space was also a shrine to the awards and exploits of his career. Terry had always thought it was naff to have every achievement on display, but she could see how it would serve to impress visitors.

She stood just inside the door and looked around. A rather grand antique-looking desk set sat on Boyd's heavy oak desk, but unfortunately the rest of it was clear. An ornate table to the left, however, had a microscope and neatly stacked files atop. The overall impression of the room was that it was occupied by an accomplished and important person.

Terry honed in on the files on the table. Very few looked recent. Just as she'd suspected, she was doing the bulk of the postmortems. She glanced through the files. The top ones were in green folders, the bottom ones in pink and blue. One of the blue folders was labelled *Eileen McCarthy*. Bingo.

A pink folder labelled *Joyce Sisters* was attached to the McCarthy file with an elastic band. She figured that meant Boyd believed there was some connection between the cases, so she took it as well and restacked the others.

With the purloined documents in hand, she walked to the

door and listened. All was quiet, so she gently opened it and looked around. The corridor was empty.

Terry slipped out of her boss's office and went straight to the photocopier. Feeling nervous and exposed, she began to feed the contents of the files into the machine. As she did, a photograph fluttered out onto the floor. Staring up at her was a young woman, her eyes open, her mouth gaping, as if mid-scream, long fair hair splayed on the once-white fabric of a pillow beneath.

Terry reached down and picked up the photo. Before her eyes, the pillow dissolved into foliage, the hair tangled and woven into it. The face began to change into Jenny's face – younger yet every bit as terrified.

Her big sister, whom she had left that evening on the path through the woods – yet again, the bratty little sister, refusing to do what she was asked, fully believing Jenny would come after her. It was a ten-minute walk on a lit road to their house against a five-minute dash through the woods, but Terry didn't like the dark. Usually Jenny gave in to her little sister's demands, but this time she left Terry to take the long way home alone. Terry's last image was looking back and seeing Jenny vanishing into the darkness.

Shaking her head as if to dislodge the memory, Terry quickly finished placing the last of the papers into the feeder and pressed Copy. As soon as the final piece came through the machine, she stuffed the pages back into their respective folders, reapplied the elastic band and replaced the originals in Boyd's office. Just as she stepped back out, she heard footsteps in the corridor. Looking around, she spotted a pile of new manila folders on the shelf behind Mrs Carey's desk and quickly shoved her copies into one, just as the office manager placed her handbag on her desk.

'Is there something I can help you with, Dr O'Brien?'

'No, no, just needed some stationery – all done now!' Terry patted the folder and gave Mrs Carey a nod.

Files clutched to her chest, she headed back to her office just in time to meet Laura returning from her photo-cataloguing tutorial.

'Have you got the file?' Laura asked quietly, seeing the bundle Terry was carrying.

'I do. Let's have a look and see what we can learn.'

Laura nodded and they went inside.

12

It was the mention of the tattoo that did it.

Terry and Laura had been going through the files Terry had copied, passing the pages to and fro between one another. The second one related to two other women, sisters who had been murdered in Ringsend in 2004. Terry put the file copies in an old yellow folder and set them aside, as she and Laura focused on Eileen McCarthy, going through each aspect of the PM, taking note of everything and cross-checking with the Farmleigh case.

'I tell you,' Laura said after a while, 'I can't wait to hear what Rachel Reece makes of this. She'll probably turn the whole case on its head – she's such a badass. She's all about getting justice for these women. She's even got that tattooed on her wrist.'

Terry looked up from the page she was reading. 'Sorry, could you rewind there for just a moment?'

Laura looked at her quizzically. 'To which bit?'

'You mentioned a tattoo.'

'Yeah. Rachel has a tattoo on her wrist, the word "justice". She says it's a message to the guilty that she's coming after them, and to the victims that she won't rest until they're at peace.'

'That's quite a commitment.'

Terry googled Rachel Reece. She clicked Images, and the podcast's one-eyed stare picture looked back at her.

In another, Rachel was strikingly made up, wearing an elegant black-lace dress, her long blonde hair cascading over one shoulder. The banner behind her was for the Irish Podcast Awards, and she was clutching a heavy-looking angular trophy.

Terry clicked on the photo and then the link to the website. The photo appeared again, followed by a close-up of Rachel smiling and kissing the trophy underneath. Terry's stomach lurched. She leaned closer, staring at the pale wrists holding the trophy.

There it was, on the back of her right wrist, the ending of a word, inked in cursive: 'ce'. There was no doubt in her mind that she was looking at the young woman whose body had been found in the grounds of Farmleigh House.

'What's wrong?' said Laura, seeing the expression on Terry's face.

Just then her phone rang. It was John Fraser.

'Terry? We need to talk. Something's come up about Farmleigh.'

'Hang on a minute.' She held the phone to her chest and told Laura to go get a coffee. 'Sorry about that. Right, you're on about Rachel Reece?'

'What? How did you know?' Fraser sounded mildly disappointed that she'd got there before him.

He explained that he'd got a call about a missing person, Rachel Reece, who had been living in Phibsborough. Her housemate had been on holiday and had only arrived back when she was confronted by the next-door neighbour, who unceremoniously dumped Rachel's cat in her arms. Seems Rachel hadn't been seen for a few weeks, and the neighbour had taken pity on the hungry animal after a couple of days.

The housemate tried contacting Rachel but her phone went straight to voicemail, and kept doing so. After six hours of listening to Rachel's voicemail greeting, her friend contacted the guards. Rachel often took off for days or weeks for her work as a crime podcaster, but she would never leave the cat alone.

Fraser had reckoned the long blonde hair and build described by the housemate could be a good fit for the body from Farmleigh.

He read Terry the full description given of the missing woman. Right down to the tattoo on her wrist: *justice*.

Terry had expected her intern might be distraught, but after a brief outburst about bastards who kill women and how women had lost their champion, Laura went straight into speculation mode. Where had Rachel gone to? What was she doing there? By the time she started in on theories of how Rachel had been lured to her death, Terry decided enough was enough and sent her off to read through the recent forensic journals and photocopy interesting articles to present at their next Case Review meeting, hoping to occupy her for at least a few hours.

Laura was right, though, there were a lot of unanswered questions around Rachel's death. They were for the gardaí to address, and right now she had other things to think about, namely a pile of updates to be done on reports, after toxicology and histology results had finally come through on a number of them. But she couldn't concentrate. She rubbed the back of her neck and sat up, her mind racing. She fished her phone out of her pocket – she'd listen to some of Rachel's podcasts to get a sense of what she was like and what she was up to.

Before she knew it a couple of hours had gone by, and she was none the wiser. As far as she could see, initially Rachel was largely just regurgitating old news reports, but there was a change in tone in the last several episodes as she made the crossover into proper investigative journalism. She would have had quite a future ahead of her.

Terry checked the time on her phone and looked at the pile of paperwork still awaiting her attention. The thought of a hot bath and some mind-numbing television won out over staying any longer. She slipped the Joyce and McCarthy folders under an atypically neat pile of similar ones on her desk. Then she picked up the Reece file and shoved it in her bag – she needed to focus on that for the case conference tomorrow.

13

The next morning Kevin Street station was buzzing. There was nothing like a break in a case to boost morale. Fraser knew how disheartening the slog in the initial phase of any enquiry could be. It was a relief to sense a lift in the mood in the room.

It was three days since the body had been found in the grounds of Farmleigh House and now they had a name. The investigation proper could begin.

For all the complexities of a large-scale police inquiry, it all boiled down to two central questions: who was Rachel Reece and why had she been killed?

Of course, none of this could be made public until the ID was officially confirmed, but Monica MacKenzie from forensics had promised her DNA lab would prioritise the case. He was also painfully aware that An Garda Síochána could be as leaky as an old sieve, so just to be sure the Reece family weren't blindsided by the press, he had driven to Donegal the previous evening to let them know the likely news.

It was the part of the job they all hated – delivering bad news to families. And God love them, the Reece parents hadn't even realised there was an issue. As far as they were concerned, Rachel was off grid doing research and would pop up when she was good and ready. He saw the shock on Mrs Reece's face when she opened the door to him along with a community garda. Gardaí calling to the house unannounced at 8 p.m. was never a good thing.

They seemed a decent family, very supportive of their daughter's choice to ditch her degree for podcasting, despite having no idea what it was really all about, satisfied when Rachel assured them she was doing well. And they couldn't argue, as she was earning enough to support herself and picking up an industry award or two along the way.

Fraser spent a half hour or so with them before heading back to Dublin. He left the local family liaison officer with them, a personable young garda who seemed sensible and sensitive. For now, the distraught parents were clinging to the hope that it might not be their daughter. That little spark of hope would fade once there was DNA confirmation.

DNA didn't lie and was not open to interpretation – it was either Rachel Reece or it wasn't. Only the results would tell for certain.

Fraser scanned the conference room. His team were all present. From pathology, Dr Terry O'Brien had been invited, along with Drs Michael Flynn and Monica MacKenzie from forensics. He had hoped that DCS Sinnott wouldn't appear, but no such luck – he'd breezed in with a couple of his lackies trotting along behind. Sinnott could never resist the opportunity to take the kudos for cracking a case. At least there was no sign of his opposite number in pathology, Professor Boyd.

Just before 10 a.m. the conference door swung open, shouldered by Michael Flynn from forensics carrying two Starbucks cups. He held the door open with his back and Terry and Monica walked in, Terry clutching her own cup in both hands, as if trying to warm herself, though hers was from a gourmet coffee pod that traded near the zoo. She was followed by a petite young woman with dark hair in a long plait, also carrying a coffee – likely the young doctor Terry had asked to bring along. They looked around for seats. Fraser nodded at Vinnie, who in turn motioned for Michael to follow him to a stack of chairs on the other side of the room.

Fraser checked his watch and made a final scan of the room, then tapped his pen on the table. 'Good morning, everyone.'

He smiled as 'good morning's echoed around the room, as well as a few groans from detectives bemoaning being dragged in after a night shift.

'Most of you will be aware that we got a lead on the Farmleigh case and are just waiting on the DNA results to confirm the ID.' A photograph appeared on the wall behind him. 'This, ladies and gentleman, is Rachel Reece.'

A round of applause broke out, everyone obviously pleased that the victim had been identified. As the noise died down, he went on to apprise them of the events of the previous few hours. He started with the missing-person report and the visit to Rachel's house in Phibsborough by Detective Sergeant

Mary Healy, who had been appointed crime scene manager for the case, with scene of the crime officers Detective Garda Vinnie Green and Detective Garda Bob Paterson. And, finally, his own visit to the Reece family and what he had learned about Rachel, at which point the room quietened as the mood dropped.

It was no bad thing to remind his team that at the heart of this, and any murder investigation, there was a grieving family.

'I should also point out at this point that Ms Reece was the niece of Edward Farrelly TD, the minister for finance. You all know what that is going to mean.'

There was a lot of murmuring and conversation among the gathered police and the forensics team.

'That's right – we are going to come under a lot of pressure from higher up, and the press are going to be all over this because of Ms Reece's celebrity as well as the political connections. So this one has *got* to be done thoroughly and one hundred per cent by the book. Not that I should have to say that, but it's always worth repeating.'

That seemed to shut everyone up.

Fraser nodded, and continued: 'Mary, can you run through the scene at the house in more detail? Vinnie, you ready with the photos?'

Both nodded and stood. Mary walked around the table to stand beside Fraser. Again, there was a round of applause, quickly curtailed by Mary bellowing at them to 'Shut up!'

Fraser smiled and motioned to her to take the floor as he sat down.

Mary cleared her throat. 'Edwardian terrace, secure.'

'Apart from the cat flap,' interjected Paterson, the self-proclaimed joker of the detective unit.

There was a ripple of laughter.

'Thank you, Bob. Mary?' Fraser indicated for her to continue.

'As I was saying, there was no sign of forced entry. There was no sign of a disturbance anywhere. There's no conclusion to draw but that she wasn't killed there. We mainly focused on the victim's bedroom, which seemed to double up as her home office. Very neat and tidy.'

'Bit like yourself, Mary,' came a voice from the back.

This time there was a collective groan. Mary ignored the heckler.

'This was confirmed by,' she looked down at her notebook, 'Maggie Steel, the housemate. She said Reece was well-organised and kept all her files in an old-fashioned sideboard in her room. We took everything there. Her laptop was missing – she usually kept it on the dressing table and didn't tend to take it out with her.'

Mary and Vinnie went through photographs of the scene, frame by frame, with Fraser interjecting here and there, allotting specific tasks to his team. Once Mary indicated she had finished, Fraser took the reins. 'Everyone know what they have to do?'

There was general nodding and an undercurrent of grumbling about specific task allocations that Fraser chose to ignore. He then turned his attention to the three doctors sitting at the opposite end of the table.

'Welcome, doctors. First, thank you, Dr MacKenzie, for prioritising the forensic evidence from this case. It is imperative for all concerned that we confirm the identification as soon as possible.'

Monica MacKenzie smiled. 'We'll do our best. Dr Flynn will be handling it, so perhaps it would be best if you liaise with him directly. Cut some of the red tape.'

'That's appreciated, Dr MacKenzie. Do you have any update for us, Dr Flynn?'

MacKenzie nudged Michael and he jumped to his feet too quickly, wobbling a little and causing his chair to tip back. He reddened. Michael was one of the best scientists Fraser had worked with, but the detective noticed he seemed uncomfortable when faced with an audience.

Michael steadied his chair and cleared his throat. 'I've ... well, I've been working on the evidence gathered both from the deceased's home in Phibsborough and from the swabs taken from the Reece postmortem.' His voice had a slight quiver, but now he was up and running Michael seemed to gain a little confidence.

'What's the timeframe, Dr Flynn?' Fraser asked.

'Um ... we should have a definitive answer tomorrow.'

'Today would be better, but fair enough.' Fraser sighed.

'I ... I can say that the woman found at Farmleigh has been dead for about three weeks.'

Fraser made a note of it. 'That's something. Anything else?'

'There's nothing to suggest it's *not* Rachel Reece.'

Fraser noticed the puzzled looks on the faces of some of his lads at that choice of words. 'So, to paraphrase what you're saying, everything you know so far fits with the Farmleigh body *being* Rachel Reece?'

Michael nodded awkwardly and sat down, visibly glad that his part of the conference was over.

Terry took the floor next. She was obviously used to summarising her reports for a lay audience, and the gardaí quickly got the gist of what she had found. The victim had been strangled, most likely not at the scene, then dumped there. It appeared to be manual strangulation, so there was little point searching for a ligature.

'It looks as if she was taken unawares. There is no evidence of a struggle and no evidence of defensive injuries.'

'Could she have been in a car?' a florid-faced detective near the back of the room asked. ''Cause a lot of them drive the girls up to the park for sex.'

Terry turned around to address the man who'd asked the question and fixed him with a stare. 'It's already established she's a podcaster not a prostitute.'

Fraser watched with some degree of pleasure as the man's face reddened and he mumbled something inaudible. He was one of Sinnott's entourage, part of the old boys' club that still lived in a bygone era. Fraser stepped in quickly. 'Was there evidence of sexual assault?' he asked Terry, knowing what she would say.

'There were no items of clothing missing, bra and pants still in place, but there were some tears that could have been made by wild animals. Other than a small bruise on the anterior vaginal wall, there were no significant injuries to the genital area, but she's been dead for some time, so other minor marks might not be obvious. The fact is I've not a lot to go on. So while the bruise may indicate recent sexual activity, I can't say she was raped. And I can't exclude it.

That's the best I can do. There is something unusual about this case. She was stabbed.'

There were mutterings and she heard someone say, 'Didn't she say the woman was stabbed. Did I miss something?'

'She wasn't stabbed to death. She was stabbed after death. With something sharp, like a dagger.'

Having delivered that bombshell, Fraser thanked her and looked down at his notes, just to be sure he had covered everything. He knew his team was rearing to get started, as was he. There was a lot to be done. Then he heard rather than saw Detective Chief Superintendent Archie Sinnott stand. His heart sank.

'Thank you, DCI Fraser. Well done so far.' Sinnott turned his attention to the room. 'Now, before you all disappear out there to get this wrapped up ...'

He smiled but the room was quiet, every eye watching him carefully. Sinnott was under the impression he was revered by his men, and Fraser was not going to disabuse him of that notion. But feared would be more accurate than revered. Feared by most and despised by some.

No one denied he was a very effective detective. As a leader, though, he was less successful.

Sinnott slapped his hand on the table. 'I trust you all to keep an open mind and that you will pursue all avenues.' He turned to Fraser. 'I'm sure you are already compiling a list of suspects. May I be so bold?'

Fraser nodded, sitting back in his seat. Sinnott was going to have his say, and there was nothing he could do about it.

The DCS turned back to face the room. 'Having heard the postmortem results, I would like to bring a name to your attention: Frank Cleaver. For those of you too young to remember, he was a prime suspect for Eileen McCarthy's murder back in 2007 – one of the cases that the young podcaster was covering. Cleaver is a known sex offender and we know that he is no stranger to the park. He was never tried for the McCarthy case – never enough evidence – did end up going down on another charge. He's been back on the streets for six weeks and, what do you know, another young woman is dead. You heard with your own ears the good doctor here,' he nodded towards Terry, 'saying she could have been raped. Is there a link between Cleaver and Rachel Reece? I want to know. So keep his name at the front of your minds and find out all you can.'

Sinnott clapped his hands to indicate that the gardaí present should get moving, then strode out of the room without a backward glance.

14

Back at the Forensic Pathology Department, Terry slipped up the back stairs to her office. She sat at her desk and pulled the Farmleigh notes out of her bag, then took the copy of the Eileen McCarthy file from under the pile on her desk.

She could recite Rachel Reece's postmortem report backwards, so she set it to the side and instead reached back to one of the shelves behind her and pulled a fresh notebook from the pile Laura had neatly stacked there. Beside it were the notebooks she'd filled with her findings and thoughts on each death she'd dealt with so far since moving to Dublin, in chronological order. They'd been scattered about the office willy-nilly, and Terry had to admit it was nice to have them all together. Her notebooks from Boston and Glasgow were stored in a large box in her dad's garage back home.

When she left Scotland he'd collected and boxed them up, muttering about how there could be hell to pay if they got into the wrong hands. Boston had been a baptism of fire. She'd been offered a residency in the Boston forensic department, after completing her postgraduate degree in histopathology in Glasgow. Shootings were a daily occurrence in Boston and she had lost count of the number of murders she had dealt with. After a couple of years there, the Glasgow forensic department had headhunted her and she returned to her home town, much to her dad's delight. There it was stabbings rather than shootings that kept her busy at the weekends.

All Terry's colleagues were fully digital, but she liked to empty her thoughts onto the page – a hangover, perhaps, from her childhood habit of faithful diary-keeping: if it wasn't written down, it hadn't really happened. Terry's notebooks, with their minutiae of observation and detail, were far more valuable to her than the official reports that became part of the evidence in the investigation of any death.

When she was at school, her arithmetic teacher had taught her that getting the right answer was only half the story; you got marks for showing how you got there, even if the answer was wrong. And, boy, did this apply in forensic pathology, where very often there was no definitive right or wrong answer – you could report on what had happened to the body, but how and why were often much harder, if not impossible, to determine.

These notebooks held her workings-out. Ten years from now, if someone challenged her on an answer, she could refer to these notes and give a full explanation as to why she had come to that conclusion.

She placed the new one on the desk in front of her and carefully wrote *Eileen McCarthy, February 2007* across the middle of the cover. She added today's date in the top left-hand corner. Then she opened the report she'd taken from Boyd's office and followed her usual procedure, reading it through, making notes and plotting the injuries on a rough body diagram. Earlier, she had compared and contrasted Rachel's and Eileen's deaths. Now it was time to concentrate on Eileen alone, and exactly what happened to her.

Eileen McCarthy had been found dead in bed in her own home. She had been stabbed about twenty times, mainly in the chest area. Boyd also described some slashes to her face and arms.

Terry turned to the section headed Blunt Force Trauma. There was mention of scratches and bruises on her neck and her Adam's apple had been crushed.

Similarity number one with the Rachel Reece case.

She flicked to the Internal Findings page. The heart had been punctured and there were several stab wounds in the lungs. There had been a lot of blood in the chest cavities. But many of the surface injuries Boyd had described on the left breast were just that, meaning they were relatively superficial. There was bruising over the ribs and down her sides and many of her ribs were cracked.

Terry studied the body diagram, trying to see patterns of injury. There was no doubt that Eileen had struggled with her attacker, and certainly quite a few of the stab wounds could have killed her. But, like Rachel Reece, she had also been strangled.

Terry closed her eyes. She could imagine Eileen in bed being attacked by a man – yes, she was sure it was a man – wielding a knife, looming over her, using his height and the fact he's upright to his advantage.

Eileen tries to grab the knife, desperate to save herself. He slashes at her arms but she keeps fighting back. He gets on the bed and straddles her, his weight bending her ribs until they snap, pain searing through her body with every breath. He drops the knife and grabs her neck and squeezes with all his might until Eileen goes limp. Her Adam's apple crushed, she fights for every last breath, and as her brain is slowly starved of oxygen, her pain drifts away but then she begins fitting. He panics, she's not dying, he lifts the knife and plunges it into her, again and again, until she stills.

Terry imagined the loneliness and terror of those final moments, just as she had so many times before, in so many cases. The evidence built the picture and it was impossible for it not to become flesh in her mind. It was that picture that drove her to do her level best for each victim. It had also contributed to her problems in Glasgow, besides her run-in with the police.

Her boss had also told her she'd spoken out of turn when she berated the histo techs for their tardiness in preparing slides vital for her to give an accurate cause of death, suggesting she asked too much of her co-workers. But she disagreed. Sometimes you had to go that extra mile. She didn't ask anything of others she didn't expect of herself.

Of course, there was one crime-scene picture she never wanted to envisage, and that was Jenny's final moments. She had been told that Jenny had been throttled. Her father could never bring himself to tell her she was raped – she had gathered that from the media's version of what had likely happened. But they didn't know, no one knew, for sure.

Scottish police would never divulge details of an active

case without good reason. So as long as Terry never saw the official postmortem report, never saw a typed description of Jenny's injuries, she would never be a voyeur at her death. That was why she had always resisted the urge to look for the report when she was working in the Glasgow forensic department. To see it would be to feel Jenny's pain.

She turned to the final page of the Eileen McCarthy report. Boyd had given the cause of death as stab wounds to the heart and lungs. He made no mention of the neck or chest injuries in his conclusions. And he didn't mention the possibility of a sexual assault. It was always the first thing Terry thought of when dealing with any female murder victim – and Eileen was in bed and had been strangled. Sex as a motive had to be considered.

Cleaver was a known sex offender – sex was his motive for attacking women. There was no hard evidence that Rachel Reece had been sexually assaulted, but Terry knew that didn't exclude it. Thankfully, the courts now accepted that not all victims of rape showed horrendous injuries. In fact, if a woman was sexually active, and particularly if she'd had children, there were often no injuries to the genital area. Often, it came down to the forensic science evidence: was there semen in the vagina and, if so, could the owner be identified?

She had come across some coy male doctors who skirted around dealing with women's nether regions. And the police were sometimes just as reticent. If a woman was murdered, why muddy the waters by bringing sexual assault into the mix? Why mention something that could be impossible to prove, unlike the killing?

At the top of the opposite page she wrote 'Further Actions:

1) Ask Michael to chase up the vaginal swabs from Rachel Reece; 2) Check what trace evidence was taken from Eileen McCarthy.'

She turned to the next page and drew two columns, one for *Reece* and one for *McCarthy*. She noted the cause of death, location, year of death and whether there was evidence of sexual assault against each.

Then she sat back in her chair. Two woman dead, murdered. Both had been strangled, but one had been the victim of a horrendous knife attack. The other, well, hell, she wasn't sure what was going on there. Why stab an obviously dead woman? That was a lot more sinister. Whatever evidence had linked Cleaver to the McCarthy killing, it was clear that if they focused too much on one line of inquiry for Rachel Reece's murder, they might be playing right into the hands of her real killer.

Fraser stared at the notes about the Farmleigh case covering his desk, then swivelled round in his chair to look at the whiteboard behind him, noting who was doing what where. There were a lot of moving parts, and it would be professional suicide if he didn't keep an open mind – despite whatever Sinnott believed. A couple of officers were talking to Reece's housemate Maggie to see if there was a boyfriend and to get a list of exes, friends and people she was at college with. There was also the possibility that she might have riled someone up nosing about in unsolved murders, even ones from nearly twenty years ago.

As if on cue, Mary Healy burst through his office door. 'Boss, I have something.'

Fraser looked at Mary. She was a straight-talking young woman from Tipperary who looked like she'd be more at home driving a tractor than interviewing murder suspects; a bit rough and ready, but she was a good forensic investigator. In fact, she was the best on his team.

'I was going through Reece's paperwork. She was very organised – her notes are in chronological order. Most of it is a lot of shit – you know how these true-crime people are. Making something out of nothing to generate content.'

Fraser tapped his teeth with the end of his pen and waved for her to get on with it.

'So Sinnott said to look for a link with Cleaver,' Mary said. 'And guess what?'

Fraser shrugged and spread his hands. 'The suspense is killing me.'

'She went to see Cleaver in Mountjoy about six weeks back, just before he was released. I'm waiting on a call back from the prison service, but if they confirm it … we are cooking with gas!' She did a little victory dance.

Fraser couldn't help but grin. 'Well done, Mary. It's a great start, but it's not the end of the job. Keep at it. See if there's anything else in there that we need to know.'

She was out of his room like a shot.

Fraser leaned back in his chair. Maybe Sinnott *was* right.

Terry had drunk two cups of coffee and spent an hour making copious notes, but she still couldn't make it fit. She took a deep breath and picked up her mobile to call John Fraser – she'd have to let him know of her concerns. She chided herself for feeling awkward – *it was only a one-night stand, no big deal* – as she prepared to channel her best professional demeanour.

He answered immediately, no trace of awkwardness in his voice. 'Terry. What can I do for you?' She wasn't sure if he was pleased to hear from her or not.

'I've been thinking about what Sinnott said about Cleaver. The postmortem findings in the Reece and McCarthy cases are quite different. He mentioned Cleaver being in the frame for McCarthy. She was viciously killed. Rachel's death is a bit more … subtle. Like it wasn't well planned. And the stabbing seems to have been an afterthought. I'm just saying, from the pathology point of view, they're different.'

'I hate to burst your bubble, but it looks like he may be right on this one.'

'But there's no conclusive evidence Reece was raped – that either of them were, in fact. And Cleaver is a sex offender.'

'You've said yourself you can't say Reece wasn't sexually assaulted.'

'I know but still …'

'Keep this to yourself, Terry, but we've made a definite connection between Cleaver and Reece, just as there had been between Cleaver and McCarthy. I can't give you the full details at the moment, as we're waiting on confirmation, but as of now Cleaver is our number-one suspect.'

'But—'

'Sorry, Terry. I have to go. I'll let you know once we have an update.'

Terry dropped her phone on the desk, deflated. She would have thought Fraser was more reasoned than that – was even her professional radar off now too? Cleaver was a sex offender – he'd first served time for sex offences when he was still in his teens – and sex offenders didn't just kill for fun.

This just didn't feel like a sexually motivated crime. For that matter, she wasn't sure Eileen McCarthy's was either. But she knew who might be able to shed some light on that. She grabbed her notebook and walked down to the reception area before she lost her nerve. She strode past Mrs Carey and knocked on Boyd's door.

'Come in!'

The door was slightly ajar so she pushed it open, stepped inside and closed it behind her.

'Dr O'Brien, how can I help you?' He glanced up at her and then immediately back down to the papers on his desk, as if she had interrupted him at a particularly crucial moment.

'Sorry to disturb you, Professor, but I was at a case conference this morning. They've identified the body from Farmleigh.'

'Mmhm.' Boyd sat up and gave Terry the full force of his attention, which was almost more unnerving.

She steeled herself. 'It's a woman called Rachel Reece. Actually, I believe you've met her?'

Boyd's face dropped for a second, then he seemed to recover himself. 'Who?'

'She came to interview you about a month or so ago for a podcast about unsolved Irish murders?'

He frowned. 'Ah, yes. It turned out we had little to say to each other. A very abrasive young woman.' He looked down at his nails. 'I'm sorry to hear of her death, of course.' Then he folded his hands and looked at Terry, as if to indicate he had said all he was going to on the subject.

'Well, as you know, DCS Sinnott seems to be working under the assumption that this murder is similar to the murder of Eileen McCarthy, back in 2007, and that both women were killed by Frank Cleaver.'

'Ah! And Dr O'Brien doesn't agree?' The smirk on Boyd's face spoke volumes.

'I'm just concerned that if they concentrate on one suspect they might miss something, or someone, else. There was no evidence that she had been sexually assaulted and Cleaver is a sex offender.' She stared at Boyd, looking for any flicker of reaction.

'Dr O'Brien, I fail to see what this has to do with me.'

Terry could see his mood darkening. 'According to the records, you did the McCarthy postmortem. I'm trying to establish if she was sexually assaulted?'

She saw Boyd's eyes flick to the folders piled beside his microscope. Her heart was beating fast. Had she put the files back correctly – had he noticed something was off?

Boyd pushed his chair back and walked around his desk, perching on the edge facing her. 'That was a long time ago. I don't remember the exact details, but if a detective *chief* superintendent is of the opinion that the two murders are linked, I am sure he has good reason for it. And it is not for you to question his line of investigation, Doctor. You are a pathologist, not a detective. That's DCS Sinnott's job and that of his team.'

He leaned forward slightly, looking her straight in the eyes, then stood. She realised she had been dismissed.

15

The National Bureau of Criminal Investigation – Ireland's FBI equivalent, as Fraser described it to Terry – was housed in Harcourt Street in Dublin's city centre. It was situated on the third floor of one of three red-bricked office blocks, set in their own grounds behind high black gates. The complex housed the headquarters of the Criminal Assets Bureau, the Armed Response Unit, the Sex Crimes Unit and most of the other special task forces that facilitated crime detection and prevention in Ireland.

Terry was there to explain to Sinnott in person why it was important to keep the lines of investigation open on the Reece murder. The detective chief stood up, rubbing his hands together, as she entered his office.

'Come in, Dr O'Brien. This is a real treat. It's usually Charlie's wizened old face I have to deal with. I hope my boys are treating you well?'

'Very well, thanks.'

'Thank you for your input into the Reece case so far,' Sinnott continued. 'The investigation is at a crucial phase, so you'll appreciate my time is precious. I apologise if I'm not giving you the time I usually would a new hire.'

'I understand,' Terry said. 'Thank you for making the time to see me.'

'Have a seat, Dr O'Brien.' He smiled as he gestured to the chair opposite his desk. 'How can I help you?'

Terry talked as quickly as she could, explaining the differences in MO and also the lack of definite evidence of sexual assault in each case, worried that she might get cut off before she had said everything she needed to. Sinnott sat back and listened without interruption, occasionally nodding.

As soon as she finished, he sat forward. Instead of being angered by her veiled criticism, he gave the impression he was genuinely interested in her concerns.

'Thank you, Doctor,' he said, steepling his fingers beneath his chin. 'I can see you're going to be a real asset to this country ... while you are with us. Of course, you realise I cannot share our intel with you. But be assured we will follow every lead, no matter how seemingly trivial.'

He leaned back in his chair again, and Terry realised she was about to be fobbed off with a *thank you, but no thank you*.

'I appreciate how frustrating it can be – particularly when you've been through this before,' Sinnott said.

Terry felt her muscles tense.

'But this is not Glasgow. I understand you had some difficulties there, getting the police to listen to your concerns about how your sister's murder was handled? My condolences on your loss, by the way.'

How the hell did he know about that? She tried to keep her voice steady. 'I– I had some questions,' she said.

Sinnott nodded wearily, as if he'd encountered this kind of distrust in police efforts many times during his long career. 'I know it might have looked like the police were closing ranks when you questioned their competence in investigating Jenny's death.'

The casual mention of her sister's name stung. How did he know this stuff? *What* exactly did he know? He had obviously spoken to someone who knew the case and it was likely that he had spoken to Boyd.

'But you can trust me when I say that, over here, we handle the job with complete professionalism and leave no stone unturned. Still, thank you for sharing your concerns, Dr O'Brien.'

As if by magic, Sinnott's secretary appeared behind Terry, and with that the meeting was over. In the taxi back to her office, Terry thought how stupid she had been thinking anyone was going to listen to her. One thing was clear – Sinnott and the gardaí weren't going to take advice from an outsider. And it was clear that's what she was here – an outsider whose personal baggage meant her professional judgement couldn't be trusted.

She was being shut out again. Just like in Glasgow.

A memory came to her of standing beside her father at the counter in the police office in Hamilton about a month after Jenny had died. It was the office he'd once worked in himself. It was the first time since the funeral she had seen him cry.

She would never forget his words. 'She was my little girl and you're doing fuck-all to find who killed her. You're supposed to look after your own.'

He had taken extended leave – Terry just remembered him being around a lot – and then he told her he had to move to a new police station, and that meant a new home and a new school for her. When he started work in the Rutherglen police office he was given a desk job. Only years later, when she was old enough to understand, did she realise that he had come to accept that his colleagues had, in fact, tried very hard to find Jenny's killer, and they were as frustrated by their failure as he was.

Terry knew that sometimes emotions can stop us accepting what we know intellectually to be true. Which was why she worked so hard at her professional veneer. It had become a shield she couldn't function without.

When Terry returned to Glasgow from Boston, she'd started to look into Jenny's investigation. The work she'd done in Boston had shown her that advances in forensic science could help solve old cases, but when she'd tried to get Jenny's case reopened, she'd met a brick wall. Been told she didn't understand, to let things lie, to calm down. 'You're not in Boston now,' they'd said.

No doubt she'd made some enemies when she started asking questions of the officers involved. She suspected the ease with which she'd been allowed leave to take this short-term post in Dublin had been a result of feathers ruffled, no matter that the party line was a clash of personalities over the expert witness debacle. But the police should have been able to stand over their work on Jenny's death, to defend it.

She hadn't wanted to take matters into her own hands.

They'd given her no choice. And in the end they shut her out too.

She couldn't face returning to the office and told the taxi driver to take her to Northumberland Road – she'd leave the office a message that she was doing paperwork from home. Her heart was racing along with her thoughts. Back at the flat, she leaned against the kitchen counter as she waited for the kettle to boil, trying to breathe in and out as slowly and steadily as she could. She made a cup of tea and, sipping the hot liquid, willed herself to be calm. She decided to call her father. He was the only one who understood.

As soon as she heard his voice, she let loose. She poured out her frustration with Boyd, the way the investigation was being handled, and the fact that Sinnott knew about Jenny. The horrible way he'd dropped her name into the conversation.

'Terry, you've got to stop this. Any good detective would have done a bit of research into your background, and police have plenty of contact with each other across the sea. And you know yourself there's a few that would put the boot in. But don't let them knowing about your sister's death change things for you. Stick to the facts and stick to the limits of your job.'

Terry was far from placated. 'Back in the day, you weren't slow to tell your pals who investigated Jenny's murder that they failed her, that they needed to do better. But as soon as I started to ask questions, you were telling me to keep my head down and let it lie. You can't even bring yourself to say Jenny was murdered.'

'Because it doesn't make any difference,' he said, his voice full of sadness. 'Not every case can be solved – there isn't an answer to everything. Come on, Terry, your own work must have shown you that by now. In time, I could see they'd done everything they could with the evidence they had. And me destroying myself over it wasn't going to bring her back. And you throwing everything away now won't bring her back either.'

She fell silent. She could hear the hum of the radio in the background. Then eventually he said quietly, 'I'm just worried about you, pet. You've been through so much and you're just getting settled. Don't jeopardise what you have.'

Terry had barely got off the phone with her dad when it rang again – this time it was Michael.

'How are you doing?' he asked.

Terry sat down heavily at the table. 'Well, I've had one bitch of a day.' She filled him in.

Michael was his usual supportive self. 'Well, I'm not surprised that Boyd is backing up Sinnott – thick as thieves, those two. But Fraser strikes me as being able to think for himself. Maybe they really do have something on Cleaver?'

He reassured her that there was no way everyone knew about Jenny and what had happened back in Glasgow when she'd tried to get the case reopened. He heard everything that was going on in their little law enforcement community from Niamh from histapathology, who was the font of all gossip in their little corner of Irish law enforcement, and so far she'd said nothing on the subject.

The pair agreed to meet up soon, and Terry ended the call and poured a glass of chilled wine. She thought about Sinnott's patronising responses, noting her 'concerns', and how he'd been so quick to let her know he knew about her past. Was he unconsciously or consciously making the evidence fit their theory – even if it meant an innocent person being accused or the real killer staying free?

And why had Boyd been so rattled by the interview with Rachel?

Terry wasn't going to let them intimidate her – she'd had enough of men implying they knew better, that her instincts were wrong. She'd been recommended for this position, and she was going to do it to the best of her ability.

She rolled her shoulders slowly, releasing the tightness. What had Rachel Reece discovered about the McCarthy murder that had sent Boyd running scared when she shared it with him?

And how could Terry get inside her head?

16

The kitchen was a hive of activity when Terry arrived at work the next day. A group of her colleagues were clustered around the TV in the break room: Niamh, the histopathology technician and inveterate gossip; Vinnie, who was leaning against the countertop, a cappuccino in his hand and his eyes glued to the screen; Tomas, his shock of dark hair even more awry than usual; and Mrs Carey, sipping daintily from a cup of tea. Laura was sat looking at her phone, seemingly oblivious to the rest. No one noticed Terry slip in – they were too engrossed in the screen on the right-hand wall, the packets of biscuits on the table largely untouched. As she made a coffee, she looked from the group to the TV. Rachel Reece's smiling face filled the screen.

Mug in hand, Terry stood silently, as mesmerised as the others. Across the bottom of the screen was the caption *Rachel Reece murder. Man brought in for questioning.*

It looked like Sinnott hadn't wasted any time.

The camera cut to a windswept reporter standing in front of the same garda station. '*Gardaí have confirmed that a man has been brought in for questioning in the Rachel Reece murder case. Rachel Reece was an award-winning true-crime podcaster who went missing around a month ago, and whose remains were discovered in the grounds of the Farmleigh Estate in Dublin's Phoenix Park four days ago. Detective Chief Inspector John Fraser, the chief investigator on the case, has appealed for anyone with information to please contact the gardaí.*'

As the news moved on to another story, the screen showing some well-dressed banker type, everyone started chatting, and Terry did her best to slip back out but was caught by Niamh's eagle eye. She practically skipped across the floor to her.

'Word on the inside is that Frank Cleaver is the chief suspect. Bastard should be hung, drawn and quartered. And then have his mickey chopped off.'

At the mention of Cleaver, Laura looked up. 'I didn't say anything, Terry.'

'I didn't think you would. I believe you are fully aware of the concept of confidentiality, unlike some.' She glared at Vinnie. 'Loose lips and all that.' She returned her attention to the technician. 'Jesus, Niamh, that's a bit extreme even for you. And he's not exactly been convicted yet.'

'Well, if anyone's guilty, it's him.'

'Come on – wait until you've got the whole story. And from a bona fide source.' Terry shot her a sharp look. 'Don't you have some histo slides to be getting on with?'

Back in her office, Terry placed the mug of coffee on her

desk and called Michael. She got straight to the point. 'I presume you've seen the latest about the Farmleigh case?'

'Money's on it being Cleaver they've brought in, so my source says anyway.'

'Your "source"?'

'Ahern. Strictly entre nous. From what he said, Cleaver is Sinnott's Moby Dick, his "one that got away". He's been waiting for his chance to put him away for a long stretch for years.'

'What's that got to do with anything?' said Terry.

'Cleaver is a really, really bad guy, Tez. I mean, he shouldn't be on the streets.'

'What has being a bad guy got to do with anything? We're supposed to serve the law, aren't we? I can't see a way that Cleaver's MO fits the Rachel Reece case.'

'Tez, this man is a violent sex offender. Do you want me to list the number of rapists and perverts in the past who started out as sexual predators and graduated to murder? Jeffrey Dahmer, David Berkowitz ... And do you know what Cleaver was serving time for before his recent release?'

'I read it was aggravated rape.'

'He beat that poor woman until she was barely recognisable. In fact, he *almost* killed her. Choked her until she passed out. Does that sound familiar?'

'You're saying he thought he had left her for dead?'

'And maybe there's other compelling evidence that you, *we*, are totally unaware of. They're not obligated to share such things with we forensic folk, after all.' There was a hint of irritation in Michael's tone – it could get frustrating being left out of the loop.

'The only relevant, and potentially damning, evidence would be the trace evidence,' Terry said, 'and I'm not aware of anything particularly compelling coming out of that. Have you turned up anything?'

It was an annoying part of the job for Terry that pathologists so rarely found out the results of the tests ordered during the course of an investigation. She collected the samples from the bodies, sent them off for testing and wrote up her autopsy reports. But the test results went back to the forensic scientists, who wrote up the forensic reports and sent them on to the gardaí. The results never came back to her.

Terry usually found out the real-world implications of the work she did along with everyone else, when it was reported by the media.

'Well, obviously, the DNA results confirmed the identity as Rachel Reece, but so far I've nothing much else. Not a hair, not a fibre, not a cell. Our killer, who may or may not be Cleaver, was either very savvy or very lucky.'

'Was Cleaver always so careful?'

'Well, they obviously didn't pull anything related to him from Eileen McCarthy or he'd have been done for it, wouldn't he?'

'Can you access the forensic report there?'

'Hang on ...'

Terry took a swig of coffee while she waited for him to reply. She opened her copy of the McCarthy file. All Boyd said was *routine forensic samples taken* and didn't itemise what they were. There was no mention of clothing in the postmortem report, but it wouldn't be unusual for it to be removed at the scene, especially if a forensic scientist asked for vaginal swabs to be taken. It all depended on the forensic strategy on the day. And also this was Ireland – she had no idea what was routine here back in those days.

'Still there, Tez?'

'Yep.'

'There's no mention of any clothing from the postmortem, but Charlie-boy took mouth, vaginal and rectal swabs. Oh, and breasts and thighs. Only DNA found was hers.'

'No semen?'

'Nope. Could have used a condom, I suppose.'

'Nothing positive at all? What samples were taken at the scene?'

'Nothing from the body. And not really anything of any use.'

'Boyd's report suggests that not only was she strangled,' Terry said, 'but, to my mind, her assailant at some point was actually on top of her. But nobody thought to take swabs from the neck?'

'Nobody thought to do a lot of things, it seems.'

'And you say there was no evidence of transfer of trace evidence from the assailant to her.' It was a statement rather than a question.

'Sorry. But that's all I've got,' said Michael.

Terry sat staring at the postmortem report for some minutes after the call. None of this was making sense. As far as she could see, there was no evidence of sexual assault in either the McCarthy or the Reece cases. And that made no sense if Cleaver was the killer.

Everyone had jumped on the stab wounds as conclusive

evidence that the MOs were identical and therefore the cases were linked, but one had been alive and stabbed, the other was already dead when they were stabbed. Why? Could it be a copy-cat type crime. And one was killed in their home while the other's body was dumped. It just didn't add up to her.

But then, maybe, he was evolving as an offender, getting wiser.

She'd found out as much as she could about Eileen McCarthy – maybe it was time to do a bit of digging about Rachel Reece. She called Michael back.

'Will you come back out to Farmleigh with me?' she asked. 'I want to revisit the scene.'

'Whatever the hell for?'

'Call it a gut feeling. Something just isn't fitting.'

'What?'

'I'll know when I see it. Will you come?'

'Why not? If there's one thing I can't get enough of, it's crawling around in ditches.'

An hour later Michael and Terry stood looking down into the muddy trench. It had rained non-stop for the last two days and the ditch now held several inches of water. 'I'm going to let you lead the charge,' Michael said, 'seeing as I haven't a clue why we're even here. At least the bloody rain has stopped. Can you imagine trying to find pupa cases in this.'

Terry ignored his rant and eased herself into the culvert. She began to wade over to the area where the podcaster's body had been removed.

'Let's just do this systematically,' she said. 'Cover the ground we covered before and see if there is anything we didn't notice.'

Michael gave one of his theatrical sighs and followed her, sloshing through the stagnant water that had gathered in the bottom of the gully.

'Don't know how you expect to find anything in this sludge. Do you think we've missed some of her belongings?' Michael asked. 'She didn't have much jewellery on. Could some have dropped off, maybe as a result of the decomposition of her flesh?'

'Maybe,' Terry said. 'Although decomposition initially causes swelling, so unless you're imagining rings flying off at high velocity due to the pressure of her fingers bloating, I'd say we'd be on to a loser.'

'Ha-ha,' Michael said without even the vaguest hint of humour.

'Come here for a second, will you?' Terry said suddenly.

Michael sloshed to her side.

'These weren't here before.' Terry was looking at the area above the spot where Rachel had been lifted out.

'What weren't?'

'These,' the pathologist said, pointing at a crop of small grey mushrooms with long stalks and smooth, pointed caps.

'Weren't they?'

'No. I remember noting this entire area was clear of much vegetation. Do mushrooms grow that quickly? I mean, they're small but they look pretty mature.'

'I don't have a scooby,' Michael said. 'Mycology isn't my area.'

'Nor mine,' Terry said. 'The soil about them is still very loose.'

'I imagine that's due to the way they root themselves,' Michael said. 'I know they have very large and very complex root systems.'

'I thought you said you didn't know anything about mycology.'

'I don't. I learned that from *Star Trek: Discovery*.'

Terry threw her eyes to heaven. 'Okay. Let's make a note of the mushrooms and keep looking.'

They did but their search turned up nothing else new.

Terry took a photograph of the fungi on her phone, and they both climbed out of the gulch and walked back towards the mansion and Michael's Honda Civic.

17

Frank Cleaver tucked his lank hair behind his prominent ears and headed out the door of Kevin Street Garda Station at a rapid stride, pulling his hood down over his eyes, more against the drizzle than to obscure his face. At least there were no photographers hanging about.

They'd brought him in for questioning for that blonde bit's murder. Stupid fuckers, clueless as usual about what they were dealing with.

He was supposed to be making a fresh start. So much for that. But fuck it, they'd nothing on him. Luckily the law prevented them from identifying him, but it was only a matter of time before one of the gutter tabloids got brazen and decided to risk it.

He was still fuming about the useless legal-aid guy who had done nothing to stop him being kept for almost a full day. It was all part of the conspiracy against him. And it was all that slag Reece's fault. Coming to see him inside. He had thought she'd be different. She'd seemed interested. But he saw the same disgust on her face as he had seen on plenty of other women's faces. Bitch got what was coming to her.

His nerves were jangling. He needed something to take the edge off before he went home.

He knew the inner city like the back of his hand and weaved his way westward and then over towards Ormond Quay. With a bit of luck, Charlie would be working. Frank didn't know his real name, but as the guy seemed to have a monopoly selling cocaine to all the rich lawyers hanging about the Four Courts, he was just known as Charlie.

Frank didn't get the appeal of hard drugs himself, but Charlie also did a good line in tranqs and roofies – that was how he got to know him. A couple of those in a drink and Bob was your uncle. Half the time the stupid tarts didn't even know what he'd been up to with them. He preferred the buzz when they put up a bit of a fight but, after his last stretch inside, he'd decided he needed to be a bit more clever: just now a couple of xannies were what he needed. Those cunts at Pearse Street had done his head in.

Charlie was on the boardwalk, a couple of boyos watching his back. Not a garda in sight. The transaction took two minutes, after which Frank set off towards O'Connell Street for the bus to Finglas, stopping off at the Tesco Express to pick up a bottle of 7-Up.

He stood at the corner of Henry Street, leaning against a shop window, keeping away from the crowd at the bus stop. He popped one pill in his mouth, unscrewed the cap from the bottle, and as he tipped his head back to take a swig, his hood fell back. He stuffed the bottle in his pocket and glanced over at the Real Time Passenger Information board to check when the next bus was due.

He was distracted by a group of girls standing under the board, dressed in crop tops and shorts. One of the girls saw him stare. Her eyes widened. Shit.

'Fuckin' perv!' Her outburst caused her friends to turn and stare back at him. 'Here, that's the sleazebucket that done time for raping that girl.'

'Fuck off,' he said. This was the last thing he needed. Typical, the story had to be big news when he was sentenced, all because they'd never nailed him for Eileen McCarthy. It hadn't stopped the bastards muddying his name all the same. Pictures all over the papers.

He flicked his hood back up as the girl surged forward. Backed against the shop window, he had nowhere to go. She stood in front of him, her hands on her hips. She leant in close and suddenly he realised what she was about to do.

She spat directly into his face. Her friends started clapping and chanting, 'Dirty perv!' Then they were laughing hysterically.

Frank rubbed his face with his sleeve and stalked off, the girls calling after him. The spitting girl's voice carried above the others. 'State of him! Fuckin' stinks too, the prick!'

He wiped his sleeve across his face again. He could feel rage building in his chest. He wanted nothing more than to grab the little cunt by the neck and teach her a lesson. It was the same feeling he had had when those McCarthy bitches taunted him all those years ago. When they were young, he'd have done anything for Eileen. And she was all nicey-nicey to him if no one else was about, but when they were in a crowd she would start on him. Usually, the other kids joined in. Vicious, they were.

Just like then, there was nothing he could do but walk away. For now. There were too many gawkers about, and he wouldn't give Sinnott the satisfaction of an excuse to haul him back in to the slammer.

There was no chance he was getting on the bus to Finglas now. Feck paying for a taxi. Anyway, there was bound to be some fucking reporter hanging around. He crossed O'Connell Street, keeping his head down. He was back on the quays before he realised where he was headed.

His old neighbour Bessie Mulligan had moved back to the city from Finglas, to Upper Mayor Street, when he was twelve. When she'd lived on the old estate, she had always looked out for him. She didn't have kids of her own and 'adopted' kids like him who hung around all day, kids who had no one taking care of them. There were rumours that her old man had been big in the drugs trade in his day. Maybe she felt bad that it was people like her husband who were responsible for his ma's problems. But he just knew that she'd feed him if there was nothing in his own house, which was more often than not.

She never turned her back on him, even after he was taken into care when his ma was sectioned. His ma was the first woman that had called him a pervert, that time he walked in on her and some john, but Bessie called him her lovely boy.

They'd stayed in touch after Bessie moved back into the city. Whether she just didn't keep up with the news or turned a blind eye to his stints in and out of prison he didn't know, nor did he want to. And it didn't matter, because she always had a welcome for him when he came by. She'd died during his last stretch inside.

After he got out, he'd taken the Luas to the Point to have a look at her old house. It was boarded up. Foreigners had moved into the houses on either side, women in them long skirts. Always on the scam, that lot. He wouldn't touch any of them with a barge pole.

He could get into Bessie's house round the back. He'd done it before. It would be a safe place for him to stay that night.

18

The afternoon's PMs out of the way – both run of the mill heart attacks – Terry spent close to two hours searching databases of Irish fungi and had been unable to find a match for the mushrooms they'd come across in the ditch.

There was, of course, a chance they were simply a naturally occurring seasonal variety she'd missed in her research, but something told her they were important. She needed help.

Terry recalled a forensic archaeologist whose talks she'd attended at one or two conferences, an expert on wilderness crime scenes. Worth a shot – if anyone could bring insight, he would be the man. She looked him up – Dr Rupert Hunt, Trinity College Dublin.

She fired him off a quick email:

Dear Dr Hunt,

My name is Terry O'Brien, and I am working in the office of the state pathologist with Professor Boyd. I could very much use your input on a case. A point has come up that comes under your field of expertise. Could you get in contact with me? Needless to say, I've sanction for your services from the coroner, so you will be appropriately remunerated.

Sincerely,

Dr Terry O'Brien

Dr Hunt would certainly have some thoughts on whether she was on to something or not.

Terry wasn't due to meet Laura until later, which gave her time to find out a bit more about Rachel Reece. She intrigued Terry. She couldn't remember being so hell bent on changing the world at that age. She had spent her first thirty years with her head in a book with no thoughts for anyone or anything other than getting through the next exam.

There was plenty about Rachel online, the vast majority of it posted by the woman herself. Terry didn't have personal profiles on social media – they were just another way for the media to keep tabs on her. And she'd had her fill of trolls in the wake of the police fiasco in Glasgow, mostly she suspected from police miffed that she had dared to question their professionalism and their ability to do what they were paid to do: investigate her sister's death. She was more comfortable being a lurker on social, with her anonymous @morticia32 accounts keeping her in the picture on stuff of interest. Rachel seemed to use Twitter mainly for promoting her podcast, occasionally retweeting things from the news about garda incompetence or violence against women.

Her Instagram was similar – lots of trailers and clips from the podcast – but it was a little more personal. Her Facebook was a ghost town – Terry could see it had once been her main platform, but in the past eighteen months Instagram and Twitter had stepped to the fore. TikTok, too, Terry discerned after creating an alias account on there.

Up to her disappearance and subsequent murder, she had posted on social media several times a day every day, including over the weekends.

Between that and the multitude of online interviews, Terry was able to glean that the podcaster had been brought up in rural County Donegal. It seemed like she couldn't get out of there fast enough – she'd finished school at seventeen and gone straight to Maynooth to study law. She'd started an MA in criminology but dropped out of that to start the podcast.

Rachel was completely open about her personal life: she was adopted and appeared to be single at the time of her death – she mentioned the perils of dating apps in one interview, but there was no evidence of dating to be seen on her pages. In fact, there were very few of the usual posts you saw on a young single-person's social media – groups of smiling people dressed-up and out for the night, living it up in town, or dressed-down and hiking in the mountains, whatever their idea of fun was.

Rachel's was mainly her work, her research and pleas for information, with the odd picture of a perfectly poured latté to break up the grid.

Anger seethed from her posts. She didn't just want to tell

the stories of these lost or murdered women, she wanted vengeance for what had happened to them. Niamh's comments earlier about the killer being hung, drawn, quartered and gelded were mirrored in some of Rachel's posts.

Death wouldn't be good enough for these psychopaths, one stated.

Yet there was also a deep empathy for the victims, a sense of grief for the deaths they had been forced to endure and an acknowledgement of the loss to the world of all they could have achieved had their lives not been cut short so brutally.

Terry was conscious of the time – she'd arranged to meet Laura for a drink in Mulhollands – but she knew she wasn't finished.

It would be good to know what Rachel had learned during her investigation into Eileen McCarthy's murder. It made perfect sense that something she had discovered prompted her killer to take such a catastrophic course of action. But what?

For that, though, she'd need a very special kind of access. She called her friend Miles, a former boyfriend from Uni who was a software coder by day and enjoyed a lucrative second career as a hacker by night. He had helped her before in accessing files the detectives in Jenny's case had refused to hand over.

'Terry O'Brien,' he said, 'how the hell are you?'

'I'm good, Miles. And how are you?'

'Can't complain, not that anyone would listen if I did. How's the Emerald Isle treating you?'

'Pretty good so far. Miles, I need your particular skillset to get hold of some information on a case I'm working.'

'Really? Can I take it as a given that you're not supposed to be accessing this information?'

'Let's just say I don't agree with the direction things seem to be going, and I'd like to test my theory.'

'Okay. What do you want me to get for you?'

She told him.

'It's pretty likely this podcaster kept backups of her files in the cloud. I can probably copy them from there and send them to you.'

'That's great, Miles. How long is that likely to take?'

'Give me a day. And you're going to owe me dinner the next time you're back in Glasgae.'

'Done. Have you still got my email address? My personal one?'

'I do.'

'Send the files to that one, just in case of prying eyes.'

'Consider it done.'

They said their goodbyes and she opened her gallery app, for one more look at the photograph she'd taken of the mushrooms that were growing right where Rachel's remains had been.

19

Michael stood just inside the entrance to Mulholland's, scanning the tables and the bar. He recognised a good few of the locals. Some nodded a greeting, while others raised their glasses towards him. The faces he didn't recognise were likely locals in for a quick drink on the way home from work.

It was a rather bland space, no denying it. The pub was resolutely old and worn, but not in the curated sense of so many of Dublin's trendified bars. Mulholland's actually *was* old style. The clientele just wanted a relatively clean place to drink and some bar food for soakage. Tables would be dragged about to suit the size of the parties, depending on whether it was a couple of guards having a drink on the way home or a group celebrating a birthday – or more likely a conviction. Successful murder trials could result in very rowdy, and somewhat messy, nights.

Detective Inspector Alan Ahern, who had been the crime

scene manager at Farmleigh, had called and asked Michael to meet him for a drink. Michael had deliberately arrived later than Ahern had suggested. There was no point looking too eager. He was just making his way over to the bar when he felt a hand on his shoulder. He spun round to face Ahern, smiling broadly. 'Thought I'd been stood up,' he said.

Michael couldn't think of a pithy comeback. He felt his face redden. Jesus, first the police conference and now here – had he lost the ability to talk to others like a normal human being? But Ahern didn't seem to notice – he had already grabbed Michael's left elbow and was pulling him towards a table at the far side of the bar where two pints sat. The two chairs at the table were placed in typical garda fashion: facing the room, backs against the wall, a good vantage point to survey the other drinkers while ensuring there were no surprises from behind.

Ahern sat and gestured to Michael to sit beside him, pulling the chairs a little closer together. Michael tried to keep his cool. He still wasn't sure if this was just a couple of colleagues having a drink or potentially something more.

Since Paul's departure, he had busied himself in the lab. If it wasn't for Terry, he'd never have ventured out, not even to the gay bars where at least he knew for sure that the majority of men were into other men. Maybe they were both being a little too co-dependent, himself and Terry. It might be time to dip his toe into the murky waters of dating again.

'Got you a pint in,' Ahern said. 'Or would you prefer something a little stronger?'

'Pint's fine.'

'Good. All work and no play, and all that. I thought it was time to drag you out of that lab and into the world.' He placed his hand on Michael's shoulder for a moment, smiling. Then he took a mouthful of beer and gave a relaxed sigh.

Michael sipped his lager and looked over the rim of the glass at Ahern.

Did that shoulder pat mean something? Or was he just being friendly? God, he's right – I have spent too much time in the lab.

If he squinted a bit, Ahern looked a bit like Paul. Both were tall and broad, although Ahern was much more muscular. And more handsome, he had to be honest. The man's features were ridiculously chiselled, like some all-American hero.

But he still missed Paul – he couldn't deny it. No amount of chiselled features could make him escape that fact. He'd always felt slightly in his former boyfriend's shadow, not quite good enough. He was always waiting for the 'it's not you, it's me' moment, but the rug had been pulled from under his feet when Paul had announced he was leaving to take care of his mother and it was best if they had a complete break.

Michael had told Paul to take some time – see if he still felt the same after a few months. Christ, he'd even offered to move to the US – how desperate did he sound? But Paul didn't budge. And it hurt.

He put his glass down and smiled at Ahern. 'Well, I'm glad I took you up on your offer.'

Ahern proved to be easy company and the chat flowed. For the first time in a while, Michael felt relaxed in another man's company. His awkwardness seemed to disappear. He went up to the bar for another round. While he waited for the drinks he looked over at the table. Ahern was on his phone, engrossed in conversation. Michael scrutinised him. If it *was* a date, was he making the same mistake again, punching above his weight. He could almost hear Terry's voice in his ear, telling him not to be stupid, to stop running himself down.

He returned to the table and placed the fresh round of drinks on it as Ahern ended the call with, 'Okay, I'll see you at the case conference. Bye.'

He put down the phone, lifted his glass and clinked it against Michael's. 'Sorry about that. Cheers, bud.'

'Cheers.' Michael smiled at him. 'So, what's the case conference about?'

'Oh, just a few updates on the Rachel Reece murder inquiry. Sinnott's got a bee in his bonnet about it. Don't suppose you've found anything new on the forensics front? Anything you haven't passed on to the team yet?' He held Michael's gaze. 'You know – it'd be great to be able to impress the boss with some new revelation.'

'Everything is being processed at the moment,' Michael said honestly. 'The results will be sent on as soon as they're completed. I wish I had more but, well, you know how it is.'

'Fair enough – I'll just have to distinguish myself in other ways.' He smiled broadly and winked at him.

Michael was contemplating how to respond when he noticed Ahern looking across the bar, his attention caught by something. He turned to see Terry and her new protégé, Laura.

Ahern stood up. 'Doc – over here!'

Terry turned, saw them and waved. Michael gave a half-hearted wave back – now he definitely wouldn't know if this was a date. The two women wove their way over to the table.

'Fancy seeing you both here!' Terry said, giving Michael a pointed look and Ahern a big smile. 'This is Laura Quinn – my new intern. Laura, this is DI Alan Ahern. You remember Michael, forensics genius extraordinaire, from the case conference of course.'

Laura nodded at them both, smiling.

'Well, Laura,' Ahern said, turning the full wattage of his attention on her. 'Pathology, eh? What's brought another young woman to follow in the doc's footsteps here?' He gave Terry an amused nod and she shot him a sideways look.

'Oh, I haven't decided for sure, but I've always been fascinated by criminal investigation—'

'Anyway,' Terry cut in, 'we'll let you get back to your drinks.'

Michael caught her eye and gave her a tiny nod of thanks. But before they'd a chance to find a seat elsewhere, Ahern stood up. 'Not at all – I have to head anyway. Here, you take my seat and I'm sure Michael will grab you another one.' He drained his pint then put his hand on Michael's shoulder once more. 'Let's do this again.'

And then he was gone into the crowd.

Michael sighed as he got up to find a chair for Laura. He wondered what had just happened between him and Ahern. If he wasn't such a trusting person, he might think the only reason Ahern had asked him out was to pump him for information on the Rachel Reece case. Everyone knew Ahern was a staunch supporter of DCS Sinnott, which did make Michael wonder.

But hey, at least he was out of the lab.

20

Terry, Laura and Michael stayed in Mulholland's until closing time that Friday night, rounding out the evening with a stop at a Turkish kebab shop. Michael made his excuses and got in the queue for a taxi home after that, saying he wasn't feeling too good.

'Was it the doner kebab or the six lagers you chugged before it?' Terry said, putting a conciliatory arm about his shoulder.

'Let's say it's probably both,' Michael said, groaning miserably.

Once his cab pulled away, Laura said to Terry, 'Will we see if we can get one for the road somewhere?'

'My flat isn't far,' Terry said. 'I've got a bottle of gin there that I've been dying to try.'

'I'm not usually a gin drinker,' Laura said, 'but there's a first time for everything.'

Ten minutes later they were sitting in Terry's front room, glasses in hand, Taylor Swift playing softly over the stereo.

Laura took a sip of the gin and nodded appreciatively.

'This is very, very good,' she said.

'It's called Glaswegin,' Terry said. 'With a name like that, I had to give it a try. Not bad at all.'

They drank for a time in companionable silence, and then Laura said, 'Poor Michael. I hope Ahern isn't giving him the wrong end of the stick.'

'What gives you that idea anyway?'

'He's a bit touchy feely. One of those guys who stares at you when he's talking to you.' Laura gave a shiver.

'I kind of got that vibe myself, but maybe he's ambi-dextrous and keeping his options open.'

'He's not bad looking,' Laura said. 'Would you?'

'No way,' Terry said firmly. 'Anyway, Michael would kill me.'

'What the eye doesn't see,' Laura said with a devilish glint.

'Not a chance! Could you imagine the rumour mill if word got out I was seeing Alan Ahern? And believe me, it would. He's part of Sinnott's crew, and that man would relish dragging my name through the muck.'

'Why would anyone have an issue with you dating a colleague – it's not like you're his boss?'

'Laura, I'm already struggling to be taken seriously. Every bloody news broadcast focuses as much on my arse as it does on what I have to say about the case I'm working. One thing you have to understand is that we are women in a male-dominated profession. Don't get me wrong, there are good guys in the ranks, but there are also a hell of a lot of chauvinistic assholes who don't reckon we've got the grit or the intellect to be effective.'

Laura nodded and sighed deeply. 'Wouldn't it be nice to think we'd gotten past that shite?'

'Wouldn't it, though?'

'So you've never dated a cop?'

Terry paused and took a gulp of her drink. 'Well …'

'Oh,' Laura said, sitting forward.

'You have to promise me this will go no further. Only Michael knows about it.'

'My lips are sealed,' Laura said, miming locking her mouth shut and throwing away the key.

'Two months before I started here I came over to a seminar on deaths in custody,' Terry said. 'At that stage I had no idea I'd be working in Dublin in the near future, so I was in the headspace that these would be a bunch of people I'd more than likely never see again.'

'Fair enough,' Laura said. 'No one could blame you for that.'

'It was a three-day seminar, lots of talks and classes and demonstrations, and on the last night I'm at the bar having a drink when this guy sits down beside me. I recognised him from one of the talks – he'd asked a question to the speaker – and I'd thought he was kind of good-looking and that the question he'd asked was an intelligent one. So we got to talking and he bought me a drink and I bought him a drink, and we decided to get a bite to eat and we talked some more and …'

'You never?' Laura said, deadpan.

'We did, yeah.'

'Good for you!'

'I thought so too! I mean, he seemed *quite* nice and it was a fun night. The next day I got my plane back to Glasgow and that was that. Then I got the job here. I'm going to be honest and say I didn't even think about that guy again ... until, suddenly, there he was working the crime scene at Farmleigh the other day. I nearly dropped with embarrassment.'

'Did he make a big deal out of it?'

'No. Not at all. He never made me feel weird, and I don't think he's said a word to anyone. No one has mentioned it to me, anyway. And if the word was out, someone would have.'

'So maybe he's actually a good guy then.'

Terry nodded. 'I think maybe he is.'

'You going to tell me the name of this mysterious gentleman? Wait a minute, if he was working on Rachel Reece's murder, I must know him. It's not Vinnie, is it?'

'No,' said Terry coyly.

Laura's jaw dropped. 'Oh my God, it's John Fraser, isn't it? Good choice, girl!'

'I'm glad you approve.'

21

Laura ended up staying over on the sofa and, much to Terry's surprise, she was awakened the next morning at 9.30 to the sound of singing from the kitchen and the smell of bacon cooking. She threw on her robe, padding out in her bare feet to discover her intern busying herself making breakfast.

'There's a cafetière of coffee just ready to go,' Laura said, flipping a rasher in the pan, 'and I have scrambled eggs keeping warm in the oven.' Just at that moment the toaster popped. 'Take a seat and I'll plate up.'

Terry did as she was bid. 'I thought you wouldn't be stirring until the crack of two or three this afternoon,' she said incredulously. 'It's Saturday for God's sake and not my weekend on call. I had booked a duvet day. Are you always this cheery in the morning?'

'I am genetically gifted with a strong constitution,' Laura said. 'I rarely suffer from hangovers.'

'That could be dangerous,' Terry observed.

'I have a limit and I stick to it,' Laura said. 'I've been well-warned by my dad, believe me.'

'Yeah. I've one of those too. But I don't often pay any heed to him.'

Laura put a plate of scrambled eggs, bacon and toast in front of Terry and, pressing the plunger on the coffee pot, poured her a mugful.

'I hope you don't mind that I …' Laura waved her hand over the table, suddenly not so sure of herself.

'Did you have all this with you in your bag, cause I'm damned sure the last time I looked in my fridge there was a lemon and a wilted lettuce. This looks amazing. It's been a while since anyone cooked something for me.'

'I just nipped out to that shop in the garage. I always think a decent breakfast sets you up after a big night out.' Laura poured herself some coffee and added milk and sugar. Terry always drank her first cup of the day black.

'I'd hardly say it was too riotous,' Terry said. 'Though my head suggests otherwise.'

After they'd eaten, Terry stacked the dishwasher and took two more coffees into the living room.

Laura, sprawled on the couch again, was scrolling through something on her phone.

'Tell me you didn't post any photos from last night,' Terry said in horror.

'No, I restrained myself.' Laura smiled. 'I was just looking at Rachel Reece's Insta page.'

'Yeah?'

'Yeah. The accepted wisdom is that she didn't have a current partner, that she was more or less married to her work. But I couldn't help but notice this guy.' She held up her phone and Terry saw a photo of Reece talking into a microphone, a professional-looking set of earphones on her head. Behind her, off to one side, was a tall young man dressed in what Terry's dad would have called a Crombie, his hair cropped close and his jawline, artfully stubbled. 'He shows up in quite a few photographs going back to April, May. Not in any of the more recent ones. Mostly they're Rachel and her girlfriends. They have that D4 look.'

'We can't all be leggy blondes. Any clues to who he is?'

'I do, as it happens. She only tags him once, but once is all it takes. His name is Kyle Brady and he's a criminology postgrad at Dublin City University.'

'You think they were an item?'

'That'd be my guess. He's possibly an ex, at any rate.'

Laura stayed until eleven and then headed into town to catch a bus back to Vinnie's place in Clonsilla, where she was staying.

After she left, Terry checked her emails. There was nothing from Dr Hunt or her pal Miles. She settled on the couch, her laptop on her lap, and decided to have a quick look at the photos her intern had pointed out to her. She found the one where Brady was tagged. It looked as if he was there when Rachel was recording her podcast. She sat the laptop down on the cushion beside her and leant back, staring up at the ceiling. Her one job was to find out how Rachel had died. She knew the mechanics of it, but not the circumstances. Maybe this guy could add some context. She picked up the laptop and went onto his page.

It was a public profile. Before she could talk herself out of it, she sent him a direct message.

Kyle, my name is Terry O'Brien. I'm a forensic pathologist, and I've been working on the murder of Rachel Reece. I believe you knew her. I'd like to talk to you about the case. Let me know if you'd be prepared to meet.

It took three minutes for Brady to respond.

3pm this afternoon. Tearoom in Kilkenny Design on Nassau Street.

Am I out of my mind doing this? Terry wondered.

She got to the upstairs café at 2.45 p.m. and found a table tucked in the corner, where she settled in with a coffee and a scone the size of a baby's head.

She couldn't predict how Kyle would react to her questions. After all, a current or ex-partner is always the most likely suspect in a case like this, and he might have something to hide. Still, she told herself, she was doing the right thing, finding out more about Rachel Reece. And they were meeting in a public place.

At ten minutes past three, early by Irish standards, she saw him approaching the coffee station, looking around for her as he ordered. He was taller than she expected, probably six foot four in his stockinged feet, and he appeared more dishevelled than in the photos she'd seen, the stubble now a scraggly beard, his hair still short but longer than it had been and untidy. The Crombie was gone, replaced by a grey hoody.

She waved to get his attention. He looked puzzled at first, then gave a tentative wave back, his reactions all a little slow.

Terry got up and walked towards him. 'Kyle Brady?' She stuck out her hand. 'Hi, Terry O'Brien. I'm sorry for your loss.'

Immediately, his shoulders slumped and his eyes filled with tears. 'I can't believe it – I just can't …'

Terry gave him the warmest smile she could muster – she was unsure how much of his grief to take at face value. Some of it could be guilt, after all.

They got some coffee and headed over to the table. Kyle, placing his cup down nervously, promptly slopped some coffee over the rim and onto the table. Terry helped him clean up the mess, then sat back and waited for him to speak.

He stared at the wet napkins for a few moments, then he raised his eyes to Terry's. 'So, you saw her body … Rachel … You saw her.' His voice was shaky.

'She's at peace now,' Terry said, despite knowing what Rachel had endured in her final moments.

'They wouldn't let me see her. The gardaí say her family don't want me to. They don't understand. Even though we split up a few months back, she was still my best friend.'

The threatened tears were now flowing. Terry handed him a napkin.

'Did she suffer?' he said through sobs. It was the question they all asked.

'I'm sorry,' Terry said, trying to sound as comforting as she could. 'I can't give you any details beyond what's already been made public – it could hamper the case.'

Kyle nodded in mute understanding.

'Look,' Terry said, 'I'm not sure if you've already spoken to the guards and I get the gist that Rachel wasn't a fan, but believe me, Kyle, we're all working to get justice for Rachel. There might be something you can do to help.'

He sat up straight and wiped his eyes with the back of his hand.

'I'm trying to find out if there was an old case she was working on that might have brought her in touch with her murderer. I'm interested in the podcast she was recording about the Eileen McCarthy case. Did she tell you anything about it?'

'Jesus, she was obsessed with that murder. That was the main reason we broke up, if you want to know. She was getting too involved. The last straw was when she went to see that man in the nursing home. She knew he had dementia, that she was dredging up terrible things for him, but she still went. We had a huge fight over it.'

'Do you know who this man was?'

'Eileen McCarthy's father. My grandad has dementia too – it's awful, he gets distressed so easily. Rachel knew how I felt – she'd even met my grandad! But even though I asked her not to go, to leave the old guy alone, she still went. She just couldn't let it lie.'

He picked up his mug, looked at it and put it down again, his hand shaking slightly. His voice became shrill.

'Jesus, we had such a row about it. I guess everything that

had ever annoyed us about each other came out. She could never let anything go – you know? Couldn't just stop and think about me for once.' Kyle stared at the table, like he'd gone somewhere else.

Terry cleared her throat. 'So what would you say she was like in the past few months – was this out of character for her?'

Kyle glanced up, slightly dazed-looking. 'Em ... I mean, she was always determined. But, I suppose, the intensity was different. She was hyper-focused on Eileen McCarthy. I wouldn't have been surprised if she had a murder wall in her bedroom. Not that she did, mind. Well, not that I knew of anyway. ' He caught Terry's eye then looked away again, across the café. 'I was worried for her – I couldn't stand to see her like that.'

'Was she working on any other cases, do you know? Did she mention anyone else she was researching?'

'No one in particular. She seemed to be looking at a whole lot of them. She was even talking about women killed in Northern Ireland. That was the last I heard from her – she said she was travelling to somewhere up north. Then radio silence. Next thing I knew she was dead.' He rubbed his forehead hard with his fingers, then put his hands over his eyes. His shoulders began to shake softly.

Kyle Brady was either a very good actor or a genuinely heartbroken ex. Either way, Terry knew she wasn't going to get much more out of him.

He stood up unsteadily. 'I need to go.'

'Thank you for your time, Kyle. I am truly sorry about Rachel.'

She watched him disappear down the stairs before draining her coffee and leaving too. There was a bus stop more or less directly across the road from Kilkenny Design, and she jogged over the street and joined the crowd there.

She hadn't been waiting more than five minutes when her phone buzzed. Taking it from her pocket, Terry saw it was an Instagram DM – @morticia32 had never gotten a DM before, because no one knew that handle was Terry's.

She opened the message.

How can you catch me now? I love my work and want to start again. You will soon hear of me with my funny little games.

How creepy! The sender name was @saucyjack. Terry thought the words had an oddly familiar ring to them but couldn't place them. It wasn't until she was on the bus and headed for home that it came to her and she felt a jolt of fear.

Terry was sure those lines had something to do with Jack the Ripper.

22

He couldn't resist. It was a distraction but he had to reach out.

The Irish Mirror had a big double page spread about Rachel Reece and there, right in the top corner of the second page, was a photograph of the pathologist. They said she was central to the effort to catch the man who killed the podcaster.

How could he resist that? The other one would have to wait.

23

Terry got off the bus a couple of stops earlier than she had originally intended and walked along Haddington Road towards home. The drizzle had let up and people were out enjoying the sun while it lasted. She found herself outside Saint Mary's church. There was no mass on and, aside from a few elderly people praying in the pews, she was alone.

The air, smelling of candle wax and incense, felt cool on her skin as she walked down the centre aisle and took a seat in the second pew from the very front.

She liked the quiet, the feeling of safety, in sacred spaces, even though she wasn't religious. And that feeling of sanctuary was even more welcome after the DM she'd just received. She looked about quickly, saw no one was paying any attention to her and took out her phone, reading the message again.

She looked it up. The three sentences had been taken from the second paragraph of a letter Jack the Ripper, or someone pretending to be him – experts were still divided on the veracity of the document – had sent to the head of the Central News Agency, a newspaper company that distributed various publications in the London metropolitan area in the late nineteenth century.

Usually referred to as the 'Dear Boss' letter – it had been addressed to 'The Boss' of the company – it was meant as a jubilant celebration of the fact that the police of the day were absolutely stymied in their pursuit of the killer.

While researching it on the bus, Terry had noticed that one word had been altered in the text sent to her.

In the 'Dear Boss' letter, the first sentence ran: 'How can *they* catch me now?' While the DM to Terry read: 'How can *you* catch me now?'

He knows I'm investigating the cases myself, Terry thought. *Whoever sent me this has to know that.*

But who could it be?

Her first thought was Kyle Brady. She had just finished speaking to him when the DM arrived, and he had her Insta handle, as she'd used the account to get in contact with him in the first place. It would be a simple thing to set up a fake Instagram account and send her the message from it.

But he had seemed so genuinely devastated by Rachel Reece's death and the emotional state they'd both been in in the months leading up to it, he didn't seem capable of such an action. Despite her early reticence, Terry had been starting to believe Brady really was upset about how things had ended between him and Rachel, and she found it hard to cast the young man as a sadistic murderer who was now turning his attentions to tormenting her.

Which didn't rule him out. Just pushed him down the pecking order a bit.

Another theory was that the message was a hoax, and someone was trying to spook her. She'd experienced this in Glasgow, anonymous messages being left on her desk or text messages from unknown numbers informing her she was being watched or that her time in the mortuary was drawing to a close. That she was a rat, overstepping her authority.

Terry didn't have to look too far to come up with suspects for that kind of behaviour here. Professor Boyd was no fan of hers, but such anonymous theatrics were hardly his style. Mrs Carey acted as his personal IT consultant, and this was way beyond her ken. Sinnott was a different kettle of fish. She had no doubt he could be spiteful, and if he decided to look into her a bit more deeply, he could use contacts in the tech squad to take a look at her social media, in which case identifying her as @morticia32 wouldn't be such a difficult job. Hell, if someone looked carefully at the accounts of her friends and family they could probably work it out.

There was a CCTV camera close to Mrs Carey's desk, so it wasn't beyond the realms of possibility she'd been spotted copying files taken from Professor Boyd's office and he'd mentioned it to his pal Sinnott.

She sat in the scented coolness of the church and pondered that. If Boyd caught her going off-piste and mounting her own investigation, though, it was most likely he would simply fire her.

Which meant that, if it *was* Sinnott, he was working from motives that were solely his own. And if the detective chief superintendent was trying to scare her, then there had to be something he wanted to keep hidden, but whatever it was, she didn't imagine it wasn't a threat to her at least.

Feeling a bit calmer, she lit a candle for Jenny and sat for a few minutes in the stillness. It was the nearest thing she knew to saying hello to her sister, to spending a little time with her.

When Jenny had been ten years old, and Terry eight, Jenny had been given a solo to sing in a school concert: the old gospel hymn 'This Little Light of Mine'. Every time Terry lit a candle for her, she thought of her big sister singing that song, standing at the front of the stage in the auditorium in their old school, the chorus ringing out in her clear, pure voice. Little did they know that one day that special light of hers would be put out.

Terry pushed the thought aside. Sitting in the semi-darkness with only the flicker of candlelight for company was soothing – here the good memories could flow, from when times were happier, and the bad ones could be held at bay.

For a while, at least.

24

Miles called her at 9 p.m. that evening with news of the files. They were in a Proton Mail account he'd set up for her and he talked her through accessing them.

'Thanks Miles, you're a miracle worker.'

'Aye, that's me, a true messiah. No bother, Terry. And remember, dinner's on you next time you're home.'

The unedited recordings were from the series Rachel was working on when she was killed, her investigation into the murder of Eileen McCarthy. Terry clicked on a file labelled 'Abandoned, Trailer'.

The background music came in first, sombre but strident, then quietened.

Terry felt chills when she heard Rachel Reece's voice – that neutral accent so many Irish people had these days, unlike her father's old-school Dublinese, but with hints of soft Donegal.

Rachel came across like many podcasters: confident with an undercurrent of excitement. Terry could envision her in the studio, script on the desk, baseball cap on her head, talking animatedly into the microphone.

On 15 February 2007 Eileen McCarthy was found murdered in her own bed. She wasn't the first woman murdered in Ireland, and she certainly wouldn't be the last, but her death is pivotal to my in-depth investigations into the women who have been murdered in Ireland since the millennium.

I am a millennium baby. I was born in 2000, and in my twenty-three years of life at least 239, yes, that's 239, women have been murdered in Ireland.

Most of them died at the hands of their partners. Many were brought to justice ... but some families never got that closure. Some women's murders remain unsolved. Investigations were fruitless, evidence was lacking or the cases fell apart. Garda incompetence? Inherent misogyny within the justice system? ...

Terry had a swig of Coke. She knew that it wasn't always that straightforward. But she also knew from experience that those involved did not take kindly to criticism or advice. She mightn't agree with Rachel's delivery, but she got where that passion was coming from. And she could appreciate why listeners would be captivated by the podcaster. She had a definite presence.

The guards neatly store these women's deaths in locked drawers, dusty and forgotten, advances in science and technology not applied, possible links between the unsolved murders undiscovered. It's pitiful. The people who have sworn to protect us failed these women.

Well, not on my watch. I'm here to see that justice is served and that none of these women's deaths remain unpunished.

The music, which had built to a crescendo, faded.

Eileen McCarthy is one of these women relegated to the cold case filing cabinet. And she's going to be the focus of my new series. Coming soon.

The trailer ended. Terry clicked on another file, *Trailer 2*.
More atmospheric music, then:

Coming soon, the shocking new episode in my series Abandoned: What Happened to Eileen.

Eileen McCarthy was twenty-six years old when she died – not much older than me. She was born and brought up in Finglas, north Dublin, and lived with her parents until a few months before her death, when she and her younger sister, Jo, moved into a flat near the family home. Eileen was a civil servant and good at her job. Those who knew her didn't have a bad word to say about her.

She didn't have a regular boyfriend, but on Valentine's

night 2007, just a normal Wednesday night, the evidence suggests a man entered her new home with a knife and cruelly murdered her.

Her sister found Eileen dead the following morning.

The Garda Press Office released a statement on 20 February that stated Eileen had been stabbed multiple times.

It was a horrendous and vicious attack. Not content with just using his knife, her attacker grabbed her by the neck, squeezing until every breath was wrung from her body.

Jesus, Terry thought, how did people listen to this stuff for entertainment? She shook her head. But despite the dramatic style, Reece was right on the money with her description of the assault.

And there was no forensic evidence that might lead to her killer? With an attack that violent and that sustained?

Reece spoke dryly and slowly, letting the unlikelihood sink in.

The best the gardaí could do was point the finger at their go-to local sexual predator, Frank Cleaver. He'd been seen coming on to Eileen in Fahey's pub in Finglas earlier that night. She rebuffed him, and witnesses report he became angry and called her a 'pricktease', a 'miserable fucking lesbian' and assured her that girls 'like her' always 'get what's coming to them'.

The music swelled and fell again.

The gardaí have refused to speak to me. Unsurprisingly. The investigation into Eileen McCarthy's murder foundered quickly. There wasn't a shred of hard evidence against Cleaver. Old boyfriends were interviewed. Work colleagues gave all the information they had. Her home and garden were combed by the forensic science team, but every single avenue of exploration drew a blank. Every step she took in the week leading up to her death was reconstructed, and a list of everyone she came in contact with was collated, each individual questioned as to why someone would have wanted to kill such a seemingly decent young woman.

And amid all of this, not a single shred of usable evidence was discovered.

When I tried to speak to the gardaí, I was warned off, told to leave it alone. Words to the effect that I didn't know what I was messing with and to leave it to the 'real' investigators.

But you know, I couldn't just walk away.

I won't give up. I'm not built that way.

'What Happened to Eileen' is my new episode, coming soon to wherever you get your podcasts. In it, I will reveal some shocking new evidence that will blow the Eileen McCarthy case wide open.

Follow me on Instagram, TikTok and Twitter for updates, and remember, if you have any information that might help, contact me on there or at rachel@ abandonedpod.org

Terry sat back into the sofa, her pulse racing.

So much of what she'd just heard reminded her of her recent experiences in Glasgow with Jenny's murder, how she had been fobbed off and told to leave it to the professionals – who were, in actuality, doing nothing.

'*I won't give up ...*'

Rachel couldn't keep that promise. But Terry could. What had Rachel Reece uncovered? Who had it threatened, and why? What had she said to Boyd that had riled him so much?

By reaching out to Kyle, she knew she was in danger of jeopardising her position yet again. She knew it was risky and could lead her into dangerous waters, but someone had to do it. She hated being told to get back in her box. What the hell did she have to lose, she was only here on a temporary basis anyway. It might just be a bit shorter than she had anticipated. Rachel and Eileen deserved better. So did Jenny.

Terry would finish what Rachel had started.

25

When Terry woke on Sunday morning, still tired and irritable, Rachel was the first thing on her mind. She knew that Fraser was working and decided she'd head in to see if he knew about Rachel's trip to Northern Ireland, and her visit to Eileen McCarthy's father. She believed Kyle was genuinely upset about Reece's death but wasn't sure if he had been interviewed yet. It wouldn't do any harm to give Fraser the heads up and, if truth be told, it might be nice to see him.

Kevin Street Garda Station was packed to bursting with arrests from the previous night's revelries. Terry squeezed through to the front of the queue, ignoring the catcalls and unsavoury comments the various hungover patrons shouted in her direction.

She'd called ahead and the desk sergeant motioned her towards the door at the far end of the room before holding up his hand and roaring at the unruly mob to settle down.

Terry nodded thanks as she made her way through the door and headed up the stairs towards the incident room set up for the investigation into Rachel's death. She could hear Fraser's voice before she reached the first-floor landing: someone was getting the sharp edge of his tongue.

When she emerged into the bullpen she could sense the tension. Normally the atmosphere in this part of a police station would be professional but relatively relaxed, the detectives chatting and joking as they went about their business. Now, all were at their desks, heads down, with only an occasional murmur from those on the phones, while John Fraser's strident voice bounced off the walls.

Fraser had taken over the office at the far end of the squad room, with only a bank of windows and a flimsy door separating him from his colleagues. Through the glass, Terry could see a young garda standing ramrod straight in front of his desk, her arms at her sides. Fraser was on his feet, leaning across his desk and jabbing his right middle finger at something that lay on the desktop between them. Only the fingers of the young officer's right hand surreptitiously scratching at her thigh gave any indication of her discomfort.

Terry hung back, waiting for the dressing down to conclude before she made her presence known. She suddenly became aware that someone was pulling at her arm.

'You okay, Doc?' DS Mary Healy stood beside her, looking concerned.

'What's that all about?'

'Christ knows. That poor girl is getting both barrels. As far as we can make out, she's in to pick up a report to take to Garda HQ and himself is not best pleased.'

Both women watched as the young garda took a bundle of papers from Fraser and made for the door. She clutched the papers tightly to her chest and ignored the office staff as she passed them and left the room. The clattering of her shoes on the wooden stairs indicated that she had broken into a run once she was out of sight.

'Bless! She'll have resigned by the end of the week!' Mary rolled her eyes.

'I don't blame her. Is that what Fraser's normally like?'

'Nah – just bad timing. He was fine until Sinnott turned up this morning. Unfortunately, the door was closed, and despite Vinnie's ear-wigging' – they both looked over at Vinnie, whose desk was directly in front of the DCI's office – 'he couldn't make out what it was about. But Fraser blew a fuse. Went fucking mental, so he did. He was straight on the phone to someone after. And that's when she turned up.' Mary nodded in the direction the young garda had headed. 'Just a case of wrong time, wrong place. It could have been any of us. Anyway, what can we do for you, Doc?'

Terry nodded her head towards the door of Fraser's office.

'Jesus. Good luck with that.' Mary blessed herself. 'I'll say a prayer for you.'

Terry took a deep breath, walked over and rapped on the door. Fraser was sitting at his desk, with the receiver of his phone clutched in his hand. To her relief, the threatening look on his face softened when he turned and saw her. He finished his call and waved at her to come in, standing up and gesturing towards a small seating area at the other end of his office – four low chairs around a coffee table. Terry took one that offered a view of the office block opposite.

'Good to see you, Terry. Tea? Coffee?'

'No thanks. I'm fine.'

Fraser sat opposite her, facing the office area. He seemed as tense as she felt. She took a deep breath and cast her eyes down as she fiddled with the buttons on her jacket. 'I met up with Rachel Reece's boyfriend yesterday.'

She looked up. Fraser was looking intently at her but he stayed silent.

'He contacted me,' she said quickly, cringing inwardly at the lie, 'looking for any information he could get. Rachel's parents won't talk to him. I didn't tell him anything, of course, but I wanted to check if you'd spoken to him yet. And if not, you might like to know what he told me.' Her voice faltered.

Fraser continued looking at her in silence, but his right eyebrow rose and she took this as an invitation to go on.

'He said Rachel had gone to Northern Ireland before her death. He also told me that she had visited Eileen McCarthy's dad. He's in a nursing home.'

'Well, I'll pass that information on to DCS Sinnott.'

Terry noted the terse note in his voice.

'I have been removed from the investigation. It would appear that the minister for justice is concerned about the upsurge in gangland violence, and the chief has decided that I should head up the new task force. He has graciously offered to take over the Rachel Reece investigation.'

Terry couldn't believe what she was hearing. 'Can he do that?'

'He can and he has. Look, I can see the logic in the transfer. There was an attempt on a gang leader in one of the estates here, a drive-by shooting, and there's real concern it's going to start a war between the two main criminal organisations. The next target probably won't be so lucky.'

'And you know the lie of the land?'

'I do. I worked with the kids in these gangs as a juvenile liaison officer back in the day, and I know all the personalities involved. The powers that be think I might be able to defuse things using a ... *diplomatic* approach. Sinnott is a respected and decorated detective. The commissioner is of the opinion that the optics of having me head up the organised crime task force and giving Sinnott the head position on the Rachel Reece case will show he has all the bases covered. I think Reece's uncle is stirring things up in the background. Which doesn't help. But it looks good to have a DCS front and centre of the murder investigation. It's *all* about the optics.' Fraser shrugged, his anger seeming to have dissipated to resignation.

Terry wasn't quite there yet. 'But Sinnott isn't exactly dispassionate about the case. He's convinced he knows who the culprit is before the investigation has even really gotten off the ground. What point is there in me giving him any new information? He'll just bury it.'

Fraser shrugged again. 'Well, that's how it is. Sinnott is your contact from now on. And you'd probably do well to keep some of those opinions to yourself.'

'Did you know about the trip to the North – did you find out anything about that?'

'It was one of the leads I intended to follow up. But I didn't get a chance.' His tone softened.

Terry rested her head on the back of the chair, mulling over what he had told her. Suddenly she sat up. 'Okay. I'll back off Rachel's case for now. But, I've been thinking' – Fraser rolled his eyes – 'I'm being serious, John. Would it classify as interfering if I have a look at the Eileen McCarthy murder? It's technically a cold case. It's only connected to Rachel because it was going to be featured on her podcast. As far as Sinnott's concerned it's not connected to the Reece investigation in a real sense, so he won't be looking into it this time around.'

'Why? Don't you have enough on your plate without dredging up old cases?'

Terry dug in. 'What if Rachel found out something that might be relevant in Eileen's murder? Maybe when she went to see Eileen's dad he remembered something that might not have seemed relevant at the time. Has anyone from the guards gone out to re-interview him?'

Fraser shook his head. 'You're not going to let this lie, are you?'

Terry shrugged. 'Sinnott is going to be up to his eyes with the Rachel Reece case. Surely he won't notice if I poke about in the Eileen McCarthy murder.'

'Terry, you're a pathologist. This is outside your wheel-house.'

'I know. But this case is not going to get the kind of investigation it deserves. And I know what it's like to be a family member of a murder victim, looking on and seeing justice slide past while the police are looking the other way.'

'Your sister,' Fraser said.

'Yes ... Look, I know I haven't mentioned it to you before, but—'

'It's okay – I heard about it and I'm so sorry. You know how coppers talk.'

'Oh, I do. All too well.'

'Right,' Fraser said. 'I'll see what I can find out about Rachel's trip up north and her interview with Eileen McCarthy's father. I suggest you leave the digging to us.' He gave her a knowing look. 'Sinnott is now running that task force and your role is clear: forensic pathologist who did the PM. I'll help where I can, but it won't be much.'

'Thanks, John,' she said, instinctively reaching out and putting her hand on his arm. He looked at her and a moment of recognition passed between them. It was the first time they'd acknowledged their brief, shared past and Terry felt a mix of awkwardness and excitement. She moved her hand away.

'Maybe we could meet up for a drink tomorrow night and I can fill you in?' he asked tentatively.

Terry didn't answer immediately. She wanted to say yes, but they were colleagues now, and she knew it was probably better not to go there. 'Maybe another time. But I'd appreciate a call if you find out anything.' She smiled to soften the rebuff.

'Of course,' Fraser said, his voice more formal. 'Now, if there's nothing else I can do for you?'

She said goodbye and left, wondering if she'd just made a ridiculous mistake by turning down a man she was pretty sure was one of the good ones.

26

It was well after lunchtime when Terry finished in the mortuary on Monday. There had been the usual build-up over the weekend. She finished with a PM on an American tourist who had keeled over on a cruise ship and Dublin was the next port of call. The coroner wanted to expedite matters, principally so that the widow could continue the cruise; she still had half the world to see.

There had been no surprises: he was an older man on medication for cholesterol, blood pressure and diabetes. He was a time bomb that, unfortunately, had detonated at sea. By the end of the day, his remains would be heading back to the US, with the rest of the American Airlines cargo, and his wife would be at the captain's table with a tale to tell.

Back in the office, there was a message on her desk in Mrs Carey's neat writing: *DCI Fraser called*.

She had to play this right. Fraser hadn't seemed particularly put out by her turning his offer of a drink into a phone call instead, but she needed him onside. She had to be sure he was still disposed to help her.

She took out her notebook and the Eileen McCarthy file, then picked up her phone. 'Afternoon, John. Such efficiency – I didn't expect to hear from you so soon.'

'I wanted to get onto it before I have to decant to Garda HQ. There's not much to tell. Eileen's father was interviewed a couple of times during the initial investigation. Reading between the lines, he wasn't exactly cooperative, but he didn't have much to add anyway. Eileen had moved out and the mother and father had no idea what she was up to or with whom. There was a cold-case review on the tenth anniversary. There's a note that an effort was made to contact him without success, and it doesn't seem to have been followed up.'

'Rachel Reece chased him, though,' Terry observed.

'Indeed. I contacted the home he's in and they say he's not fit to be interviewed. I've a solicitor's details if we want to take that route – that's out of my hands now, of course, but it looks like a dead end in any case.'

'It was worth a try. Thanks anyway.'

'No worries. And if you change your mind about that drink ...'

Terry felt a flicker of pleasure to know he was still keen. 'You know, maybe I will take you up on it.'

'Brilliant. I'm free tomorrow night.'

'Me too.'

'How about Croke's over on Nassau Street? It's usually quiet on a Tuesday night.'

'Perfect. I'll see you there around eight?'

'I'll be there. Oh, one more thing on the Eileen McCarthy case. Her sister—'

'Jo, isn't it?'

'Yeah, Jo. She seems to have vanished without a trace.'

27

The young man lying on the mortuary table the following morning was twenty-three years old, around the same age as Laura, but their lives couldn't have been any more different. No wonder Terry's intern looked subdued. The man's mother had told the young garda who responded to her call that he had 'a bit of a drug problem' and 'some mental health issues'. His girlfriend had broken up with him and he had shut himself in his bedroom. His mother found him suspended by a belt from the curtain rail.

'Forensic pathology is a harsh mistress,' said Terry. 'The fragility of life, eh?'

Laura exhaled. 'You said it.'

The young man was dressed in jeans and a T-shirt, both rather grubby. Lying on the autopsy table was the black plastic belt, now in three pieces, which had been around his neck. His face was pale, which meant she could reassure his mother that he had died almost instantly. No time to reconsider.

There were no tell-tale signs of intravenous drug use – his poison was obviously of the softer kind. Time and toxicology would tell. The only mark on him was from the ligature around his neck. His organs were healthy and even his Adam's apple wasn't broken. It hardly seemed fair that there was so little to find. *What a waste of a young life*, Terry thought, not for the first time.

In time, there would be an inquest and she could answer the family's questions, but for now she wrote in her notes: *Consistent with hanging from a high suspension point*. The next move was the coroner's.

Terry sent Laura over to the state lab with the toxicology samples, hoping it would clear her head. If Laura wanted to become a forensic pathologist she needed to learn to compartmentalise. There was a time and a place for emotion, and it wasn't in the postmortem room.

Terry was at her desk when Laura returned later in the morning. The Eileen McCarthy file was open in front of Terry and she'd been looking again at the @saucyjacky DM she'd received.

'You're a true-crime afficionado,' she said as Laura took the chair opposite her.

'I am.'

'If someone sent you this, what would you make of it?' Terry passed the phone across the desk.

Laura scanned the message. 'Aren't those lines something to do with Jack the Ripper?'

'Yes,' said Terry. 'It's from a letter written to a newspaper editor. Its authenticity is pretty hotly disputed, but it's considered important because the author signed it "Jack the Ripper", which is why that serial killer is known by the title today.'

'Yeah, I've read about that,' said Laura.

'I've read the whole letter,' Terry said. 'He brags about the police not being able to catch him and says he's going to continue killing, gives details about what he's going to do next. The whole letter is … boastful, I suppose.'

'This person's username on Instagram is @saucyjacky,' said Laura. 'You get the significance of that, right?'

'Yep,' said Terry. 'The next message that was sent to the Central News Agency after this one is known as the Saucy Jacky postcard.'

Laura sat back and looked at Terry. 'People who identify with one of history's most vicious and notorious serial killers are probably not the type you want sliding into your DMs.'

'Probably not, no.'

'You got this on Saturday afternoon?'

'I did. After I'd interviewed Kyle Brady.'

Laura's eyes opened a little wider. 'You got in contact with him?'

'Yep.'

'Is that … *usual* for a forensic pathologist?'

'No. It's not.'

'So why—?'

'You don't need to get involved in any of this, Laura – it's certainly not part of what you came here to do! I just wanted to know what your thinking on it was.'

'I'd say its purpose is much the same as the Dear Boss letter. If you take it that it's from the person who killed Rachel Reece, they're pretty much saying they're going to kill again.'

'But also, just as with the Dear Boss letter, this could be a hoax, couldn't it? Someone trying to scare me?'

'Why would they want to do that?'

Terry thought about shutting down the conversation and just asking Laura to put her handwritten notes on that morning's PM into the online system, keep things professional. But if Terry was going to utilise her own resources to learn all she could about Eileen McCarthy in a bid to learn more about the Rachel Reece case, then Laura, who was bright, resourceful and trustworthy, could be a useful part of that.

'I don't think the investigation into Rachel Reece's murder is going in the direction it should,' Terry said. 'So I'm, let's say, *quietly* looking into it myself. A murder enquiry is like a giant jigsaw. There are many dissectologists involved.'

Laura cut in: 'Pathologists?'

'No. People who do jigsaws.'

'Oh!' She looked a little puzzled.

'What I mean is the gardaí start with the edge pieces, the outline, then look for the pieces that identify the perpetrator. The forensic pathologist starts with the picture of the victim and then tries to help fit in other pieces that will help reveal the bigger picture. The problem is, some people try to force pieces in. Try to make them fit. I'm worried that that could happen here. I'm just …'

'Checking that the right pieces are in the right places?'

'Exactly.'

'Won't that get you in trouble?'

'Only if the powers that be find out. I don't want to interfere with the investigation or imply that the gardaí are not doing a good job.'

Laura thought about that. 'So where do we start?'

28

The Oak Nursing Home in Donabate had obviously been a rather grand country house in its time. The grounds were well kept but there was no getting away from the function of these places – patients confined to their rooms or lined up in the day room, a waiting room for the end of life. Terry shivered at the thought.

She and Laura had arrived there by taxi that lunchtime. Terry was determined to see what she might find out if she could get to speak to Liam McCarthy directly. What might he have told Rachel Reece when she visited?

It took half an hour to make the journey, which Terry reasoned would probably be closer to forty-five minutes on the return jaunt as Dublin's traffic, always bad, intensified towards rush hour. They could stay late when they returned to finish up their day's work.

The reception area of the home was like a boutique hotel's

– muted colours, tasteful furnishings and fresh flowers. There was also a nice buzz about the place and a pleasant lavender scent, which didn't seem to be masking the stench of urine and boiled cabbage.

A woman in her mid-twenties smiled from behind the desk. Terry smiled back. She wondered how much the staff knew about Liam McCarthy's history and if they'd be wary about new visitors coming out of the blue. She decided to go with the cover story she'd concocted with Laura in the taxi.

'Hi there. My name is Terry O'Brien, and this is my sister, Laura. We're old neighbours of one of the residents here, Liam McCarthy? I live abroad but am back in Ireland for a few days and thought to pay a visit. He was great friends with our dad, Lord rest his soul – he would have wanted us to visit.' She did her best to look solemn and the young woman's facial expression, which had run the gamut from suspicious to curious, now shared Terry's concerned look.

'I know what you mean. If my gran ended up in here and no one visited, I'd be fuming. And it's not that easy to get here – people are always complaining. Anyway, maybe a visitor would perk Liam up. He's a bit moody today – won't come out of his room.'

'We don't want to upset him.'

'Oh, you could do that without even trying. Maybe an old friend is just what he needs. I can't leave my desk – Harry Houdini over there is just waiting for his chance to do a runner.'

They looked over to where she indicated. Hovering near the door was a man, well into his eighties, so stooped he was almost bent in half. The only thing keeping him upright was the Zimmer frame he was hanging on to.

Good luck to him, Terry thought. *He must be more spry than he looks.*

'Liam's in room 213, just up those stairs. He's got really bad arthritis. Rarely leaves his room now. Maggie is keeping an eye on that corridor – just check in with her.'

'Thank you. We really appreciate it.'

Terry and Laura climbed the stairs to the first floor. Terry had expected the décor to become more hospital-like the further she was from the main public area, but the hotel vibe continued up to and into room 213. The aforementioned Maggie didn't seem to be about so they slipped inside, closing the door softly.

It was simply furnished but clean and tidy. Opposite the door there was a large orthopaedic chair, angled to take advantage of the view of the grounds. Perched on the edge of the seat, ignoring the vista, was a tiny old man, captivated by a large television screen positioned to be viewed from the bed, attached as it was to the opposite wall and taking up most of it. The flatscreen was showing an advert for Coca-Cola in which many colourfully and scantily clad young people were skateboarding, wind-surfing and doing other extreme physical activities, cans of the soft drink improbably clutched in their hands as they did so.

The duo walked towards the room's occupant. At the sound of footsteps, he turned but his attention immediately returned to the screen.

'Mr McCarthy. My name is Terry and this is my colleague, Laura.'

Terry stood right in front of the old man. His eyes never wavered, and he continued staring straight ahead. She found his silent stare quite disconcerting.

'Laura and I work with the gardaí and we're looking into Eileen's death again.'

At the mention of his daughter's name the old man's eyes flicked to some framed photographs arranged on the window ledge. Then he stared blankly at her again.

'May we ask you a few questions about Eileen?'

He continued staring. Terry felt increasingly uncomfortable, unsure how to proceed.

'Is there anything you remember about your daughter that you'd like to tell us?' Laura asked. 'Any information you can give us would be helpful.'

Without warning, Liam McCarthy turned to Terry and grabbed her right forearm, his fingers digging into her flesh. She tried to prise him off but he wrapped both hands around her forearm tightly and held on.

Laura stepped in and tried to loosen the old man's vice-like grasp, with little success – it was clasped tight. Eventually, the grip slackened, and as it did, the old man let out a deep, heartfelt sob.

'Mr McCarthy?' Terry looked at his face. Tears were running down it. He began to stroke her arm softly.

'Jo? My Jo?'

'No, Mr McCarthy. I'm not Jo. I'm Terry. Terry O'Brien.' She gently took his hand and placed it back on the arm of his chair.

The old man continued weeping. 'Jo, get Irenie. I can't find

Irenie. Why won't she come? Is she looking for Eileen? Jo, love, get your mam.'

The crying increased in pitch, a keening lament so loud it was bound to alert someone. Terry knew she had only a few moments. She leaned over and looked in his eyes. 'Mr McCarthy. What do you remember about Eileen's death?'

'He took her away from me,' McCarthy said. 'Why did he want Eileen?'

'Who took her?' Laura asked. 'Who took Eileen?'

'The big man said he'd get him.' His rheumy eyes were darting back and forth rapidly, and he was wringing his hands, murmuring to himself. 'That's why he wanted to find you, Jo. Your mam told him where you were. Where is she? Get Irenie, Jo.'

Terry realised this whole idea was futile. She felt bad that she had caused the bereaved man such distress. 'It's all right, Mr McCarthy,' she said softly. 'I'll go and get one of the nurses.'

'No!' He tried to haul himself to his feet, his voice now at shouting pitch. 'He'll come for you now, Jo. Run.'

He steadied himself and turned to Terry just as the door was flung open. A tall muscular woman in her fifties, clad in a nurse's uniform, entered the room. 'What's all this racket about?' she said.

The old man ignored the nurse, jabbing a finger at Terry and Laura as they moved to leave. 'Neither of you would ever listen to me,' he said, and then, just as suddenly, he slumped back in his chair and turned to face the window.

29

Terry and Laura got back to the office just before 3 p.m. They were removing their coats when the desk phone rang.

'Dr Rupert Hunt is here to see you,' said Mrs Carey. 'Will I send him in?'

'Dr Hunt?' Terry said, surprised. 'I thought he might ring or email ahead, but fair enough.'

'Mm-hm,' said Mrs Carey. Clearly her visitor was within earshot.

'Okay,' said Terry. 'Could you send him to the conference room and I'll be there in a minute?' She hung up and turned to Laura. 'I've to pop out for a moment. Will you enter my notes from this morning's PM into the system? I shouldn't be too long.'

'Yeah, no worries.'

Terry headed for the door, but as she did, Laura said, 'That visit wasn't a waste of time, you know.'

Terry paused. 'I don't see that we learned much.'

'I did a four-week rotation in geriatric medicine, so I know a bit about the ageing process. Even people with severe dementia can and do have windows of lucidity, which can often be triggered by a name or a piece of music or a photograph, something from their past.'

'So, you think we might have triggered something in Liam McCarthy?'

'He thought you were Jo. He said a "big man" came looking for her, who said he'd "get him". And her mam told him where Jo was, so it seems they did know. Maybe someone they thought was trying to help them find the killer was the killer.'

Dr Rupert Hunt stood to greet Terry when she entered. He looked like a man who spent a lot of time hunched at a laptop.

Terry was hard pressed to put an age to him – probably somewhere between forty and fifty. For all he was stooped, there was something lofty in his presence, the bearing of an academic so steeped in learning he was floating above the world of mere mortals. His eyes were piercing and very blue, his nose was sharp and straight, and when he smiled he revealed a set of perfect white teeth. She noted he had the long, dextrous fingers of a musician when he reached out to shake her hand. She was struck by his clothes, no corduroy trousers or tweed jacket, the uniform of the typical academic. He was wearing a mustard coloured jacket and had a colourful scarf draped around his neck. She sat down opposite him.

'Dr O'Brien,' he said, smiling warmly. 'I'm sorry to show up unannounced, but I was intrigued by your email.'

'Thank you for coming,' Terry said, motioning for him to sit. 'The case I'm asking you to give me some help with is quite a high-profile one. I know you've consulted with the gardaí in the past, so you don't need me to lecture you on confidentiality.'

'I fully understand and have no worries, I can be trusted with sensitive information.'

'Good. You've come across the murder of the podcaster Rachel Reece in the media?'

'Of course. Tragic. I was quite a fan of her work, I must admit. True-crime podcasts are my guilty secret. Please don't judge.' He smiled and leaned a little closer towards her, clasping his hands together and resting them on the table in front of him, displaying perfectly manicured nails. Suddenly aware of her own neglected ones, she placed her hands on her lap.

'On a return visit to the crime scene, I discovered a patch of mushrooms that hadn't been there during the previous visit, which was only a matter of days before. I checked various resources on Irish fungi but couldn't find a match for them.'

'I see. And you think this has relevance to the case?' She could see his interest. He unclasped his hands and laid them flat on the table.

'I don't know. They weren't there before. They don't seem to belong. I just … I want to know what they are and why they're there, I suppose.'

'Do you have a photograph?'

She got the shot she had taken up on her phone and passed it to him.

He sat back looking at the image. 'Hmmm. I think I know what these are. But I need to see the site.'

'Is it not possible to confirm it any other way?'

He handed back her phone. 'It's not that simple. Every plant and organism is part of the wider environment and impacts on the body in a particular way. That impact is recorded by the bones, which act like the body's hard drive. I've developed a theory, which my research has borne out many times, that the relationship between the site of burial and the story the bones tell is quite an important one.' He was lecturing to her, his hands sweeping through the air, punctuating his words. Grandstanding came to Terry's mind.

'Rachel wasn't buried, Dr Hunt. She was dumped.'

'I bet the landscape had started to claim her when you found the body, though.'

She had to admit he was right. 'I could find some time tomorrow to bring you out, I suppose,' she said.

He relaxed back into his chair and began buttoning his jacket. 'And I'll need access to the body. To get a clear view of the bones I'll need to remove tissue from several of the limbs.'

'How are you going to do that?'

'A solution of water and hydrochloric acid.' He seemed almost gleeful at the thought, a classic nerdish academic.

'Nice.'

'I don't know about that. But it is effective.'

'Okay. And I can take you through the site at Farmleigh tomorrow at ten.'

'I'll see you there.'

They both stood.

'Just to reassure you, I have no intention of nay-saying

anything you've done on the case so far,' Dr Hunt said as they shook hands once again. 'I hope I can add something to the tragic story of this young woman's death. You might be surprised what the bones can tell us if you know how to listen to what they say.'

'Well, you're the Bone Whisperer,' Terry said. 'Isn't that what they call you?' *That, or tosser*, she thought. She hadn't quite got the measure of him. As her dad would say, if he was chocolate he'd eat himself.

'It's not a moniker I relish,' Hunt said, smiling. 'Sounds rather grim. My students call me Rupert the Bear, presumably because I like scarves and am a bit large and lumbering. I think that suits me much better, don't you?'

'Sounds as if they like you,' Terry said.

'Nice to think so,' Hunt said and, with a nod, headed out the door.

30

Fraser was about to get into his car in the car park of Kevin Street Garda Station when he heard his name being called. Dusk was starting to fall and the traffic was still bumper to bumper on the road outside.

Looking around, he saw the portly figure of DCS Archie Sinnott strolling towards him.

'John, how are you?' he asked, leaning against the Audi's bonnet while he got his breath back. Fraser bristled internally – the model may have been over ten years old with around 200,000 kilometres on the clock, but his car was his castle.

'I'm good,' Fraser said. 'What brings you here?'

'I had a meeting with your sergeant,' said Sinnott. 'You're working late.'

'I'm wrapping things up,' said Fraser. 'There are a few loose ends to be sorted on one or two outstanding cases.'

'I heard Terry O'Brien came to see you yesterday morning.'

Fraser raised an eyebrow. 'And?'

'What did she want?'

'To clarify a point of information in the PM on Rachel Reece,' Fraser lied. 'Apparently the terminology they use in Glasgow is a bit different to how things are recorded here, and she was worried she'd set out some of the details in language me and the team wouldn't understand. We checked and she hadn't, so it was all good.'

'I see. Well, I want you to be wary of that woman. I've just learned she left Glasgow under a bit of a cloud. I don't think her stay here will be a long one. Professor Boyd is looking for any reason to give her the heave-ho.'

'She seems to be doing a pretty good job from what I've seen,' Fraser said, honestly this time. 'She knows her trade inside and out, if you pardon the pun, and her team all like and respect her.'

'She doesn't know her place, though,' Sinnott said, his tone exaggeratedly regretful. 'She overstepped her boundaries in a major way in Glasgow, from what I've been told. Tried to have a cold case reopened, and when the commissioner wouldn't do it, she set out to investigate it herself. And there were other issues too – she knew better than the police how to do their job.'

'This wouldn't happen to be her sister's case, by any chance?' Fraser asked.

'What does it matter? She's a pathologist, not a detective.'

'With respect, Boss, if a member of my family had been murdered and the case had never been solved, I might think about going rogue myself. Can we really fault her for it?'

Sinnott sniffed and gave Fraser a hard look. 'This isn't a

summer camp we're running here, John. There is a chain of command and a delineation of duty *for a reason*. We cannot have any Tom, Dick or Harriet thinking they can take the law into their own hands. That, as you should know, leads to anarchy.'

'I'm just saying that maybe she deserves some slack. Let what happened there stay where it is. Give her a chance to prove herself.'

Sinnott came in very close to Fraser, so close the detective could smell sweat and Brylcreem. 'I heard another rumour too,' he said, in a hissed whisper, 'about you and Dr O'Brien. That you and she might have had a bit of a fling a while back. Now, I'm not one to listen to gossip, but I will advise you, as a friend, to maintain a professional distance. You're on the up and up, John. I'd hate to see anything ruin that for you.'

Fraser stepped back and stared at Sinnott, who stared right back, unflinching.

'Well, good talk,' the detective chief superintendent said eventually. 'I'll let you get on with your evening.'

Fraser nodded and watched his boss swagger away. He remained standing beside his beloved vehicle for a couple of minutes, till the rage bubbling below his cool exterior began to subside.

31

Croke's of Nassau Street was a trendy, up-market bar that sold a lot of craft beers and artisan spirits. The list of gins the pub stocked was longer than many Chinese restaurant menus Terry had encountered.

The tables and chairs were all from different sets, giving the place a higgledy-piggledy look that was actually quite pleasing. Terry ordered a Bacardi and Coke and took a high stool at a table crafted from a wooden barrel with spaces for the punters' legs cut out of it.

Those punters consisted of men with long beards and top-knots and women in vintage dresses with visible tattoos.

Thin Lizzy was playing on the stereo: 'Don't Believe a Word'. Terry liked rock music and had always been a fan of Phil Lynott. If Croke's weren't such a hipster venue, she might come again.

She was taking the first sip of her drink when Fraser arrived, looking about until he spotted her. He waved, got a pint of some kind of cloudy ale and joined her.

'What the hell is that?' Terry asked. 'It looks as if they're cleaning the pipes and you're drinking the result.'

'It's called Liffeyside Ruby Ale,' Fraser said, 'and I am assured it has a light effervescence and rich, hoppy flavour.'

'I'll take your word for it,' Terry said, laughing.

'I like beer that's got a bit of character.' Fraser grinned. 'Yeah, I'll drink Heineken if that's what they're serving, but given the choice, I prefer something more interesting.'

'I admire your spirit of adventure,' Terry said. 'Cheers.'

They clinked glasses and drank.

'I just had an interesting chat with DCS Sinnott about you,' Fraser said, putting his glass down.

'Oh yeah?'

'Yup. Apparently you left Glasgow under a cloud of controversy and I should steer clear of you if I want to maintain my career trajectory.'

Terry shook her head in annoyance. 'Looks like Boyd has been talking,' she said.

'Just be careful,' Fraser warned. 'He was going on about you overstepping. Which is exactly what you're planning on doing here too.'

'You're not backing out on me, are you?'

'No. I'm just letting you know they're on your case for some reason. I don't know if it's Boyd's jealousy because the media loves you or because he's worried that you're a better pathologist and will show him up. He's been top dog for too long.'

'Well he wouldn't be the first man to be threatened by a young pup,' Terry said.

'Well, anyway,' Fraser said, 'I wasn't scared off, and here we are. Thanks for agreeing to come out, by the way.'

'Thanks for asking me again.'

'I've wanted to since I saw you at Farmleigh.'

Terry smiled. 'Oh, have you now?'

'I have. I mean, yeah, we both thought that night at the conference was going to be just a one-off, but I'll be honest: as soon as you were gone I wished I'd at least taken your number.'

'You just had to ask.'

'So?'

'I … I had a lot of fun. I suppose I was just enjoying the moment.'

'So is this you enjoying the moment again?'

Terry thought about it. 'Why don't we see what happens? I don't think we need to force things, do you?' she said.

He put his hands up and smiled. 'No, not at all.'

'Good. Now, tell me about Jo McCarthy.'

'There's not a huge amount to tell. More or less a month after her sister's murder, Jo's boyfriend called Pearse Street Garda Station, claiming she was missing. Her parents were contacted, but Mrs McCarthy claimed she'd just gone off on her own in an attempt to get over what happened to Eileen.'

'What did Mr McCarthy say?'

'The report I read doesn't have a statement from him.'

Terry glanced down at the table. 'I spoke to him earlier today. Now, before you go off on one,' she said quickly, 'I just thought it would be nice to visit an old man with no family.'

Fraser rubbed his hands over his face. 'Great. My little talk with Sinnott suggests he's not best pleased with you, your inclination to visit lonely old people in nursing homes notwithstanding. But hey, I'll plead the fifth.'

Terry took a sip of her drink. 'Was any follow-up ever done on Jo's disappearance?'

'Not formally, no. Because the parents were claiming she'd just gone on a holiday, there was only a quick look at her room. No forensics. She was never officially a missing person.'

'Yes, I suppose if there was no real reason ...'

'About a year later Sinnott sent a detective to do a supplementary interview with Mr and Mrs McCarthy to see if they'd remembered anything new about Eileen in the days before the murder. Apparently they reported that Jo was still away, and might not be coming back.'

'Did they say where she'd gone?'

'The detective asked. Sinnott wanted her checked out as well, so he needed some sort of contact information.'

'And what did they say?'

'That she was travelling in Europe and wouldn't be back any time soon.'

'They didn't have a number for her?' Terry asked, her eyebrow raised.

He shrugged. 'No. None.'

'Or an email or even a postal address?'

'They didn't have a postal address. A couple of emails were sent to the address they provided, but no response was ever received.'

Terry sat back in her chair and looked at the ceiling. 'So, these people have had one daughter brutally murdered, and their other kid pisses off around Europe without so much as a postcard or a forwarding address. And no one thought that strange? Is that normal for Ireland, people falling off the grid? And nothing?'

'Not even a social media post about it,' Fraser said. 'I checked today. Jo had a MySpace page which she updated regularly. It stands to reason she'd have moved with the times. But this woman has no online presence whatsoever.'

'She never surfaced at all then? Vanished into thin air?'

'It seems so. And no one made a fuss about it. Which is very, very strange indeed.'

Terry shook her head, flabbergasted.

'So what do you think happened? Is it possible the murder scared her so much she left Dublin and her life here to set up somewhere else?'

'I mean, it's *possible*,' Fraser said. 'But how many people actually do that? Just up and go? Never contact their family or friends again?'

'Not many. People usually stick to their routines and the safety of the familiar. But if she didn't disappear on purpose, what *did* happen? And why did the McCarthys tell this fairy story?'

Fraser was quiet for a moment. 'Maybe it's what they wanted to believe. The thought of losing two daughters was just too much for them?'

'That's a hell of a lot of denial to live with for so long,' Terry said.

'And a hell of a lot of pain,' Fraser added.

32

DCS Sinnott drove past Frank Cleaver's house. The curtains of the mid-terrace home were drawn, but he could see a flickering light indicating that the television was on. Cleaver was back in Finglas.

It was unlikely Cleaver had the balls to do a runner, but Sinnott was determined to keep an eye on him nonetheless. If he so much as spat in the street he'd be hauled in. It was no surprise he'd been in and out of prison for years – he didn't seem to have the wit to cover his tracks.

Sinnott had followed him on Friday night, too, after he'd been released from questioning in Pearse Street Station. He'd witnessed a group of girls harassing him at a bus stop and was disappointed that Cleaver didn't react but instead walked off. If he had even looked like he was making a move towards any of the girls, Sinnott would have had the excuse to haul him in again.

The chief superintendent had checked out the house Cleaver had gone to that night. It had belonged to an old woman who had lived on Cleaver's estate at one point. They must have stayed in touch. She had died a while back and the house had been lying empty since.

Sinnott sat in the car outside the Finglas house for about ten minutes, not really caring if Cleaver saw him, and then headed, satisfied that the suspect was home for the rest of the night.

He planned to return early the following morning to see what the pervert's daytime movements might reveal.

I warned you that if you ever got out, I'd be on you both night and day until you slipped up, didn't I, Frankie boy?

Every detective had their 'one that got away'. That case they lay awake at night mulling over, trying to identify the one thing they'd missed that had caused the case to flounder.

Frank Cleaver was Sinnott's such case.

He'd worked round the clock to close the Eileen McCarthy murder, skipping meals, catching an hour of sleep here and a light doze there for months. When his own DS told him to close the book on it, he came close to torpedoing his own career by grabbing the washed-up old fucker by his lapels and shaking him.

How could he walk away while that poor girl's death was still unsolved?

Sinnott had joined the gardaí because he believed society should have rules and regulations, that the bad guys should be held accountable for the crimes they committed. Yes, Frank Cleaver had been caught many times for other, smaller offences and had done time behind bars.

But the life he had snuffed out – Sinnott was convinced of it – was filed as 'unsolved'. This criminal was once more walking the streets, a free man, while Eileen McCarthy would never again step out in the sunshine or enjoy a drink with her friends.

Sinnott had promised the girl's parents he would catch the bastard who'd done it, the man who'd carved up their daughter and crushed her windpipe. He'd vowed the monster would end his days behind bars.

And he had not followed through on that promise.

He had let them down.

Now Mrs McCarthy was dead and her husband had lost his reason.

But that did not mean Sinnott was released from his oath. *All a man has is his word*, his father had told him. It was a truth he held dear. When Cleaver slipped up, he, Detective Chief Superintendent Archie Sinnott, would be there to see it and to bring him in.

And this time, he'd get the fucker to talk.

33

At midnight Terry and Fraser stepped out of Croke's and onto Nassau Street.

'So …' Fraser said, shoving his hands deep into his pockets.

'So, indeed,' Terry said, trying not to laugh at the look of anxious expectancy on Fraser's face. 'I'm going to walk to the taxi rank and make for home.'

'On your own?' Fraser asked, still looking hopeful.

'On my own, yes.'

Fraser looked a bit crestfallen.

'I had a great time with you, John. But—'

'Ah, the inevitable "but",' Fraser said.

'No inevitable "but". Just,' she smiled up at him, 'let's take it slowly, get to know each other. I know almost nothing about you other than you're a good detective and a beer nerd.'

'What do you want to know? Ask me anything!'

Terry laughed. 'I will. But you'll need to ask me out again first.'

Fraser was about to do just that when his phone rang.

'Sorry to disturb you, sir. Sergeant Willis here from Command and Control. I believe you're the DCI on call this evening.'

Terry was standing close enough that she could hear what was said at the other end – the desk sergeant was one of those people who shouted down the phone.

'No, I'm not,' Fraser said, puzzled. 'Murphy was supposed to be on call tonight.'

'She was, sir, but she got called away. An emergency at home, I believe. You're next on the roster we have here.'

Fraser thought for a moment. He was pretty sure he wasn't due to be on the duty detective list for another month, but this was a typical Sinnott move. He'd pissed his boss off and this was the reward he was reaping.

He shook his head to try and rally himself; he had drunk three pints of pretty strong ale. He certainly wasn't fit to drive. But there was nothing for it. He'd have to grit his teeth and tough it out.

'What have you got?' he asked Willis.

'A body in the Phoenix Park. A young woman.'

Fraser's eyes widened, and he saw Terry's do the same. 'Near Farmleigh?'

'Not far – down towards Kilmainham way. The local uniforms think it's just a junk—eh, a drug death.'

'What makes the local guys think that?'

'One of them says he recognises her jacket – says she was well-known to him. Dr Maher was called in to declare her dead. He doesn't think it's suspicious. He said he didn't see any marks of violence on her, but our lads say she's past her sell-by date. So it might not be easy to tell at first sight. Could be a case for the pathology people.'

Fraser knew why the sergeant was a bit hesitant about taking the doctor's word. Maher was not the most meticulous garda doctor, but he was always available. He didn't like getting too close to the bodies, particularly if they were pungent. As a result, he had missed a few injuries in the past. It didn't usually matter, as the pathologist would pick them up at postmortem, but under the circumstances it was best not to take any chances.

'Let's not press the panic button yet. Contact DI Ahern from my SOCO team, tell him I'm SIO and he's scene of crime manager. Get him out to the scene, I trust him to make the call, and if he's happy, transfer the body to the city mortuary. Oh!' He winked at Terry. 'And maybe give Dr O'Brien the heads-up that there's a body coming in for postmortem tomorrow.'

'I'll do that, sir.'

'Goodnight, Willis.'

'Have a good rest of your night, sir.'

The call ended and Fraser looked at Terry. 'What do you make of that?'

'I won't know until I get her on the table,' she said. 'Could be drug-related. But it seems a bit of a coincidence, doesn't it?'

'And it could just be that,' Fraser said. 'Come on. I'll walk you to the taxi rank.'

As they strolled towards the bustling thoroughfare of Dame Street, Terry couldn't help but think of the DM she'd received.

... I love my work and want to start again. You will soon hear of me with my funny little games.

Well, I'm not laughing, she thought. *If this is you, Saucy Jacky, there's nothing funny about your games at all.*

34

It was after closing time when she left the bar with the police detective. He hadn't expected that. He hadn't noticed Fraser going in, but then, he was only interested in the women.

He didn't like how it made him feel, seeing her with another man. Not when he had decided she was his to take. It made him want to strike out, but he had learned patience.

One time, his urgency to act had almost resulted him in being caught and caged. That was in the early days. He had worked hard since then, honing his craft. Perfecting each strike. Amateur errors were no longer a threat to his success.

From the dark interior of his car, he watched the detective talking on his phone as the pathologist stood off to one side, waiting for him to be done.

He would never treat her like that.

He knew all about Fraser, about them all. But they knew nothing about him.

Fraser might act the big shot, he probably had his eyes on the commissioner's job, but he was forty-two, divorced and childless. That summed him up – impotent, ineffectual. He was simply a nice guy and not good enough for the pathologist.

35

There were plenty of cars and a lot of people in the mortuary car park when Terry arrived the next morning at 8 a.m. Some of the crowd stood in small groups chatting and smoking, relatives, she assumed, of the young woman found in the park.

She received some curious looks and spotted a few of the assembled onlookers muttering to one another when she passed by, but she kept her gaze averted and made for the front door. She still hadn't got used to the idea that in Ireland people actually knew who the state pathologist was.

She rang the bell at the mortuary door, keeping her back to the throng. As she waited for Tomas to answer, she made the mistake of looking over her shoulder, and a woman from the nearest group peeled off and advanced towards her.

'You're that woman, aren't you? The one who does be on the news? My sister Tina's in there and those fuckers aren't letting us in. She was found in the Phoenix Park last night.'

Tomas half opened the door and Terry offered an apologetic smile to the woman as she squeezed through the small gap. As the door closed behind her she heard her shout, 'Are ya gonna tell us what's goin' on?'

DI Alan Ahern was sitting in Jimmy's office nursing a cup of coffee and looking rumpled and unshaven. He was staring into his drink and didn't notice her arrival.

'Morning, Alan. See you got the short straw. Come in to the pathologist's office when you're ready.'

He gave a vague smile and returned to focusing on his cup. Terry walked along the corridor to the room the pathologists used as their mortuary office. It was sparsely furnished but functional and provided some privacy when they had to talk to family or the gardaí. She sat down at the desk. Tomas appeared and placed a mug of coffee and a copy of the coroner's request for an autopsy in front of her. There was little information about the circumstances of the woman's death: Tina McCabe was her name. Terry swivelled the chair round to face Ahern, who was still clutching his cup as he lounged against the door jam.

'Tina McCabe?'

'Ran a quick fingerprint last night. Ran it through the database. Hence that mob out there.' He was referring to the family in the car park.

'The coroner seems pretty sure this is a common-or-garden drug death. Did you find anything relevant at the scene? Any drug paraphernalia?'

'The doc had already been by the time I got there,' Ahern said. 'The body was in a little den, a clearing in the middle of some bushes. There was a lot of stuff in there – looked like she'd been camping out. The body was wrapped in a sleeping bag. The junkie who found her thought she was just sleeping. Does heroin affect your sense of smell?'

'That would make an interesting research project,' Terry said. 'But the simple answer is I don't know. Did it look like she'd taken something?'

Ahern shrugged. 'It's the most likely cause of her death. Dr Maher wasn't too concerned.'

'From what I've heard he rarely is.'

'He did say he couldn't rule out whether she had been strangled or that there might have been a wound somewhere that he couldn't see.'

Strangled, Terry thought. *The coincidences continue.*

'In other words,' she said, 'he's covering himself, just in case? He probably has a six-foot-long stethoscope so he doesn't have to get too close to his live patients. I'll be able to make up my own mind anyway once I get started.' She stood and stretched. 'That bunch of people outside, they're family, I'm guessing?'

'The local gardaí informed them,' Ahern said. 'The first uniform on the scene said he recognised her jacket and knew where her family lived. I got them to wait until I ran the print. The whole lot of them have a loyalty card for the garda station, frequent flyers one and all. They were told to wait and that someone would get in touch later today.' Ahern shook his head. 'But there was no stopping them once they heard she was here.'

'Okay. Well, keep them at bay for now. I haven't seen her yet, but from what I've heard she'd been dead for a few days before she was found, so the smell will be pretty noxious. Can you fend them off?' she asked.

Ahern got to his feet. 'I'll give them the party line: "We cannot afford to contaminate evidence at this sensitive stage of our enquiries." I'll use my charm.'

'Well, you've got plenty of that to go around.' Terry fixed him with a deadpan look and he smiled and headed off down the corridor.

In the mortuary, she gingerly opened the body bag, keeping her distance to allow the pungent gases to escape. She was struck by the appearance of the young woman within. Despite the discoloration of her skin due to early decomposition, Terry could see that she looked similar in age to Rachel Reece. However, this woman's relationship with drugs had taken its toll: her hair was greasy and tangled, her clothing worn and stained.

Terry's eyes were drawn to a red spot in the groin area of her tracksuit bottoms. Once the clothing was removed, it was obvious that the layers she had been wearing had disguised the extreme ravages of her lifestyle. Terry could follow the woman's journey with heroin as she descended further into its grip: the scars on her arms and legs, then the sinus in her right groin, where she had injected shortly before she died. In fact, that was likely the last thing she had done.

Laura appeared at her shoulder then took a step back when she saw the state of the young woman lying on the mortuary table. 'God, she's just skin and bones!'

'I know, right? An advertisement for not taking drugs,' Terry said, trying to lighten the mood. She remembered how shocked she had been at the first bodies she'd seen, and this was all new to Laura, who was doing her best to look stoical.

'Have you found anything yet?'

'Nothing shouting out at me. But ... I don't know.' She looked up. Ahern was in the observation room scrolling through his phone. She rapped on the glass separating them as she flicked on the microphone. 'Alan, have you any photos from the scene?'

'The local scene-of-crime officer was out. I'll give her a bell. Anything in particular you're looking for?'

'I want to see where and in what position she was found. And what happened to the sleeping bag?'

'She took all the stuff that was lying about, as far as I know. She was supposed to take it up to FSI this morning. I'll check.'

Terry turned to Laura. 'I'm maybe being a little too cautious.' She walked around to stand at the right side of the body. The intern took up position on the other side.

Terry pointed out the tell-tale signs of a life of intravenous drug abuse. 'There's no doubt about her lifestyle choices. But there's a couple of things I'm not so happy about. Look at the colour of her face.'

'It's a bit dark and blotchy looking.'

'Congestion and cyanosis are the technical terms.' Terry smiled at Laura. 'But from the tip of her nose to her chin the skin is slightly paler. And look at these haemorrhages on her sclera.' Terry stretched the eyelids, exposing the white of the eyes. 'These are called petechiae, classically seen in deaths due to strangulation. Not a diagnosis, mind you, but nevertheless ...'

'You think she's been strangled?'

'No. I'm not saying that. I'm keeping an open mind as to what happened to her. Even drug addicts get murdered. So far the findings are pretty non-specific. This could all be due to respiratory arrest due to drugs – literally, she would turn purple as she ran out of oxygen. And if she collapsed face down all the blood would rush to her face. And where her face was pressed in to the ground it would be pale. Just like that.' She pointed at the area around Tina's nose. 'Although she could have been smothered. But let's not jump the gun.'

'Is that why you need the photographs?'

'Sure is. Let's have a coffee while we wait for the SOCO.'

Garda Clodagh Rafferty was a tiny bundle of energy. She spoke nineteen to the dozen, but the gist was that the local gardaí had unzipped the sleeping bag before she arrived. She took photos of the young woman before the doctor came and helped him turn the body face up. Her photographs were as sharp as she was.

'There's the needle and syringe beside her right thigh.' She pointed at one of the photographs. 'I bagged everything and dropped the bags in to the lab. Looked like a typical drug den. There were a few empty vodka bottles, cheap and nasty stuff.'

'Do you mind staying and taking some pictures of the PM?'

'No problem,' she said, and Terry commenced.

As Terry dissected the neck, her thoughts drifted to Rachel, how different her life had been to this poor woman's. But at least this lost soul had family out there, even if they hadn't been able to help her out of her cycle of self-annihilation. She wondered if Rachel had any brothers or sisters, a pretty younger sibling who looked just like her – she hadn't come across any on Rachel's social media, and she hadn't thought to ask Kyle.

'How did you do that dissection so neatly?' Laura piped up, breaking through her reverie.

'Well, I have done it a few times before ...' She smiled at Laura, who looked more relaxed now. 'Watch and learn!'

There were blotchy haemorrhages in the soft tissues of the neck, but her Adam's apple wasn't broken. Terry looked up at the viewing gallery, where Ahern was sitting alone. She waved to get his attention and leaned over to speak into the microphone.

'Looks like it's drug-related all right. She's recently injected in her groin. I'm still a wee bit concerned about the haemorrhages on her face and neck, but I've covered all bases just in case some information turns up later. Cause of death is down to toxicology now. I've done a dipstick test on the urine and it's positive for opioids and benzodiazepines. Just need alcohol on board and you have the holy trinity of the drug addict's life.'

She turned to Laura. 'Can you label the blood bottles, please? Use the name on the coroner's request form.'

She turned back to Ahern. 'If you decide to use the family for a formal ID, you need to warn them she's not looking her best. Tomas will do what he can in the meantime.' She sighed and looked at the shell on the table before her that had once been a human life. There was something nagging at her but she needed more than gut feeling to declare this another murder. As her old boss used to say, If it walks like a duck, but she always wondered about drug addicts' deaths. They knew to the last grain how much junk they could cope with. So what went wrong this time? It did no harm to keep an open mind. There was more to learn about the circumstances of Tina McCabe's death.

36

Terry was just back at her desk when her mobile rang – she was pleased to see it was Fraser.

'Good morning, Terry. Any update on the body from the Phoenix Park?'

'It looks like a drug death, right enough, but two deaths in the park does seem like a big coincidence. Anyway, it's in the hands of the state lab now. You'll get the tox results through in a couple of weeks.'

'Well, unless something turns up that suggests it's not what it seems, it's one less case for me to worry about, I guess.' Terry heard him exhale and his voice softened. 'Last night was very pleasant.'

'Pleasant? Okay, Mr Darcy'

Fraser laughed. 'Okay. Enjoyable, fun.'

'I'm kidding. I wouldn't say no to a rerun.' Terry was surprised at how much she meant this.

'Me neither. Let's organise that as soon as we can.'

'Let's.'

'Okay, so I've been busy making a few calls on your behalf. I got on to my contact in Northern Ireland, Angela Kirkpatrick – she's a DCI I worked with some time back. The body of a man murdered up there was dumped over the border and I was the DI on call. It was tricky working both sides of the border but, in fairness, some aspects of the investigation required a little southern charm.'

'I didn't know that was a thing.'

'That's because you Scots are so dour you wouldn't know charm if it bit you on the backside.'

'Touché, DI Fraser.'

'Anyway,' he went on, sounding pleased with himself, 'I asked her to make a few inquiries, try to find out if Reece had been sniffing about, trying to get some info from the PSNI. Or if she had come to her attention by asking around about women missing or murdered over the last twenty years.'

'Any luck?'

'Not really. But Angela knew who Reece was. Big fan of the podcast, apparently, which I was surprised to hear. But she said stuff like that is turning out to be helpful in some instances, particularly for historical cases. It seems, especially in the North, people can be reluctant to speak to the police but are more than happy to spill their guts to some kid with a microphone. That said, Angela was sure if Reece had been asking around she would have known about it.'

Terry thought about that. 'I guess it would depend on how blatant Rachel was about it. She may have been going after the less obvious sources, under the radar.'

'Maybe. Angela said if Reece had been looking for a case or two for her series, she has a long list she would have been happy to share.'

'So, we're not any clearer as to what Rachel was up to?'

'There's that *we* again – I'm off the case, remember? Speaking of *we* ... how about dinner this weekend? A proper date?'

'I could do with a decent meal,' Terry said. 'I'll let you choose the venue.'

'I'll see if I can find somewhere that serves haggis and deep-fried Mars bars.'

'Washed down with vintage Irn-Bru. Sounds perfect. Call me when you have somewhere booked.'

They signed off and Terry cracked open a can of Coke, thinking about what she'd just learned. She wasn't convinced that Angela would have known if Rachel had been poking around. Rachel was smart, and if she didn't want to bring herself to anyone's attention, Terry suspected she would have known how to keep her investigations on the downlow.

She still wasn't sure about Kyle Brady but if he was right and Rachel had found something that took her to Northern Ireland, was it that something that got her killed?

37

By the time Terry got to Farmleigh later that morning, with Michael who'd agreed to join her, Dr Rupert Hunt was already there, leaning against the bonnet of a silver sports car.

A flamboyant dresser, he was wearing a red suede jacket with a silk paisley scarf slung about his neck, hardly suitable for the job at hand, Terry thought, though at least his sturdy black hiking boots were up for it.

'Dr Hunt, this is my colleague, forensic scientist Dr Michael Flynn. He's working the case with me. He was there when I found the mushrooms.'

'Very pleased to meet you,' Dr Hunt said, shaking Michael's hand vigorously. 'Two heads are often better than one. And please, call me Rupert.'

'That's a snazzy set of wheels, Rupert,' Michael said, looking at the car in admiration.

'It's a 1994 Marcos Mantara Spyder, a British-made

vehicle, and quite rare. It took me quite a bit of searching to find a model in good condition. It's all completely original, right down to the radio.'

'Very cool,' Michael said.

'Yes, wonderful,' said Terry in a clipped tone. 'Shall we get to the scene?'

'Lead on, MacDuff,' said Rupert.

'Hey! That's my line,' said Michael, beaming at the older man, who patted him on the shoulder.

'Both hilarious and original, gents,' said Terry dryly.

'Can I ask you something, Terry?' Rupert said as they made their way towards the site.

'You can,' said Terry.

'Are you the same Dr O'Brien who published a paper in the *International Journal of Forensic Pathology* earlier this year on bone-markings in wilderness environments?'

'Yes, that was me,' Terry said.

'It was a fascinating read. I was riveted. I published one on a similar theme myself. Based on remains discovered in the Wicklow Mountains, some contemporaneous, others megalithic. You might be interested in it.'

'I'd love to read it,' said Terry, chuffed that he knew her work. They were going to get on well.

When they arrived at the ditch, she pointed to the spot where Rachel's remains had been discovered. 'You can see where we removed some of the soil. She was right there.'

'Yes, I can identify that quite plainly. There's nothing to prevent me getting in there for a closer look?'

'Knock yourself out.'

The forensic archaeologist removed his jacket and scarf,

carefully folding and placing them in the leather satchel he was carrying, and slid stiffly into the trench. With much sloshing and straining through the mud, he made his way over to the spot where Rachel Reece's remains had been discovered. For a couple of minutes, he observed the scene with eerie calm, moving gently around the boggy earth while Terry and Michael waited above the ditch. He then took some images and spent a little while on his phone.

'Anything interesting?' Terry finally asked.

'You could say that,' he said. 'You'll have to come down.'

Rupert waited for them both to reach him, holding some bracken and meadow grass aside so they could see what he was focusing on.

'What are we looking at?' Terry asked.

'The earth in this particular area is remarkably nutrient rich,' he said, taking up a lump of chocolatey brown, moist soil from the side of the bank and rubbing it between his fingers. 'It's why the plant growth is so lush. We're standing in a naturally occurring grow-bag. Because the trees lean in towards one another, creating a kind of amphitheatre, every time they drop a leaf or a piece of bark falls off or a bird leaves a dropping, it's falling into this bowl in the earth and enriching it. What's most interesting, though, are the mushrooms you asked me here to look at.' He pointed to them.

'What makes them so interesting?' Terry asked.

'You were right, Dr O'Brien,' he said, gazing at the crop of fungus through his glass. 'These are quite special.'

'Why?' Michael asked. 'You see fungi everywhere at this time of year, particularly in damp, cool places like this.'

'They're of interest,' he said, 'for precisely the reason Terry suggested: because they do not belong here. As I suspected, they're called *Hebeloma aminophilum*, also known as "the ghoul mushroom".'

'Charming,' Terry said.

'The ghoul mushroom is part of a family of fungi called saprotrophic mushrooms, and they are fascinating organisms indeed.'

'You'll have to be more specific,' Michael said. 'They just sound creepy to me.'

'Saprotrophic mushrooms feed on rotting matter. One group specialises in rotten wood, for example. But there is a genus, which the ghoul mushroom belongs to, that feeds on decaying flesh. I would guess that, as Ms Reece's body decomposed, particles were absorbed by the soil here, and our friends feasted on it. This is a young but healthy crop.'

'Which means they *do* belong here,' Terry said.

'Not quite. *Hebeloma aminophilum* does not grow wild in Ireland. It is native to Australia. You said that Ms Reece had been dead for a matter of days. Her body would have been like an incubator for ghoul mushrooms, and what we're seeing here is ... overflow, for want of a better word.'

'I still don't get it,' Michael said.

'You mean they're not there by natural means?' Terry said.

'They can't be. How they came to be here is anyone's guess.'

'We need to get back to the lab,' Terry said, and hauled herself out of the ditch.

38

The three stood in Michael's work area in the Forensic Science Ireland building with Rachel Reece's test results laid out on the table about them, as well as bags containing her clothes and the contents of her pockets. Rupert set up his laptop on the bench beside the stereomicroscope, downloading the relevant information on mushrooms, as Terry and Michael set about the job of inspecting Rachel's belongings.

'I want to know if those mushrooms were planted there on purpose while Rachel lay there or after her body had been removed,' Terry said.

Michael sounded convinced. 'Seriously?' he asked. 'Isn't it more likely the spores managed to get out of some wacky mycologist's eco tunnel and found their way to that ditch?'

'Just humour me,' Terry said. 'If I'm wrong, I'm wrong, and we'll go back to the drawing board.'

'Where should I start?' Michael asked.

'The two areas on Ms Reece where spores might attach themselves are on her hair and clothes,' Rupert said.

'Okay,' Michael said. 'I have some hair samples here. Let's get them under the microscope and take a look.'

He placed a few strands on a slide and slid it under the clips on the device's viewing stage, then peered through the viewfinder.

'All I can see is the hair shaft. Her cuticle is in a shocking state and she's a natural blonde. But nothing else,' he said after a few seconds. 'But don't take my word for it.'

He stood up and Terry took his place.

Of course he was right – the hair shafts were clean as a whistle.

Next, Michael carefully removed Rachel's clothes, one item at a time, from the evidence bags where they had been stored.

'I'll try her T-shirt first,' he said, 'seeing as it would have been exposed.'

He picked up a small square of clear adhesive tape and methodically pressed it over the surface of the garment, then repeated the process he had just performed with the hair.

'All I can see are fibres and a few hairs, which match her head hair,' Michael reported.

Terry once again confirmed the absence of spores.

'Maybe a sample from the bottom half of the body,' she said. 'Can we try again? Maybe her skirt?'

Michael sighed but did as she asked.

'Okay,' he said, after gazing at his second sample for several long moments. 'This time, there's something present.'

Terry had a look and saw tiny brownish specks dotted about that looked like over-ripe lemons. She reached down and twisted the objective lenses, upping the magnification. What she was looking at was like a coral reef with shot-out appendages that looked a bit like misshapen arms. Some of the spores seemed to be just husks, outlines without anything inside.

'Rupert, can you take a look and tell me what we've got?'

'Of course.' He lowered his eye to the viewfinder and gazed for what seemed like forever.

'Well?' Terry asked nervously.

Rupert straightened up and nodded. 'Those,' he said, 'are the spores of *Hebeloma aminophilum*.' He turned the screen of his laptop towards them. 'This is what you are looking at.' It was a paper on the lifecycle of the ghoul mushroom, and one of the photographs of the spores was identical to what they were seeing down the microscope.

'I think we need to talk to Sinnott,' Terry said. 'Someone has deliberately planted freaky mushrooms on a body. That's not normal. I've seen folk leave flowers at a murder scene but never mushrooms. This just might be a quirk of the killer. And he might have done it before. We are straying into serial killer territory here.'

39

Michael and Terry were at Harcourt Street along with Dr Hunt to meet Detective Chief Superintendent Archie Sinnott, who looked harried when they arrived into his cramped office on the third floor.

'I can't give you long,' he said, doing his best to make an apologetic face – for Rupert's benefit, Terry assumed. 'But I'll help out where I can.'

Rupert wasted no time. 'Drs O'Brien and Flynn kindly brought me out to look at the crime scene yesterday. It yielded some interesting and, I believe, useful results.'

Terry went on to fill Sinnott in on the presence of the ghoul mushrooms at the scene, and Michael continued, explaining how samples from Rachel Reece's clothing showed spores also.

'I don't understand how this is useful,' Sinnott said. 'Couldn't the spores that the mushrooms came from have arrived on the wind, blown from somewhere close by, and landed on Ms Reece's clothes?'

'If that were the case there would have been a distribution of the spores – a thin layer of them, on the part exposed to the prevailing wind,' Rupert said. 'What we found was that their presence was very localised.'

'Which means?' Sinnott asked.

'Which means they were deliberately put there,' Terry said. 'And the spores developed into the mushroom crop we found weeks later. I think—'

Sinnott cut her off. 'You're sure these spores are from your ghoul mushroom and not one of our local ones that could have been picked up anywhere?'

'They're distinctive in appearance,' Rupert said. 'There can be no doubt.'

Sinnott sighed. 'So where does that leave us?'

'You're looking for someone with a knowledge of rare mushrooms and how to propagate them,' Rupert said. 'That should narrow the search a bit.'

Terry butted in. 'As I was about to say, I think this is a signature, a calling card if you like. Something deliberately left by the killer. It doesn't mean anything to us at the moment, but it has some significance to them. I would also say it rules out Frank Cleaver,' she added.

'Why do you say that?' Sinnott asked. 'He may have researched that kind of stuff while he was in prison.'

'And I have no doubt you'll check that out,' Terry said, 'but Cleaver is a sex offender. I'm not denying he is a dangerous man, but this is all too … contrived for someone like him. We're looking for a completely different kind of criminal.'

'This individual is toying with you,' Rupert said. 'There is a kind of artistic swagger to what they're doing.'

'Thank you for your *professional* analysis, Dr Hunt,' Sinnott said, his tone suggesting he thought the notion a bit ludicrous. 'We'll add this evidence to the rest and see where it leads us. But as of right now, Cleaver is still our main suspect. Is there anything else? I have places to be.'

'What if the killer kills again?' Terry said.

'He won't,' Sinnott said. 'Because I'm going to bring Cleaver in again for questioning.'

And with that the meeting was over.

40

Things were lining up beautifully, but he had to be patient, to follow the rules he had set himself right back at the beginning.

He made a commitment after his first time. He would only target one group. Sisters.

His own had it coming. Sadistic to the core. When he came for them, he had expected them to say sorry, beg his forgiveness, to even plead on one another's behalf, but to his surprise and amusement, they turned on each other.

He would have done his mother as well but the old slag was riddled with cancer. A long slow death was good enough for her. If only she had been there to witness the death of her precious girls. He liked the symmetry of his sisters' deaths. From then on, each new death would be a pair, one a mirror image of the other.

The pathologist had a sister. After she was murdered the

pathologist changed her name from Anne Therese to Terry. He understood the need to shake of the past. But he knew it was impossible. Her sister's murder was probably the beginning of the pathologist's relationship with death. Did she realise that the callous murder of her sister had sealed her fate? That it would lead her to him?

The sisters should be united in death and he would see to it. What one man had started, he would complete. It was her destiny.

He hoped she would appreciate the thought he put in to each death. That was what he lusted for.

When they were finally together, he wanted her to feel safe in the knowledge that she was not just going to die, but that her death was going to be something special.

He watched her as she got out of the car and walked towards the mortuary building. She stopped and looked at her phone. Something was troubling her. He could put an end to that.

41

Rupert dropped Terry back to the mortuary in his Spyder while Michael took the opportunity to have a wander down Grafton Street.

'I fear the pressure may be getting to your DCS Sinnott,' the forensic archaeologist said as Terry was about to get out.

'There's something up with him, that's for sure,' Terry agreed.

'Is it possible he's taking this case personally?' Hunt asked.

'I think that's a given,' Terry said. 'He's obsessed with pinning Rachel Reece's death on Frank Cleaver, as if doing that will in some way make up for the fact he couldn't get Cleaver for Eileen McCarthy's death. It's become a crusade.'

'And, alas, history informs us that the crusaders were misguided and did far more harm than good,' Rupert mused.

'I don't think anyone has told Archie Sinnott about that. But then ...' She sighed and rubbed her eyes. 'I don't know ... a lot of the detectives seem to believe it could be

Cleaver, and sometimes I even get to thinking *myself* that it could be.'

'What does the evidence say?'

'That's the problem,' Terry said. 'It's as confusing as all hell!'

'Then perhaps it would serve you to keep an open mind until you have reason to close off all other avenues and focus on just one.'

'You're right,' Terry said. 'I know you're right.'

'I'll drop by tomorrow to harvest some bones from the Reece remains,' Rupert said.

'You still want to do that? Well, you played a blinder on this so far, I'll give you that,' Terry said.

'And I shall take it,' Rupert said, his face lighting up in a smile.

He was actually kind of attractive when he smiled, she thought, climbing out from the low sports car. When she checked her phone as she climbed the steps to the front entrance, her stomach dropped. There was a DM alert on the screen. Her heart raced as she opened it.

I am Saucy Jacky and my latest victim has already been stalked and killed and you guys didn't even realise it was me.

Terry felt a sudden coldness all over. It was time to tell Fraser what was going on.

Laura was in her office.

'I got another message,' Terry said, opening Instagram and showing the intern.

She read the words closely, and then turned to her laptop, typing rapidly.

'I thought so,' she said. 'It's not quite right, but it's definitely another serial killer quote.'

'Not Jack the Ripper this time?' Terry asked.

'No. We've come a bit more up to date,' Laura said. 'Joseph James DeAngelo, known by many monikers, but probably most famously as the Night Stalker.' She read from the screen. 'Between 1974 and 1986 he murdered thirteen people, raped at least fifty – there's some conjecture as to whether it was him or not in a few cases – and burgled at least a hundred and twenty properties across the state of California.'

'Liked to try his hand at everything,' Terry said.

'Oh, definitely. In March 1977 he rang the Sacramento sheriff's department and said: *I am the East Side rapist and I have my next victim already stalked and you guys can't catch me.*'

'It's pretty close all right,' Terry agreed. 'Mine says: *I am Saucy Jacky and my latest victim has already been stalked and killed and you guys didn't even realise it was me.* Past tense.'

'DeAngelo wanted the police to know he was going to rape again,' Laura said. 'Jacky wants you to know he *has* killed again, but that you – and the gardaí – didn't peg the death as his handiwork.'

'Which death, though?' Terry asked, puzzled. 'It couldn't be the American tourist, unless Saucy Jacky is a pirate. There's been nothing else out of the ordinary. Except for Tina McCabe, the drug death. Though I wasn't one hundred per cent convinced of that.'

Laura nodded slowly. 'Even drug addicts can be murdered, wasn't that what you said?'

'But why kill a drug user? It doesn't fit with Rachel's death. It makes absolutely no sense.'

'You did say that you were keeping an open mind ...'

'Well, something did turn up this morning.' Terry told her about the mushroom-spore findings.

'So,' Laura said, 'if this guy fancies himself as famous – or is it infamous? Doesn't matter, whichever it is, could spores be his calling card? How cool would that be?'

'Jesus, there's nothing cool about it, Laura. I mean, this guy could just be a regular nutter, a hearse chaser – a fantasist. I've come across his type before. But what if ... what was it Rupert said? If he's the killer and he's toying with us? With me.'

Michael was annoyed.

'Terry, the gardaí are pretty sure that death was down to drugs. It's not a priority. I've already got a backlog of stuff because of all the shenanigans with the Rachel Reece stuff.'

'If you could bump it up the list, I'd be really grateful. Genuinely. Something has cropped up that makes me think it might be linked with Rachel Reece's death.'

Silence at the other end of the phone. Then: 'It's a good thing I love you.'

'So you'll prioritise it?'

'Yes. For you.'

'Thank you!'

'You're welcome. I have to finish up something first, but then I'll start looking at the Tina McCabe clothing you sent over.'

'Brilliant. Call me if you find anything.'

'More mushrooms?'

'It's a hunch.'

Terry hung up. As she did, she noticed Laura was looking a bit worried. 'What's up?'

'Okay,' Laura said. 'So far, Jacky is communicating with you using edited quotes from serial killers. You said that Dr Hunt believes he's making a statement by using the mushrooms. Well, maybe the same is true of the serial killers he chooses to reference.'

'Go on,' Terry said. 'I'm listening.'

'It says here the Saucy Jacky postcard, which is where your guy got the name he's using, referred to two of the Ripper murders, but was posted to the Central News Agency before the deaths had been publicised in the press. It's one of the reasons a lot of people believe it's genuine. And here we have your Jacky seeming to hint at another death, a murder in fact, that has managed to slip under the radar. The gardaí haven't sussed it, you haven't sussed it, and the media haven't got wind of it. There was no press here when the body came in, was there?'

'No. I'm afraid the death of a drug user living homeless in the Phoenix Park doesn't make for a great headline,' Terry said.

'There's a conflicting theory about the Saucy Jacky postcard, though,' Laura went on, stabbing at the screen of her laptop. 'Some people believe it was a hoax and had been written by a journalist for the Central News Agency in a bid to keep the Ripper in the news, to spark further interest in the case. And sell newspapers, I guess.'

'You're saying this could just be someone taunting me, taking the piss? Come on, even Michael wouldn't go that far.'

'No, I'm wondering if that might be a clue to who he is,' Laura said. 'Could our killer be a rival podcaster? Or maybe a writer?'

'It's as good a theory as anything,' Terry said. 'Let's suppose the whole Ripper reference has a meaning. He stabbed and strangled his victims. And that brings me back to Eileen McCarthy, the unsolved murder Rachel was interested in. Maybe this guy has been active for a while and maybe Rachel had sussed something out.'

'There are some grainy pictures of the Ripper's victims. They're pretty gruesome. Jesus, he was vicious.' Laura's fingers flew over the keyboard. 'Now this other fella was a different kettle of fish. He shot his victims. Night Stalker by name and stalker by nature. He sounds a bit more methodical than Jack. Took his time. But he did kill a couple, the Maggiores, who he thought were on to him.'

Terry nodded slowly. 'The only definite link between Rachel and Tina is geographical. Reece was researching Ripperesque murders, but Tina, maybe, like the stalker's couple, she was just in the wrong place at the wrong time. She was living rough in the Phoenix Park. Is it possible she saw something? Let's see what Michael comes up with.'

42

Terry headed into the kitchen to make coffee. Niamh was there flicking through the channels on the television, a half-full mug of milky tea and a severely depleted packet of chocolate digestives in front of her.

'Laura not with you?' she asked. 'I thought I spied her earlier.'

'She's gone to a crime scene with Vinnie – aggravated burglary.'

Niamh flicked onto Virgin Media where a young blonde woman in a red dress with perfectly coiffured hair was speaking solemnly into a microphone. '*A man has been taken in for questioning for a second time in relation to the murder of award-winning true-crime podcaster Rachel Reece.*'

Terry wondered on what basis they'd dragged in Cleaver again – assuming it was Cleaver, but as far as she knew there were no other suspects in the pot. Either way, the coroner was going to get antsy. He'd want to release Rachel's body to the family.

Niamh sniffed loudly. 'Seriously, what kind of slimy fucker could do a thing like—'

'Shhh! I want to hear this,' said Terry.

She leant over and picked up the television remote and pressed the volume button.

'*The Garda Press Office has issued a statement outlining that they wish to question a man further in relation to the podcaster's disappearance and death. The same man was held for twenty-four hours earlier this week, but the statement indicates some new information has come to light. This morning, Minister for Finance Edward Farrelly, who is the maternal uncle of the deceased podcaster, had this to say.*'

The image changed to the grave-looking politician, whom Terry took to be in his late fifties. He had receding grey-streaked hair and was wearing a charcoal suit with a wide blue pinstripe.

'*Rachel's death has devastated our family and left a space that cannot be filled in all our lives. She was a brilliant, dynamic young woman with a bright future ahead of her. She fought for justice and that is what she deserves. I have full confidence that An Garda Síochána are doing everything they can, as expeditiously as possible, to bring the person who did this to justice.*'

Right, Terry thought. *Subtle. Pressure is being brought to bear, and Sinnott is only too happy to take the lead position in the lynch mob that's going after Frank Cleaver.*

She was glad his attention was on the investigation and

not badgering her to let Rachel's body go. Even though it wasn't her decision to make.

Niamh took back the remote control, muted the TV and looked at Terry. 'Maybe we've got him this time. Cleaver.'

'You think he did it?' Terry asked her.

'Are you saying you don't think he's our man?'

'Well, I reckon there's pros and cons that he did it,' Terry said. 'The evidence is far from definitive, which is probably the biggest con.'

Niamh shook her head. 'I don't know, Doc, but this is a man who loathes women and he has previous form attacking women in the Phoienix Park. And now they've got something new on him. So, yes, I think they are probably on the right track.'

As soon as Terry got back to her office, she called Fraser.

'What's the story with Cleaver?' she asked. 'Have they found new evidence? You heard about those mushrooms we found at the scene?'

'Terry,' Fraser said with mild irritation, 'do I have to keep reminding you, I'm not on the case any more? Sinnott certainly hasn't told me anything about any new evidence, nor any mushrooms. But Reece did visit Cleaver in prison. We're still waiting to interview the prison officer on duty in the visitor's room at the time but it was a terse meeting by all accounts. He obviously set his sights on her after that.'

She sighed. 'Shit. What was she thinking going to see a sleazebag like him?'

'People in glasshouses—'

'That's different. I'm not talking to criminals. Part of me

wants it to be Cleaver and be done with it. But just being a creep is not enough to convict someone of murder. It's not difficult to see him as a sexual predator, but we're not even sure Rachel was sexually assaulted. *You need the evidence.*'

'Terry, you're preaching to the choir. But there's nothing you or I can do about it.'

'Do we know if he's ever moved out of the jurisdiction? Maybe Rachel went up North because she thought Eileen McCarthy's killer could have been active up there. Or maybe even in Scotland. I mean, it's a short ferry ride away.'

'Well, I drew a blank in the north. And as far as I know there's no connection between him and Scotland.'

'Was it ever looked into?'

'Him having any dealings in Scotland? Not that I'm aware of. But then, why would it?'

'Don't mind me. I'm just thinking aloud. I can't get past the fact that everything we have on Cleaver is circumstantial, or based on gut instinct. There has to be something more tangible, and it'd be good to find it.'

'I'll admit, there are some doubters on Sinnott's team,' Fraser said, 'but he has more than a few loyalists too, good cops who are convinced of Cleaver's guilt. At the end of the day, though, Terry, it's out of our hands. He's in being questioned as we speak, and they'll either let him go afterwards or they won't. The wheels of justice roll ever onwards, as my old sarge used to say.'

'You're right, of course,' Terry said. 'I'm just frustrated. If it's Cleaver, I'd like to be able to say with absolute certainty.'

'Me too,' Fraser said. 'Me too.'

43

Terry's head was thumping. She and Laura had spent the afternoon with Niamh in her tiny lab dicing tissue samples from this week's cases for the histopath tech to process. Her headache was due to the combined effects of Niamh's incessant chatter and the formalin fumes. The lab tech tended to switch off the ventilation system when she was talking to ensure Terry heard every precious word. Health and safety be damned.

Terry was packing up for the evening when her mobile phone buzzed, Michael's name flashing on the screen.

'Hi, Michael. What have you got for me?'

'So far nothing. I've been over the McCabe clothing with a fine-tooth comb. Zilch. I've just got her knickers to do. And the less said about that the better.'

Terry laughed. 'I won't delay you so. Bye for now.'

She replaced the handset and called Fraser. She needed to

know more about Tina's death. And Fraser was the man to help her. She was just heading into town to meet him when Michael called her back.

'Knickers clean as a whistle. From spores at least.'

'Thanks, Michael. What about the sleeping bag?'

'What sleeping bag?'

Terry and Fraser met in Croke's an hour later.

'I thought we were planning a dinner date next,' he quipped as soon as he was sitting down, a glass of non-alcoholic craft beer in front of him – this time he was on call.

'And we'll do that,' Terry said, with a brief smile. 'But I called you here because I need your help.'

Fraser nodded. 'Go on.'

'There's some stuff I need to tell you.'

She explained that on the basis of what they had discovered regarding the ghoul mushrooms at the scene and the spores on Rachel Reece's clothes – and her nagging suspicion that Tina McCabe's death was somehow related – she was checking her out too.

'Hold on,' Fraser interrupted. 'Wasn't she deemed a drug death? Wasn't that what you told me?'

'I was … well, I was sort of directed to look at her case again,' Terry said. Then she told Fraser about the DMs she'd been receiving, passing her phone over so he could read them for himself.

'Terry, why the hell didn't you tell anyone about these?'

'I thought the first one was probably a hoax, someone in the department trying to wind me up. I only got the second one this afternoon. And I *am* telling someone. I'm telling you.'

'This is worrying, Terry,' Fraser said. 'If this – this Saucy Jacky legitimately is the person who killed Rachel Reece, then he has an unhealthy fascination with you. That's not good news.'

'I don't like it myself,' Terry said. 'But maybe we can use it. Laura is convinced these messages are all clues, just like Dr Hunt reckons the ghoul mushroom is a message in and of itself. I think we need to give him space to keep sending them so we can decipher what they mean.'

'It's too risky.' Fraser shook his head. 'He could escalate, decide sending messages isn't enough. If he worked out that's your secret Instagram handle, he can probably find out where you live just as easily.'

'We don't know he's the killer, and even if he is, he's playing a game.'

Fraser sighed and took a sip of his beer. 'You're right. We don't know it's the killer but we don't know it's not. You need to take this more seriously,' he said.

'I will. John, can I ask you to come with me to the Phoenix Park this evening?'

'Why?'

'That last message is implying we've missed a murder. That can only be Tina McCabe.'

'Not unless there's a body still to be discovered.'

'Which is why I've asked Michael to check if the same spores were on Tina McCabe's clothing. That way we would have a direct link between the two murders.'

'And has he found anything?'

'Not yet. But there's a slight hiccup. She was wrapped in a sleeping bag, which it turns out was left at the scene. If the killer is using the same MO, spores would have been scattered on top of her body.'

'And?'

'And onto the sleeping bag, which we don't have. I rang the SOCO when I realised it wasn't with the rest of the clothes, and she told me she'd left it with the woman who found the body.'

'I'll have a word.'

'She thought she was doing a good thing leaving the bag, that it would be of use. And it wasn't actually flagged as a suspicious death so technically she didn't do anything wrong. But I have to retrieve it to check it out for spores. And I want to see if there are any mushrooms at the location. So I need to go back to the park. Will you come with me?'

'Well, I'm damn well not letting you go alone!'

She leaned over and kissed him on the cheek. 'Thank you.'

'Dates with you are nothing if not interesting, Terry, I'll say that much.'

44

Dusk was settling over the park when they arrived. The street lamps gave the place a pleasant glow and, as they got out of Fraser's car, Terry could see deer off among the trees, keeping their distance from the joggers and dog-walkers who were still very much in evidence, despite the lateness of the hour.

They had arranged to meet Clodagh, the scene-of-crime officer, in the car parking area just in front of the entrance to Garda HQ. Terry still couldn't get over the audacity of Rachel's killer, dumping her body so close to HQ. That might be the reason the gardaí were so antsy about the murder. It was right under their noses.

The small white SOCO van was tucked into a corner and the young garda was leaning against the bonnet smoking. Fraser walked over and tapped her on the shoulder. She spun around and quickly stamped out her cigarette. 'Oh, sorry, boss. I was just—'

'Thanks for coming out, Clodagh,' Fraser said, pretending he hadn't noticed her breach of protocol despite the cloud of smoke. 'Dr O'Brien wants to have a look at the scene. Maybe you could drive us over, as you've been there before? Hopefully we won't keep you long.'

They got in the van and the young garda drove up to Wellington Road, parking close to the monument.

'The body was found down there.' She pointed in the direction of Kilmainham. 'Just watch your feet.'

The den was well hidden within a large clump of bushes. Fraser told the two women to wait in the open. Clodagh handed him a hefty torch.

Within moments, he came out. 'It's all clear. No sign of any sleeping bag, just cardboard and black bin bags.'

Clodagh and Terry entered the den, and the SOCO showed them where the body had been lying. The ground sloped down towards the perimeter fence, which Tina McCabe's head had been close to.

Terry gestured for the torch and searched the ground in and around where she was found. 'No mushrooms. But I'll take a few soil samples in case the spores haven't had time to germinate.'

The two women were kneeling side by side, scooping soil into the small sterile containers Terry had stashed in her handbag earlier at the mortuary, when they were startled by Fraser shouting 'Oi, you!' to someone.

They got up and scrambled back into the open. Fraser was holding someone by the arm. The person had their back to Terry and was brandishing a vodka bottle with the dregs left in it at Fraser. They were skinny and dressed in a grubby red tracksuit.

'Get your fuckin' hands off me or I'll shout "rape".'

'And I'll have you done for striking a guard with a bottle. Drop it!'

'Fuck off!'

Fraser held fast and his prisoner jerked their head backwards, trying to butt him in the face.

'That's her,' Clodagh exclaimed, 'the one who took the sleeping bag!'

The woman turned towards her voice, dropping the vodka bottle. 'Oh! It's you. I done nothing. I'm just a bit pissed. I don't have any drugs. Don't do them.'

Fraser relaxed his grip. 'We're just looking for something,' he said.

'Well, I haven't got it! I never took nothing.'

Terry walked over and motioned for Fraser to let her go. *She can protest all she likes*, she thought, *but she* is *a drug addict. Just like her friend was.* 'I'm Dr O'Brien. I'm the one who examined your friend Tina. I'm trying to find out what happened to her. Do you still have the sleeping bag?'

'It was mine.'

'I understand, and I'm happy to buy it off you.'

'It wasn't cheap. And I'd need to get another.'

'Well, I'm sure we can sort you out. But unless you take Revolut ...' Terry looked over at Fraser, one of the few people she knew who still carried cash, and mouthed 'twenty'. She turned back to the woman. 'DCI Fraser here will give you twenty euros compensation and I'll get someone to make sure you get a new one.'

'I knew he was a guard.' Her eyes darted to the bottle lying at her feet. She held out a hand.

Fraser laid the note on her upturned palm, making sure not to make contact.

'Thanks.' She shoved the money in her pocket. 'But I don't have the sleeping bag any more.'

Fraser made to grab her arm again but Terry pulled him back. 'What did you do with it?'

'I sold it.'

'Of course you did,' said Fraser.

Terry shot him a look. 'Can you tell me who you sold it to?' she said.

'Walk up towards Castleknock gate,' the woman said. 'You'll find a tall girl, red hair. She's called Bernice. She used to look out for Tina and me. I needed a few quid.'

'Okay, thank you,' Terry said. 'Look after yourself.'

They walked back to the van.

'*She'll* be on your table before too long,' Fraser said.

'She might get herself together,' Terry replied. 'Where there's life there's hope.'

'I admire your optimism.'

'Fake it till you make it,' Terry said, and laughed without much humour.

Clodagh drove them up to the Castleknock gate and stayed in the van while Terry and Fraser reconnoitred. They spotted Bernice from some distance away. She was perhaps six foot two in her heels and had long red hair running almost to the small of her back. She was standing with two other women who were obviously sex workers. They turned and watched Terry and Fraser walk towards them.

'Threesome? That'll cost ya,' Bernice called out.

Terry started to laugh with real humour this time. 'No, nothing like that. You knew Tina McCabe.'

Bernice stared her down. 'Time is money. By which I mean if I'm talking to you, I'm not earning.'

Terry nodded. 'I get that. I'll only keep you a few minutes.'

'And tell *him* to stand a ways off,' Bernice said, glowering at Fraser.

Terry turned and gave him a look. He walked away a few yards and leaned against a tree, within earshot.

'I was given your name by a friend of Tina's. I'm looking for the sleeping bag you bought from her.'

Bernice smiled. 'Mags. Shit. That girl can't keep her mouth shut, especially when she's off her head. I gave her a fiver for that ratty auld yoke. Felt sorry for her. You can have it for fifty, though.'

'Be real,' said Terry. 'Twenty.'

'Deal,' she said.

Terry turned to Fraser again, who rolled his eyes and reluctantly dug into his pocket for a second time.

Bernice looked back over her shoulder at her two companions. 'Sylvie. Go get that piece of shit I got off Mags.' She turned back to Terry. 'And don't give it to this nice lady.' She nodded towards Fraser. 'He'll take it off you.'

Terry took a chance to ask about Tina.

'She was a junkie,' Bernice said, quieter now so Fraser couldn't hear. 'But she was a good kid all the same. I did my best to keep her safe. Looks like I failed.'

'Did she have any friends she saw regularly?' Terry asked.

'Tina didn't have friends, leastways none that didn't come

out of a needle and into her arm. Addicts get like that once they reach a certain stage. I was the closest thing to a friend she had.'

'Where did she get her drugs?'

Bernice shook her head. 'Your pal there will arrest whoever I point the finger at. I know how it goes.'

'We're not here to bring down a drug dealer,' Terry said. 'It's Tina I'm concerned about. I want to know how she died. And if there's dodgy gear out there I need to know.'

Bernice was quiet for a moment, then said, 'She used to get her gear off a bloke who sells over near Farmleigh.'

'You're sure of that?' Terry asked.

'I'm certain,' Bernice said. 'She was over there all the time.'

45

'She was right, you know. Bernice,' Fraser said to Terry. Clodagh had dropped them off and taken the sleeping bag, assuring them she would run it over to FSI straight away. Now, they were standing next to Fraser's car on White's Road, bounding the north side of Farmleigh Estate, about a hundred yards from Chesterfield Avenue, the main road running through the park. A skinny track-suited man sporting a baseball cap with an enormous peak was lounging under a streetlamp at the junction, ideally placed to nip out onto the main road to service a punter or duck back along White's Road towards Castleknock, should the need for a hasty retreat arise. He had looked decidedly cagey when they'd turned in to the road.

His tracksuit was covered in zippered pockets, and every fifteen minutes or so someone would arrive, hand him money surreptitiously and he would open one of the pockets, remove the small package of drugs and hand it to them, the money disappearing into the pocket to replace its former contents.

'What was she right about?'

'I really do want to arrest that guy.'

'That's not exactly what we're here for,' Terry said.

'It's very likely some of his drugs killed Tina McCabe,' Fraser said. 'God knows how many other deaths he might be responsible for.'

'If her death *was* accidental,' Terry said.

'Well, yeah, I suppose,' Fraser agreed.

Terry looked around. There was dense greenery on both sides of the road.

'I think that's the fence Rachel Reece's body was dumped over,' Fraser said, nodding towards the left.

'Is it? I'm not sure from this angle.'

'I reckon so.'

'If it was dark, like it is now, could Tina have seen anything from back there?' asked Terry, nodding in the direction of the dealer.

Fraser strolled over and stood at the fence. 'She'd see a car,' he called to her.

'Yes. But could she make out someone manhandling a body over the fence?' Terry called back.

'I guess so.' Fraser strolled back to the pathologist's side.

'Is this the spot, though?' Terry wanted to know. 'If it was further along it would be more difficult to see clearly.'

'There's only one way to find out.'

They drove back to the main entrance of Farmleigh. Fraser showed his ID to the security guard and explained their visit. They parked outside the house and trudged across the grass and scrub. Somewhere to Terry's left a vixen screamed. Bats flapped overhead, chasing moths in the glow from the streetlamps.

They were near the north-east corner of the field when they encountered a wall of stinging nettles almost as high as themselves, which blocked their way.

'It doesn't take long for nature to reclaim the land,' Fraser remarked.

'It would have been easier if we'd just walked the long way round, like I did with Michael and Rupert,' said Terry as they circumnavigated the forest of nettles. Fraser said nothing but ducked into a gap in the dense greenery that formed a natural barrier, sandwiched between Beech Lane and White's Road, and vanished into the darkness. Terry followed. The path executed a straight line: the garda search unit had flattened everything in their way. It was twice as wide as Terry remembered. In the tunnel the air was still and close, rich with the smell of chlorophyll and damp earth.

And suddenly they were in the clearing.

'This is where she was dumped,' he said.

Terry joined him. There was the ditch, full now of black ground water, with a fence rising behind it. Fraser leaped over the ditch and climbed onto the lowest rung of the fence, peering over onto White's Road.

'As near as dammit as to where we thought,' he said.

'Tina could have seen the killer tossing Rachel's body over the fence,' she said. 'He killed her because she saw him. Drug-addled as she was, he was scared she might be compelled to talk.'

'Let's get out of here,' Fraser said. 'I think you've got what you came for.'

46

'So what next?' Terry asked as they made their way back to the car. 'Will you talk to Sinnott?'

'I don't want to burst your bubble, but I can't see how this will make any difference to him,' Fraser said. 'It could still have been Cleaver. I don't think it was but if, and it is a *big* if, that poor girl was killed because she saw the body being transported, that doesn't mean it wasn't.'

'I know. I'm working on that.'

'I think there's a way to go yet. We still haven't a definite link between the Reece and McCabe deaths.'

'I'll call Michael first thing in the morning and get him onto the sleeping bag. And I'm open to any other ideas about where I might look.'

'Well, if anyone comes up with anything, I'll be sure to pass it on.'

'Thanks for nothing, John.'

'Hey, c'mon. Who's walking the land with you in the middle of the night when he could be at home reading his Terry Pratchett book?'

'You like Terry Pratchett?'

'Well, I've read the Discworld series probably five times from start to finish, so ...'

'You're that much of a nerd?'

'Is the pale horse upon which Death rides named Binky?'

'What?'

'Exactly, Terry. Exactly.'

Next thing, from out of nowhere, an almighty force hit Terry on the side of the head and everything went black.

She opened her eyes to darkness and the sound of shouting. She was lying on the ground at the edge of the forest. She put her hand to her head and felt a raised bump but it wasn't bleeding. Whatever force had hit her must have knocked her out for a minute.

She'd landed badly on her hip, which was aching and sore. Rolling onto her stomach she got her legs underneath her and managed to stand upright. As soon as she did she was assailed by a wave of nausea and thought she was going to throw up, but it passed as quickly as it had appeared, and she stood blinking in the moonlight.

And what she saw horrified her.

John Fraser was grappling with a man who seemed to dwarf him in size. The attacker, who was dressed all in black with a balaclava over his face, had Fraser by the throat and was trying to choke the life out of him. The detective brought his fists down on the arms of the attacker – once, twice, three times – with all the force she could muster. But the blows had no effect and, dark as it was, as she stood there frozen, Terry could see Fraser's face was turning a deep scarlet.

In desperation Fraser reached under his jacket and pulled out his handgun, but the big man sensed the movement and, releasing one hand from the detective's throat, knocked the gun from Fraser's grip with a ferocious blow.

This was enough relief, however, for Fraser to deliver a kick to his assailant's groin. The black-clad man staggered backwards, letting go of Fraser, who didn't give him time to recover but lunged forward, striking out with both fists.

Suddenly, though, the dark figure had a knife in his hand, and slashed out at Fraser before he could get close enough to deliver a blow.

Fraser cried out and fell back. Frighteningly quickly the assailant was on his feet and Terry knew she had to do something, and fast. Casting about, she picked up a tree branch lying on the ground near her foot. As the attacker loomed over Fraser, knife raised, she rushed forward and struck him on the head as hard as she could.

To her horror the first blow seemed to have no effect. She swung the branch a second time, hitting the back of his head with an audible crack. This time he was knocked over backwards but almost immediately he rose to his feet again and was gone from sight at lightning speed, through the nettles.

The detective groaned as Terry knelt beside him. 'John, are you okay?'

'Bastard cut me,' he said. 'Is he down?'

'He was. And I thought he was out, but then he jumped up and charged away – I can't believe the speed.'

'Fuck it!' he said, staggering to his feet. As he cast around looking for where his gun had landed, Terry could see a patch of blood spreading across his shirt.

'Let me see that wound,' said Terry.

'It's not deep,' he said hoarsely.

'Do you have a degree in medicine?'

'No, but I have been cut before.'

'Show me!'

Fraser let Terry open his shirt and shine the light from her phone on the wound. He was right: it was shallow. The skin had been opened and blood was seeping from what looked to be a jagged cut.

'Did you see the blade he used?'

'No. But believe me I felt it. He might have dropped it. We'll find it if he did.'

'I can't clean the wound here,' said Terry, 'but I'm going to try and bind it.'

Terry unwound the scarf from her neck as Fraser called for back up and wrapped it around the detective's mid-section. He winced as she pulled it as tight as she could.

'Is it better I pass out from not being able to breathe rather than loss of blood?'

'Stop complaining, you big jessie. And try not to bleed too much on my good scarf, it's Alexander McQueen.'

'How apt,' he said, looking at the signature skull design.

So much for carrying out my investigation in secret, she thought, as they waited for the response team.

47

They made their way slowly back towards the road to wait for the patrol cars.

'Do you think that was … him?' Terry asked.

'I don't know,' Fraser said. 'But guess what?'

'What?'

'Cleaver is in custody. So there's no way he could have committed *this* particular crime.'

Two patrol cars and an ambulance arrived ten minutes later.

Terry and Fraser were both questioned separately.

Fraser described the assailant to the guard interviewing him. 'He was tall – six four or five, maybe. And very fit for a guy so big. Most blokes of that size lumber, but this one moved as if he weighed next to nothing.'

'He injured you?' The guard indicated the bloodstain on Fraser's shirt.

'Cut me. It isn't a serious wound.'

'And he got away while you were down?'

'Yeah. Terry thought he'd be unconscious after she clocked him over the head. Instead he was up again in moments and off like lightning.'

'Okay. First things, first. Let's get you to hospital to have that knife wound looked at. We'll pick this up again later.'

Terry was sitting in the ambulance having a large graze on the left side of her head cleaned when Fraser climbed in beside her.

'You do know how to show a bloke a good time,' he said.

'Never a dull moment with me,' she said as the doors were closed and they headed to the A&E department at St James's, just across the Liffey.

Three hours later the pair were deemed fit to be discharged. DS Mary Healy and her colleague Bob Paterson were in the waiting room.

'Chief's been on, boss. We've to get you home and keep an eye on you tonight. He wants you both in tomorrow morning.' Mary turned and threw the car keys at Bob. 'You drive, I'll ride shotgun.' Terry noticed Mary checking the gun beneath her jacket.

Fraser was stretched out in the back seat, looking sleepy from the painkillers he'd been given. Terry sat bolt upright, squeezed in beside him.

'Mary,' Fraser struggled to sit up, wincing a little, 'it makes more sense to have us both in one place.' He turned to Terry. 'If it's all right with you, I'll stay at yours? The couch will be fine – I doubt I'll sleep much anyway.'

Terry nodded. She felt her face redden as Mary glanced round.

'Suits us, boss,' Bob said. 'There's one of them twenty-four-hour garages along from the doc's flat. No offence, John, but you're in the middle of the fucking country. Not great for night surveillance.'

Once they were inside her flat, Terry produced the bottle of gin and poured them each a double measure.

She sat down beside him on the couch. 'Thanks for staying tonight. I wasn't keen on being on my own.'

'Or having Bob Paterson sitting in your kitchen all night.'

They sat for a bit, lost in their own thoughts, sipping their drinks.

'Could it have been someone linked to the dealer we were watching who wanted to warn us off?' she asked.

'Could be,' he said. 'Best to keep an open mind at this stage.'

'I suppose so. But ...'

'You think it could be whoever is behind those messages,' Fraser finished the sentence for her, 'Saucy Jacky.'

'Maybe. Or maybe my imagination is just running riot. I don't know.'

'Let's run with it, then. Do you have a theory on who the messenger might be?'

'Well, the first DM arrived just after I'd met with Rachel's ex.'

'Kyle?'

Terry nodded. 'And whoever just attacked us – well, Kyle is really tall, so was he.'

'I think it's tenuous, but I'll see about bringing him in for questioning again.'

'That'd be good,' Terry said. 'Can I ask you something, John?'

'Fire ahead. Just keep in mind I'm weak from blood loss and slightly stoned, so anything I say could be considered of questionable veracity.'

She smiled. 'Okay, here's my question: you told me that Sinnott warned you that colluding with me might impact on your career.'

'I did tell you that, yes.'

'And you are, unless I am very much mistaken, a blue-blooded copper with no intention of a dramatic career change any time soon.'

'You are not mistaken.'

'So why, taking all of that into consideration, are you agreeing to help me out when you've been explicitly warned to keep away from me?'

Fraser sipped his drink. Terry felt a low swoop in her tummy as he turned to face her. 'Terry, I think it's pretty clear at this stage that I like you.'

'I sort of know that, yes.'

'Well, let's just say, I can see you're in deep with this one, and I don't want to see you get hurt.' Fraser smiled and gently touched the plaster that had been put over the injury on the side of her head where she'd been hit. 'Not doing a very good job of it, am I?'

'I think we both know it could have been a hell of a lot worse if you hadn't been there.'

'Well, I'd be dead if you hadn't hit the fucker with a tree branch! Let's leave it at we rescued each other.'

'Is that from a movie or something?' Terry asked.

'Damned if I know,' he said, and leaned in to kiss her.

48

The surge of jealousy hit him like a sledgehammer when she arrived home with the detective. He wanted to kick the door in and crush the man's skull with his bare hands.

He could imagine her watching him do it, silent as she observed the full extent of his passion. Once she had observed him at work, she might even go with him willingly, recognising that destiny had brought her to him, and him to her.

He saw the front door to her building close, and he knew that in twenty-two seconds the light would go on in the window on the second floor.

They seemed at ease in each other's company, she and the detective. He was sure that, for her at least, this was a front, to lull the detective into a false sense of security. Why, unless she needed something from him, would a woman like the

pathologist ever choose to spend time with a dolt like him?
She had to be stringing him along.

That made him feel a bit better.

The light went on as if on cue, and she stood in front
of the window, framed for just a moment, arms cruciform,
before pulling the curtains closed. He felt a rush of desire
for her. When it happened, he planned to make it last.

He would finish her, eventually, with his hallmark
combination – the knife and the choke – placing the
mushroom spores in her dark places afterwards.

But he had something special in store for her. This would
be a trophy killing. He would steal her heart as she had
stolen his.

And they would all wonderwhy this one was so different
to the others.

They would never know this was an act of love. A song of
praise written in blood and bone and pain and fellowship.

It would be his finest work.

All he had to do now was wait.

49

Terry woke the following morning with a throbbing
headache. She rolled over to see Fraser still there,
sleeping fitfully, snoring away. An unpleasant sound, but not
altogether an unpleasant sight, she had to admit.

She was not a romantic by nature, preferring to see the
world through a lens of common sense and precedent.
Common sense dictated that jumping into a relationship with
a colleague, particularly a rapidly rising senior detective, was
not exactly sensible. Particularly as she was the new girl in
town. It might make other detectives wary around her. Even
worse, some of them might fancy their chances too.

For women in her line of work, being truly equal wasn't
the same as being seen to be equal, she knew only too well.
Neanderthal thinking hadn't as much gone as been driven
underground, where it flourished among a vocal minority
in bars and locker rooms. Terry was wary of this and did

her best when on the job to keep things professional. Cool detachment was the order of the day.

Precedent had shown her that forensic pathologists suffered a high incidence of divorce and she knew Fraser already had one of those in his baggage. The job was all-consuming, making no allowances for birthdays, high days or holidays. It took a special partner to put up with that. Someone had to give. For that very reason, relationships within law enforcement were doomed to failure. Policemen, particularly career-climbers, like forensic pathologists, were focused on one thing and one thing only, and that was their job. It would eventually lead to tension. Two takers, no givers.

Terry knew all of these things, yet waking to find John Fraser lying beside her was invitation enough for her not to care about doing the wise thing and calling it quits. She liked Fraser, was certainly attracted to him, both mind and body, and she had to admit they got on great together. She wasn't looking for marriage and wasn't even sure she wanted a long-term partner. What would be would be. For now, she was happy to allow their relationship to take its course and just see what developed.

Fraser wasn't like the usual cops she encountered. He was as tough as any of them, and obviously a damned good detective, but he was also quiet and thoughtful and, most of all, respectful. She knew he would never brag about their relationship, would never put her in a position which could impact her career.

He stirred beside her, opening one eye and smiling sleepily. 'What time is it?'

'Just after seven.'

He winced and put a hand on his bandage as he sat up. 'We're due at Sinnott's office at 8.30. Can I use your shower?'

'We might save time if we went together.'

'And we'd save water, too,' Fraser agreed in mock seriousness. 'Which is good for the environment.'

They just about had time for breakfast.

'I see I'm not the only one with secrets,' Fraser said, the radio playing quietly in the background as they sat at the small kitchen table.

'I don't follow,' Terry said.

'You're one of those weirdos who puts Marmite on their toast,' he said.

'I like it.'

'I don't know if our relationship has any future then,' Fraser said, looking dejected.

'When was the last time you tried it? I bet you were a kid.'

'It doesn't matter how much I try to develop my palate,' Fraser said. 'I will *never* share your appreciation for that stuff. Yuck!'

'Never say never, John – oh, shush for a minute!' She reached over and turned up the radio.

'*Gardaí have this morning released without charge a man being held for questioning in the Rachel Reece murder case*,' the newsreader said.

Terry and Fraser looked across the table at one another.

'What do you think that means?' she asked.

'Nothing,' Fraser said. 'I wouldn't read too much into it.'

'Well, we've got the sleeping bag now,' Terry said. 'Which might help us to link Rachel's and Tina's deaths.'

'We do,' Fraser grinned, 'along with a few extra war-wounds for our troubles.'

'How about we go to work,' Terry said, 'and see if last night's adventure actually makes any difference to what we already know.'

50

S he knew it was going to be a challenging day.

She had so much to do and she had to show that she was capable of doing it – she couldn't afford to let this attack on her give Sinnott or Boyd the excuse to sideline her.

They arrived at Harcourt Street expecting a bollocking, but Sinnott had been surprisingly supportive. The best news was that he was putting Fraser on the inquiry. Sinnott made it sound as if it was so he could keep an eye on him, but Mary told her separately that Minister Farrelly, Rachel Reece's uncle, had stormed into his office demanding assurance that the best men were on the case. His sister, Reece's mum, had been particularly impressed by the detective who had driven all the way to Donegal to deliver the news to them personally. And so it was that Fraser was pulled back in.

The bad news from her meeting with the DCS was that Terry had been given garda protection, in the form of two young cops, Tony and Pádraig – the ones who'd driven her to Famleigh when the body was first discovered.

Terry was due at the inquest regarding the bouncer's death that afternoon. She would be in and out in ten minutes. All the coroner wanted from her was the cause of death. A life snuffed out in six words, *blunt force trauma to the head*.

She'd also been informed by email that the family of the American tourist were suing the shipping company, and she'd been asked to expedite her report. Most likely the wife didn't get the sympathy, or the preferential treatment, she thought should be forthcoming during such a trying time.

Before she went to her own office, Terry popped in to FSI to make sure the sleeping bag had been delivered to Michael by Clodagh.

'What the hell happened to you?' he said, pointing at her head when she walked in. A large sealed evidence bag, likely containing the tattered and filthy sleeping bag, was sitting on the bench.

'It's a *long* story,' she said and filled him in on the events of the night before. He was concerned but there was an impatient edge to it. Was he annoyed?

'Terry, do you think it's time to let go of this … it's becoming obsessive. And dangerous.'

Now it was her turn to be annoyed. 'Really, Michael? Obsessive? Or maybe I'm just trying to do my job. And it would help if others would get on with theirs!'

'Are you for real? I've been busying my arse for you these past few days. By the way, there wasn't a single spore on Tina McCabe's clothes – I checked every square inch.' He paused and looked down at the evidence bag. 'So, this is the missing piece of the puzzle, I suppose?'

'Yes.' Terry said. 'Myself and Fraser went and got the sleeping bag last night, so here's hoping. Give it a look over and see if you find any spores. If you don't, review everything else we sent over, would you? I want to be as thorough as I can on this. Oh! A word of warning: it stinks.'

'Nothing I'm not well used to. I'll call with any news.'

'Cheers. I've a statement to prepare' – she pointed at the Elastoplast above her right ear – 'so I'd best get moving.'

'See you later. And sorry. I just worry. You don't seem yourself. Look, let's meet later for a drink and talk it all through. Mulholland's at eight?'

'I'll be there with my posse in tow. I'm on a leash now.' She pointed out the window at the garda car parked outside.

'I guess we'd better behave ourselves then.'

Vinnie was waiting for her when she got back to the mortuary.

'Morning, Doc. I've been sent over to take a few photos of your injuries. You and Fraser are the talk of the station. Sinnott's doing his nut. The last thing he needs is someone like Fraser out of action.'

'Have you seen John?' Terry asked.

'More of him than I wanted to.'

'Any chance I can get a look at the photos? Just in case they need an expert opinion. The A&E doctor was brand new, and he kept referring to the injury as a laceration – a real rookie mistake.'

'If you say so. Now, where do you want to do this?'

She had just walked Vinnie to the front door after he'd finished taking the photos when her phone buzzed. Picking it up she saw it was another Instagram DM. *Fuck.* She opened the app.

She was relieved to see it wasn't another message from @saucyjacky, but instead from someone calling themselves @simplyclaradwdy:

> *I hope you don't mind my reaching out. I got your DM link from Kyle Brady, who tells me you're working on the Rachel Reece murder and spoke to him, wondering if he had any information. I'm Clara Dunwoody. I was Rachel's foster sister, we were raised together. Could we meet as soon as possible? My mum is going out of her head with worry and if there's anything you could tell us we'd really appreciate it.*

The message brought her back to those awful days after Jenny's death. She knew how much comfort it could give a family to have their questions answered, in as much as she could. And, who knew, maybe Clara had insights about Rachel that could be useful to her investigation. Terry accepted the message and messaged back:

> *Are you free this morning? How about 11.30 in Bewley's Café on Grafton Street?*

If that suited, it would give Terry time to head in before the inquest. The response was almost instantaneous:

I'll see you there. I know what you look like from the news, and my profile pic is accurate except my hair is lighter now.

Terry liked the message, then headed straight back to her office.

She had finished writing up her incident statement by 10.45 and passed it to Laura, who'd agreed to proof it. 'I just need to pop out for a wee bit,' she told the intern.

'For God's sake mind yourself,' said Laura. She'd been shaking to hear about what happened in the park the night before despite Terry's reassurance everything was under control.

'I'll do my best. See you in a while.'

51

Bewley's Oriental Café was situated near the top of Grafton Street, across the road from Dubray Books, and was one of Dublin's most famous landmarks, with its Victorian facade and stained-glass windows.

Tony insisted on parking outside which, as it was a pedestrian street, drew more attention to her than she wanted. She went inside and looked around for Rachel Reece's foster sister. There was no sign of her and she was starting to wonder if the whole thing had been a set-up when a voice came from behind her. 'Hello? Dr O'Brien?'

She turned and there was the girl from the profile picture. Terry did a double take. Clara was a little smaller than Terry's five foot six inches, slim, with a long face and pale complexion framed with ash blonde hair that hung below her shoulders. She was dressed in a leather jacket, blue-and-red chequered trousers and a white shirt, knotted to show off her midriff. Terry put her in her mid-twenties. She was a dead ringer for Rachel Reece. She'd mentioned in her message they were foster sisters. But they could easily have passed for blood relatives as well.

'I'm Clara. Thank you for agreeing to meet me so quickly.'

'You're welcome,' Terry said, shaking her hand. 'I'm sorry for your loss.'

'Thank you,' she said. 'We're all reeling. It's just so hard to believe.'

'Of course,' said Terry, 'it's a huge shock.'

'And the gardaí are telling us it could even be days yet before the body is released? It's been almost two weeks!' Terry recognised the plea in her voice – she knew how difficult it was for families in cases like this one, the interminable wait to give their loved one a proper send-off, as police and forensic investigations took precedence.

'I'm afraid I can't say precisely,' said Terry, but hopefully it won't be too long now. Let me get you a coffee.'

When they were seated, Terry asked her if she'd been interviewed by the gardaí.

'Yes,' she said quietly. 'A detective spoke to me shortly after … after Rachel's body was found.'

'So why are you so anxious to speak to me?'

'I … I had the impression the guy, the detective, was just going through the motions. I answered all his questions, of course, but when I offered information, it was as if he wasn't interested.'

'What kind of information?'

'Well, I told him Rachel had been getting a lot of shit online. Death threats and all that.' Clara's voice had become shaky, and she swallowed hard, trying to compose herself.

'Poor girl. But that stuff is par for the course – not that it makes it right. It's just, there are a lot of nasty people out there. It's why I had to close down my own social media.'

Clara leaned forward, steadier now. 'Yes, but she said there was one who was constantly on her case.'

'Did she have any idea who it was?'

'She had her suspicions. I don't know if she was just being paranoid, but she was worried that whoever it was would find out where she lived. And she told me she'd been getting weird calls on her phone – number withheld, but when she'd pick up there'd be no one there, just noises in the background.'

'Did she say what kind of noises?'

'She said it sounded like a building with lots of people, a train station, maybe, or a shopping centre. A lot of banging and shouting.'

'Did anything happen?'

Clara glanced around quickly before answering. 'We were having a drink in Phibsborough – this was three days before she vanished. When we came out there was a man hanging about. He followed us but then disappeared.'

'What makes you think he was following you and not just heading home himself?'

'Well, that's what I presumed at the time. I thought she was overreacting.'

'Weren't you worried when you didn't hear from her for a couple of weeks?'

Clara looked down at the table. 'I … I knew she was on a deadline to get this new podcast up and running, so I thought she was on one of her research trips and keeping her head down.'

Terry sipped her coffee. 'What did you advise her to do when she told you she was worried?'

'I told her to call the police,' Clara said. 'But she wouldn't hear of it. Said she didn't trust the authorities. "They're afraid I'm going to show them up," she said. "They're not going to help me."'

'That's a pity.'

Clara's eyes filled with tears. She closed them and breathed deeply before speaking. 'Rachel was very proud. And I know she could be arrogant and a bit of a know-it-all, but I have to tell you, Dr O'Brien, she was not just my foster sister. She was the most loyal friend I've ever had. She would give you her last euro if she thought you needed it, and if you called her in the middle of the night with a problem, she'd drop everything to be by your side. And she was fearless. She would stand up to anyone. That's probably what got her in trouble.'

'Sounds like quite a woman,' Terry said.

'She was,' Clara said. 'She really was. The podcast – yes, it made her famous and it made her controversial, and I know she enjoyed that. But that wasn't why she did it. She wanted to do good. To make a difference. To find the truth. That wasn't fake. She was passionate about what she did.'

'Clara, do you know if Rachel went to the North of Ireland before she died?'

'Yes, she did. It was part of her research for the new episode she was doing on Eileen McCarthy.'

'What was she hoping to learn there?'

Clara thought for a moment. 'She was looking for Eileen's sister, Jo, who had apparently disappeared. Rachel got a tip-off that Jo had fled to the North because she was afraid she'd be killed, too.'

'What kind of a tip-off?'

'She told me it was anonymous. Sent to her via Instagram. The message was deleted shortly after she received it. But I have my suspicions. She had been in contact with some guy who was in prison. I reckon he was the one that told her.'

'Do you know where in the North she went?'

'No. Sorry. She just took off. She had a habit of doing that. She was always like that, even when we were at school. She just got so wrapped up in things.'

'Thank you, Clara. That's very helpful.'

She gave a wan smile. 'I'm glad. I really hope you catch the man who killed her.'

'So do I. In your message to me, you said you're afraid. Why?'

Clara stirred her cappuccino, which she had barely touched. She looked up at Terry, her eyes wide. 'The man Rachel and I saw that night, he was a very tall man in black.'

Terry felt a shiver of recognition. 'What about him?'

'I think he's following me, now.'

Terry watched Clara disappear into the crowd on Grafton Street and stood for a moment, thinking about what she'd just heard.

Rachel Reece's foster sister was being followed by the same person who, she claimed, had followed and possibly threatened Rachel. She said she'd seen him outside her flat and the IT firm where she worked. And, Terry pondered, this was the second set of sisters to present themselves in the tangled web of this case.

She would have to explore the possibility further.

52

He stood across the street from the café in the shadows of a shop doorway and watched the girl say goodbye to the pathologist. It was exciting to see both of them together.

The girl exuded cool confidence. But he knew different. He liked her clothes and her long blonde hair that hung loose down her back, shining in the sun. He had to resist the urge to reach over and touch it.

She was so like her foster sister they might have been twins. He was torn, but she would have to wait.

She gave the pathologist a hug walked off down the street. On her own she was more wary. She knew he was there. He had seen to that.

He might as well keep the pressure on. Today anyway.

He kept a good distance.

She was soft, this one, not like her sister, who was loud and full of anger. He followed her through the bustling streets of Dublin's city centre but his mind kept going back to the pathologist.

She was where his immediate interest lay.

He had to admit, she fascinated him.

He stopped in his tracks and watched the foster sister of his kill walking away into the distance, then he turned back.

53

Terry called Fraser when she got back to the office and told him what Clara had just shared with her. 'You need to get her some kind of protection. Whatever it takes, get Sinnott to sanction it,' she said. 'Look what happened to us. Her description matches the guy who attacked us, and she says this same person was following Rachel Reece.'

'We still don't know if our attack was random or targeted, or if it was the killer. But you're right, that's all compelling. I'll ask him to reach out to her,' Fraser promised. 'The attack in the park is being taken seriously.'

'She's being stalked,' Terry said. 'I'm not. Tell him I don't need to be babysat. Let her have Tony and Pádraig. He whistles all the time, Pádraig. And talks about his dog.'

Fraser laughed. 'Well, you're stuck with them, I'm afraid.'

'Please just get something arranged for Clara, John. I'll talk to you later.'

She was still in her office – Laura had gone to lunch with Vinnie – reading over her notes for the inquest that afternoon, when her desk phone jangled. It was Boyd's extension.

'Dr O'Brien, could I see you in my office, please?'

'I'll be right there.'

'Thank you. I won't keep you long. I know you're busy.'

That's comforting, Terry thought, and went to meet her fate.

Boyd was gazing at the screen of his laptop when she went in and motioned for her to sit.

'I received a report this morning regarding a police detective dialling 999 last night from a field in Farmleigh,' he began, 'a field that adjoins a recent crime scene. The transcript of the 999 call suggests he was in the company of one of my staff. He requested garda support, having been injured in an altercation.' Boyd closed his laptop and steepled his fingers. 'Have I left anything out, Dr O'Brien?'

'No,' Terry said. 'I'd say that's a good summary of what happened.'

'The information I was sent, as a matter of courtesy, posits that you were following up on some evidence that had been omitted from the cache taken at a recent crime scene. One that, as far as my knowledge extends, has nothing whatsoever to do with the Rachel Reece murder. So what in heaven's name were you and DCI Fraser doing roaming about right next to the Reece crime scene in the middle of the night?'

'We were following up on the Tina McCabe case,' Terry said. 'I hadn't been called to the scene and I just wanted to check it out. The postmortem is inconclusive, and the sleeping bag she was wrapped in was left at the scene. DCI Fraser is the senior investigating officer on the case.'

'How convenient.'

'I wouldn't say that.'

Boyd gave her a hard look, which softened when he saw the plaster on her temple. 'You were hurt,' he said.

'Fraser was slashed with a knife,' Terry said. 'He came off worse than I did.'

'How did these injuries come about? And the *real* story, please. Not some cock-and-bull nonsense.'

She detected a thawing in his relationship with her. Pity it took a whack to the head. She touched the plaster. Stuff it, she could come clean on this one. That way she could deflect him from her other unscheduled outings. It was one thing to visit a scene, something else completely to go off interviewing witnesses.

In a suitably wavery voice, she told him about going to the park to get the sleeping bag, and how Bernice told them where Tina got her drugs. How they'd gone up there, seen Tina McCabe's drug dealer hanging about and realised how close it was to the Reece crime scene. 'It made me wonder if Tina could have been at the location on the night Rachel Reece's body was dumped and saw something.'

'That's a bit of a leap,' Boyd said. 'You think the McCabe woman was murdered?'

Terry considered telling him about the DMs from Saucy Jacky, but decided to reserve that information until she had harder evidence.

'It's a possibility,' she said. 'On the way back from having a look at the ditch where Rachel Reece's body was found, we were jumped.'

Boyd nodded. 'The Phoenix Park can be a dangerous place at night,' he said.

'No argument there, Professor.'

'Dr O'Brien, I have already spoken to you about keeping within the very specific confines of your post. Do I need to remind you again?' He was shaking his head but for once he sounded more resigned than angry.

'No, sir. Everything happened as I told you.'

'There's nothing else you wish to share?'

She crossed her fingers behind her back. *Not at this time, anyway*, she thought. 'No, sir. What you have in the report you were just reading is the whole of that story.'

'Very well. I am choosing to take you at your word, in spite of your history.'

'Thank you,' Terry said. 'I think.'

He looked at her for a moment, one eyebrow slightly raised, then said, 'Dr O'Brien, I did not call you here to discuss your night-time wanderings.'

'No?'

'I received a communication from the Department of Justice today requesting I extend your contract of employment.'

Terry blinked. 'Oh. That's unexpected. Can I ask why?'

'I believe it's down to your … approval rating, for want of a better term. The public likes you, and that reflects well on the minister for justice, who very much enjoys good publicity. But be warned, he can turn just as easily. It seems that you are helping to make all things forensic popular. And God knows we desperately need to attract new blood.'

'Professor, with the greatest of respect, I don't want to keep this job because I look good on the telly. You're the very one who's been telling me to keep away from journalists and focus on the work.'

Boyd looked somewhat chastened. 'I ... I did not like the tone of some of the articles I read or the reports I saw on the television. However, I understand you cannot control how these things are edited. Regardless of what I think, those in the corridors of power like what you're doing for our little corner of law enforcement and wish to retain your services.'

'And how do you feel about that?'

It was Boyd's turn to blink. 'I beg your pardon?'

'You're my boss, Professor. I don't want to take on a job you aren't happy for me to have. I've been under the impression you were looking for an excuse to get shot of me, if I'm being honest.'

Boyd looked at the desktop for a moment, as if gathering his thoughts. 'You are an excellent pathologist, Dr O'Brien. I can see that. I accept that I could be a bit more open-minded about the way you conduct your affairs, but I will not have my authority challenged – as your superior it behoves me not to. However, I do believe we could work together, and work together effectively.'

Terry couldn't help but smile.

'Well in that case, I accept.'

Boyd nodded. 'Excellent. I'll inform Human Resources.'

He stood, offering his hand, which she shook. 'Here's to new beginnings.'

'I'll drink to that!' she said.

Terry had a few minutes to spare before heading to the inquest, and she googled *murdered sisters Ireland*.

The list was not long.

Among articles on Ireland's notorious Scissor Sisters – gruesome perpetrators, not victims – and tribute pages to siblings who had died in road traffic accidents or separately as a result of gangland activity, she found one instance of two sisters who had been murdered as part of the same attack.

In 2004, Anne and Kitty Joyce had been found murdered in their home in Ringsend, both victims of what looked to be a frenzied knife attack. The killer had never been found. Terry had almost finished the first article she opened when she realised something about the case was familiar.

She sat back in her chair, trying to work out where she had come across the Joyce sisters, when her eyes fell on the yellow folder at the bottom of a now messy pile on the corner of her desk. It was the second file she'd taken from Boyd's office – the one that had been attached to Eileen McCarthy's with an elastic band.

She reached over and pulled it out, flipping it open.

As the article had stated, in June 2004 sisters Anne and Kitty Joyce had been killed in their home in Ringsend. Anne had been twenty-eight years old, Kitty thirty-two. Both had been stabbed and both postmortems were performed by Dr Charlie Boyd.

The format of the reports was different from the one the office now used. She noted that the chief state pathologist at that time was Professor Brendan Cunningham. She'd never heard of him. But she made a mental note to ask Mrs Carey about him.

The reports were unusually concise, sparse on details such as the circumstances surrounding the deaths and the scene – usually considered crucial information in any PM report. However, it was the brevity of the descriptions of the injuries the women had sustained that was most frustrating. Particularly as she didn't remember seeing any accompanying photographs in the files in Boyd's room.

She was used to reviewing other pathologists' reports, and photographs were essential – a permanent record of a pathologist's findings. Even when double-checking her own reports against the photographs taken, she noticed patterns she had not seen at the time of the dissection or slight nuances she had missed. During the postmortem, the pathologist was necessarily close to the body: the photographs allowed you to step back and see the bigger picture.

Kitty had been found in the kitchen in a pool of blood. Her throat had been cut and she had been stabbed multiple times. Anne was in the living room. She had also been stabbed over and over, but there were slashes on her face and arms. It was possible Kitty had been taken by surprise but Anne had put up a fight.

There was no mention of any possible weapon and there was just the bald statement 'routine trace evidence taken'. Clothing wasn't even mentioned. At least the toxicology results were noted as being negative for both women: no drink or drugs involved, legal or illegal.

There was no note of an inquest or of court attendance, but she could check that out – at least, Mrs Carey could, if necessary.

Terry read the report one more time and put it back in the pile. She could see no connection to Rachel Reece, but figured that, if Boyd had been looking at it at the same time as he had pulled the McCarthy file, Rachel Reece might have been asking about it as well. Was it the similarities in the deaths, vicious stabbings and strangulation? Eileen's murder was more controlled, less frenzied – a sign of an evolving MO? Had Rachel assumed Jo was dead and therefore the link was that they were sisters? If so, now she was dead was Clara at risk? She already thought she was being stalked. Terry needed to impress on Fraser again the urgency to get her protection.

54

The inquest to the bouncer's death was as straightforward as predicted. The grief-stricken family held their emotions in check as Terry took the stand and answered questions from the coroner on the cause of death: 'An extradural haemorrhage due to blunt force trauma to the head.' That was all, the details would follow in due course.

As she passed the family on her way out, a woman she presumed to be Robbo's mother intercepted her. 'Please tell me he didn't suffer,' she said. Terry was used to this. These were the details that were so important to families, and she had a variety of ways of answering the question to provide as much solace and as little pain as possible, while remaining truthful. In this case, it wasn't hard.

'He didn't,' she said. 'He would have died peacefully in his sleep.'

'Thank you,' she said, relief washing across her stricken face.

As they parted ways, Terry felt her phone vibrate in her pocket. Outside on Store Street, she looked at it. Another DM notification. She opened it tentatively, hoping it was from Clara Dunwoody. No such luck.

I love to hunt. Prowling the fields and walkways of the park or the residential areas of the city looking for fair game – tasty meat. The wemon of Dublin are z prettyist of all. I must be the drugs pumped into their veins. I live for the hunt – my life. Let me haunt you with these words; I'll be back! I'll be back!

Terry sat down on the steps outside the building and read the words again. She googled the first two lines and learned they were – in slightly edited form, once again, to suit the circumstances – taken from a letter left at the scene of a double homicide committed by David Berkowitz, known as the Son of Sam killer.

John and I could have been a double killing, Terry thought, feeling sick to her stomach. *He's telling me he'll try again.*

This message seemed to bring a lot of the strands together.

He says he lives for the hunt, she thought. *Prowling the park or the city. He stalked poor Rachel, terrified her before he finally killed her. And now he's moved on to Clara.*

She wondered if she herself would be walking home one evening only to see a hulking dark figure standing in the shadows of a nearby doorway. Fraser had warned her about it right from the start, that if this man could find her on social media, hidden as she tried to keep herself, it would only be a matter of time before he worked out where she lived.

I must be the drugs pumped into their veins, the message read.

He's admitting to killing Tina McCabe, she thought. *He's confessing to the murder.*

How did he do it? Did he wait until Tina had injected herself and was semi-conscious before he gave her more, causing an overdose? Or did he buy the drugs for her – did he get hold of diamorphine, pure heroin, perhaps, so pure her body wasn't able to cope with it? She knew he was clever.

Remembering what Laura had said about the identities of the authors of the original messages being possible clues, she googled Berkowitz. He was ex-military, serving with the army. Fraser had said the man who attacked them was extremely strong and freakishly agile. Did this hint at a man with military training?

Apparently Berkowitz claimed in the 1990s – he was arrested and sentenced in 1978 – that he was part of a cult and that the killings he committed (he pled guilty to eight but was suspected of many more) were part of some kind of ritual sacrifice.

Was the killer saying his motives were spiritual?

Were these killings and all the odd aspects that went along with them linked to a satanic cult? And had Cleaver ever expressed any interest in such things? From what she knew of him, he was simply a common-or-garden rapist and sadist. What about Kyle Brady? He didn't seem the satanic type, but then, was it possible to tell? Maybe he had a room full of occult paraphernalia.

She picked up her phone and called Rupert Hunt – this was precisely his freaky wheelhouse of social anthropology.

'Terry, great timing,' he said, answering promptly. 'I have my report on the Rachel Reece crime scene ready.'

'Good stuff,' she said. 'I was ringing about putting some more work your way, actually.'

'Why don't you come over to my office and tell me about it? Two birds with one stone – I can talk you through the report.'

'I can be there in twenty minutes, if that works?'

'I'll await your arrival.'

'See you soon,' said Terry, and walked around the corner to Talbot Place where Tony was waiting for her.

55

R upert Hunt's office was a large high-ceilinged room in the older part of Trinity College, off College Green. Two of the walls were lined with bookcases and display cabinets; the other two displayed primitive art, ancient-looking maps and a framed selection of the degrees he had secured over the course of his career as a social anthropologist and an archaeologist.

Rupert stood stiffly when she came in, his hunched frame betraying a vulnerability at odds with his air of grand accomplishment. He walked around his large desk and they shook hands, then Terry wandered over to one of the display cases.

'Are these archaeological specimens?' she asked.

She was looking at a selection of tools and utensils, all of which had been fashioned from either bone, wood or stone, as well as a large cracked urn, the kind of artefacts you might expect to find during an archaeological dig.

'Not all, they're a mix of ancient and ... shall we say more modern,' Rupert said.

'They're quite impressive,' Terry said.

'Why thank you,' he said, sounding genuinely pleased. 'And thank you for coming. I thought it useful to have a chat before I file my report on the Reece case. Please, take a seat.' He indicated a leather-backed chair on the other side of his desk.

He picked up a book from his desk and passed it to her. The cover was a patchwork of photographs, some in black-and-white, some in colour, of women, all who looked to be between the ages of eighteen and forty. It was titled *Lost in Plain Sight: Decoding the Mysteries of Ireland's Vanishing Triangle*. The author was Rupert Hunt, PhD, MLitt, BSc.

Terry opened the cover and read the inscription inside, which looked to have been written in fountain pen: *To Dr O'Brien – in memory of ghouls and ground water. Rupert Hunt.*

'Thank you,' Terry said. 'You'll have to forgive me, but what's Ireland's Vanishing Triangle?'

'It refers to an area of about eighty square miles, with Dublin at its uppermost point, in which thirteen women went missing during the late 1980s and early 1990s. All of the cases remain unsolved.'

'And how does a social anthropologist or archaeologist apply their trade to missing persons cases?'

'Are you familiar with the field of semiotics?'

'Not especially but I think I'm about to be.'

Rupert smiled. 'Indulge me. It's the study of how human beings encode the world around them using signs and symbols. Anthropologists study the meaning we as a species place on shapes and colours, for example – even down to calling the area in which these women disappeared a triangle. It isn't, not even close, but it makes it easier for people to comprehend, fits something that is in fact quite chaotic into a kind of order. And that, Terry, is what anyone who works in law enforcement is really attempting to achieve: order from chaos; meaning from something that is often meaningless.'

'So you look at the details of the cases and try to find a code to decipher? I guess it's not much different from me and patterns of injuries.'

'In a nutshell, yes. The women were within a certain age profile, late teens to late thirties, with one lady in her early forties. They all disappeared close to their homes. No substantial clues or evidence have been found for any of them.'

'That doesn't look like much of a pattern to me,' Terry said, trying not to sound too sceptical.

Hunt smiled. 'You'll have to read the book to learn more.'

'I will, thank you.'

'Excellent. Now, before we get to my report, you said you had another job for me?'

'Yes. Well, more a question, really. Have you turned up much ritual murder in Ireland through your work?'

Hunt leaned forward slightly. 'Do you mean in the present-day?'

'Yes. There was a scare in Scotland last year when it was reported some kind of satanic cult was operating in Glasgow. The trial is still pending. Has there been anything like that here?'

'I believe there was an isolated case in the 1970s, but other than that I'm not aware of anything of that nature. Is this pertinent to a case you're working on?'

'It was just something someone alluded to,' said Terry. 'Normally I don't give these theories much credence. Remember the fiasco in Orkney way back in 1991, when do-gooder doctors started making allegations of satanic child abuse on the back of dubious findings. Turned out to be a load of nonsense but it ruined the lives of a lot of people. I prefer to stick to the facts,' Terry said. 'Why don't you tell me about your report.'

'Happily. Let me get it on the screen ...' He fiddled with his laptop for a moment. 'Thank you for sending a copy of your findings. Professor Boyd arranged for me to harvest some samples of bone, and I can state there was nothing unusual about them. Ms Reece was a healthy young woman with good nutrition, though I did note a slight calcium deficiency.'

'I'm impressed with the efficiency of your laboratory. Not getting enough dairy?' Terry asked.

'Or drinking a lot of caffeine,' Rupert countered. 'It was very slight, though could have increased over time. But not pertinent to our investigation.'

'No,' Terry agreed.

'Obviously the most interesting and unusual aspect of this case is the presence of ghoul mushroom spores,' he went on. 'I have some theories on why this might have occurred. The most obvious reason to have peppered the body with saprotrophic spores would be so the mushrooms would bloom and then consume the body, thereby destroying the evidence.'

'How long would that take?'

'Several months, probably years, but the body would be completely absorbed.'

'Completely? Bones and all?'

'Yes. If Rachel Reece's remains had not been discovered when they were, they might never have been found at all.'

Terry nodded. 'It's an interesting idea, but if that was the motivation, why dump her in such a public place?'

'Well, indeed. It's a theory, but not one I subscribe to.'

'Okay. What else have you got?'

He sat forward. 'Did you know that mushrooms share more with animals than they do plants?'

'I had heard that, yes.'

'So, they do not exhibit any of the behaviours one would expect to see in a plant. They secrete a digestive enzyme, for example, to break down their food before they absorb it. You'll see that too in insects like flies. I should also point out that the DNA of whatever a saprotrophic mushroom eats *can* be extracted from it.'

'Really? I'm sure FSI would love you for that.'

'Yes. By scattering spores over the remains, the killer was giving Rachel Reece the chance to live again in a different form. Her genetic signature would literally become a part of the mushroom. Rachel's DNA – her life force, if you will – would become the power source for this other remarkable yet wholly alien being.'

'That's a nice idea,' Terry said, yet again trying to rein in her scepticism, 'but it seems a bit fanciful. I thought you were a man of science.'

'Is it art or is it science? So here's my third and final suggestion: in Australia the aboriginal people revere the ghoul mushroom, prizing it and understanding it as a sign of the interconnectivity of all beings in creation. The spores are highly sought after.'

'And how does that help *us*?' Terry asked.

'If I'm right, the killer wasn't trying to disappear Rachel Reece or transform her,' Rupert said. 'By leaving ghoul mushroom spores with her body, he was honouring her.'

As Terry headed back to her office in the garda car, she thought about Rupert's theorising. The only transformation she could see was from living to dead. And the killer may well believe he was honouring Rachel, but if he did it was a delusion. How could brutally killing someone be an act of honour?

56

Michael was in Mulholland's by the time Terry got there that evening. He had a pint in front of him and a Bacardi and Coke ready and waiting for her.

'You look like you've had a long one,' he said.

'Don't even get me started.'

'And where's your big strapping garda protector?'

'Sitting outside in the car like the good boy he is,' she said.

'Would you not at least offer him a fizzy drink and packet of crisps for his troubles?'

'Wouldn't want to come on too friendly a mistress,' she said, smiling. 'Lest he get too comfortable in the job.' She raised her glass to him. 'Thank you for this. You said you had some news?'

'I did. I do. Alan Ahern and I are dating. I think.'

Terry took a large swallow of her drink. 'You think? I mean, how do you not know?'

'We went out the other night, just him and me – not here, obviously. And afterwards, he stayed over at mine.'

'Meaning ...' Terry said, looking at her friend expectantly.

'Yes, well, he didn't sleep on the couch!' Michael said, swatting her playfully on the shoulder.

'Good for you,' Terry said, grinning. 'So let me get this straight: you went out together, you've sealed the deal – so why are you still uncertain?'

'He ... well, he's not great at returning texts. Or calls.'

Terry gave him a hard look. 'Nothing. Are you saying he's ghosted you?'

'I wouldn't call it that.'

'You've been messaging him and he hasn't responded?'

'Yeah.'

'That's what they call ghosting, Michael.'

He rolled his eyes. 'Whatever. Maybe he's just busy.'

'Let me summarise this for you: he went out with you, slept with you and then stopped calling you. He is what we women call a wee shit. Didn't your mother warn you about men? They're only after one thing. Move on. You've a few frogs to go before you meet your prince.'

'I'm supposed take relationship advice from you?' he said, looking at her askance.

'What's that supposed to mean?'

'C'mon Terry. You run every time someone tries to get close to you. I might be naive, but you're afraid of intimacy.'

'That's not fair,' she said, feeling stung.

'The truth hurts,' he said. 'I processed your drug-death sleeping bag, by the way,' he said.

'And?'

'There were no spores present. Sorry.'

Terry couldn't help but notice that his tone didn't quite match his words. 'What about the other trace evidence?'

'Nothing on any of the swabs. Nothing in her clothes, which I checked again for you. Hair was clear, oral swabs clear, breasts, thighs ... Tez, there were no spores from ghoul mushrooms or any other fancy fungus on that woman.'

'Crap. Michael, I know there's something off about this death. Could there be something in the drugs that killed her? Maybe I could follow up with toxicology and—'

'Not so fast,' Michael said. 'I chased up the tox for you. There's an opioid and a benzo present – it'll take weeks to get the levels – but she had a blood alcohol of two forty. You don't need to look too far for the cause of death. She fucked her brain up on drink and drugs. End of.'

Terry took some more of her drink. 'Maybe we missed something else,' she said. 'Can you look it over again?'

Michael bristled. 'I didn't miss a bloody thing, Terry. I went over every single piece of evidence multiple times to be sure, and that meant I had to work late to get my own jobs finished. I've put everything else on the back burner for you these past few days, and to be honest, I'm getting a bit fed up of it,' he said, his voice rising.

'I know, and I'm sorry, but I wouldn't ask if it wasn't important.'

'Important to who, though?'

A few people turned to look at their table.

'Keep it down, Michael. You *know* how busy I've been with this case. I thought you'd have wanted to support me.'

'Support you? *Support you?* What about me, Tez? Have you once asked how I was doing through all of this? Have you had any idea that my social anxiety has been going through the roof these past weeks? Did you think to ask me how I was coping with the whole Paul/Alan Ahern business? Did you even wonder?'

Terry opened her mouth to respond, then closed it again. He was right. She hadn't thought about her friend in any other context than as her 'man on the inside' in Forensic Science Ireland. It had been insensitive of her. The case was her priority, yes, and she did need the examination of the evidence fast-tracked, something she hoped Michael would understand. But she couldn't deny that she was riding roughshod over everyone, Fraser, Michael, even Laura and Niamh to some extent. Not to mention fibbing to Boyd. She knew she needed to get a grip. And yet ... something was driving her on and she couldn't seem to stop it.

'I'm sorry you feel I was less attentive than I could have been,' she said, doing her best to sound contrite. 'I didn't mean to make you feel used. Honestly, I didn't.'

'Too little too late, Tez,' Michael said, pushing back his chair.

This probably isn't the moment to ask him to take a look at Eileen McCarthy again, she thought, as he turned and headed towards the exit.

57

Terry surveyed the grubby office kitchen at the end of the following day. Mugs piled in the sink, out of date Fire Brigade calendar on the wall, the oddity of a periodic table beside it that no one had ever owned up to putting there. Not surprising really that Fraser had been distinctly nonplussed when Terry suggested dinner at her office, in response to his offer to eat out.

She knew Sinnott would be keeping an eye on her, and Fraser couldn't afford to piss him off either. Neutral ground, with a professional reason for them both to be there, was best under the circumstances.

'M&S special deal, complete with wine,' Terry said, placing the food down in front of him.

'Nice,' said Fraser. 'Nearly as fancy as Marco Pierre White's.'

'It's not the food, it's the company. So suck it up.' Terry

pressed the start button on the microwave with a flourish. She filled two water glasses with wine. 'Crystal's in the dishwasher.'

They clinked.

After taking a large drink, Fraser put his glass on the table. 'So I brought Kyle Brady in for questioning today.'

'Yeah?' Terry said, 'and how did that go?'

'Well, his devices were all confiscated and handed over to the tech squad,' Fraser continued. 'Apparently, the Saucy Jacky account is what's called a ghost account, meaning there've been no posts, there's no profile picture, and the only person messaged from it is you. It was set up using a VPN, a virtual private network, which means the IP address that set up the account is hidden and encrypted. Can't be accessed, in other words.'

'So there's no way to link it to Kyle,' Terry said.

'Nope. He fell apart under questioning, crying and sobbing the entire time. Saying he loved Rachel but she hurt him, put her work first, and he couldn't cope with being with her, even though he loved her.'

'Sounds like a confession to me, or the start of one,' Terry said.

'I'm afraid not,' Fraser said. 'This was Brady's second time being questioned, and last time he was in, he gave an account of his movements from when Rachel Reece was last seen alive. Which tallies well with Michael's maggots telling him she had been dead for about three weeks before her body was found. The investigators have been checking his story, and he's come back in the clear – he couldn't have done it.'

'So what we have at the end of the questioning,' Terry

said, 'is that he couldn't have killed Rachel Reece and there's nothing to link him to the DMs either.'

'That's about it. The evidence indicates that Kyle Brady is innocent. We released him earlier this evening. Leaving Cleaver alone in the picture again.'

They were quiet for a while.

'You know,' Terry said, 'I've followed my training. With a lack of concrete evidence tying Cleaver to the case, I've done all I can to investigate what might prove or disprove it. I've come up with nothing. I still don't think he's the man – the science doesn't lean that way … But maybe it's time for me to let it go. If it gets that far, the courts will decide.'

Fraser raised a glass. 'To hanging up our spurs,' he said.

Terry raised her glass too and tried to put on a happy smile. But happy was the last thing she felt. She felt exhausted and defeated from the events of the previous days and was glad when John didn't mind her saying she wanted to spend the night alone. Tonight, she needed her own company.

58

The pathologist had not gone home yet that night.

It seemed the mortuary was her home and her flat merely where she slept.

He understood that. He had a place, a hideaway, simple and a bit rough, but very much like home. It was quiet and secluded, hidden from prying eyes, a place where he could be himself.

More of a home than any of the so-called ones he'd grown up in.

He suddenly wanted to know if the pathologist missed her home, the street where she and her sister had gown up. If it was a good home, a happy one. He wondered if her parents had had a close relationship, or if they'd fought.

He was alone now, just as he had been for most of his life. Soon, though, he would be with her, just as it was meant to be.

59

Next morning, Fraser called her early.

'I'm sorry, Terry, but you're going to have to stay under police protection for a while.'

'You're joking!' she said. 'John, seriously, you don't think that's a bit of an overreaction?' From her vantage point she could see Pádraig in the driver's seat picking his teeth. 'I thought it would blow over in a couple of days.'

'You've no idea how serious they're taking this attack, Terry. The fact it happened in the park … And just so you know, it's all across the Sunday papers. Someone leaked it, I thought we might have been able to keep it under wraps. And now, with the DMs … Sinnott is insisting.'

Terry groaned.

Fraser continued, 'Not only that, but I'm afraid our techies are going to need your phone for a few days. It may contain evidence as to where these DMs are coming from.'

'You've got to be kidding,' said Terry. 'You might as well take my right arm.'

'Sorry, but it has to be done. We'll have it back to you just as soon as possible. I'll organise to get it picked up.'

Later in the morning, after she'd texted her contacts to say she'd be without her phone for a days and to email her, she got called into work for a PM. On the way she instructed Pádraig to stop off at the Spar where she picked up the main papers. News of the attack was everywhere. She kept her head down as she paid at the counter, sure people were looking at her. Once back in the car, she scanned the headlines, which ranged from the mundane – 'Top Pathologist and Murder Detective Assaulted in Phoenix Park' – to the more sensational – 'Scot Doc and Cop in Knife Attack Horror.'

She called Fraser again. 'So, given that we're now national news, is there any word on the attack?'

'A team did a grid search of the area, which turned up a grand total of nothing. There's a gate at the far side of Farmleigh, and some tyre tracks were found there, so they reckon he had a car waiting.'

'Any luck with that? Were they able to take casts of the tracks?'

'Another dead end, it seems. The tyres are as common as muck. They're found on every model of hatchback in Dublin and beyond.'

'Shit,' Terry said.

'They did find footprints near where I went down,' Fraser added. 'The ground was very boggy. The technical bureau took casts of those too.'

'Any better luck?'

'They were for a size twelve foot, which is not that common, though not rare enough to be a major help. The prints were for a boot that can be bought in about half the footwear shops in the country and is readily available online.'

'Whatever did we do before databases,' Terry said. 'The thing I was most interested in was the knife he used. Did they find that?'

'They did not. Either he never dropped it at all, or he managed to grab it back up before he ran off. They searched the field up and down. There was no sign of it.'

'Bugger. No fingerprints then. What about the branch? I hit him twice!'

'And you've got a pretty good back-hand. But all FSI got were some fibres, which they assume were from the balaclava.'

'What were the fibres, as a matter of interest?'

'Synthetic, some common form of polyester.'

Terry shook her head. 'So, we've got nothing.'

'We know he wears a size twelve boot and more than likely drives a hatchback,' Fraser said.

'And imports balaclavas from the north,' Terry added.

'Fuck it, we've practically got him cornered,' Fraser said with a rueful laugh. 'But seriously, watch your step, Terry – who knows where this bastard is or what he's up to.'

'Oh, don't worry – I've got it covered. I've got Tony and Pádraig watching my back,' she said with more than a hint of sarcasm.

Why does being protected feel so much like being under house arrest? Terry wondered. *And is that what this fucker wants? For my movements to be restricted?*

And as the thought occurred to her, she reckoned it might just be true.

60

Fraser was called to Sinnott's office at 10.30 that morning. It might be Sunday but until Reece's killer was under lock and key, it was all hands on deck.

'I'm not going to keep you too long. I just wanted to tell you that I think it's time we arrest Frank Cleaver for the murder of Rachel Reece. I want to thank you, John, for the work you did on this case. I know I drove you hard, but it was worth it in the end.'

Fraser shook his head. 'Sir, can I ask on what evidence I'm to sign off on Cleaver's arrest?'

'New evidence came to light, John. Literally within the last twelve hours.'

'Can I ask what the nature of the evidence is and why I wasn't informed of it?'

Sinnott's jowls reddened and he cleared his throat. Reaching for the handset of his desk phone, he picked it up and pushed a couple of numbers on the dial pad. 'Mary, can you pop in to my office for a few minutes?' He turned his attention back to Fraser. 'Our tech boys have been going through Ms Reece's devices and equipment. As she has quite a number of storage devices on which she keeps recordings and research documents, this has taken a lot of time. Most of it was not relevant to this investigation. However, yesterday a file was recovered from the deleted items on one of Ms Reece's phones. She had several which she used for different purposes – personal, research, interviews. The file that was retrieved was on the phone she used for research and is in the form of a voice note sent as a multimedia message. It seems Cleaver managed to get his hands on a mobile phone while he was in prison, and after Ms Reece interviewed him, he sent her this message. Can we play it, Mary?'

Mary, who had just entered the office carrying a slightly out-of-date touchscreen phone, nodded and fiddled with the device. Suddenly Frank Cleaver's guttural tones filled the office.

'*Hiya. Guess who? You told me to call if I thought of anything else. All I can think about is getting my hands on that tight little arse of yours.*' Cleaver coughed loudly, cleared his throat and continued. '*Don't tell me you don't want it too.*' He sounded breathless and there was a squeaking noise in the background. '*You won't have to wait too long. I'll be out soon and I'll come looking for you. You'll get what you deserve.*' They heard a groan and the message ended.

'The dirty bastard was wanking,' Mary said, shaking her head in disgust. 'Fucking scumbag. Sorry, sir.'

'Jesus H Christ,' said Fraser.

'Yes, well. That is what we are dealing with,' said Sinnott.

'But, sir, a threat is just a threat. It's not enough to secure a conviction,' said Fraser.

Sinnott's eyes narrowed. 'I do not agree. What we have there is not simply an idle threat. It's a statement of intent.'

'Sir, why wasn't I told about this before now?'

'The tech team brought this file to me late last night, under my instruction to come direct to me with any breaking evidence that will eradicate any doubt of Cleaver's guilt.'

'And you didn't think to inform me, as lead investigator, even as a matter of courtesy?'

'I'm informing you now, Detective Chief Inspector. I would have thought you'd be happy to see our man in custody. It would be another win in a very short time for you as lead, wouldn't it?'

Fraser had a lot of things he wanted to say, but he kept them to himself. 'What's the second piece of evidence?'

'Reece thought that someone was following her,' Sinnott said. 'So we checked the CCTV in her neighbourhood, going back to when Cleaver was released. Sergeant, please continue.'

'We found CCTV footage from a supermarket near where she lived,' Mary said. 'In it, Cleaver is very clearly seen approaching Rachel. We can't hear what was said, but he grabs her by the arm and is obviously shouting and acting *very* threateningly. She strikes him – delivers a punch to his throat, actually, fair play to her – and gets away. But there's no doubt: Cleaver made a threat in the voice message you just heard, and now we have footage of him accosting her afterwards.'

'We have to assume that the next time he caught up with her, she didn't get away,' Sinnott said. 'Are there any further questions?'

Fraser couldn't believe what he was hearing.

'We got the bastard,' Sinnott went on.

'Isn't this all a bit premature, sir?' Fraser said. 'With respect, a good barrister would tear the evidence you've got apart and have the case dismissed, and the DPP will see that and refuse to proceed. If you really want Cleaver locked up, and I know you do, we need to have some kind of physical evidence linking him to Rachel Reece's death. I know it's frustrating, but we have to be patient.'

'Cases have been tried on circumstantial evidence successfully,' Mary said, clearly annoyed that Fraser was raining on their parade.

'Not at the level of a murder inquiry,' Fraser said. 'The gravity of the charge and the severity of the sentences mean the case we present *has* to be rock solid. What we've got right now is shaky at best.'

'I am your senior officer, John, and you'd do well to remember that. I want Frank Cleaver arrested! Today!' Sinnott said, his voice trembling.

'Sir, I am the lead investigator on this case,' Fraser said, his voice steady, 'and I will not sign off on the arrest.'

Sinnott had gone an alarming shade of puce. 'Then I will have you removed from the role – *again* – and get it done myself!'

'I'm here at the minister's request,' Fraser said, 'and I took an oath to discharge my duties with fairness and impartiality. I intend to do that, which means ensuring we act with purpose and in good faith, no matter the circumstances or the history involved.' He stood. 'These new pieces of evidence are good and will help to build a case. But we should be channelling our energies into finding some hard physical evidence and not trying to create a case out of clues we know will not ultimately get us where we want to go. If you both take a step back and leave the emotion out of it, you'll see I'm right.'

'Get out of my office!' Sinnott shouted, getting to his feet and pointing at the door.

For once, Fraser did as he was told.

61

Terry didn't know the DS who turned up for the postmortem on the suspicious death she'd been called in for, but luckily she could reassure him that it was an accident. A young man from Bristol, over in Dublin for a stag do, who was enticed by the heady charm of Temple Bar and ended up in the canal, too drunk to swim and save himself. The DS barely said thanks as he high-tailed it out of the mortuary, although Terry was sure Jimmy's gruff manner had something to do with the poor guard's hasty departure.

She left Jimmy banging about the postmortem room and walked up the stairs to her office, stopping for a moment to look out the window in the reception area. The quiet was welcome. The garda car was sitting outside the front of the building, a grim reminder of her present circumstances.

She wondered what to do next. Yes, she had promised Fraser she would give up on her fixation with the case, but then he had phoned to tell her what had happened in Sinnott's office and she couldn't get it out of her mind. The whole thing still didn't feel right to her.

Cleaver was a bully and a predator, a violent rapist and a truly dangerous person, there was no doubt about that. From Fraser's potted version of events, it sounded as if Cleaver had been harassing Rachel from prison, and that he was likely the man she thought was following her. It seemed that had Rachel not defended herself when accosted outside the supermarket, something very bad would certainly have happened.

Fraser said that Cleaver had threatened her, had said she was going to get what she deserved. While it sounded like he intended to rape and brutalise her, that did not amount to a plan to murder.

Of course, violent sexual assaults do go wrong and can result in accidental homicide. Maybe this time he went too far.

Maybe.

She opened her laptop and went to the folder of files Miles had accessed for her. She clicked on one labelled 'Eileen McCarthy Excerpt 4, Episode 1' that she'd been meaning to listen to.

Synthesiser music built to a crescendo then faded and Rachel Reece's soft but urgent voice began:

According to information given at a garda press conference Eileen McCarthy was stabbed multiple times in a horrendous and vicious attack. Not content with such violence, her attacker grabbed her by the neck, squeezing until every breath was wrung from her body.

*Yet there was no forensic evidence, despite the ferocity
of the attack?*

Reece spoke these words dryly and slowly, letting the
unlikeliness sink in.

*The best the gardaí could do was point the finger at
a local sexual predator, Frank Cleaver. Cleaver has
a history of sexual violence, but not of murder. He
propositioned Eileen in a pub where she and some
friends were drinking on the night of her death and
reacted angrily when she rebuffed him. Cleaver is an
easy target.*
    But is he the right one?

The music swelled and fell again.

*The gardaí have, despite repeated requests, refused to
speak to me, but I was able to talk to a neighbour of the
McCarthys who is still living next to their family home.
She had known them since they'd moved in, not long
after Eileen was born.*

Another voice came in. An older woman, and a real Dub.

*Ah, Eileen, she was such a pet. Now, she could act the
maggot all right when she was a young one. Irenie, God
rest her soul, was run ragged with the pair of them girls!
But sure, didn't they turn out grand? They had it all
ahead of them … Poor Eileen. The family fell apart after*

*what happened. Jo took off and Irenie was never right
after it – how could she be? No wonder their da ended
up in that home.*

Reece's voice returned.

*That was Annie Byrne. She described the McCarthys as
good neighbours. Irene McCarthy, Eileen's mother, died
a few years after Eileen's death – 'of a broken heart',
according to Annie. And her sister Jo, seemingly unable
to live with the constant reminders of her beloved sister,
left Dublin shortly after Eileen's death. Mr McCarthy
suffers from severe arthritis and Alzheimer's and has
been in a nursing home since 2016. It seems that, in his
mind, he continues to live in 2006, when his family was
still together. Which is a mercy, really.*

The excerpt ended – obviously something Rachel had been
planning on slotting into the first episode of her unbroadcast
new series.

Terry thought about what she had just heard.

The previous sections she had listened to made no bones
about the fact the gardaí had warned Rachel off. Boyd also
sent her packing. Why did they not wish to discuss this case?
The PM report was a functional but sparse piece of work.
Rachel Reece openly suggested in her recordings that Eileen
had been failed by the investigation, and Sinnott's fixation on
the case seemed to indicate he felt so too.

What was going on? Why such a level of secrecy? A
popular true-crime documentary series might be a good way

of encouraging the public to come forward with clues that might help solve a cold case.

Yet instead of cooperating, as she had seen the police do in other media explorations of unsolved murders – both active and retired officers – they had tried to shut her down. There was nothing much she could do today. She was still on call. She would sleep on it.

The idea was to get a good eight hours but she couldn't shut off. At 4 a.m. she lay awake thinking. Eileen McCarthy was from Finglas and so was Frank Cleaver. Finglas was a big place, but it was possible they'd known one another before Cleaver approached her in the pub that night. The neighbour Rachel had interviewed, Annie Byrne, might know. She quickly looked up the PM report. Eileen's parents had done the formal ID on the day of her postmortem and the address was on it: 22 Ardmore Road.

Terry was due at a brain cut at 1.30 p.m. the next day and had a pile of histo samples to prepare for the lab, but she figured she could get to those during the afternoon. The morning was her own. Tony dropped her at the department and told her he would be in the main car park.

Terry went in through the main door of Office of the State Pathologist and climbed up to the reception area. Mrs Carey was already at her desk.

'Morning Mrs Carey,' she called out as she walked. 'I'm just going to dictate yesterday's case and then I'll be down in the mortuary for the rest of the morning.'

'Right you are,' said Mrs Carey.

Terry walked on down the corridor to her room. She

dropped her Dictaphone and notes on the desk. Then she called a taxi and slipped down the back stairs.

Not long after, she stood outside a row of terraced houses and tried to think how Rachel would approach this. She looked at the house to the right of the McCarthy home. It was a bit shabby in comparison to the others. It was likely whoever lived there had been here a long time. She knocked a couple of times and rang the bell, but no one answered.

She turned around just as a door two along opened and a woman came out and stood on the path, her arms folded. She looked to be in her forties, dressed in jeans and a T-shirt, with her hair in a high ponytail. She eyed Terry beadily.

'You looking for something?' Her voice carried a note of warning.

'I was hoping to speak with Annie Byrne.'

'You're not one of them loan sharks, are you? Chasing her 'cause her kids aren't paying, bleeding her dry?'

'No! Nothing like that. My name's Terry. I work with the gardaí, and I was hoping to have a word with her about old neighbours of hers, the McCarthys.'

'Well, Annie's not here, she's in hospital. Hip replacement.'

'Oh. I hope that goes well for her,' said Terry

The woman made a show of scrutinising her, then turned to go back inside. 'Come on in,' she said from over her shoulder. 'I'm Louise Christie, by the way. I was pals with Eileen and Jo in them days.'

Over a mug of strong tea in her tiny, immaculate kitchen, Louise filled Terry in.

'I was a few years older than the McCarthy girls and babysat for them when they were young. We stayed friendly but didn't pal about. I had other stuff on me mind. See, I started going out with Eddie – a right useless fucker – and moved in with him for a bit. It didn't last, though I tried me best, God knows I did. When it all fell apart I moved back here to look after me da when me mam died.'

'That was kind of you,' Terry said.

'Ah, he was a decent old skin, me da.'

'I can see you thought a lot of him.'

Louise nodded and looked wistfully out the window.

Terry thought she'd better get the conversation back on topic. 'What was Eileen like?'

Louise brought her gaze back into the room and sniffed, rousing herself from her reveries. 'Eileen was a handful. She had her mother's heart broken when she was a young one. Herself and Jo ran with a right shower. But Eileen was the ring-leader – Jo just tagged along. I mean, if you look at it now, most of the stuff they got up to was pretty tame. No drugs – those girls never got involved in all that shite. It was more a bit of shoplifting, cider in the park, that kind of thing.'

Louise took a puff of a small vape tucked inside her right palm, then turned her head away from Terry as she released a plume of vanilla-scented vapour towards the kitchen wall.

'Did you know any of the boys she was friendly with back then?'

Louise rolled her eyes. 'Most of them got their arses kicked eventually, bucked up their ideas and did all right for themselves. A couple turned to the drugs. *That* didn't end well. Never fucking does.'

'Do you remember a boy called Frank Cleaver?' Terry asked, trying to keep her tone casual.

'Little Frankie? Eileen made that fucker's life a pure misery. He was one of them smelly kids – may God forgive me for saying it.' Louise blessed herself, casting her eyes up to the ceiling. 'But he always gave me the creeps. Still, when I think back though, what fucking chance did he have? That mother of his – she should have been sterilised at birth. Luckily she was so pissed most of the time she never got pregnant again. If it hadn't been for auld Bessie, up at the top of the road there, he would have starved to death. Anyway, he trailed about after Eileen like a lost puppy, even though she gave him hell – called him a little pervert and everything. Now, everyone round here knows the gardaí liked him for it, for killing her like, but I never thought he was the one who done it. As far as he was concerned, she could do no wrong.'

'Did Eileen's parents think he was guilty?'

Louise shook her head. 'No. He was messed up, and I know he ended up going down for assaulting some young one, but he wasn't a killer. He could never do something like that to Eileen, anyway.'

'What about Jo, Eileen's sister, what happened to her? Do you keep in touch?'

'No – she was a nice enough girl but she lived in Eileen's shadow. After Eileen was murdered she didn't know what to do with herself. She took off, and we never heard nothing about her after that. I dunno where she is now. Never came back here is all any of us know, and good luck to her. I'd fuck off and never look back if I could.'

Terry wished she had thought to record the conversation

on her phone – *Rookie mistake*, she thought. *Rachel would have been all over that.*

'Was there anyone in their group that Eileen was particularly close to?'

'Nah. She was the queen bee of that lot, but she wasn't thick. She had no intention of ending up in some pokey flat with a couple of kids. She got her shit together before the Leaving Cert – ended up in the civil service. She done well.'

'Any boyfriends?'

'None that I know of. I'm sure she had her offers – she was a stunner. And she could be nice when she wanted to. I remember one lad, wasn't from round here, just appeared at Bessie's now and again – another one of her waifs and strays. He was one of those fellas you hardly notice – you know, nondescript, a bit older than the others. I think he'd been in care and was living on his own in one of them halfway houses, and Bessie used to give him a home-cooked meal every now and again – she used to get a few quid off the health board to keep an eye on kids just out of care. Jo fancied the arse off him but she never stood a chance against Eileen. And Eileen had no notion of him, but that wasn't the point. Everyone called him BJ.' Louise looked at Terry. 'You know, *Blow Job*. It was 'cause of they were his initials – BJ. I never knew his real name.'

Terry nodded as if this seemed like a perfectly reasonable nickname. 'Does Bessie still live round here?'

Louise laughed. 'Fuck no. She was ancient even back then! She moved out years back – always wanted to go home to Sheriff Street. Annie kept in touch with her, but she died a while back.'

Terry stood up. 'Louise, thanks for your time, I really appreciate it. I'll let you get back to your day.'

'I hope that was some help to you,' Louise said. 'It's funny, all them people is gone except for Frankie Cleaver. He's still knocking about. Till he ends up back inside again, of course. That's the way with a few of the lads from around here. Stuck in the revolving door.'

'You've been a great help,' Terry said. 'Can I leave you my card? When Annie gets out of hospital, maybe you could give me a call?'

Louise took the card and used a pineapple-shaped magnet to stick it on the door of her fridge. 'You gonna catch the fella who done for Eileen?'

'I hope so,' Terry said. 'I really hope so.'

62

Michael looked up when Terry arrived into his lab the following morning.

'I come in peace,' she said. 'And I bring gifts.'

Michael snorted and went back to his microscope. 'Terry, leave me alone, will you? Let's give each other some space.'

It was Terry's turn to snort. 'Do I not get some say in all of this? We've been friends for a long time, Michael, and I think it's fair to say we've had our share of bust-ups. If memory serves, sometimes I've been the one at fault, which I surely am in this instance, but there have been more than one or two occasions when you were the one who messed up. What I don't recall, though, is me ever making you jump through hoops to be forgiven. That's a new one on me.'

Michael spun in his chair. 'Tez, when you moved to Ireland it was supposed to be a whole new start for us,' he said, his voice indignant. 'Paul had ditched me, and I really needed my best pal. I thought it would be like when we were at uni. But no, you disappeared into your new job, and when you're not doing it you're either playing Jessica Fletcher or becoming best buds with John frigging Fraser.'

'Oh, Michael, you big eejit!' Terry said, shaking her head in exasperation.

'I'm sorry, but that's how I feel! And it's important to own your feelings, Terry.'

'Oh, for Christ's sake. You've been at those self-help books again. What have I told you? Look, you're my best friend – well, equal parity with Becs. And I'm sorry. Truly I am. I know I took advantage of your good nature. I won't let it happen again.'

'You'd better not! And I want to feel you're making more of an effort with me. I think I deserve that.' He folded his arms.

'Ah, come on, stop being so precious,' she said, laughing.

'Terry, I mean it! Stop making a joke of everything.'

Terry fixed her face to look as serious as she could. 'I'll do my level best, I promise. How does that sound?'

Michael seemed to accept that. He threw a glance at the bag she was carrying. 'You mentioned a present?'

Terry reached in, producing a sealed lunchbox. 'I scoured the northside for some really good cakes. Think Greggs.'

'Yum Yums?'

'Well, nearly. I couldn't find genuine Yum Yums. So I got some jam doughnuts and squashed them flat.'

'Oh, I do miss the finer things in life.'

'You'll regret it when you can't fasten that waist button.'

Michael hopped off his chair and gave her a hug. He then

grabbed the bag of doughnuts and ripped it open, spilling sugar onto the bench. 'Shit. MacKenzie will go apeshit if she catches us.' He used his sleeve to wipe the benchtop and they tucked in.

'What do you make of Rupert Hunt?' he asked.

'Bit of a know-all,' Terry said, 'but he's fine as far as I can see. Watch that jam.' She leaned over and wiped at the lapel of his lab coat.

'I'm not sure about all that guff about weird mushrooms,' Michael said, his mouth full. 'But it was quite fun. I do like working with you. You know that?'

'We make a good team. I'm the brains, you're the brawn.' She squeezed his bicep and laughed.

'Why is it so important to you to prove the link between Tina McCabe and Rachel Reece?' Michael asked her, flexing enthusiastically. 'I mean, you're pulling out all the stops.'

'Because it'll help prove the theory we're dealing with a serial killer,' Terry said.

'How?'

'There's Eileen. There's Jo, her sister, missing. . Then there's Tina. I think she could have seen the killer dumping Rachel's body – and she ended up dead. If we can confirm there is a link between Tina's death and Rachel's, we'll demonstrate we're dealing with someone for whom killing is so easy it's become a reflex action – Tina is dead because this individual didn't want to leave any loose ends, and they were shrewd enough not to leave a forensic trail. I do think they might be arrogant enough to leave a very subtle calling card, though. In other words, we're dealing with a serial killer.'

'You're spending too much time with Laura. She's been bending my ear about Bundy.'

'Well, she's given me some useful leads. Actually, would it be okay if I bring Laura over to have a look at the sleeping bag?' She watched his face. When he didn't react she went on. 'No spores were found on Tina McCabe, right? So it follows there'll be no spores on the inside of the bag, as the lining would have been in direct contact with her.'

'You're not starting that again, are you? *Locard's principle, every contact leaves a trace.* Don't be so patronising. I know all that shite.'

'Of course you do, and so I asked you to take samples from the outside of the bag. But I think I gave you a bum steer. *Mea culpa, mea culpa.*' Terry beat her chest with her right fist.

'What the hell are you on about?'

'I checked the photos again. At the scene the SOCO took photos with the sleeping bag open and then when she closed it back up. And here's the thing: Tina was using it inside out. So, the yellow lining was actually the outer surface.'

'Ah shit, Tez. You can't make me handle that again. It was putrid.'

'Hence Laura. She'll be your assistant. Deal?'

Michael put the last of his doughnut in his mouth and licked the sugar off his fingers. He stuck his sticky hand out. 'Deal. Give me a few days to clear my own backlog, and we'll make it happen.'

She hugged him.

'Oh, and I've got some good news,' he said once she let him go.

'You do?'

'Ahern called me. We're going out again tonight. And he suggested I bring my toothbrush. I'm staying at his place.'

'What took him so long?'

'He says he's worked off his feet right now. I imagine you can identify with that.'

'Well, make sure he treats you right,' Terry said, 'and have fun.'

'I bloody well intend to,' Michael said and gave her an exaggerated wink.

63

By 7 p.m. that evening Terry had finished the histo slides and had her coat on, ready to head home. As she was leaving, she noticed a pile of mail precariously balanced on Mrs Carey's desk that Tomas had left there. She went to fix it and noticed a thick envelope addressed to her, with 'Eileen McCarthy PM Photos' written across the top right-hand corner. Vinnie had come through.

She went back into her office but took one look at her once-again messy desk then grabbed a fresh notebook and headed instead to the conference room. She spread the photos out on the table so she could view them all with ease.

There was a lot to see: the injuries on the neck, the defensive wounds on the hands, wrists and upper arms. And the wounds to the chest area.

There were five stab wounds and a large slash over the left breast. She looked closer, then pulled back again and viewed the photos from a distance. The wounds appeared to form an outline of a heart shape, with a line cutting across. There were two stabs wounds above the nipple, one either side and one directly below; the latter designed to be a fatal wound, as it was directly over the heart. The slash across was the final flourish. If she was correct, the upper four wounds would be shallow, perhaps not even deep enough to do much damage to the lung, but nonetheless painful and bleeding, designed to invoke fear. She looked again from even further away. That was key to recognising specific patterns, being able to take a step back. Too many forensic pathologists couldn't see the wood for the trees. This time the motif was clearer. A broken heart.

She cleared a space on the table, sat down and smoothed out the first page of the new notebook. In a column on the left side, she listed *Rachel Reece* and *Eileen McCarthy*.

In a row across the top, she listed *Strangled*, *Stabbed*, *Signature Mark*, *Sex Assault*, *Clothing* and *Forensics*.

Writing it down on paper allowed her to organise her thoughts. She placed ticks and crosses in the columns where she could, question marks where she wasn't sure and an asterisk against them all in the Forensics column. She would need to speak to Michael about the forensic evidence, but for now she would concentrate on what she knew.

She had a sudden thought. She went back to her office and picked up Rachel's file, opening the postmortem photos on her laptop. She flicked through them until she got to the torso. She stared at the three stab wounds on the breast. Fuck, could this be an aborted attempt at the broken heart? Or was she seeing patterns that didn't exist? And anyway the stab wounds weren't identical, she was sure different knives had been used and Rachel was stabbed after she died. She'd leave it for now. She went back into the conference room to Eileen. It still wasn't clear to her as yet why Rachel had appeared to think Cleaver wasn't responsible for Eileen McCarthy's murder. Although, to be pedantic, Rachel was scathing about the gardaí homing in on Cleaver and apparently not considering other possible suspects. Rachel hadn't actually said it *wasn't* him.

She picked up two of the photos and went through to the histo lab to check if Niamh had looked at the McCarthy slides she'd asked for when she came back from seeing Michael. She found two trays with a Post-it for her attention on them, took them back into her office and sat down at her microscope.

It didn't take long to confirm that Eileen had been pretty healthy. All her major organs were boringly normal.

The second tray of slides contained the sections of skin that had been taken from the knife wounds. The first slide was labelled *SW4*. Boyd had placed numbered stickers beside each wound and stab wound number 4 was adjacent to the left nipple. The photograph had been taken with a ruler laid beside the gaping stab wound and it was about two centimetres wide. The ends of the wound were pointed, the gaping hole the shape of a rugby ball. Two sharp edges to the blade, she thought. She would expect such a knife to have a sharp tip in that case. She picked up the close-up photo of the breast area: the margins of all the stab wounds were red, not bloody, but looked abraded.

She put the slide on the stage and rotated the lenses, selecting the lowest magnification. Down the scope she could see that the surface layers of the epidermis at the margin of the stab wound had been scraped off, exposing the dermis, the layer beneath it. Whatever had pierced the skin had a blunt tip, and there was an irregularity to this wound, too. As if the tip was not evenly contoured, the way blades usually are. She would have to go back to the report and get the dimensions of each of the stab wounds, the width and the depth, and she would be able to determine the size and shape of the blade. But not tonight.

There were also sections labelled *left shoulder*. She checked the photos: there were two cuts, caused by the blade slicing across the skin. These weren't typical incised wounds, which would be a straight line; the edges of these were uneven. *This is not making sense*, she thought, *this is the kind of injury made by a serrated blade*. She had seen hundreds of examples in Glasgow, where steak knives were often the weapon of choice.

Her eyes flicked over the tissue. It appeared more cellular than she expected. She switched to a higher magnification. The cells were polys – polymorphonuclear leucocytes – the healing cells. Lots of them. She checked the next slide. Same.

The knife cuts on Eileen's shoulder had been inflicted some hours before her death. She hadn't been killed immediately. She was tortured and then killed.

And the killer had punched out the shape of a broken heart into her chest.

64

Terry stood up from the microscope to rest her eyes and let out a long, slow breath as she surveyed the piles of files that had once again formed around her office. Death, the gift that kept on giving.

A human life was a complex thing – full of potential yet could be snuffed out in an instant, the result of an uncontrolled impulse or an accident of fate. Death could catch a person anywhere, for a myriad of reasons or for no reason at all.

And perhaps, she thought, that bitter truth might be the answer to another pressing question: where Jo McCarthy, Eileen's sister, might be. She called John from the landline.

'Hi, just a quick one. I've been having another look at the McCarthy file – I've got the photos and histology now. But I had a thought. You know your friend in the North, Angela?'

'Yeah?'

'I know you asked her about Rachel. But ... maybe it's worth looking at it from a different angle. If Rachel had been trying to trace Jo, Eileen's sister, and had found her, Jo would surely have come forward by now. Unless you're living under a stone, you can't miss the news reports on Rachel's death.'

'You think Jo's dead?' Fraser asked.

'Maybe. Angela told you they had a long list of women who had been killed but whose cases remain unresolved.'

'And you want me to ask Angela for that list?'

'Please, John. I think it'd be really helpful.'

'Terry, no one else is working the Eileen McCarthy case,' Fraser said, picking his words carefully. 'Cleaver has been arrested for Rachel Reece, and those working *that* case are channelling their efforts into building as much evidence as possible to secure a conviction. I thought you were hanging up your spurs.'

She was quiet for a moment. 'I mean, I am. Sort of. Look, it just doesn't *fit* for me. None of it. I might be on to nothing, but I have to try. For Rachel. And for Eileen.'

'And for Jenny,' Fraser said.

Terry bristled. She knew he was right, but his stating it rankled her. A silence hung between them for a few moments.

'So, are you going to ask her for me?' said Terry.

'Yes, I'll ask her.'

'Thanks, John.'

She replaced the handset and felt the familiar sense of blank emptiness that always came when she was unexpectedly reminded of Jenny's death. There was a time when the only ways she knew to cope with the pain were to either stay in bed and let sleep anaesthetise her, or drink until she was so numb the feeling might just as well not be there.

Time and experience had taught her other coping mechanisms, but were they any better? All she knew was that work was a relief.

She picked up the photos of the wounds again, holding them in turn at arm's length, focusing on the details of each wound. She thought about the blade again. What could she tell about it?

The stab wounds looked to have been made by a dagger-like blade, both edges sharp, the hole made in the skin having an oval shape, but the tip was blunt. It had taken some effort to puncture the skin, and the cuts made by the blade being drawn across the skin were irregular, which suggested the cutting edge was not straight, but notched or serrated. Curious, it just didn't make sense, a knife that was like a dagger but not really. Why would the edges of such a blade not be straight? There was a group of parallel scratches running across the skin below the left breast caused when the blade had been pulled out from one of the stab wounds. These were the tell-tale marks of a serrated blade but they were not equidistant. This wasn't a standard knife. Killers were much more predictable in Glasgow; steak knives, bowie knives, swords and machetes, the sharper the better. There was something peculiar about this knife; why bring a duffer of a knife to the party? Was it symbolic?

The photograph of Fraser's wound showed a four centimetre cut with wavy margins. Ordinarily, she would have no hesitation in identifying the weapon as a serrated blade, a common or garden steak knife or similar. But now she was second-guessing herself. Could the same weapon have caused Eileen's and Fraser's wounds?

65

That night back at her flat Terry pulled up online databases of knives and blades on her laptop. She hadn't a clue what she was looking for, but she was certain she'd know as soon as she saw it.

Survival knives could be easily bought over the counter without any proof of either identity or character in countless shops all over the city of Dublin, never mind the rest of the country.

The problem was that very few of these blades were fully serrated, usually having an isolated area of the knife that had serrations, while the rest was traditionally straight-edged. It looked as if the entire weapon that had been used to torture and kill Eileen McCarthy was serrated.

But not evenly – the 'teeth' of the serration seemed to be of different sizes, as were the gaps between them.

A company named Gerber made a blade they called their

Ultimate Survival Knife whose serrated section was designed with a varied serration pattern, but even this had a uniformity to it, the different distances running in a set pattern.

The closest she came to a knife that could have made the wounds to Eileen was a modified bowie knife, based on the model Paul Hogan used in the eighties movie *Crocodile Dundee*, which had a variegated serrated edge on the upper part of the blade. Yet the cuts she was looking at were far too small to have been made by such a large knife – bowie knives were virtually machetes.

After almost an hour and a half she gave up.

Whatever kind of blade had been used, it was unusual.

And she was beginning to believe it was not built by a standard smith.

Next morning in work she slipped down the back stairs to the mortuary and changed into scrubs. Tomas had left the coroner request forms in the changing room for her to read while she was getting ready, and Laura was already in the autopsy room, bustling about organising equipment. The bodies were on the postmortem tables when she walked in.

She checked the body on the nearest table, making sure the name on the form matched the name on the wristband. He was described as a seventy-six-year-old man with a history of heart disease, found dead at home by his home help. The reason given for the postmortem was that *the house was insecure* – the back door had been slightly ajar. She thought the coroner was being ultra cautious. Tomas pointed at the man's lips, which had a blue tinge, and stated, 'Heart attack.' She knew he would probably be right.

On the other table was a middle-aged female described as an alcoholic. She was bright yellow and covered in bruises: liver failure, Terry was sure – jaundice and blood-clotting problems.

Both bodies got the full treatment, scrutinised outside and in, toxicology and histology taken just to be certain there was nothing missed. But she was pretty certain their families would have nothing more to worry about than the cost of the funerals.

She and Laura had a cup of tea with Tomas before Terry headed back to her office. Mrs Carey called to her as she reached the top of the stairs. 'A woman rang and left a message for you.' She peeled a Post-it note from its yellow pad and handed it to Terry.

Annie out of hospital, it read, followed by a mobile number.

'She gave her name as Louise,' Mrs Carey said.

Terry's morning was full, as she had reports to prepare for the coroner, but she decided she'd call over to Finglas at lunchtime. It might be worth a punt. Maybe Annie would have something to add about the McCarthys, and Jo in particular.

She called Louise and asked her to let Annie know she was coming.

'She's had a hip replacement, so she won't be going anywhere further than for a walk up and down the street,' Louise informed her. 'You won't miss her, so don't worry.'

Terry took a taxi over, giving Pádraig the slip once again by exiting the back way. What he didn't know wouldn't hurt him. She instructed the driver to wait and stood patiently after knocking on the door. Annie was bound to be a bit slow after her surgery. She looked around her. The garden appeared neglected and there was a hanging basket next to the door that had seen better days.

'Who's there?' The voice from behind the door was surprisingly strong. Terry had envisaged a frail old woman, bent over, shuffling along the hall. Louise had been as good as her word, because Annie didn't hesitate and opened the door as soon as Terry said who she was.

Annie Byrne stood upright, a stick in her right hand, held as if she was ready to use it as a weapon rather than a walking aid. She eyed Terry up and down then turned and called back over her shoulder, 'Come ahead in. Close the door behind you and put it on the snip. Those bastard moneylenders have a habit of barging in.'

Terry did as she was bid, remembering that Louise had indicated Annie's children were in strife with the local payday-loan racketeers, and followed her into the kitchen.

Annie pointed her stick at Terry. 'Sit!'

The old woman busied herself making tea, refusing any offer of help. There wasn't even a shake of the hand that put a china cup and saucer on the table before Terry.

'I hear you've been asking about Irenie's family. God rest her soul. That old bastard made her life a misery. They met in hospital, you know. She said it was a one in a million chance they got together. She did her best, but I wasn't surprised that the girls got out.'

'How so? Was he violent?'

'You don't know the half of it. But I kept my word to that poor woman. Told no one. Did you know she went to the priest, that sanctimonious git Father McGill? He told her she had made her bed, and it was the Lord's will she remain in it and try to help her husband to change. You wouldn't credit it.'

She sat down heavily across from Terry. 'So what are you after? Same as that young blonde one? God help us from these do-gooders, raking over the past. Nothing good ever comes from it.'

Terry tried to gauge how much Annie Byrne knew. She decided it was best to be straight with her. 'Did Louise tell you that Rachel Reece, the woman who interviewed you, was killed?'

'I saw it on the telly when I was in hospital.' The woman visibly slumped, and now her hands trembled a little as she lifted her cup and took a sip. She fixed her gaze on Terry. 'Was it Liam?'

Terry sat back. 'What? Why would you think that? Mr McCarthy is in a home.'

Annie struggled to her feet and walked slowly to the sink. She grasped the edge of the draining board and kept her back to Terry. 'He was a vicious bastard. Irenie was terrified of him. He suspected I knew what was going on, but I would never have said anything while Irenie was alive. Sure, I was never convinced he was doolally – that would be too bloody good for him. He should have to remember what he did to his family. Though I don't think he ever raised a hand to his girls.'

Terry got up and stood beside the old woman. 'Sit down, Mrs Byrne. Drink some tea.' She gently guided her back to the table.

'That was why Bessie, our old neighbour, left, you know,' Annie continued when she was seated. 'She'd had enough. She never said, but I think he threatened her.'

Annie got up again and shuffled back to the sink. She pulled open the drawer to the right of it and lifted out a photo album. Terry saw that most of the photos underneath it, inside the drawer, were loose. Annie sifted through them and handed one to Terry. 'Irenie, me and her girls. It was Eileen's grad. Irenie was a fine-looking woman, but Eileen, she was a beauty.'

Terry looked at the four women smiling at whoever took the photo. Eileen was very pretty. She must have been about eighteen, blonde hair in curls and a face full of make-up. Beside her was a younger, less vibrant version: mousey hair, a bit hunched over, acne showing on her face. Annie pointed at the figure. 'Poor Jo, always in Eileen's shadow.'

A younger Annie stood on the right side of the group, her stance making her look more like a security guard than a kindly neighbour. At the other end was Irene McCarthy, thin with wispy brown hair and a smile that didn't reach her eyes.

Annie handed Terry another photo. This one had been taken inside one of the terraced houses. 'That's me and Bessie in her front room, just before she moved away.'

The two women were seated on a green floral couch. The window behind was elaborately dressed and the room was crammed with furniture, ornaments on every surface. Bessie had been a tiny twinkly-eyed woman with long hair that, even in the photo, was obviously dyed black.

Annie sat back down. 'Bessie had notions, God love her.

She wanted to be an actress when she was young. I thought it was a bit over the top myself, but she and I were best friends for a lot of years, and that means you have to put up with each other's foibles. How she crammed all the knick-knacks from her theatrical days into that wee house she moved to I'll never know.' She smiled. 'We had some laughs, though. That was probably one of her waifs and strays taking the photo.'

'Did you know the children she fostered?'

'Oh, it was nothing official, like. She just liked to help people out, and when a social worker found out, the health board offered her a few quid as a support worker for youngsters who had just left care. She'd be busiest with them over the summer – they'd be round her place from dawn till dusk. During the rest of the year, they'd have courses or work experience to keep them busy.'

'Did you know a boy whose nickname was BJ? Louise mentioned him.'

'I remember him, yes.'

'Can you recall his full name?'

'No. They all just used to call him BJ. I know he was Bessie's favourite, mind. Clean. A gawky-looking lad, mousy hair, flattened nose and too many teeth for his mouth. He had a bit of a reputation, used to get in fights and that. But Bessie would have none of it. He was always very polite to me, though. He was smart as a whip, too. Had some sort of a smart job – maybe in a gallery or something? I don't remember rightly, something the health board set up for him. He was hoping to go to college, but I'd heard that from some of Bessie's waifs before. Most of them never made it. I don't know if he did or not.'

'I'd like to talk to him. He was friendly with Eileen, wasn't he?'

'Oh yeah. They all ran together at one time.'

'Would you have any idea how I could find him?'

'He'd been in a care home over in Cabra – they might know. Though he's long gone out of there, and kids like that, you never know where they end up, God love them.'

'Your children wouldn't have kept in touch with him?'

'They were that bit older, so they were more pally with Louise. Grand girl that. But BJ? No. I haven't seen him in years. He stopped visiting Bessie after a while, like most of them do. Only a few ever kept coming.'

'Like Frank Cleaver,' Terry said absently, her mind on how she might track this BJ down.

'Yeah. Frank was always loyal to Bessie, as she was to him. Him and BJ were pals too. Bessie loved that lad. No matter what he did.'

Terry finished her tea and stood up. 'Thank you, Annie. I appreciate your time. Do keep me posted if you think of anything. Now I'd best run, I've an appointment at two.'

'No rest for the wicked, eh,' Annie chuckled, 'or for those who try to catch them.'

Terry smiled and told Annie not to get up, that she'd show herself out, then made for the waiting taxi.

She had her hand on the handle of the rear door and was about to get in when a movement caught her eye. In an alley across the road stood a figure dressed in black, a hood obscuring the face. Their eyes locked as he stared at her intently. Tall, broad, menacing. Time seemed to slow down. She was aware of the sounds around her – mothers chatting as they pushed buggies down the street, a refuse-collection truck about a hundred yards to her left, idling as its workers collected the bins and wheeled them to it to be emptied. Her mind felt strangely clear.

In a sudden burst of speed and motion, she stepped around the rear of the taxi and began to walk briskly towards him. He immediately spun and disappeared up the alley. Bolstered by her stalker's retreat, she continued until she was standing exactly on the spot where he had been. He must have been fast, as there was no sign of him in the alley.

When she arrived back in the office, an Insta DM was waiting for her on her laptop.

Let's dispense with the serial killer quotes and speak plainly. We'll meet soon, Dr O'Brien. But not today. You and I have a few moves left in the game before things reach their climax. In the meantime ... I'll be watching.

The time stamp was minutes after she saw her stalker.

66

That evening, Fraser turned up at Terry's work. 'At your service, Dr O'Brien. Gave the boys a night off. You're staying in mine tonight,' he said.

She had called and told him about her encounter in Finglas and the DM, which she had also forwarded to him.

'I've sent a team to check the alleyway, and we're going over CCTV in the area as well,' he told her. 'We might get something.'

'You won't,' she said as they walked to where his car was parked. 'I bet you a steak dinner there won't be any cameras on that alleyway, and that it leads to a bit of waste ground where a car could have been waiting, and the waste ground probably has several exits and two of those lead to by-roads with no speed cameras.'

Fraser looked at her reproachfully. 'You've been watching too many crime dramas,' he said. 'Why don't we just wait and see?'

After a few moments, she went on. 'Is it possible Cleaver had an accomplice? Someone who was in on the killings with him?'

'And then there were two. Multiple deaths, multiple killers. I'm not sure about that Terry.'

Terry thought about it. 'Maybe you're right. Serial killers tend to be narcissistic psychopaths. They don't make great team players. They'd end up killing each other.'

'Well, that would save us a lot of bother,' Fraser said, laughing dryly. 'Could it be someone who was involved with Eileen McCarthy and had been hurt by her too – you've said she was a bit of a wild one. Maybe the whole Rachel Reece thing has drawn them out?'

Terry shook her head. 'And I guess two killers living in one area is statistically unlikely.'

'How long have you been here in Ireland?'

'I'm talking serial killers. You know fine well that's what I mean.'

'Have you thought this guy you saw might have nothing to do with Rachel Reece or Eileen McCarthy,' Fraser went on. 'The work you do, it's not beyond the realms of possibility you've riled up someone. You've handled a few gangland shootings. Those guys play dirty but I don't think they'd be daft enough to take a pop at you. This smacks of someone who wants to put the fear of God in you.'

Terry sighed. 'I'd thought of that, but the messages this guy sends suggest he knows about the case. I believe he's involved. And … whether I like it or not, I'm on his radar.'

'Terry, you've got the weight of An Garda Síochána behind you,' Fraser said. 'He'd be a fucking idiot to think he can snatch you from under our noses. Although if you insist on dodging your escort, there's not much we can do.' She'd had to tell him about giving Pádraig the slip.

'Okay. Point taken. But serial killers tend to reach a point where they almost want to be caught,' Terry said as they crossed O'Connell Bridge. 'Because of the criminal nature of what they do, they can't claim credit for their work. That very often drives them to distraction, which is why so many of them end up writing to or calling the police, taunting them, looking for recognition and even praise.'

'And that's what this guy is doing?'

'It's just a thought. He wants me to pay attention.'

'Well, he's achieved that.' Fraser brought the car to a stop at a red light.

'He says we've got a few moves left before the game reaches its climax,' Terry said. 'Which means he's preparing for the end.'

Fraser turned and looked at her and, for the first time, she saw real fear in his eyes.

67

Coming so close to her in the alley had almost finished it.

He had wanted to end it there and then, had seen the chance to loop his arm around her neck and whisk her away through the maze of alleys to his waiting vehicle.

The desire had been so strong he had been forced to do the only other thing he could think of: run away. By the time he got to the car and gunned it out of the abandoned building site where he'd left it, he was sweating rivulets and sucking his breath in and out frantically.

He had driven as fast as he could without drawing attention to himself, barely even recognising where he was going until he found himself close to his special place, where he planned, very soon, to bring the pathologist.

He had, over the course of his life, studied how to inflict pain. He knew the human body intimately, and how much it could be damaged without ending the individual's life. He knew where to cut to cause maximum pain and where to cut and cause a heavy bleed that would weaken and frighten them, make them believe they were going to die. But not yet.

It was all part of the game he so enjoyed.

He got out of the Ford Fiesta and went into his workshop. He made some tea with the old electric kettle there and began to plan.

He wanted the moment with the pathologist to be special. Nothing hurried or too frenzied. They'd get to spend sometime together. When she saw her end was coming, they would be gazing into each other's eyes.

And in those final moments, she would thank him for her death.

68

Fraser dropped Terry to work the next morning. She'd been subdued all the previous evening and there was little he could do to lighten the mood. He placed a hand on her shoulder as she was getting out of the car. 'Tony will pick you up from work today, okay?'

'I guess.'

'Don't look so dejected.'

'I know, I'm just … pissed off about it all.' She shook her head and got out of the car, closing the door with more force than she had intended.

When she got into the office, she noticed a new email headed *NI deaths* in her inbox. She clicked it open. There was no message, only a Word document attached. She smiled. Angela had come good.

She looked at the list of women killed in Northern Ireland from 2007 to the present. It was less than half of the number south of the border over the same period, but it still made grim reading. These women had been wives, mothers, sisters, daughters, loved by family and friends. And now they were just another statistic.

She got up and walked into the empty kitchen – thankfully, it was too early for the morning coffee break. She gathered her thoughts as she waited for the kettle to boil.

When in doubt, have more coffee.

Back in the office, she set her mug down on the blotter. She decided she would concentrate on the five years after Eileen's death, which narrowed the list down considerably. Of course, there was no Jo McCarthy included, but that didn't mean much. If Jo was fleeing the same fate as her sister, she would have changed her identity.

Angela had included a short summary of each death, including the victim's profile, the circumstances of their death and the cause of death. There were no photographs.

Terry opened up a new Word document and started copying and pasting the most likely candidates. She excluded any women over thirty. She decided to ignore general descriptions of the women – if Jo changed her name, she would certainly have changed her appearance. Terry also decided to work on the premise that if Jo was killed, the modus operandi would be similar to Eileen's. With this in mind, she dismissed a hit-and-run incident, a shooting and two head injuries.

That left six women. Three had been killed by their partners. The three remaining were unresolved. Interestingly, one was unidentified. Of the other two, one had had her throat slit and the other was a single stab wound to the abdomen, which had punctured the aorta.

Terry's instincts were on alert as she read through Angela's notes on the unidentified body. This was a key piece of evidence, something she knew would be a critical building block in her theory that these deaths were linked.

Incomplete, partly skeletonised remains found in Kilbroney Forest Park, County Down, on 2 February 2008.

No clothing or possessions.

Dentist suggests early twenties (dental chart available).

Clump of dyed black hair with skull (found distant to the 'body'/animal scavenging).

Pathologist found notches on ribs 'consistent with knife assault', and also mentioned some discolouration of the costal cartilage, suggested ochronosis.

DNA profile obtained but no match on UK database (missing persons). N.B. No match with any missing person in Ireland (whole).

No group claimed responsibility.

Larynx never recovered. State of remains precluded any comment on sexual activity, consensual or not.

Remains unsolved.

Unsolved, Terry thought. A lost soul, on the run and far from home. Isolated and vulnerable.

Jo, could I have found you?

Terry read through the details one more time. One jumped out at her, something she had noticed when she'd looked at the photographs from Eileen McCarthy's PM but had dismissed as unimportant. Now she saw it in a new light.

She took Eileen's photographs from her desk drawer and spread them out like a pack of cards. She had been so focused on the pattern of the knife wounds she hadn't bothered to look more than once at the internal images, relying instead on Boyd's description in his report.

Luckily he'd had the photographer take one of the ribcage with the skin peeled back. And there it was, the thing she'd noticed first time but not given it a passing thought. The cartilage linking the ribs to the breastbone wasn't glistening white as it should have been but had a mottled grey appearance. If this was what she thought it was, it could be a familial condition that would be shared by siblings.

She went straight to Boyd's office, where she met Mrs Carey on the way out carrying several files and a mug. She greeted Terry and held the door open for her.

Boyd was over at his microscope as she entered. He turned to her and held up a glass slide. 'One less for the gardaí to worry about. Hypertrophic heart. The young chap found dead behind the shopping centre at Blanchardstown last Friday night. Natural causes. Sit!' He waved at the seat on the other side of his desk and sat down opposite.

'Prof, do you have the Eileen McCarthy file? There's something I'd like to check.'

'Anything in particular?'

Was that a defensive note in his voice? She knew exactly what was in the report – she'd made a photocopy of it, after all – but she had to give him the opportunity to come to the same conclusion she had. Accusing him of missing something would only be counterproductive. She needed him onside.

'Was there any mention at the time of a family history of alkaptonuria?'

'Alkaptonuria. Black urine disease. I don't think I've come across it in a case before. Why would you consider it? What has the family history of an old case of mine got to do with anything you're dealing with?' There was a note of warning in his voice.

'Something or nothing is the honest answer.' She had come this far – what was there to lose, aside from her job? She ploughed on. 'Eileen McCarthy's name has come up time and again in the Rachel Reece investigation. And now there has been a suggestion that her sister may have been murdered.'

'Suggestion?'

'Well, I have reason to believe she was murdered in the north. In fact, I think I might have found her.'

'I'm confused. What has this to do with the death of the Reece woman?'

'The gardaí, including DCS Sinnott, are now of a mind that we could be dealing with someone who has killed before.' Another white lie to add to the others. She hadn't a clue what Sinnott thought, but Fraser was coming round.

'A serial killer in Ireland?'

Terry said nothing. She hoped the mention of Sinnott would suffice to gain his cooperation.

Boyd kept his eyes on her as he stretched across his desk and pulled a pile of files over. He carefully chose a blue folder, the colour used for the files for the year of Eileen McCarthy's death, 2007. He opened it and took out the report it contained.

'There's no mention of that in the coroner's request. Nothing from the gardaí either.' He raised his eyes to Terry. 'Hold on!' He leafed through the report again. 'Ah! *The rib ends were dusky*. You think that is ochronosis, black cartilage?'

'Maybe. It's not a diagnosis you make with the naked eye.' Terry tried to sound nonchalant. 'Would there be any histology?'

Boyd looked down at the report, turned to the last page and read: '*Histology confirmed that there was no evidence of natural disease which caused or contributed to her death.*' He looked up. 'Does that answer your question?'

'Not really.'

Boyd sat quietly for a moment. 'Let's come back to my original question. What bearing does this have on this alleged serial-killer theory?'

'None,' she said. 'But it might be important in finding Eileen McCarthy's sister.'

Boyd gave her a hard look.

'Jo McCarthy took off shortly after her sister Eileen was murdered,' Terry went on, 'and seems to have disappeared. I thought finding her might shed some light on the circumstances. As I said, I think I might have traced her.'

'*Might?*'

'As I said, I think she may have been murdered.'

Boyd's face was crimson. 'Dr O'Brien! I was prepared to cut you some slack, but now I think I may have made a mistake.'

Terry stood her ground. 'The body of a young woman was found in Northern Ireland, early 2008. She was murdered. The body was never identified. The pathologist at the time in

Belfast, I can't remember his name, described a discolouration of the cartilage around the ribs and diagnosed ochronosis, the dark discolouration associated with the genetic condition alkaptonuria, which is fairly uncommon, so this is an important point. I think it may be Jo McCarthy'

The atmosphere could be cut with a knife. Boyd, his face red, picked up the handset on his desk phone and punched in a number.

He turned again to Terry. 'The presence or absence of alkaptonuria would have had no bearing on Miss McCarthy's cause of death, nor would it have assisted in identifying her killer. It would have been immaterial to any investigation. However, now that it has been brought to my attention, and that confirming the diagnosis may identify a Jane Doe—' He cut off as the call was answered. 'Niamh. I want you to look out the histology slides for Eileen McCarthy,' he said, 'number 51 of 07. Thanks.'

Terry's stomach dropped – those slides were already sitting in her office, given to her by Niamh. Thank God he hadn't given Niamh enough time to say anything, but who knew what she might say later.

Boyd immediately made another call. 'Tomas, can you check the retained specimens in the basement for number 51 of 2007? Bring anything you find up to Niamh.'

He turned his attention back to Terry. 'Luckily I decided back in 2002 that we should retain all specimens for twenty years. But let me tell you, *Detective* O'Brien,' he said, 'this better be leading somewhere or there will be questions to answer. Ms Reece had the impertinence to question my competence and professionalism. It is hard to explain to those with preconceived ideas that even death is not always black or white.'

'I wish. Mainly it's a murky grey. What did she want to know?'

'That was the issue I had, she didn't want to ask questions. Instead, she hurled a series of accusations at me. Including colluding with the gardaí to cover up their inadequate investigation of the McCarthy death. I told her in no uncertain terms that that was not the case. I hold my hand up to not recognising the cartilage changes, but that omission would not have affected the investigation.'

'I agree. But did you think there was anything odd about the case?'

'I did think that the knife injuries were not typical, but no knife was ever recovered.'

'I'm having the same thoughts myself.'

But while her boss was doing his best to look stern, Terry could see that she had his attention.

Back at her desk Terry DM'd Clara Dunwoody from her laptop and asked her to call her office number. Moments later they spoke, and Clara asked about Rachel's case.

'We've nothing concrete as yet, I'm sorry,' said Terry, 'but we've got a few leads.'

'Well, that's promising, I suppose.' Clara sounded flat.

'Are you getting on okay with your police protection?'

'Yes, James and Ben are both very nice. It's a comfort having them there.'

'Any sign of your stalker?'

'No, not at all. I wonder if the two boys have scared him off.'

'It's possible.'

'I mean, there were times before where I could *feel* he was there, even though I didn't see him. But to be honest, since I talked to you, I haven't had that sense, not once. Maybe I was imagining things.'

'Well, here's hoping.' Terry did her best to sound cheerful.

'Let me know as soon as there's a break in the case.'

'Don't worry, Clara. You'll be informed.'

'Thank you, Doctor. I appreciate the chat.'

'No worries.'

Terry hung up, wondering if Clara's stalker really had been scared off. Or if he'd just transferred his interests to her.

69

Terry had another look at Eileen McCarthy's histology slides, but she already knew they'd tell her nothing. Boyd had only sampled the main organs. There was heart, lung, liver, kidney and spleen. But no cartilage or bone. A dead end.

She sat back, feeling deflated, just as Niamh appeared in her doorway. 'Doc, Tomas brought up a couple of bags of stuff connected with those slides. More samples, I think.'

'Where are they?'

'Follow me. And by the way, I wouldn't have mentioned anything to Boyd, don't worry. I know what people say about me, but I can keep my mouth shut when it matters.'

When they arrived at the lab, Laura, who was bent over a microscope, looked up and waved before returning to her task.

On the dissecting bench were two freezer bags, the kind people use in their kitchens for storing food. The labels identified them as 51/07 EMcC. The small bag contained scraps of heart and the other internal organs. Nothing that hadn't been processed.

She turned her attention to the bigger bag. This was more like it. Through the clear plastic she could see what looked like a couple of ribs partly submerged in murky fluid. She carefully cut the bag open and tipped the contents into the colander in the sink. There were two short segments of rib and some other bits and pieces.

Carefully she lifted out the bones and rinsed them in cold water. The ribs had been cut in half during the postmortem, the front halves saved. She would need Michael to have a look at them and tell her which ribs they were, but she suspected they were from the left side of the ribcage and probably the fifth and sixth, the ones in front of the heart.

Each rib showed one cut end and one smooth rounded end. She felt along the borders and found a nick in each bone that lined up when she laid the bones one on top of the other. A knife had penetrated between the ribs notching the bottom edge of one and the top edge of the other as the blade had slid through, seeking out the heart.

And she could feel that the notches were slightly jagged and uneven.

She ran water over the gubbins in the bottom of the colander. She shook it as if she was divining for gold. If she had been she would have been a very rich lady, for there, lying on the shiny steel, was a long narrow piece of tissue looking like the false witch's nails she had seen kids wearing at Halloween.

It was the piece of cartilage that had joined one of the ribs to the breastbone. It should have been creamy white, but instead it was a strange grey colour.

She called Fraser. 'I think I've found Jo McCarthy.'

70

Fraser agreed to contact Angela for access to the full file on the investigation into the death of the unidentified woman. He also undertook to make an application for access to the medical records of the McCarthy family. But that would all take time.

'You know what the data protection laws are like,' he said. 'Even for a murder investigation they make you jump through all kinds of hoops.'

'Thanks, John. I appreciate your trying, anyway.'

'No worries.'

They were both quiet for a moment.

'Sorry for slamming the car door this morning,' Terry said, breaking the silence.

'It's okay. I know it's hard. Nearly as hard as you slammed that door.'

Terry couldn't help but smile. When their call ended, she sat for a moment, thinking about how to circumvent her problem. She reached for her phone again. 'Hi, Rose, Terry O'Brien here.'

'Terry, good to hear from you.'

Dr Rose Farrell was a forensic pathologist who had done her forensic training in Edinburgh. She had been a paediatric pathologist but was enticed to the dark side after she got involved in a case where a mother was accused of smothering her baby. Rose diagnosed a genetic heart defect and argued that the pathologist who had carried out the postmortem on the baby wasn't trained to recognise natural disease in children. The mother was found not guilty and Rose had found her calling. She was renowned for her no-nonsense approach. She had joined the Belfast Office of the State Pathologist about a year before Terry moved to Dublin.

'I've been meaning to call you. I could do with a female ally in Ireland, even as far afield as Belfast.'

'Ah! Charlie Boyd getting to you, is he?'

Terry could hear the amusement in Rose's voice. 'You could say that.'

'Something tells me that's not why you're phoning, though.'

'You know me too well.'

Terry quickly went over the two killings. Rachel Reece's murder had been widely reported so Rose was aware of it, but she knew nothing of Eileen McCarthy.

'And how can I help?' Rose sounded puzzled. 'Is there a link between the recent murder and this woman McCarthy?'

'I think so. The intriguing part, and this is where you come in, is that Eileen's sister, Jo, may have disappeared soon after her sister's death. Rachel Reece, who was investigating Eileen's death at the time she was murdered, seemed to believe Eileen's sister had travelled to the North. And I thought, *What if she was murdered too?*'

'That's a bit of a leap, even for a forensic pathologist.'

Terry told her about Angela Kirkpatrick getting involved and how she had narrowed down the list of women murdered in Northern Ireland within a couple of years of Eileen McCarthy's murder to one, and mentioned the similarity in the discolouration of the cartilage and her suspicion of alkaptonuria as a familial trait.

Terry had expected some resistance so was surprised when Rose readily agreed to email the postmortem report. Not only that, she said she would send any photographs and check if there was any histology.

Shortly after, Rose called Terry back. 'I've got the report. Dear oh dear! It's shocking what some of the old boys churned out. Noel, the last-but-one chief state pathologist, was a strange one by all accounts. He was a bit of a Scrooge, had some odd ideas too. If a body was unlikely to be identified, he wouldn't use departmental funds on *unnecessary investigations*.'

'So, what did he do in this case?'

'Not much. But it would appear he wasn't a complete tit. He did keep tissue, just in case. As luck would have it, I have a jar, a very large jar, full of all sorts.'

'Brilliant, Rose.'

'Look, I'll have to check with the coroner if I can process

it. Leave it with me.'

'Rose, you're a star.'

Ten minutes later an email pinged into Terry's inbox. She double clicked on the Word document attached.

'*Dyed black hair, blonde at roots, 20 inches long ... multiple knife notches on the ribs ... grey discolouration of costal cartilage ...*'

There was a second file attached, *2/2008 Photographs*. There must have been about eighty thumbnails. Noel Barker might have scrimped where *his* budget was concerned, but he had no such concerns for the other state departments.

The body was laid out in its anatomical position. She could see why it had not been identifiable. The head, or rather the skull, was detached, propped up by a sponge. The right hand and ulna were missing. The right leg was largely skeletonised from the knee down, the toes nibbled. There were patches of skin remaining on the trunk.

Scavengers had made their mark. Terry guessed there had only been a half-hearted attempt to conceal the body, her killer relying on the remote location and exposure to the elements to hide his tracks. Flies and animals would be attracted to bleeding injuries and she could see small toothmarks on the edges of the skin remaining. There was a large hole in the skin over the left side of the chest, exactly where there had been stab wounds on Eileen.

Luckily the knife had struck bone or Dr Barker would have been hard pressed to be certain the woman had been stabbed, as her internal organs had provided a tasty meal for the forest fauna. Terry magnified the nick and could clearly make out its rough, irregular nature, almost like a saw cut. A notched blade.

The body had been photographed from head to toe. If Dr Barker was a man of few words, going by the brevity of the report, he liked a visual record. Terry methodically went through the photographs. She had seen enough to know there was a good chance she was looking at Jo McCarthy. The histology would be the clincher.

Her serial-killer case was building and she knew it.

71

At 5.30 that evening, Terry was finishing up a report on a hit-and-run death that had come in the previous week when a knock came on her office door and Fraser entered, unannounced.

'What brings you here?' she said.

'Just passing,' he said. 'Decided to call by.' He took a bundle of files off her guest chair and sat down. 'No Laura?'

'She's doing some work with Michael right now. I thought it would be good for her to see the whole gamut of the forensic world.'

'I'm sure he's taking good care of her.'

'No doubt.' Terry looked at Fraser quizzically. 'So, what really brings you here?'

'There was something I wanted to talk to you about,' he said. 'We're almost ready to charge Cleaver. I thought you'd want to know.'

'Any new evidence?'

'There is. CCTV of Cleaver breaking into Rachel's back yard from a neighbour's camera – he used their garden to gain access. He was testing the back door and windows of her house.'

'That's still circumstantial.'

'Agreed. But it speaks to intent. And a T-shirt's been found in a drain one street away from Cleaver's house. Rachel's housemate says she had one similar.'

'Seriously?' Terry said. 'Intent. Intent to what? Hanging about someone's back garden doesn't indicate murderous intent. And a T-shirt? In Michael's words, are you fucking joking me? And what do Michael and Monica MacKenzie say? Do you have any proper physical evidence?'

'Yes.'

Terry blinked. 'What?'

'I was saving the best for last. We got a search warrant for Cleaver's house.'

Terry nodded. 'What did you find?'

'A hair. It was on a doorjamb in an upstairs room.'

'And that's been sent to FSI? DNA tests being done?'

'Fast-tracked. The minister himself directed it. Results due in a couple of hours.'

'Good luck with that. Even if it is Rachel's, it still doesn't mean—'

'Terry, without video footage of him murdering her or a signed confession, there's always a margin for doubt, but if you put everything we have together ... well, it's up to the DPP. Sinnott's ready to charge him, and I have to say, I think this one will go all the way to court.'

'And what about the mushrooms? Where do they fit? You know that calling card isn't Cleaver.'

'Who knows – maybe it was an accident? A bird swallowed them and shat the spores out or something. I don't know, Terry. But what we have – it's enough to move.'

'Okay, John. But if you do charge him, let me know if his solicitor wants a defence postmortem done on her remains. Tomas will need to get the body out of the freezer to defrost.'

'Shit. Really?'

'If I didn't freeze the body, it would be nothing but a rickle of bones. And I've still got to take a sample of the vaginal bruise to see if it was fresh. If there was going to be a defence postmortem, the other pathologist would need to see the injury before I start chopping it up. But if Cleaver's defence team aren't calling for one, I need to get on to that double quick so the boys in the mortuary can reconstruct the body before the undertakers whisk her away.'

He nodded and stood. 'Okay, I'll let you know as soon as I hear. I'd best get back. There's a lot to do.'

'Okay. I'm going to take it easy tonight, have a quiet one,' said Terry. 'Talk tomorrow.'

She finished up her work absentmindedly after he left. Even in the face of everything Fraser had just told her, she felt sure they were on the wrong track. The MO emerging was of a serial killer with a sophisticated mind, one whose methods were evolving to become more controlled, exacting – even under stress. They took extraordinary care not to leave trace evidence and their calling card suggested this was no ordinary crimina. From everything she'd read about his methods, Cleaver was as ordinary as they came – rough, tough and totally lacking finesse. Though sexual assault couldn't be ruled out of the McCarthy and Reece cases, Cleaver's brand of sexual violence would inevitably leave a trace.

The question was whether, in the face of government pressure and a building media storm over the Rachel Reece murder, it would make any difference, now they had what they needed to arrest him.

72

The following day was Friday, and Terry had to deal with a fire death in Galway. Technically, Boyd was on call for road trips, but he'd had some lunch thing at the College of Surgeons and it would do no harm for her to get the brownie points by offering to go. It turned out to be a long day. The Fire Brigade weren't happy letting the forensic team into the scene, and it was mid-afternoon before the technical bureau had it secure and photographed.

The body was finally taken to the regional hospital and she managed to sweet-talk a radiographer into X-raying it. She soon has confirmation that it was indeed a man, he'd had a hip replacement and only about four teeth, so must have run into a dentist at some point when he lost the others. The outside of the body was charred but the insides were relatively preserved, enough for her to confirm he had died from the fire fumes. She even got blood for toxicology and DNA. It was one in the morning when Pádraig dropped her back at the flat. At least she could have a lie-in as Boyd was on call for the weekend.

She tossed and turned all night, finally getting up at 5.30 to make coffee. She pulled back the curtain and looked out the front window. Tony, who had replaced Pádraig, was sitting outside in the patrol car. She rapped hard on the window and mimed drinking a cup of something. He didn't need persuading. Within a minute, the tall, weathered-looking guard with the build of a rugby player was at her door.

'Can I ask you something?' she said when he was seated at the table, mug in hand.

'Go for it,' he said.

'Do you believe I'm being stalked?'

'You and DCI Fraser were attacked, weren't you?'

'I've still got the scars to prove it,' Terry said, tapping the plaster on her temple.

'And the DCI said when you gave me and Pádraig the slip and headed to Finglas, you saw someone watching you.'

'Well, I thought I did. He scuttled off pretty sharpish,' Terry said.

'Your description of the guy in the park matches your guy in Finglas. So, yeah, could be someone is watching you.' He took a big mouthful of coffee, half-emptying the mug.

'Have you or Pádraig seen anyone since you started keeping an eye on me?'

'No. Doesn't mean there's no one there, though.'

'Have you seen anything suspicious?'

'No. But like I said ...'

'Yeah, yeah, I get it. Can I ask who you think this potential stalker might be?'

Tony shrugged, refilling his coffee mug from the jug Terry had made.

'I'm asking you. I want to know what you think.'

The big guard looked embarrassed. 'I ... well, some of the lads think you've got yourself a fan.'

Terry laughed out loud. 'You think this is just a true-crime nutter?'

'I do. A lot of us do.'

'Based on what?'

'I don't think I should say any more.' Tony looked embarrassed. 'I shouldn't have opened my mouth.'

'Go on. Tell me.'

'Okay. Well, Doc, some of those true-crime fans are seriously weird.'

'Yes, I know. A lot of them are forensic pathologists.'

'No, seriously, Doc. They get fixated on people like yourself. You're in the papers every time there's a suspicious death. They think they know you.'

'Well, they don't. Someone hit me on the head with a stick and stabbed DCI Fraser? How does that fit? It's hardly a sign of hero worship.'

'I never said the guy was sane,' Tony said. 'See, that's why they put us in uniforms. We all look the same. You don't.'

'Wow,' Terry said.

'You did ask,' Tony said. 'Sorry.'

She watched him from the window as he returned to the

car. He checked up and down the street, picked something out of his teeth and climbed into the driver's seat.

They all think the same, she thought. *That I brought this on myself, attracting some crazed weirdo – not that the serial killer has fixated on me. Rachel was right: they wouldn't have taken her seriously if she'd reported her stalker.*

73

He loved knives.

They were one of the oldest tools humans used as a species. As a young man he had marvelled over worked flint pieces, their edges so sharp he was certain you could shave with them.

He had seen a knife once made of crystal – it was Mayan, more than a thousand years old, and was in a museum in Mexico. He had stood gazing into the display case, transfixed by its beauty.

The first time he'd realised the majestic power of a knife he had been thirteen and in the care home. He was in the kitchen, and one of the girls had been ragging on him yet again.

One of the staff had been preparing dinner and had left to go to the bathroom. In a fit of pique, he had grabbed the small sharp knife the woman had been using to peel potatoes.

'If you say one more word, I'll cut your tits off!' he'd said.

The bitch had backed off after that. She'd told on him, he denied it. Sister Bridget had stuck up for him, she always did, and nothing had come of it.

Well, almost nothing.

He began to fantasise about what it would have been like to actually cut her.

Now, sitting in this office, the building quiet with only the cleaners about, he fantasised about cutting the pathologist. He dreamed of the joy it would bring, and he smiled. Not long now.

This one was different, though.

He would not just take the pathologist. He stared at the empty bell jar on his desk. Soon it would contain her heart.

74

Terry spent the morning mindlessly watching TV, flicking from one channel to another until finally settling on an episode of *Murder, She Wrote*. Jessica Fletcher was on holiday in Ireland meeting her Irish cousins – who had the most dubious Irish accents Terry had ever heard – when people started to get murdered, the deaths all of potential benefactors to a will that was about to be read.

'I don't know why you're never a suspect, Mrs Fletcher,' Terry said to the screen. 'Surely someone has noticed you're a common denominator in hundreds of murders at this stage.'

Her WhatsApp buzzed on her laptop – a message from Annie Byrne who'd been trying to call her. Christ, it was a nightmare having no phone. She texted her back to say she'd WhatsApp call her and moments later they were speaking.

'You said to call if I thought of anything,' said Annie.

'I did, yes.'

'Well, Louise took me for a cup of tea in a café we like over Cabra way yesterday, and while we were over there we ran into Sister Alphonsus – she's pally with Father Ward. Always complained about Bessie's flower arrangements. It was her that put Bessie in touch with the care home that young lad BJ was in. Not that she would have anything to do with the kids. Bride of Christ my arse. Pardon my French, Doctor. She told me that the nun who worked in the home around that time was Sister Bridget. She's retired and has been in a nursing home since she got the Covid. She's getting out soon and they're going to ship her over to their headquarters, whatever they call it, to spend her retirement. It's someplace in England, so if you want to talk to her, you don't have much time.'

'I appreciate that, Annie, thanks a million.'

'Sister Alphonsus said she'd tell Bridget you'd be in touch. I said it could be this weekend.'

'That's great. I really appreciate it. Have you got the address?'

The carer at the home agreed Terry could visit the nun as long as she kept it short, as she was in frail health. 'What's it about anyway?' she asked.

'One of the boys in the care home,' explained Terry. 'I just want to ask her a few questions.'

'She's one of the nicest women I know,' said the carer. 'She's still very emotionally invested in the children she cared for, and when they get into trouble it does affect her. Do you know, she still gets cards from some of them.'

'Don't worry,' Terry reassured her. 'I've no reason to think the person I'm asking about has done anything wrong. I just want to track him down so I can see if he has any information that might help with a case I'm working.'

'Grand so. I'll let her know you're here.'

The nursing home was very different to the one Eileen's father lived in. His was like an old-school hotel, while St Mary's was brand spanking new, every item of furniture looking as if it had just been taken from the showroom floor of IKEA.

Terry was shown into a sparsely decorated room with a small table and four chairs. A teapot, mugs, milk, sugar and a plate of chocolate digestives were set out on the table, and a tiny, round, smiling-faced woman with a cloud of white hair was sitting waiting for her, dressed in a blue cardigan and skirt, a crucifix on a gold chain hanging under the collar of her white blouse.

'I'm Sister Bridget,' the old woman said, standing shakily and taking Terry's hands.

'Thank you for agreeing to meet me, sister,' said Terry. 'I wanted to talk to you about a young man the kids used to call BJ. I believe he would have been in the residential care home from the early nineties until maybe 2005, 2006?'

'Bobby, yes,' the old nun said. 'Bobby Joyce was his name.'

'Joyce, did you say?' said Terry, her antennae raised.

'That's right. I think he was with us from a bit earlier than that, though. He was taken into care in the 1980s, unless I'm much mistaken. He did stay a bit longer than most because he had nowhere else to go and was doing some courses. The law states that care residents can remain in care into their twenties so long as they're in education. He'd had a very tough time at home. Why are you asking about him?'

'I know you're bound by confidentiality,' Terry said, 'and I respect that. But he was friends with two young women who were murdered, and I'd really like to talk to him about them. Are you still in contact with him?'

Bridget sighed and shifted in her seat. She lifted her crucifix to her lips and kissed it. 'Do you think he had something to do with their deaths, these two poor women?'

'Why would you ask that?' Terry wanted to know.

'Bobby – he was an angry boy. All the time angry. He'd been badly let down by his family, his mother and sisters. It was as if … well, as if now he was away from them he wanted to hurt the world before it hurt him. We worked very hard with Bobby on controlling his rage, but it was always a problem.'

'Did he get into fights?' Terry asked.

'At first, yes. He hurt a couple of the boys who bullied him, put one of them in the hospital. The boy broke Bobby's nose, but that seemed to only make him angrier. He was one of those children who had been so abused that he didn't seem to feel pain any more. After that the kids knew to leave him alone.'

'Did he receive therapy?'

'He was sent to a child psychologist over in the Mater. I'm afraid I don't recall his name.'

'Did he get on okay in school?'

'Oh, he was clever. Gifted, I'd say. We always encouraged the clever ones. He did well in primary school and was in honours classes right the way through secondary.'

'Did he go to university?'

'Ah …' Bridget said, and looked down at the table for a moment. 'He should have. But in those days child services were not well resourced. He was sent to do some courses in further education colleges, I know, but most of our children are set up with jobs ultimately. That would have happened for him, too.'

'Do you know where he was employed?'

Bridget puzzled over that. 'I was never involved in the after-care programme,' she said. 'When they leave us, not many of them keep in touch.'

'Where might I find out?'

'If you call After Care Services at Cabra Social Work Department, someone might be able to tell you.'

'Thank you, Sister,' Terry said and bent down to pick up her bag from the floor as she stood up.

'You're welcome. I hope you find him. I worry about him, sometimes. He had such a lot to deal with, poor Bobby. Before and after he was with us, life was cruel to him.'

'Do you remember if he had sisters?' Terry asked.

'Yes. God rest them.'

'What happened to them?'

'Bobby's two sisters were found murdered five years after he left St Matthew's. Poor Bobby. The gardaí treated him like a criminal.'

'He was brought in for questioning?'

'Yes. They even spoke to me at the time. I told them about his anger issues when he was young but that I didn't think he was capable of doing something so heinous. He hadn't seen his sisters for years. His family abandoned him. Maybe I was wrong.' The nun slumped back in her chair.

'Did you see him after that?'

'No. I still get Father Ward to offer a mass on the anniversary of their deaths. God rest their souls.'

Terry thought about the pink folder she had found on Boyd's desk the day she went looking for the McCarthy file. She hadn't known how the Joyce cases were relevant, but now she did. And Rachel Reece had followed this trail before her. She needed to look at those files.

75

'Let me guess,' said Fraser when she was seated opposite him in Kevin Street thirty minutes later. 'You didn't want to turn up *wherever* you were going in a garda car, and you've given the boys the slip, again.'

'In a word, yes. But, John, listen to me. You know it hasn't sat right with me that Cleaver murdered Rachel Reece.'

'I do.'

'We know Rachel Reece had been looking into the McCarthy murder, and it seems reasonable that something linked to it may have been behind her death.'

'And you think we didn't think about that? You do know how murder investigations work? Do you know how many statements have been taken? Not to mention that Cleaver is a link! I'm sorry, Terry, but you're in danger of pissing me off as well. Sinnott did warn me.'

'Sinnott. Of course. Back to the old boys' club. Well, did your *old boys* look at Bobby Joyce?'

'As a matter of fact, yes. After you messaged me his name on your way here, I put a call into HQ. I'm waiting for the files to come through, but it seems that he was questioned at the time his sisters were killed, and had a firm alibi. Not that there was any evidence to pin on him – or anyone else, for that matter.'

'Okay. But—'

'No buts, Terry. His name also came up at the time of Eileen McCarthy's murder, but by that time he appeared to have vanished into thin air. There is no way round it. The investigation leads us to Cleaver's door. Rachel visited him in prison as part of her investigation, and he responded by making a threat against her, seeking her out once he got out of prison, even going so far as to break into her yard to scope out access points to her home.'

'It sounded more to me that he threatened to find her when he got out and rape her. Not kill her. Frank Cleaver has never killed anyone, as far as you know, and I don't believe he intended to murder Rachel Reece either. In fact, I just think he got a kick out of putting the fear of God into her. And you've got nothing else. I bet that T-shirt was a red herring.'

Fraser shrugged. 'Terry, we have a hair from his home that belongs to Rachel. The DNA is back.'

'Yes but how did it get there?' Terry asked. 'Rachel visited Cleaver in the prison. A hair could have come adrift and he could have taken it, or he might even have removed it from her shoulder or sleeve when she wasn't paying attention.'

'That's a reach, Terry, even for you. And what, he took it

home and somehow it got caught on the door handle? And was still there weeks later?'

'It could have been planted.'

'Who by?'

'I don't know. It just seems too ... *convenient.*'

Fraser sighed and rubbed his eyes. 'Terry, convenient or not, it is hard evidence. Sinnott is of the opinion it's enough on top of what we already have on him.'

'And you agree.' It was a statement. She realised that Fraser wasn't so firmly in her corner as she'd thought.

'Right, forget Cleaver. Go on: Eileen McCarthy. Let's hear your theories.'

Terry had nothing to lose. 'Rachel investigates Eileen McCarthy. As you know, Eileen's sister, Jo, went missing shortly after Eileen's death. We now know Jo was also murdered. Then there's Rachel's foster sister, Clara Dunwoody. The description of the man who's following her matches the description of the guy who jumped us in the park, and I'm pretty damn sure he's the same guy I saw in Finglas. And he's categorically *not* Cleaver. You'd fit two of Frank Cleaver into this guy.'

'Well, I'll agree with you there – Cleaver's no Mr Universe,' Fraser said. 'But again, you're making one mighty big assumption about this big guy. As you would say, it's a bit too convenient, one man responsible for everything. I think there's a much simpler explanation for our attack, to do with drugs. So I would leave us out of the equation.'

'Rachel Reece and Clara Dunwoody,' Terry continued. 'Eileen and Jo McCarthy. Two sets of sisters.'

'Two doesn't necessarily make a pattern,' Fraser said. 'And

what about Tina McCabe? You seem convinced she fits in here too.'

'She's a spanner in the works, I agree,' Terry said. 'But I still believe her death has something to do with it.'

'There is not one shred of evidence to say she was murdered,' Fraser said, staring at her steely-eyed.

'Not as *yet*,' she said.

'Look, you may be right about our attack being linked to McCabe, but not in the way you suggest,' Fraser said. 'You're still not convincing me on the rest.'

'Here's the clincher,' Terry said, leaning forward. 'The Joyce sisters were murdered a few years after Bobby got out of care. I think Rachel Reece made this link when she was researching Eileen's murder, and asked Professor Boyd about the Joyces as well when she came to interview him that time. I found the file on their PMs in his office attached to Eileen McCarthy's with an elastic band.'

'So?' Fraser said.

'Bobby Joyce *knew* Eileen and Jo McCarthy.'

Fraser nodded. 'So let me see if I have your reasoning: Reece links Bobby Joyce to McCarthy and that leads her to the Joyces, therefore Bobby Joyce is the killer. Have I got it right?' He stared at her, his face impassive. 'I suggest, Terry, that before you go about making such accusations, you do what you know best: go back to the pathology on these cases and get me some kind of physical evidence that'll tie it all together.'

'Well, the old nun immediately asked if I thought he'd had anything to do with the McCarthy deaths. But, okay, Michael and Laura are looking for mushroom spores on Tina

McCabe's sleeping bag. That would link her and Rachel for definite. If I can find them on the others, we'll know that this is the calling card of a serial killer. And whatever evidence you have for Cleaver killing Rachel Reece, you will never be able to make the case for him as the mastermind between a string of murders. You'll have to widen the search.'

Fraser looked at her doubtfully.

The Forensic Pathology building was quiet when Terry arrived back. The yellow folder was still in her office, at the bottom of the pile on the corner of her desk. She pulled it out to re-familiarise herself with the Joyce case but she couldn't focus. Her meeting with Fraser hadn't gone to plan. Not for the first time, she wondered if she had made a mistake trusting him. From now on, she would have to rely on her own instincts.

The lack of photos in the Joyce file was bugging her. Where the hell were they?

She tore down to the records room, her footsteps echoing in the empty halls, and punched her code into the digital door lock. She made her way to the shelves for 2004 and located the empty space the Joyce file had recently occupied. Nothing. 'Fuck,' she muttered, casting about for anywhere the photos might have fallen out.

She called Vinnie, who never seemed to be on a day off. 'I'm looking for photos for a PM report dating back to 2004. Any idea where they might be?'

'All those photographs were sent to be digitised.'

'How long ago?'

'About six months. The process seems to be going *very* slowly. Can I ask how far in the file is?'

'It's 34.'

'You might be in luck. If you go to the rear of the filing room there's a trolley the photographs are left on in batches to be picked up when we have time to process them. They're safer in your place – things tend to wander over here in HQ. If they haven't been taken yet, they'll be there.'

She did as he suggested. The trolley was where he'd indicated, and she rifled through the sets of envelopes, each labelled with a name and a number. The Joyce file was the third one in.

This time, she went straight to the conference room, spilling the photos out on the long table and arranging them into two sets, one for each of the sisters.

The first thing that struck her was the ferocity of the attacks. They were frenzied. The wounds had been delivered with such force they went right through to bone – Anne had almost been decapitated so ferocious was the cut to her throat.

He was barely in control of himself, Terry thought. *It's like he was on the verge of just letting loose and tearing them apart.* She envisioned him, wild-eyed, the hand clutching the knife slicing through the air over and again. Blood spewing out. She screwed her eyes shut but she couldn't see the knife and she couldn't see his face.

Her eyes ran down the set of prints until she found the ones she was really looking for – the wide shot of the women's torsos.

And there it was: the cuts were deeper, more open, less refined in their execution, but the jagged, rough markings of an unusual blade were clearly visible, as was the distinct five-stroke broken-heart pattern. It was present on both women, just as it had been on Eileen McCarthy.

As it most surely would have been on Jo McCarthy, too, if she'd been discovered before the animals and the elements got to her. Terry knew she was right.

'I'm coming for you,' she said, her voice low. 'You got away with it for a long time, but I'm coming for you.'

76

Terry spent a quiet Sunday alone. She declined Fraser's suggestion of a movie, instead opting to spend the night with a bottle of Sancerre and a few episodes of *Schitt's Creek*, ensuring oblivion and only a slight hangover. He'd sounded a bit hurt – maybe Michael was right and she was afraid of intimacy – but right now it just felt better to be alone. She was tired of people doubting her – deep down, she did enough of that herself for a small army. Whatever silly thoughts she'd briefly had that herself and Fraser would uncover the truth of Rachel's murder together, she knew now she had to let it go.

The night she slept fitfully, waking from her recurring nightmare of Jenny. But this time it ended differently. Her sister was screaming at her to run, but instead of taking off along the path as fast as her legs would carry her, now

Terry turned and faced a tall, dark figure. She began to walk towards him but he was gone.

The following morning, after PMing two drop-deads and a drowning, she called Michael. 'How's the work on the sleeping bag going?'

'Slowly. We're leaving nothing to chance, so we've approached it like a grid search. So far, no spores have turned up, but we've a little under half the outer, or is it inner, layer to get through yet.'

'Thanks, Michael. I appreciate it.'

She was on her way up from the mortuary when Mrs Carey called down to say that a courier had just arrived with some further samples for her. When she went to sign for them, she discovered that Rose, as good as her word, had secured the histo work from Jo McCarthy.

She grabbed the evidence bags and dropped into the histo lab. She emptied the contents onto the dissection bench and spread them out. There it was, a small plastic bag labelled *head hair*. The DNA profile of the person she believed was Jo McCarthy was on the Northern Ireland DNA database, and eventually this would be released to FSI for comparison with Eileen's DNA. But this way Michael could have a result within the day, and Jo's DNA profile would be entered on their own DNA database. Another missing person crossed off the list.

She headed over to forensics, where Laura and Michael were sitting either side of the double-headed microscope, seemingly oblivious to the stench that hit Terry despite her heavy-duty face mask and the room's state-of-the-art ventilation.

Both looked up as she entered. 'Any luck?'

Michael smiled. 'I think we might be on to something. We started at the bottom and we're working our way up. This last lift was about halfway up and there are a couple of spores.' He stood up and rolled his shoulders. 'Just going to sample the next area.'

He walked over to the large island bench where the sleeping bag was laid out. Terry, breathing through her mouth in a futile effort to counteract the putrid smell, followed him over.

'Laura! Bring over the tapes labelled 5 and 6.'

Terry stood out of his way, watching as he pressed the clear sticky tape onto the material. He handed number 5 to Laura and picked up number 6 and continued the process. Then Laura and Michael took up their positions at the double-header again.

Terry pulled on a second pair of gloves, first squirting some scented liquid soap onto the pair she was already wearing, which would stop her hands stinking for the rest of the day. She carefully flattened out the bag. In the photographs the SOCO had taken at the scene, the material was ripped towards the head end. She assumed, given Tina was sleeping rough, the bag had been damaged on briars or something. Now looking at it, she wasn't so sure. 'Michael. Can you have a look at this?'

She heard his stool scrape back and he appeared at her side.

'Did you look at the tears in the material?' she asked.

'Not yet,' said Michael.

'Thing is, I don't think they are tears. I think the material has been cut with something sharp.'

'What? Let me get a closer look.' He grabbed the handle on the large magnifying glass suspended from the ceiling by a mechanical arm. 'Maybe.' He stepped to the side to allow Terry to see through the magnifier. The ends of the damaged threads were cleanly cut, not raggedly torn.

'Can you take some extra lifts from the damaged area before I touch it? I'm just going back to my office to pick something up.'

Michael and Laura were back in position, engrossed in the images down the microscope, when she got back.

'Got to hand it to you, Tez. You were right,' said Michael. 'Spores à gogo. Tons of them.'

Terry felt her pulse quicken. 'I knew it,' she said, more to herself than anyone.

She smoothed out the bag and took a clear acetate sheet from the folder she had returned with. She placed it over the cuts in the sleeping bag and traced each onto the sheet. She folded the bag in half, clearing a space on the bench. She laid the acetate sheet on the bench and placed a photograph from the folder beside it. There was no doubt. The pattern of cuts in the sleeping bag matched the pattern of the stab wounds on Eileen McCarthy's chest. Five stab wounds forming a heart shape and a cut running across.

77

Michael wasn't long bursting Terry's bubble.

'I thought Rupert Hunt and his theory on the meaning of mushrooms was looney tunes, Tez – granted, it looks as if he may have been on to something there. But heart-shaped cuts on a sleeping bag?'

She held the acetate up to the window and traced around the pen marks she had made. 'Tell me you can't see it!'

'Maybe, but if you oriented the bag slightly differently you'd get a different shape. Is it not a bit contrived?'

'Who are you, the fucking defence?'

'Don't get snarky. I'm just saying tread carefully.'

'What do you mean?'

'Whatever you bring to Sinnott needs to be watertight.'

Terry knew Michael was right. She had to be certain of her facts or they would just shut her down, even Fraser.

'What if we find spores on Eileen McCarthy and the Joyces? They'd have to listen to me then.'

'By we, I assume you mean me. You want me to go and find the trace evidence for three ancient murders. Do you know how much crap there is in the evidence room?'

'I know, I know,' she said trying to placate him. 'Laura?' The young doctor looked up from where she was busying herself with slides. 'You don't mind helping Michael, do you? I'll be in the histo lab with the McCarthy bones. Oh, and Michael? Add *DNA profile* to your to-do list.' Terry handed him a bag with hair in it. 'I think this belongs to Jo McCarthy.'

Niamh had already started preparing the ribs from the sisters when Terry returned to the office. Normal processing would take a couple of days, so Terry had asked her to prepare frozen sections of the cartilage, using the cryostat to produce ultra-thin slices ready for examination in minutes. This method was not ideal for tricky diagnoses, like cancers, but good enough for what she wanted.

'Here you go, Terry – those slides are Eileen's.' She pointed at the cardboard slide tray sitting next to her microscope. 'Jo's will be another ten minutes.' She continued putting the fragile glass cover slips over the tissue she had carefully placed on the glass microscope slides. 'I had a quick look – just checking the quality. But it seems your diagnosis is right.'

Terry noticed the textbook open on the bench, images of connective tissues with blobs of yellow–brown pigment, the images labelled *Ochronosis*. She picked up one of the slides and put it on the microscope stage under the x40 lens. She adjusted the eyepieces, bringing the tissue into focus. There they were, clumps of brownish pigment. Ochronosis. Niamh set down Jo's slides. Identical. There was no doubt that they were sisters. She high-fived Niamh and walked along to her office.

An hour or so later Michael called. 'Well, Terry, I've got to hand it to you for sheer doggedness. Your instincts were right. Spores on the vaginal swabs of McCarthy and the Joyces. They had been commented on in the original reports as "fungal infection, not specified". Two different scientists reported them so they wouldn't have made the connection. Probably need to show them to Rupert to be sure.'

All the self-doubt that had been building fell away, and Terry felt a flood of relief. 'We've done it, Michael. We've made the connection.'

An hour later, Terry was sitting in Hunt's first-floor office in Trinity College's anatomy block, scanning his bookshelves with their huge tomes on semiotics, sociology and wildlife. He'd agreed to see her at short notice, and she was now waiting for him to return from the anatomy lab where he was checking the slides she'd brought to confirm the spores as those of the ghoul mushroom.

'You're admiring my library?'

Before she could answer, a young man appeared in the doorway behind Hunt. 'Dr Hunt. Sorry. Am I too early?'

'No. Come on in. This is Dr O'Brien. And Dr O'Brien, this is Sandy, one of our undergrads. I'm helping him with his dissertation.'

The student nodded and went over to the conference table next to Hunt's desk, where he left a folder full of papers.

Hunt turned back to Terry. 'Sorry about the interruption.' He pointed to the tray of slides. 'You are quite correct. These are indeed ghoul-mushroom spores. Where did they come from?'

'Just tying up loose ends on that case.' She flicked her eyes towards the student, who had settled in a chair and was obviously listening to their conversation.

'Ah! Of course.' Hunt mimed zipping his lips closed.

Jimmy greeted her when she returned to the mortuary that afternoon, sticking his head out of his office. 'What's up, Doc?' This was his latest irritating habit.

'Hi, Jimmy. I just want to take another look at the Reece specimens.'

'Hang on, I'll pull those out for you.' He walked past her, brown lab coat flapping, and went straight into the PM room, bypassing the changing room. By the time she had changed into her scrubs, he had the large silver tray containing the perineal and neck dissection specimens on the table.

'Knife, Doc?' Jimmy was lounging against the sink with a PM40 knife in his ungloved hand. She watched as he scraped his left thumb over the cutting edge of the blade. He saw her looking. 'What? You can't check if it's sharp with your gloves on.'

'Thanks, Jimmy. I've something to do – I'll be back in a

minute. And put on gloves and an apron.' She went back into the changing room and pulled her phone out of her bag. 'Michael. The sleeping bag. Those tape lifts you took from the stabbed area, could you check for DNA? Our killer might have handled the blade to check its sharpness.'

She sampled the vaginal bruise and put the fractured Adam's apple in a formalin-filled jar, with instructions to Jimmy to bring them up to Niamh in the histo lab. She then climbed the stairs back up to the office area, grabbed a coffee and sat down at her desk.

She called Fraser. 'Are you free?'

'I am. I've just had a very interesting conversation with a professor from the National Museum about Bobby Joyce.'

'Oh.' Terry was thrown for a moment – maybe he was taking her more seriously than she'd realised. 'Can you come to FSI? Michael, Laura and I have some stuff we'd like to walk you through.'

An hour later, Fraser listened intently as they explained their findings. 'Hats off to you,' he said when they were finished. 'This is hard forensic and pathological evidence that links the deaths of Reece, McCabe, McCarthy and now the Joyces in a way no one can dispute.'

'Well, I still need to revisit Tina. And I have to finalise the histology of the vaginal bruise in Rachel's case.'

'And then all you need is a killer to pin them on,' Fraser said. 'And we don't know it isn't Cleaver. Sinnott will go ballistic if she's challenged further on that score, believe me.

But I must admit, my mind isn't made up. And I've been doing some digging elsewhere.'

Soon after, the four of them were sitting together in the staff kitchen having a coffee, as Fraser filled them in on what he'd uncovered about Bobby Joyce.

'BJ, as he was known to his friends, was a resident of St Matthew's Unit in Cabra from 1986 until 1998. I talked to the psychiatrist, Dr Theo Brennan, who saw him for twelve months in 1992 into 1993. After a lot of toing and froing and protesting about psychiatrist–patient confidentiality, he dug out the file. What he had to say was very interesting indeed. If only he'd been more forthcoming during our original investigation into the sisters' deaths.'

'You must have been very persuasive,' Terry said.

'Actually, I threatened to come back with a warrant,' Fraser said. 'Anyway, according to the good doctor, Bobby Joyce sent up a good few red flags. He was torturing animals before his voice broke, and when he was sixteen he abducted one of the girls from the unit, took her to a disused storage shed at his school, tied her up and frightened the shit out of her. If her screams hadn't been heard by the school porter, who had called in to borrow a tool to do some DIY in his own home, Byrne believes Bobby would have seriously harmed her. As it happens, the porter hit the lad over the head with a hurley stick and was able to rescue the girl. Joyce maintained she was his girlfriend and it was just a bit of fun.'

'Jesus, why wasn't he sent to a juvenile detention centre or something?'

'He was supposed to be transferred to St Lawrence's, a juvenile assessment centre, but they didn't have a bed for him,' Fraser said. 'So Sister Bridget, who seems to have had a soft spot for the boy in spite of everything, offered to be responsible for him if they would allow him to stay at St Matthew's. They moved him to a separate building on the grounds for six months, where he lived away from the other children and was home-schooled. Dr Brennan saw him three times a week, and at the end of that period it was decided he could go back to living with the other kids.'

'Seriously?' Laura said. 'What happened to the girl he'd attacked?'

'She was seen at the sexual assault unit, but was virgo intacta. Nonetheless, they decided it was best to move her and her sister to another unit.'

'She had a sister?' Terry asked.

'Oh, she did. The sister didn't like Bobby – she said he made suggestive comments to her and had made threats against her. It was thought best to get them both away from him.'

'How was he after he went back to join the rest of the kids?' Michael wondered.

'There were no more incidents, but Dr Brennan thinks that was mostly motivated by the fact Bobby felt he had been severely punished. He didn't want that to happen again, so he learned to be careful, to curb his aggression – in the home, at any rate.'

'Did Dr Brennan say whether or not he thought this was something Bobby could do over the long term?' Terry asked. 'Suppress his violent tendencies?'

'I asked him that very question,' Fraser said. 'He indicated that, without therapy, he did not think it likely Bobby could keep his anger in check over the long term. It seems Byrne recommended the lad be sent for various types of interventions to address problems with anger management, PTSD, narcissistic personality disorder, disassociation ... none of which were ever followed up on. I think Byrne was scrabbling about for some sort of diagnosis to pin on him.'

'So Bobby was left to deal with his issues on his own, pretty much,' Terry said.

'Like a lot of kids in care, it doesn't matter how bright you are, your choices are limited. There was no pressure on him to do much with himself, despite being assessed as within the gifted range intellectually. It appears he did some further education courses at the local college, and then they organised a placement in the National Museum.'

'Doing what?' Michael asked.

'I talked to Dr Liam Franey, who is in charge of the neolithic and megalithic exhibits. He remembered Bobby, gave him a mixed review. It seems Bobby wasn't good front of house – Dr Franey called him uncouth. I think there was a bit of a culture clash. At any rate, there was a PhD student there at that time, Ash Sweeney, who was studying ancient weapons, and that's the area where Bobby showed the most interest. Apparently Sweeney took him under his wing. Tried to train him up.'

'So what happened to Bobby Joyce?' Terry asked.

'Dr Franey banned him from the museum around 2004 – Sweeney had finished his PhD and returned to Australia, so there was no one to speak up on the lad's behalf. Joyce went to view the exhibit Sweeney had last worked on and overheard two women making comments and laughing. He lost it and started screaming at them, behaving threateningly. That was the last straw for Dr Franey.'

'That's the year his own sisters died,' Terry said.

'And after that he seems to have disappeared. Mary is trying to contact Professor Sweeney to see if he's kept in contact with him.'

'But didn't you question him after Eileen was killed?'

'His name was definitely in the mix, it came up when the team were trawling her old friends, but from what I can glean from the investigation at the time, he wasn't to be found and no one admitted to seeing him much after his sisters died. Bobby Joyce has done a remarkable job of keeping under the radar for so long.'

'A ghost killer?' Terry said. 'Another little obstacle to make finding this guy even more difficult.'

78

The following morning Terry arrived in to a PM on an old man who had been found dead in front of the TV by his carer. It proved to be the result of a stroke, a rupture of a small aneurysm on the circle of Willis, the ring of arteries on the undersurface of the brain, blood pulsing out and flooding the skull cavity and compressing the brain. It must have been lying dormant for years. Though that would be no consolation to his children and grandchildren.

When the PM was complete, she left Laura to suspend the brain in a bucket of formalin and headed to her office.

The one thing that was still niggling her about the killings, which she now knew for sure were all linked to Rachel Reece, was the blade used to stab and slash Eileen, Jo and the Joyces. What kind of weapon could have created those wounds?

She took out the photos that showed close-ups of the

wounds again, taking a magnifying glass and examining each one in detail.

She had assumed the blade was serrated, but as she looked more closely, she realised that wasn't exactly true. Rather, the blade's edge wasn't an even line. It was as if the surface of the blade was coarse, slightly jagged.

She went through to the lab where Niamh had left Eileen's and Jo's ribs in a couple of colanders in the sink. She picked one from each of the women, put them on sheets of blue paper towels and took them over to the stereomicroscope to view the knife injuries.

This was puzzling. Metal blades by their nature have smooth surfaces, while this one, she could see, ground the bone's edges as it sliced through them, like a saw. Instead of a narrow V cut into the bone this was a broad groove, the sides of the groove rough. She flicked a switch on the side of the microscope and a scale appeared beside the image she was looking at down the lens. Most blades are a millimetre or two thick; the blade causing these injuries was at least five millimetres thick.

Back in her office she took out Eileen McCarthy's postmortem report and pulled the Eileen McCarthy notebook from her shelf. She transcribed the measurements of the stab wounds, width and depth, and plotted them on a graph. The outline of the blade used to kill Eileen appeared. She repeated this with the Joyces. She stared at her drawing. The blade was dagger shaped, as she had suspected, but it was shorter, none of the stab wounds being more than eight centimetres deep, and wider than the daggers she was familiar with. It was like a stubby Highland dirk, but from the irregularity of the incised wounds, this blade wasn't honed by any master of metal.

She called Rose.

'Gosh,' the Belfast pathologist said, looking at the images Terry had emailed her. 'Those are odd.'

'I know. What's really stumping me is the composition of the blade. It's not serrated exactly ... Do you know what's coming to my mind, and this is going to sound weird, but bear with me: it's like they were cut with an irregular piece of stone.'

'I see what you mean,' Rose said. 'It's probably a custom-made weapon.'

'Yeah, which doesn't help me much in tracking it down – with the History Channel being so popular, every hipster out there is doing blacksmithing courses and making their own bowie knives.'

'Most of those are useless as anything other than orna-ments, though,' Rose said. 'This one is sturdy. It's gone through a good few ribs and is still going strong.'

'How do you mean?'

'Killers sometimes fetishise objects and work them into their MOs. Might this be a piece of a shovel, for instance, or rebar?'

'The rebar might work in terms of thickness but I don't think so.'

'I'm just saying we tend to go for the obvious, which is usually right. But who's to say what a deranged killer might arm themselves with. And when that happens we have to get a bit creative.'

'I'll keep it in mind.'

'Listen, I have to go – due in court in an hour. Talk soon.'

Terry put down her phone and sat back. Maybe she was thinking about the blade from the wrong angle – maybe Rose was right and it wasn't a standard knife at all, but some other kind of cutting implement. But what, exactly? She'd put in a call to Rupert Hunt. Perhaps he might have some ideas.

79

She was coming to him. He knew she would.

It was time to prepare. He had no further use for the podcaster's laptop, that he would add to his trophies at the workshop.

He opened the display cabinet and took Ash's knife from his collection. That he would use to torture and kill. His artistry, the heart, required more finesse. He tested the weight of each of his recently forged flint blades before selecting one. This was perhaps his finest yet. The pathologist was deserving of such perfection.

He would have to hone it to razor sharpness for the deepest cut, the one that would release her heart into his hands.

He sat at his desk and uncapped his fountain pen and wrote her a note. He placed the envelope on his laptop. He would instruct the student to hand it to her.

He opened the drawer and removed three plastic cable ties to fashion handcuffs.

His briefcase packed he watched the clock tick down the time.

80

Back at the lab, Terry opened the large glass pot Jimmy had brought up from the mortuary and tipped the piece of tissue onto the chopping board. She dried it off and sat it under the stereomicroscope. She could now make out a faint yellow tinge around Rachel's vaginal bruise. It wasn't a fresh injury. She had had sex with someone, but it was hours if not a day or so before she died. She went looking for Niamh to ask her to fast-track the histology. She was right, this was definite proof. Rachel hadn't been killed in the course of a rape. Sex, the evidence suggested, was not the motivation for her killing.

She was due to meet Rupert at his office at 5 p.m.

Tony parked in Setanta Place and strolled down to the university with her. 'I'll be at the café in the quad, late lunch,' he said. 'Come on back to me when you're done with the boffin.'

'I shouldn't be too long.'

'I've got my newspaper, so take your time.'

She walked across the campus to Rupert's office. The door was ajar. She knocked and waited. When there was no response, she tentatively pushed it open and scanned the room. There was no sign of Rupert but the student she had seen earlier was seated behind the professor's desk, earbuds in and oblivious to her presence. He jumped as she waved her hand in front of his face.

'Sorry to startle you.' She smiled at the young man, discomforted by being caught in his tutor's chair.

'Hi. Weren't you here earlier? If you're looking for Dr Hunt, he's had to go out. He said to give you this.' He picked up a manila envelope lying on top of Hunt's laptop and handed it over to her. 'I was just finishing off my essay.'

'Don't let me stop you. Thanks for this. If he does come back tell him I'll rearrange our appointment.' She turned to go but stopped at the door and looked around. Something had caught her eye: a small display case with an array of what looked to be primitive stone blades. Strange that she hadn't noticed them before. As she headed back to find Tony, she opened the envelope. Inside there was a hand-written note in exaggerated italic writing.

Sorry to miss you – I had to bold out. Meet me at the Brown Thomas car park. I have to collect some notes on an article I'm working on. We can talk on the way.

She went to text Tony – she could not get used to being without her phone – but she figured they wouldn't be long.

Dr Hunt was leaning against the wall inside the opening to the car park, dressed in a less flamboyant way than usual.

'Thanks for this,' she said as she fell in beside him.

'Delighted to help if I can. Now, my car is parked on the second floor. My workshop is down at the port. I thought I might kill two birds with one stone, so to speak.'

'How's that?'

'Well, I've a few bits and bobs I need for a little experiment I'm planning stored there, and I also have some books and reference volumes I've collected over the years which might be of interest to you. Now where is this drawing you told me about?'

As they waited for the lift he looked at her crude representation of the blade that had killed at least four women.

'I'm interested in what kind of weapon that could be.'

Hunt studied her drawing. 'I would say it might well be a vintage cutting tool.'

'Like an antique?'

'Yes, or one made recently but crafted using *traditional* techniques.'

He pressed the fob as they arrived on the second floor and the car locks sprung up. 'Apologies for this old jalopy of a thing,' he said, 'the Spyder is being serviced.' They got in and he nosed the vehicle out of the parking space.

An uneasy feeling settled over her. 'Are there many people making knives using traditional methods?' she asked.

'No. It takes quite a degree of skill and a great deal of knowledge about the materials used. I favour flint. It can be honed to a razor-like sharpness but retains its integrity. This is more robust shall we say?'

'You've made weapons using traditional methods?' she asked, her mind turning to the display case back in his office.

'When I was young I worked with a wonderful man in the National Museum,' he said, smiling warmly. 'Ash Sweeney. He was aboriginal. A kind soul. He encouraged me to follow my passions.'

'So you trained in the museum?' Terry tried to keep her voice steady.

'No. My talents weren't appreciated the way they should have been. I realised the musty museum wasn't for me. So I joined my early mentor in Australia. That's where I did my PhD.'

'And that was where you came across the ghoul mushrooms?'

'It was. Let's just say, they called out to me.'

Terry kept her gaze straight ahead. *They called out to me.* His calling card. She felt a cold chill wash over her. She turned to him, suddenly struck by the size of him as he sat to his full height, his stoop gone.

'Everything okay?' he asked.

'You know what, I've just realised that Tony will be looking for me – I'm under garda protection at the moment. I'd actually better get back.'

He braked suddenly and she jolted forward. She felt a brief sting in her neck, then nothing.

81

Fraser sat in the conference room in Harcourt Street Garda Station, glowering at the team of detectives who had, for the last couple of weeks, been working the Rachel Reece case. None of them looked happy.

'I don't understand how a man who was supposed to be under round-the-clock surveillance managed to vanish into thin air,' he said, his voice teetering on the brink of real anger. 'You are all on this team because you're supposed to be the best we've got, the pick of the crop. So how, would someone please explain to me, did this happen?'

'He sneaked out the back of his house,' Jones, a young detective whose dark hair was cropped down to little more than stubble, said. 'There's a network of alleys running behind it, and once me and Bill had copped it, he was well gone. I'm sorry, sir. This is on us.'

'You knew the alleys were there and you didn't have the

rear covered?' Fraser asked, his voice tight. 'That's a mistake I wouldn't expect from a rookie in Templemore.'

'We'd been covering both exit points for a fortnight,' Bill Rafter, a blocky man with curly blond hair, piped up. 'He *never* used anything other than the front door. Which meant that one of us was always hangin' about in an alleyway for hours every shift with nothin' to show for it. We decided yesterday to call off the alley duty and both pass our tour in the car.'

'And that was a mistake, wasn't it, Detective?' Fraser snapped. 'Because as soon as your backs were turned our boy took his chance and legged it.'

'I agree we made an error of judgement,' Jones said.

'It was a little more than an error of judgement,' Fraser said, speaking the words quietly, though everyone in the room heard the weight of what he was saying. 'You disobeyed your orders and have been found negligent in your duties. I'm writing you both up.'

'Yes, sir.'

'Understood, sir.'

'Now,' Fraser continued, signalling the dressing-down part of the meeting was over, 'does anyone here have an idea where Frank Cleaver might be?'

'Can I suggest we start by interviewing his cronies on the quays?' Mary said.

'It's worth a try, but I don't harbour great hopes of any of them feeling inclined to give up an associate,' Fraser said.

'We'd best check rail and bus out of Dublin,' Trevor, a grizzled detective who was a contemporary of Sinnott's, said.

'That's a given,' Fraser said. 'Get on it, will you? We've lost enough time already.'

'If he's spooked he might be on the lookout for something to calm his nerves,' Mary said. 'I'd guess staking out his dealers might be worthwhile.'

'Good thinking,' Fraser said. 'Put together a team and get on that right away.'

'Consider it done, boss.'

'I want Frank Cleaver found by the end of today,' Fraser said. 'Are we clear on that?'

'Yes, boss!' the men and women in the room said in a chorus.

'Good. Then go and get it done. And Mary, keep an ear to the ground for any info on Bobby Joyce.'

The group broke up as the various detectives set about the tasks they'd been set. Fraser was making for the door when his phone buzzed in his pocket. 'What is it, Tony?'

'I think we might have a problem.'

'I'm having a lot of those this afternoon. Go on – I'm listening.'

'The doc has gone AWOL.'

82

When Terry awoke she realised she could not move her arms or legs. She was lying on a hard surface. The last thing she remembered, she was in a car with Rupert Hunt. A moment of dawning. Cold fear. Doors locking. And a sensation, like a scratch or insect sting, and then nothing.

She hoped against hope this was a variation of her usual dream, and she would wake up in her bed in her flat. She took a deep breath through her nose and opened her eyes. It was hard to focus – her sight and her brain were fuzzy. She had no idea where she was. There was a corrugated metal ceiling high above her. A humming sound was coming from her left, and she turned to see a generator of some kind. She moved again to get up but couldn't. Looking down, she saw that her hands and feet were bound with cable ties. She was handcuffed and hogtied.

Straining her neck, she could see that the room was long. She was lying on an old rug on the floor. The windowless space was illuminated by a single bulb dangling above her. She could make out a jumble of pallets stacked against the wall in front of her and, to the side, an assortment of old furniture. Beside an upturned sideboard there were spades and ropes and a massive roll of plastic. Equipment for an archaeological excavation.

With a struggle, she shuffled to her knees and managed to get upright. Towards the end of the space were a couple of old armchairs and books stacked beside them – and just beyond that was a work area, a long table with what looked like jigs and clamps attached to the edge, and standing beside it, dressed in black, was Rupert Hunt. He was turning a whetstone with a pedal to sharpen a knife.

He looked up and spotted her. She shook her head, trying to remember. Rupert Hunt and Bobby Joyce. The museum. Hunt was Bobby Joyce. It didn't make sense.

'I see you've returned to the land of the living,' he said, taking his foot off the pedal and walking towards her. 'I was worried I might have put a little too much *sedative* into the mix – it's hard to gauge the doses on the arrows. But I had to get you here without a kerfuffle and I had other things to see to.'

She tried to speak and realised she couldn't move her mouth.

'I guess you're wondering where you are. This is my workshop. I mainly use it for storage these days.'

He walked over to her and effortlessly placed his hands under her oxters as she struggled uselessly. He carried her to the seating area, placing her in one of the armchairs. He sat opposite.

'You appreciate why I have to tie you up. If I didn't, you'd try to run away, and the struggle that would ensue would force me to … speed things towards their conclusion, and I don't want to have to do that. I want us to be able to take things at a leisurely pace. And you've already upset my plans. Clara was supposed to be next. But you were pushing the gardaí in my direction and I needed time to complete things. Now, if you promise not to scream I'll take that tape off and we can have a civilised chat.'

Terry tried to keep her breathing steady as he leaned over and ripped the tape from her face. 'What do you want? Why… why have you brought me here?'

'To tell you. To show you.' He stood up in front of her, arms outstretched. 'That old fool Boyd shut me out. I waited for him to pick up the clues I set. Waited for him to seek my expertise. I knew one day I would meet a worthy adversary. Despite Sinnott's men trying to thwart you, you recognised my genius, you followed my trail. But you still hadn't made the leap required to be able to see me for who I really am.'

Her head was thumping. 'You're Bobby Joyce.'

'No. Bobby Joyce legally disappeared when I changed my name by deed poll. He's still in here, of course, poor thing.' Hunt pointed at his chest. 'He comes out sometimes, when I need him to. But the public mostly sees Dr Rupert Hunt. And that's the way I plan to keep it. But Saucy Jacky also served his purpose, rather elegantly I thought.'

Her blood ran cold. 'You killed Rachel Reece.'

'Oh, now, don't be like that. Really, that was all Bobby's work. Nice job he did too.'

'You are Bobby, you sick fuck.' She tilted her head back and screamed for help.

'And that was what Rachel did too,' he said, when she finally stopped. 'I had to stop her. Silly girl. She had managed to find out that Bobby Joyce was Rupert Hunt. She tracked down Ash, he knew about my metamorphosis from Joyce to Hunt, encouraged me even to reinvent myself, shake off the shackles of my past. He's so proud of what I have become, following in his footsteps, but only in an academic sense, you understand. I couldn't have her ruining that.'

He sighed, then roughly dried tears and snot from her face with a white handkerchief before covering her mouth again with a strip of gaffer tape. 'Now, if you're a good girl, Bobby might not appear. For a while anyway. He's the one who's very handy with the knife. He's anxious to meet you. He's been watching you.'

83

Fraser called Terry's number three times in a row, but each time it went to her message minder. He'd had it dropped back to her office that afternoon – was it possible she didn't get it? He left one terse voicemail: 'Terry, I am assuming you slipped past Tony for some reason best known to yourself. If so, could you please have the decency to let me know you're okay, and get back to safety as soon as you possibly can? You've got protection for a very good reason, and I'm concerned.'

He sat behind his desk holding the phone for several minutes, hoping it would ring, but it didn't. Swearing, he set it on the corner of his desk and returned to work.

Cleaver's disappearance was infuriating and could be interpreted in several ways.

It might indicate the man was guilty of the Rachel Reece killing after all, and that he knew the net was closing in on him.

If that was the case, then all the work Terry, Laura, Michael and he himself had done on the Bobby Joyce angle was for nothing, at least when it came to finding Rachel Reece's killer. Though even if Bobby hadn't killed the podcaster, it looked likely he had murdered several others, so the work overall wouldn't be wasted. But finding him was like looking for a needle in a haystack.

Another possibility was that Cleaver thought that Sinnott was hell-bent on arresting him, whether he'd killed Reece or not, and he wasn't going to take the chance of going down for a crime he hadn't committed. But surely he wasn't daft enough to believe that.

There was a third version of events, which posited that Cleaver's flying the coop had nothing whatsoever to do with the investigation and was down to something else – maybe he owed someone money or just couldn't tolerate being cooped up in the house constantly with detectives outside.

Following that line of reasoning didn't offer Fraser anything, so he let it go. A team of trained detectives were scouring the city looking for Cleaver. Fraser just had to remain positive and trust he would be located, and soon. He was still a suspect but there was something else he needed to draw him on. Just this afternoon the information had come through that Bobby Joyce's alibi for the Joyce sisters' murders was none other than Frank Cleaver.

84

Terry watched as Hunt paced back and forth in front of the workbench. He turned and picked something up. 'This is what you were looking for.'

In his right hand he held a knife fashioned from dark stone. It was crude and rough, just like the ones in his office. She kept her eyes on it as he pulled a sheet of paper from his jeans pocket. She recognised it as the graph paper with her drawing.

He held the paper and the knife in front of her. 'Well done, Dr O'Brien, a very good match. But what you didn't guess was that I fashioned a canine radius into the handle.' He turned the knife this way and that. 'A fine piece of work. Dr Sweeney – he allowed me to call him Ash, you know – was a craftsman. I never could match his expertise in replicating ancient tools. But they require a lot of effort to kill.' He returned it to the table and picked up a piece of sharpened flint. 'He told me about the ghoul mushrooms too. That was a nice touch, I thought. I honoured the dead in honour of Ash.' He started laughing. 'I waited a long time for someone to realise their significance – to even find them – but only you came close. And that was only by chance, a quirk of fate. I had to scatter the spores over the last two bodies rather than *impregnate* them. Deflowered, so to speak, with a syringe full of spores. I like to imagine the whores being devoured from deep within.'

He walked towards her, knife in hand.

'You know about my trademark, don't you?' he said, lifting the knife above her and drawing a heart shape in the air. He slashed the tip of the knife down, stopping millimetres from her left eye. 'Oh, Terry. No need to look so wild-eyed. I'm not going to start carving out my love for you just yet.'

He returned to his seat and leaned back into it.

'It was Anne, my loving big sister, who gave me the idea. She sent me a Valentine's card after I'd been taken into care with a big red heart on the front. Anne had taken a black marker and drawn a line across it, and inside she had crossed out the message and written *You broke our mother's heart*. She was a vicious bitch. The day I carved that symbol into her, it was cathartic. Of course, I never had time to get it onto Rachel – rushed job and all. She found me at the museum workshop in Collins Barracks. Wanted to talk about Bobby. Can you accidentally kill someone? Well, once I'd started I had to complete the ritual, but you know how blood makes such a mess. The heart must wait until after I had dumped her body. I'd just started on it when that junkie stuck her nose in. That left me with loose ends. Very inconvenient.

That won't happen again. But perhaps you found it in that junkie's sleeping bag – clever girl that you are. I had to improvise. Bobby didn't want to play that night and I do find stabbing rather distasteful. Although, I'm prepared to make an exception in your case.'

Terry watched him, her body trembling. She felt groggy, pins and needles prickling the ends of her fingers and toes as he lifted her over to an area of floor where he had spread clear plastic. The scratch in the car was a sedative injection, she knew, as she tried in vain to fight back, her body devoid of strength. Tears streamed from the corners of her eyes.

He laid her out on the plastic and straddled her, using his weight to hold her still. 'Are you ready, Dr O'Brien?'

Using the flint blade, he cut the buttons from her shirt, one at a time. A muted whine escaped from her bound mouth.

'Come now, Terry. Such fretting will do you no good. This is just the beginning. There is so much more to come. You would be better off accepting your fate.'

He pulled her shirt open and used the knife to sever her bra straps and cut the band that held the cups in place, lifting them off and tossing them aside. Her whines became louder.

'Sssshh,' he said.

And then he drove the knife into the upper part of her left breast. The pain was excruciating. Her vision blurred. As darkness settled over her, all she could think about was Jenny.

85

Tony sat opposite Fraser, looking contrite. 'I brought her to Trinity College to meet the archaeologist guy.'

'Do you mean Hunt?'

'Yeah.'

'So how the fuck did you lose her?'

'She was supposed to meet me back at the café.'

'What fucking café? What part of "keep a close eye on her" did you not understand?' Fraser thumped his desk and a half-full mug of coffee tipped over, spilling its contents across his papers. 'When did you last see her?'

'A couple of hours ago when I dropped her to Trinity. A lad in Hunt's office says he went off to check out the site for their dig. He thinks it's in Wicklow. He saw Terry but she left after a few minutes. Hunt's not answering his phone either – I've tried a few times. I went round the campus, into the bookshop, the library. Nothing.'

'Jesus. Right, I'll see if I can't get hold of Hunt.'

'Okay, boss. She told me this guy works with you, so I figured it was okay to let her go and talk to him.' Tony fiddled nervously with his keys, setting Fraser even more on edge.

'It was. But as protection detail you should have walked her to the door of his office and waited outside. It's not rocket science, Tony. And stop with the keys!'

'Yes, boss, sorry. But you know the doc. She's very … independent.'

Fraser sighed. 'I know, Tony. I know. Go back to Trinity and see if she or Hunt turns up back there.'

'Will do.'

'And when you find her, do not let her out of your sight!'

Fraser felt impotent. Waiting was not his forte. He picked up the phone again. 'Mary, any luck on Cleaver?'

'Bob Paterson's gone out to that old dear's house up near Sheriff Street. I'll chivvy him along. So far no joy in terms of bus or rail. I have three teams of two scoping the dealers we know he buys regularly from. And Jones and Rafter are back out at his house, in case he shows up there. I'll keep you posted.'

'Thanks, Mary. I've another job for you. Dr O'Brien seems to have gone astray.'

'Has that tosser Tony seriously lost her again?'

'She was due to meet Rupert Hunt in Trinity College but he wasn't there. Neither of them can be contacted. Would you get a home address for him and head over and see if he's there? Some student says he was going to Wicklow, but I wouldn't bank on that.'

'Roger that, boss. I got a number for that Aussie bloke Bobby Joyce worked with too. I'll text it over.'

'Good work, Mary. Keep me posted.'

He was mopping up the spilled coffee when his phone pinged. It was Professor Sweeney's number.

It rang once before going to voicemail. 'Hello, this is Ash Sweeney. For the next month I'll be unavailable by any phone other than satellite, because I'm in South America on a dig. If it's urgent, you can email me and I'll tend to whatever it is you need on my return. Otherwise, I'll chat when I'm back. Bye for now!'

He decided to try calling Hunt himself. It was picked up after three rings.

'Dr Hunt, this is Detective Chief Inspector Fraser.'

'Hello, Detective Chief Inspector,' he said warmly. 'How can I help you?'

'I'm looking for Dr O'Brien. I believe she was due to see you this afternoon?'

'Yes but I needed to get down to the site of the dig in advance of the students tomorrow. I left an envelope with what she was looking for with my student. Is there a problem?'

'Did she say where she was going?'

'No, and I didn't ask her. Is everything all right?' Hunt said, a note of concern in his voice.

'Yes, I'm just trying to get hold of her. Nothing urgent.'

'Ah, well, if I hear from her, I'll let her know you called and tell her to get in touch.'

'Thanks, Doctor. I'd appreciate that.'

'My pleasure.'

Fraser hung up, feeling irritated and helpless.

86

When Terry regained consciousness she stayed still for a moment and took stock. It was difficult to breathe and she was aware of a pain in her chest, as if something was pressing on it. The place was quiet. Her hands were bound in front of her and she raised them to tentatively touch the wound in her chest. She felt a deep gash in the skin and her hand felt sticky. He must have pulled out the knife.

She pictured her injuries. A deeply penetrating wound. The knife Hunt had brandished had matched her crude drawing but he didn't use that on her. Instead he'd used a flint blade, probably the same one he used on Rachel. She guessed it was about ten centimetres long, long enough to penetrate her chest. She braced herself against the pain as she moved her finger in the hole to gauge the depth of the injury. There was no resistance. Her lung was surely punctured. She would be bleeding into her chest and the air escaping from the hole in her lung would be building up too. Between the blood and air, the pressure in her chest would grow, squashing her lung and then her heart. With luck, the knife might not have cut an artery and the bleeding would be slow, but she had to act fast.

Raising her head slightly and scanning around in the silence, it seemed as if Hunt had left. She knew what she had to do. In A&E, she had been a dab hand at inserting chest drains. She'd never imagined having to do it to herself.

She managed to roll over and get to her knees again, then rolled into a sitting position and, using her feet as levers, scooched over to the wall and struggled to her feet. The pain was intense and her breathing was becoming laboured. She scanned the floor. She'd noticed a pile of disused lab paraphernalia lying in a corner earlier, which included a Bunsen burner. If she could remove its rubber tubing, it was just possible she could fashion a drain for the air building in her chest.

It was her best chance. As she shuffled across to pick it up, she noticed a narrow piece of grey stone lying beneath his work table, about fifteen centimetres long. She took it in her hands.

It hadn't been sharpened, so it took a bit of effort to get through the rubber of the Bunsen burner, but it did the job and she had a piece of tubing about twenty centimetres long. She manoeuvred her arms to stick the flint in her jeans pocket.

Then, clenching her teeth, she pushed one end of the tubing into the hole in her chest, which was just below her collarbone.

For a second the room pinwheeled and shuddered in front

of her eyes. She paused, waiting to regain stability, then pushed again. Her screams from beneath the tape sounded like keening. Sweat rolled down her forehead and back. Steadying herself as best she could, she took a slow, deep inhalation through her nose and continued in fits and starts, stopping when the agony became too great.

She continued the process until blood started trickling out and only about five centimetres of the tube was visible. She then slowly pulled the tube back out, centimetre by centimetre, until it stopped pouring blood. She felt immediate relief from the pressure in her lungs as the air escaped through the tube. As gently as she could, she pulled another couple of centimetres out and tucked the free end into her shirt pocket.

Now she could make a start on her bindings. She steadied herself against the workbench leg and was just about to pull out the flint from her pocket when the door opened and she turned to face a smiling Hunt.

'You've been busy while I've been away,' he said. He took his time walking towards her. 'Very nice handiwork, Doctor.' He leant over her and patted the tube. 'Just what I would have expected from a woman with your considerable talents. The will to live is powerful. Eileen had it strongest of all. She was so full of life. She loathed Bobby. Was vile to him. But when I came back from Australia as Hunt she was all over me. Bobby was furious. So he took care of her but that was more work for me. I had to find Jo.'

Hunt bent down. 'It's futile to try and escape. I can see I'm going to have to wrap you up good and tight before I settle you down for the night. I can't have you leaking blood over the floor. And you're going to need your sleep. Incision two happens tomorrow, and I might have a few other treats in store for you as well.'

He grabbed her by the hair and dragged her back to where she had been lying.

She tried to fight him, but it was a fruitless exercise. The only comfort she had was the knowledge of the flint in her pocket.

87

Frank Cleaver surfaced at 10.30 that night, and it was, as Mary had suspected, his drug habit that drove him from cover.

DI Roger Harrington called it in. 'Boss, I'm on Merchant's Quay and our boy has just approached a known dealer. He got off the Luas coming from the Point direction. How d'you want us to play it with Cleaver?'

'Take him in. Now,' Fraser said. 'Bring him to Kevin Street. I'll meet you there.'

'Do you want him arrested?'

'Not yet. Just bring him in. I'm fed up of the game-playing. Let's sweat him one last time and see why he ran.'

Fraser had just hung up when he got a call from Michael, who sounded panicked.

'Detective Fraser, I can't get hold of Terry.'

'When did you last hear from her? We've been trying this end as well.'

'I've not been talking to her since she was up in my lab yesterday. I was looking for her this afternoon – I've some DNA results and she'd said to let her know as soon as I had them. But no one has heard from her since earlier today. I've been round to her flat and there's no answer, no lights on, and she's not picking up her phone. Look, normally I wouldn't make so much of it – it's only been a few hours – but with everything that's been going on, I'm worried.'

Fraser sat forward in his chair, the uneasy feeling he'd had all evening beginning to grow. 'I've been working under the assumption she's gone off on one of her wild goose chases. She'd been to see Rupert Hunt and seems to have taken off somewhere else, but where?'

'She was going on about the knife wounds and trying to work out what type of knife caused them. She thinks it's something odd – I'd say that's what she wanted to talk to Dr Hunt about. She might have gone to the museum,' said Michael.

'That's possible. It's just up from Trinity. She's not still there at this time of night, though.'

'Do you think she could have gone after that Bobby Joyce guy she was going on about? When she gets the bit between her teeth she can be a little ...'

'Headstrong?'

'I was thinking pig-headed, but yes. Do you think she could be in trouble?'

'Look, sit tight,' said Fraser, trying not to let his voice betray how worried he really was. 'We're doing our best to locate her. I'll be on to you as soon as we have news.'

88

Darkness had long fallen by the time Hunt left the workshop again, turning out the lights as he left. The clunk of a heavy padlock and chain told Terry that any thoughts of escape were futile.

She lay in the dark, thinking about how her life had come to this pass.

Had she done something to invite it? Had she driven this awful, deranged man to want to hurt her? She had only been doing her job. Okay, she had stepped beyond the fixed nature of what she was supposed to do, but it was all about finding justice for Rachel, and she felt no guilt about that. She had done what she felt she had to do, and she was at peace with it.

What she was not at peace with was the possibility she was going to die. She had so many things she still wanted to do. She loved her job, loved her friends, and there was what had happened to Jenny – she had only scratched the surface of it.

She had sworn to live life to the full for her, and no deranged psychopath was going to get in the way of that.

She would fight. She didn't quite know how, yet, but she was not going to let him kill her.

Her makeshift chest drain was keeping her lung inflated, but even with that, the sense of a weight pushing on her chest was increasing. By morning she knew she would be fighting for breath. How much longer could she last, particularly if he cut her again?

She was starving. Hunt hadn't left her any food, but he had loosened the cap on a sealed bottle of water and placed it beside her before he went. He had taken great pleasure when he whipped the tape off her face. She forced herself to drink. She had lost a lot of blood, and she knew she needed to remain hydrated if her system was to replenish it.

She tried to sleep. The pain from her wound nagged at her and several times she woke up sweating and shaking, sure he had returned and was looming over her. Without windows to give her a sense of the light outside, she had no idea what time it was, but eventually exhaustion took hold and she slipped into an uneasy doze, and didn't awaken until she heard the chains rattling and a key turning in the padlock.

She sat up painfully and managed awkwardly to pull the flint from her pocket. She palmed it, pushing the end of it up her sleeve to hide it.

The she prepared herself for what was to come.

89

'Interview commencing 11.45 p.m., Kevin Street Garda Station, DCI John Fraser and DS Mary Healy interviewing Frank Cleaver of Killowen Drive, Finglas. For the tape, Mr Cleaver has refused legal representation at this time.'

'Damn fuckin' right I have. Shower of wankers. Useless cunts.' Frank Cleaver stared at Fraser and Mary across the table in the interview room.

The room itself was a simple square box. Its walls, painted magnolia, were a mess of graffiti that had been scratched on them over the years. In one corner a camera had been affixed to record the interview sessions, and the table and chairs, which were bolted to the floor, were all metal, the Formica tabletop pitted and grooved with the initials, messages and vulgarities scratched there over thousands of interviews over several decades.

'Would you like some tea or coffee?' Fraser asked.

'No, I would fucking not like tea or coffee,' Cleaver growled. 'I want to be released. I done nothing. If you had anything on me, I reckon I'd have been arrested by now.'

'Not necessarily,' Fraser said. 'We might be looking for the smoking gun.'

'What's that supposed to mean?'

'Why did you run?'

'I didn't. I went to stay with friends for a few days. I didn't want your two gorillas following me. I'm entitled to a bit of fucking privacy. It's me constitutional right, so it is.'

'Where did you go?'

'Mate o' mine has a flat on James's Street, near the Guinness Brewery.'

'And he invited you over for a bit?'

'I asked him, if you must know.'

'Could you tell us this friend's name?' Mary asked.

'Nope. I will not. He was doing me a favour, and I'm not letting youse fuck him about as well.'

'You're not making this easy on yourself,' Fraser said.

Cleaver shrugged.

They sat, Cleaver staring at the tabletop, Fraser and Mary both eyeing him. He seemed angry, it was true, but there was a sense of nervousness about him, too. The constant surveillance had worn him down.

He's a bundle of anxiety and neuroses, Fraser thought. *It won't take much to break him.*

'Talk to me about Bobby Joyce,' he said.

'BJ? From years back?' Cleaver said, looking up at him, puzzled. 'What about him?'

'Seen him recently?'

'Nah.'

Fraser could see he had touched a nerve.

Cleaver looked away. 'He got too big for his boots. Went off somewhere after his sisters were killed, didn't want nothing more to do with the old gang. I thought he'd taken it bad. When he came back a couple years later he was … different. I dunno.'

'How was he different?'

'He was acting the maggot, the big I am. Fuckin' arsehole.'

'What do you mean?'

'Started talking right posh and he looked different.'

'He'd cleaned himself up?' Fraser offered.

'Maybe. Yeah, I s'pose you could call it that.'

'You and him were close, though, weren't you?'

Cleaver glanced up nervously. 'Maybe. At one time we was buds, yeah. What's that got to do with anything?'

'Just keep answering our questions, please,' Fraser said. 'You were his alibi when he was interviewed at the time of his sisters' murders.'

'So? That was bleedin' years ago.'

'Was that alibi genuine, Frank? Was Bobby Joyce really with you on the night his sisters were murdered?'

'I told you. It was a fucking long time ago.' Cleaver shifted in his seat.

'Answer the question, Frank,' Mary said. 'It's a simple yes or no.'

'Fuck you,' Cleaver said. 'I don't have to say nothing.'

'Where did Bobby live when he came back?'

'Don't know. Might have been Ringsend again. Can't remember.'

'Can you remember the address?'

'What's in this for me? Gonna do me a deal and let me the fuck outta here?'

Fraser sat back. 'I don't think I can make any promises just yet,' he said. 'But it would go easier on you if you cooperated with us.'

'I've changed my mind. I want one of them free solicitors. No comment, fuckwits,' Cleaver said, then folded his arms tightly.

Fraser terminated the interview.

90

Hunt propped Terry against the wall on the large sheet of clear plastic, spreading what looked to be blue kitchen roll at her feet.

'Soakage,' he said calmly, registering her gaze. He punched her shoulder, sending waves of pain through her body.

She closed her eyes until the worst of it subsided. When she opened them she couldn't see Hunt, but she could hear him moving about at the other end of the room.

She looked down at her shirt. It was soaked in blood but the tubing was still in her pocket. She relaxed her shoulder and saw that the tube hadn't been dislodged and was still snaking through her ribcage. But the drips from her pocket told her the level of blood inside her chest was rising and being syphoned off by the tube. It was draining blood and not air.

She was nearing the tipping point and needed to act fast.

She slowly manoeuvred the shard of flint down her sleeve and clasped it between her hands, holding them in prayer pose.

Hunt stepped over her, grabbed her by the feet and pulled her flat to the floor in the centre of the plastic. Tears streamed down her face but she didn't resist.

'Prayers won't help you now. This is all your own fault. Now you'll see that your meddling has consequences.' Hunt's voice had changed, the cultured tones replaced by a thick Dublin accent. The significance dawned on her with horror as a bead of sweat ran down her back. Bobby Joyce had come to play.

Hunt straddled her, lifting her arms and putting them over her head, and pulled open her shirt, tugging out the tube in her chest. He then leaned over her as if to kiss her, his back arching.

She only had one chance to stop him. She pushed down the fear and dread and looked steadily, defiantly, into his trance-like eyes. She registered a momentary flicker of confusion in his gaze, then cold satisfaction.

'This is going to hurt,' he said as he pulled back his arm and raised his knife.

'Not as much as this, you motherfucker,' she said as she swung her arms over and slammed the flint into the back of his chest with all her strength. He shuddered as she hit bone, shock writ large on his face as she twisted the flint in her hand and pushed it further in.

'What ... the fuck?' he screeched. 'You dirty bitch.'

The flint cut into her hands as he struggled to remove her arms from around him, but she held it tight until she was satisfied the job was done. When she went to pull it out, she heard a crack as part of it came away in her hand.

Hunt lashed out with his knife, slashing into her abdomen with agonising force. He tore at his clothes furiously, twisting this way and that as he tried unsuccessfully to get at the flint lodged in his back. With a low howl, he collapsed onto her. Pain seared through her as she struggled to get free from under him, every breath a marathon effort as the light began to fade.

91

Fraser and Mary sat in the station kitchen, each nursing mugs of now-cold tea.

Fraser looked up at the clock. It was 2.30 a.m.

He stood up abruptly. 'It's been too long,' he said. 'Terry would have been in touch by now. Where is she?'

'I think we have to admit she's in trouble, boss.'

He looked at Mary and saw the worry he felt reflected in her eyes. He started pacing. 'Well, we know it's nothing to do with Cleaver. Terry linked all the deaths to one killer, and it all seems to be pointing to Bobby Joyce, but where is he?'

'Could he have taken her somewhere like he took Reece?' Mary said.

'Terry thought he had kept McCarthy alive and tortured her. We might still have time.'

'Time to do what, though?' Mary asked. 'We've nothing to

go on. We don't know where this guy even is. He's a ghost, boss.'

'We've got someone who knows him in custody,' Fraser reminded her.

'Someone who won't talk.'

'So we make him talk!' Fraser thought about it. Only one thing occurred to him, and it was a gamble.

But he had no other option.

Shortly after, he and Mary walked into the same interview room where they'd spoken to Cleaver the night before.

'Frank Cleaver, I'm arresting you for the murder of Rachel Reece,' he began.

'What? No! You can't! I didn't do it, for fuck's sake!'

Fraser looked at Mary, who shrugged. 'You've given us nothing to work with, Frank,' she said. 'We tried talking to you last night, but you weren't interested in answering our questions.'

'Ask me again then! Come on – you know I didn't do that woman. I'm not a killer! I never killed nobody. You know what I done, and I know what I done, but never that.'

'Did you lie when you gave Bobby Joyce an alibi for the time his sisters were murdered?' Fraser asked.

'You're looking for me to incriminate myself! Where's my lawyer?'

'Better to go down for lying on the record than for murder, Frank,' Fraser shot back. 'Answer the question, or I'll continue with the arrest.'

'So I fucking lied!' Cleaver shouted. 'He was me buddy! He told me the cops were giving him a hard time because of him being in care. For fuck's sake, man, his sisters were dead. Of course I helped him out. I mean, what sicko would kill his own sisters?'

'You said he went away. Where did he go?'

'Oz, or maybe the other one.'

'You said he changed.'

'Yeah. He had a nose job and got his teeth fixed. Fucking Ken doll. And then he got that fancy job in Trinity. He could've helped me out. Fucking mean git.'

'He worked in Trinity College?'

'Yeah. Don't ask me doing what.'

Fraser looked at Mary.

'He started dressing different too – he used to look just like the rest of us: hoodies and tracksuits and runners and all. Then it was all weird-coloured suits and fancy scarves. Like fuckin' Doctor Who.'

Shit! Fraser thought. *Shit, shit, shit!*

'Mary, can I see you outside?' he said, then to Cleaver, 'We'll be back in a moment.'

They stepped out.

'It's Hunt,' he said as they closed the door behind them. 'Bobby Joyce is Hunt! Fuck!'

'I can't fucking believe it,' Mary said.

'You checked his house yesterday?'

'We called over like you asked,' she said. 'No one was home.'

'Where is it?'

'An estate in Lucan.'

Fraser's mind was racing. 'So lots of houses around?'

'Plenty, yes.'

'Any sheds or outbuildings on the property?'

Mary's forehead furrowed in concentration. 'A small garden shed out back, but it's wooden. Not likely to hold much. There's one of them plastic tunnel things for growing veg and stuff. Looked like it was overrun with weeds.'

Fraser gave a curt nod. 'Right, get out there again and check the place over. Bring two others with you and proceed with caution. Consider Hunt armed and dangerous. I believe he has the doc – do you understand?'

'Loud and clear, boss.'

'Okay, go,' Fraser said, and went back inside.

'This next bit is very important,' he said, fixing Cleaver with a stare. 'Did Bobby have anywhere out of the way – a place he went to work or hide out? Somewhere deserted?'

Cleaver thought for a moment. 'When he was working in that museum place – he was still pally with us then – he was hanging out with this big black guy, Ash he called him. They had a place out in Ringsend in the docks, I think – they were making stuff out there. Don't ask me what.'

Fraser ended the interview and called Mary before he headed for his car. 'I'm on my way to Ringsend. You continue to Hunt's place but tell the other teams to hightail it towards the Dublin docklands.'

92

As Fraser drove, he called Ash Sweeney's number again. Nothing. He rang the Dublin Port Authority and explained what he was looking for and that it was urgent. It only took a couple of minutes for the voice at the other end of the line to come back. There was no Bobby Joyce but there was a Robert James Joyce who rented a storage unit on Behan Dock in Ringsend. 'That dock hasn't been used these past ten years. I didn't think anyone worked out of there anymore, to be honest.'

He got the eircode and headed straight there, perhaps five minutes away. He grabbed the garda radio and put a call out for all cars in the area to head for the quays.

He fought the rising panic and drove.

His phone rang – Mary.

'No sign of Hunt at his home. But there's a flash car in the drive. No sign of the doc either.'

He hung up and kept driving.

There were five storage units on the dock but only one that looked like it might still be in use – a new-looking padlock and chain was hanging open from the door handle, and a Ford Fiesta was parked beside it. Fraser left the Audi a couple of hundred yards up the quayside and jogged, keeping low, his weapon in hand, towards the container. Three garda units had arrived around the same time, and he motioned for the others to hold back and stay low.

He listened closely for a couple of moments – there were no sounds from within. He reached up and turned the handle slowly. When he felt the catch release, he flung it open, his gun extended before him, and called out: 'Gardaí! Get down on the floor or I'll shoot!'

And so it was he found them, Terry and Rupert Hunt, in an ever-widening pool of blood. He ran to where Terry lay, calling for backup and an ambulance. Her pulse was very weak, her breathing rapid and shallow. He gently laid her on her right side and, as he did so, she opened her eyes and focused on him for a moment.

'I told you it wasn't Cleaver,' she said.

And then she was gone again.

93

Consciousness came and went. She preferred the darkness, because when she was awake there was confusion and pain and nausea. She was aware of people around her bed, talking in hushed tones. She didn't have the strength to even open her eyes. She listened. Michael, Fraser, Laura. And then she heard that familiar north County Dublin accent, tempered by thirty-odd years in Glasgow, and she knew everything would be fine. Her dad.

Finally, she woke and did not feel the need to go right back to sleep. The lights were low and the room was quiet.

A nurse appeared, coming in to check on her, a young man with a shaved head and dark brown eyes. 'Nice to see you back with us, Dr O'Brien.'

'Where am I?'

'You're in St Vincent's Hospital. You've had major surgery.'

'I'm thirsty.'

'I'll get you some water. Mr Ferguson, your surgeon, will be delighted you're awake.'

'How long have I been out of it?'

'A couple of days. Your visitors have gone home for the night. Best get some sleep. There's a garda on post outside your door. He'll see you aren't disturbed.'

Early next morning, the surgeon explained that the stab wound had punctured her lung and that, although her makeshift drain had been effective, she had required some surgery and a more professional chest drain. She had lost a considerable quantity of blood, but her other wounds were fairly superficial and she would make a full recovery. They had found a toxin in her blood but it hadn't been identified yet: the toxicologists were working on the theory that it was plant-based, they're liaising with colleagues in Australia. She vaguely remembered some type of blowpipe in Hunt's car. That was a first, she thought, knocked out with a poisoned dart.

She was sitting up, wrestling with a cup of coffee with her bandaged hands, when Fraser peered in her door. 'You up for a visitor?'

'Just don't make me laugh. It hurts.' She patted her chest and winced.

He sat down beside her bed. 'They tell me you're going to make a full recovery.'

'They make them tough in Glasgow. What about Hunt?'

'Do you remember what happened?'

Terry's head ached. She'd had flashes of what had passed in her waking moments, but it was a blur. 'Hunt is Bobby Joyce, isn't he? He was going to kill me?' Fraser nodded. 'Clara, he didn't get her, did he?'

'Clara is fine.' Fraser reached for her hand. 'Hunt is in Beaumont and won't be going anywhere fast. The neurosurgeon had to remove a piece of flint from his spine. God knows how you managed to drive that through his back.'

'A Glasgow lumbar puncture.'

'Well, it saved your life. His spinal cord is partially severed. They're not hopeful he'll get the use of his legs back.'

'Never say being a pathologist doesn't have its uses outside the mortuary. We know the weak spots. When in dire need, et cetera.'

Fraser squeezed her hand. 'Anyway, we won't be able to interview him for a while, but your friend Cleaver is being very cooperative. He knew Bobby but had no idea about Hunt. He can't get his head around it. I find it difficult myself.'

'Bobby became Hunt. Hunt is his public persona, he said that himself. Bobby is his alter ego. A split personality.'

'Laura informs us it's one of those dissociative disorder things. But we'll leave that to the head doctors in the Central Mental Hospital.' He smiled.

'He admitted killing his sisters, and Eileen and Rachel. Even Tina. There's probably more bodies. More sisters,' said Terry.

'Work to do. We've been checking out Hunt's haunts. We've retrieved CCTV footage from the National Museum up at Collins Barracks where he was working on a new exhibition and we've picked up Reece going in.'

'He said he had to shut her up. She had worked out who he was.'

'It's not far to Farmleigh from there. Handy place to dump

a body. We found her laptop in the workshop. Looks like the sick fucker was using it to send you those messages.'

'Poor girl. Poor women. None of them deserved this.'

'No, they didn't. And there are more. We found bones in his garden in what look like stone chambers, under a patch of mushrooms. Michael is working on them. He says they are cist graves, an ancient Celtic system of burial. There were two complete corpses in them.'

'Any idea who they could be?'

'We have our suspicions. Terry, there's one more thing.'

'What?'

'Did Hunt mention Jenny at all while he had you?'

'No.'

'We've been going through the contents of his office in Trinity. Our tech boys have interrogated his laptop. Seems he's a member of some sick dark-web group who share his *interests*, shall we say. Anyway, he's been in touch with someone about Jenny.' Fraser waited for her to say something.

Terry fiddled with the bedclothes and stayed focused on them as tears began to stream down her face. 'And? Did you find out something?' Her heart was pounding.

'Not yet,' Fraser said. 'But we're looking into it. I couldn't keep it from you.'

Terry nodded. 'Thanks, John.'

Once he had gone, she lay back and thought about Hunt, and what she'd had to do to survive him. She knew he was a dangerous man – a damaged man, whose actions had taken many lives and wrecked many more. But she felt nothing.

Closing her eyes, she slept soundly.

She dreamed of Jenny.

Acknowledgements

Life is short but it is full of opportunities; it would be rude not to take them. I have been guided through this new phase of my life by some tremendous people. First on the scene was Faith O'Grady, agent to a reluctant writer. Thanks for having my back. Next came Ciara Considine, publisher with Hachette, who undertook to help turn this sow's ear into a silk purse. She had her work cut out. She in turn introduced me to some fabulous writers who gave me masterclasses on writing thrillers. Shane Dunphy taught me how to add tension and colour to a story, it was much appreciated. Brian Finnegan, author and fellow lover of musicals, was there to talk me through plot development. I think he thought my ideas were better than my singing. We'll see.

And then there was the editing. Painful but necessary. Thanks to Emma Dunne for picking up the obvious errors. But you had it easy in comparison to the secretaries that for years have had to knock my reports into shape, especially Daphne Paton and Lorraine Johnston.

And to my long-suffering family who have championed me throughout, even though I have ignored them for days at a time: Philip my husband and my childers, Kieran and Sarah, thanks.